OXFORD WORLD'S CLASSICS

MRS DALLOWAY

DAVID BRADSHAW is Professor of English Literature at Oxford University and Hawthornden Fellow and Tutor in English Literature at Worcester College, Oxford. Among other volumes, he has edited *The Hidden Huxley*, Waugh's *Decline and Fall*, Ford's *The Good Soldier*, Huxley's *Brave New World*, and the *Cambridge Companion to E. M. Forster*, as well as Oxford World's Classics editions of Lawrence's *The White Peacock* and *Women in Love*, and Woolf's *Selected Essays*, *Mrs Dalloway*, *To the Lighthouse*, and *The Mark on the Wall and Other Short Fiction*. In addition, he has edited *A Concise Companion to Modernism* (Blackwell, 2003) and, with Kevin J. H. Dettmar, *A Companion to Modernist Literature and Culture* (Blackwell, 2006). He is a Fellow of the English Association and Victorian and Modern Literature Editor of the *Review of English Studies*.

OXFORD WORLD'S CLASSICS

For over 100 years Oxford World's Classics have brought readers closer to the world's great literature. Now with over 700 titles—from the 4,000-year-old myths of Mesopotamia to the twentieth century's greatest novels—the series makes available lesser-known as well as celebrated writing.

The pocket-sized hardbacks of the early years contained introductions by Virginia Woolf, T. S. Eliot, Graham Greene, and other literary figures which enriched the experience of reading. Today the series is recognized for its fine scholarship and reliability in texts that span world literature, drama and poetry, religion, philosophy and politics. Each edition includes perceptive commentary and essential background information to meet the changing needs of readers.

OXFORD WORLD'S CLASSICS

VIRGINIA WOOLF

Mrs Dalloway

Edited with an Introduction and Notes by
DAVID BRADSHAW

OXFORD
UNIVERSITY PRESS

OXFORD

UNIVERSITY PRESS

Great Clarendon Street, Oxford OX2 6DP

Oxford University Press is a department of the University of Oxford.
It furthers the University's objective of excellence in research, scholarship,
and education by publishing worldwide in

Oxford New York

Auckland Bangkok Buenos Aires Cape Town Chennai
Dar es Salaam Delhi Hong Kong Istanbul Karachi Kolkata
Kuala Lumpur Madrid Melbourne Mexico City Mumbai Nairobi
São Paulo Shanghai Taipei Tokyo Toronto

Oxford is a registered trade mark of Oxford University Press
in the UK and in certain other countries

Published in the United States
by Oxford University Press Inc., New York

British Library Cataloguing in Publication Data

Data available

Library of Congress Cataloging in Publication Data

Data available

ISBN 978–0–19–953600–9

9

Typeset in Ehrhardt
by RefineCatch Limited, Bungay, Suffolk
Printed in Great Britain by
Clays Ltd, St Ives plc

CONTENTS

BIOGRAPHICAL PREFACE

VIRGINIA WOOLF was born Adeline Virginia Stephen on 25 January 1882 at 22 Hyde Park Gate, Kensington. Her father, Leslie Stephen, himself a widower, had married in 1878 Julia Jackson, widow of Herbert Duckworth. Between them they already had four children; a fifth, Vanessa, was born in 1879, a sixth, Thoby, in 1880. There followed Virginia and, in 1883, Adrian.

Both of the parents had strong family associations with literature. Leslie Stephen was the son of Sir James Stephen, a noted historian, and brother of Sir James Fitzjames Stephen, a distinguished lawyer and writer on law. His first wife was a daughter of Thackeray, his second had been an admired associate of the Pre-Raphaelites, and also, like her first husband, had aristocratic connections. Stephen himself is best remembered as the founding editor of the *Dictionary of National Biography*, and as an alpinist, but he was also a remarkable journalist, biographer, and historian of ideas; his *History of English Thought in the Eighteenth Century* (1876) is still of great value. No doubt our strongest idea of him derives from the character of Mr Ramsay in *To the Lighthouse*; for a less impressionistic portrait, which conveys a strong sense of his centrality in the intellectual life of the time, one can consult Noël Annan's *Leslie Stephen* (revised edition, 1984).

Virginia had the free run of her father's library, a better substitute for the public school and university education she was denied than most women of the time could aspire to; her brothers, of course, were sent to Clifton and Westminster. Her mother died in 1895, and in that year she had her first breakdown, possibly related in some way to the sexual molestation of which her half-brother George Duckworth is accused. By 1897 she was able to read again, and did so voraciously: 'Gracious, child, how you gobble', remarked her father, who, with a liberality and good sense at odds with the age in which they lived, allowed her to choose her reading freely. In other respects her relationship with her father was difficult; his deafness and melancholy, his excessive emotionalism, not helped by successive bereavements, all increased her nervousness.

Stephen fell ill in 1902 and died in 1904. Virginia suffered another breakdown, during which she heard the birds singing in Greek, a language in which she had acquired some competence. On her recovery she moved, with her brothers and sister, to a house in Gordon Square, Bloomsbury; there, and subsequently at several other nearby addresses, what eventually became famous as the Bloomsbury Group took shape.

Virginia had long considered herself a writer. It was in 1905 that she began to write for publication in the *Times Literary Supplement*. In her circle (more loosely drawn than is sometimes supposed) were many whose names are now half-forgotten, but some were or became famous: J. M. Keynes and E. M. Forster and Roger Fry; also Clive Bell, who married Vanessa, Lytton Strachey, who once proposed marriage to her, and Leonard Woolf. Despite much ill health in these years, she travelled a good deal, and had an interesting social life in London. She did a little adult-education teaching, worked for female suffrage, and shared the excitement of Roger Fry's Post-Impressionist Exhibition in 1910. In 1912, after another bout of nervous illness, she married Leonard Woolf.

She was thirty, and had not yet published a book, though *The Voyage Out* was in preparation. It was accepted for publication by her half-brother Gerald Duckworth in 1913 (it appeared in 1915). She was often ill with depression and anorexia, and in 1913 attempted suicide. But after a bout of violent madness her health seemed to settle down, and in 1917 a printing press was installed at Hogarth House, Richmond, where she and her husband were living. The Hogarth Press, later an illustrious institution, but at first meant in part as therapy for Virginia, was now inaugurated. She began *Night and Day*, and finished it in 1918. It was published by Duckworth in 1919, the year in which the Woolfs bought Monk's House, Rodmell, for £700. There, in 1920, she began *Jacob's Room*, finished, and published by the Woolfs' own Hogarth Press, in 1922. In the following year she began *Mrs*

Dalloway (finished in 1924, published 1925), when she was already working on *To the Lighthouse* (finished and published, after intervals of illness, in 1927). *Orlando*, a fantastic 'biography' of a man–woman, and a tribute to Virginia's close friendship with Vita Sackville-West, was written quite rapidly over the winter of 1927–8, and published, with considerable success, in October. *The Waves* was written and rewritten in 1930 and 1931 (published in October of that year). She had already started on *Flush*, the story of Elizabeth Barrett Browning's pet dog—another success with the public—and in 1932 began work on what became *The Years*.

This brief account of her work during the first twenty years of her marriage is of course incomplete; she had also written and published many shorter works, as well as both series of *The Common Reader*, and *A Room of One's Own*. There have been accounts of the marriage very hostile to Leonard Woolf, but he can hardly be accused of cramping her talent or hindering the development of her career.

The Years proved an agonizingly difficult book to finish, and was completely rewritten at least twice. Her friend Roger Fry having died in 1934, she planned to write a biography, but illnesses in 1936 delayed the project; towards the end of that year she began instead the polemical *Three Guineas*, published in 1938. *The Years* had meanwhile appeared in 1937, by which time she was again at work on the Fry biography, and already sketching in her head the book that was to be *Between the Acts*. *Roger Fry* was published in the terrifying summer of 1940. By the autumn of that year many of the familiar Bloomsbury houses had been destroyed or badly damaged by bombs. Back at Monk's House, she worked on *Between the Acts*, and finished it in February 1941. Thereafter her mental condition deteriorated alarmingly, and on 28 March, unable to face another bout of insanity, she drowned herself in the River Ouse.

Her career as a writer of fiction covers the years 1912–41, thirty years distracted by intermittent serious illness as well as by the demands, which she regarded as very important, of family and friends, and by the need or desire to write literary criticism and social comment. Her industry was extraordinary—nine highly-wrought novels, two or three of them among the great masterpieces of the form in this century, along with all the other writings, including the copious journals and letters that have been edited and published in recent years. Firmly set though her life was in the 'Bloomsbury' context—the agnostic ethic transformed from that of her forebears, the influence of G. E. Moore and the Cambridge Apostles, the individual brilliance of J. M. Keynes, Strachey, Forster, and the others—we have come more and more to value the distinctiveness of her talent, so that she seems more and more to stand free of any context that might be thought to limit her. None of that company—except, perhaps, T. S. Eliot, who was on the fringe of it—did more to establish the possibilities of literary innovation, or to demonstrate that such innovation must be brought about by minds familiar with the innovations of the past. This is true originality. It was Eliot who said of *Jacob's Room* that in that book she had freed herself from any compromise between the traditional novel and her original gift; it was the freedom he himself sought in *The Waste Land*, published in the same year, a freedom that was dependent upon one's knowing with intimacy that with which compromise must be avoided, so that the knowledge became part of the originality. In fact she had 'gobbled' her father's books to a higher purpose than he could have understood.

Frank Kermode

INTRODUCTION

A Well of Tears

Jacob's Room (1922) ends with a poignant *tableau vivant*. The shoes of Jacob Flanders, a victim of the First World War, are held out by his mother in his overwhelmingly empty yet eerily occupied room. Virginia Woolf was as conscious as anyone in the 1920s of the paradoxical legacy of 'the bloody war'[1] of 1914–18— how what it had taken away was continually brought home to people—and her next novel, *Mrs Dalloway* (1925), is the second of three she published during that decade (the third, *To the Lighthouse*, appeared in 1927) which explore, among other things, the social and psychological impact of the War.

The image of Betty Flanders holding out her dead son's shoes is called to mind soon after the beginning of *Mrs Dalloway* when Clarissa thinks of 'Lady Bexborough who opened a bazaar . . . with the telegram in her hand, John, her favourite, killed' (p. 4). This reference to a moment of mental and emotional arrest, following almost immediately after the first of Clarissa Dalloway's flashbacks to when she was 'a girl of eighteen' at Bourton (p. 3), develops into a key theme in the novel: in differing degrees, the plights of Lady Bexborough, Clarissa, Peter Walsh, and Septimus Warren Smith all lay bare how the trauma of a moment can check the progress of a life. Like the chiming of Big Ben, the past is both 'irrevocable' (pp. 4, 99) and ever present in *Mrs Dalloway*, and the retrospective cast of Clarissa's mind is epitomized in her choice of reading: she 'scarcely read a book now, except *memoirs* in bed' (p. 7; emphasis added).

The novel is set on an imaginary (see note to p. 123 on pp. 182–3) and very hot Wednesday in June 1923. While Clarissa can 'thank Heaven' that the War is 'over', for Lady Bexborough, and 'for some one like Mrs Foxcroft at the Embassy last night eating

---

[1] *The Diary of Virginia Woolf*, ed. Anne Olivier Bell and Andrew McNeillie (5 vols.; London: Hogarth Press, 1977–84), ii. 51.

her heart out because that nice boy was killed' (p. 4), its hurt is undiminished. Though the social changes which the War accelerated are apparent to Peter Walsh on his return from India (pp. 61, 137), and he is a beneficiary of 'the great revolution of Mr Willett's summer time' (p. 137), introduced as a daylight saving measure at the heart of the conflict in 1916, the War's darker vestiges continue to obtrude amidst 'the bellow and the uproar' (p. 4) of London. The sky-writing aeroplane, for example, 'bore[s] *ominously* into the ears of the crowd' beneath (p. 17; emphasis added) because for Mrs Coates and her fellow Londoners its sudden drone still prompts the fear of aerial bombardment five years after the War has ended (though unsystematic and barely comparable with the London Blitz of 1940–1, being bombed from the air was as terrifying as it was unprecedented during the First World War). Even the 'indomitable' Helena Parry was 'disturbed by the war . . . which dropped a bomb at her very door' (p. 151). More generally, there are frequent references to and invocations of 'the dead' (pp. 15, 17, 56, 74, 93, 123, 125, 153) in the novel, and at one point a line of boy soldiers is seen marching up Whitehall past the War Office (now forming part of the Ministry of Defence), having laid a wreath against that most pain-filled and loss-laden of all empty spaces, the Cenotaph (from two Greek words meaning 'empty tomb'; p. 43), completed in 1920 as Britain's national memorial to her 'Glorious Dead'. Elsewhere, the 'embittered' (p. 10) Doris Kilman, victimized during the War because of her German origins, German friends, Germanic name and gutsy honesty (p. 105), observes people 'shuffl[ing] past the tomb of the Unknown Warrior' (p. 113) in Westminster Abbey. The corpse it holds could even be that of her brother, killed in the War, despite his name, fighting for Britain (p. 105). In these various ways, Woolf drives home her sense of the War's ongoing tragic aftermath, its refusal to leave hold of the living, the persistence of memory.

   A profound sense of absence is felt not only by those characters who have lost brothers, sons, and comrades in battle. Peter Walsh, for example, has spent most of his life 'overcome with . . . grief' (p. 36) because of Clarissa's rejection of him in favour of

Richard Dalloway, and Clarissa herself has 'borne about her for years like an arrow sticking in her heart the grief' (p. 7) of having broken with Peter. Hugh Whitbread always makes Clarissa feel that she 'might be a girl of eighteen' (p. 5) and beneath her guise of the 'perfect hostess' (pp. 6, 53) that is exactly what she is, trapped (like Peter, p. 130) in the time warp of Bourton in the 1890s, when her life was brought to a symbolic halt after she opted for a prudent marriage rather than giving rein to her heart. Now a frail 51-year-old, Clarissa's emotional suspension finds release in the 'schoolgirlish' (p. 5) spring of her language—'What a lark! What a plunge!' (p. 3)—and if Septimus's own fatal plunge and his wife's sedative-induced dream of 'opening long windows, stepping out into some garden' (p. 127) are clearly anticipated on the first page of the novel when Clarissa recalls how 'she had burst open the French windows and plunged at Bourton into the open air' (p. 3), the triggering of such a vivid recollection of something so long ago by something so slight as the word 'hinges' (p. 3) reveals just how close the past lies to the surface of Clarissa's mind. At different points in the novel, Clarissa (p. 37), Lucrezia Warren Smith (p. 56), Septimus (pp. 18, 119) and Peter all start crying, all, like Peter, 'suddenly thrown by those uncontrollable forces' (p. 39), 'these astonishing accesses of emotion' (p. 68), which the War and their pasts have bequeathed them, and in so doing they lend weight to Clarissa's conviction that 'This late age of world's experience had bred in them all, all men and women, a well of tears' (p. 8).

Shattered Nerves, Disabled Lives

As well as the pleasure of trying to fathom what Woolf gives us, her texts offer the extra satisfaction of musing on what she withholds. Septimus Warren Smith, for example, is a curiously grandiose name for a poorly educated clerk from the provinces. Is his 'fantastic Christian name' (p. 72) really the one with which he was baptized, its Latinate ring evincing his parents' hopes for his social advancement? Or is it the forename which the pre-War aspirant poet gave himself, topped off with a suitably distinctive two-part surname? Certainly, there is no mention in the novel of any of the six older siblings the name Septimus implies, and the philoprogenitive connotations of his Christian name, coupled with the unavoidable association of 'Warren' with the teeming fertility of rabbits, serve only to spotlight the barrenness of his marriage.

It is typical of Woolf's fiction in general that on first reading *Mrs Dalloway* many details pass by almost unnoticed before retrieving the reader's attention and demanding closer scrutiny. Some details turn out to be significant, some do not, and with others it is impossible to say. Who is the typist, for instance, whom Clarissa hears on returning to her house from Bond Street (p. 25)? It is most likely Miss Kilman, typing up work assignments for Elizabeth, or Elizabeth, typing up her response to such assignments, because Clarissa would seem to have no need of a typist and Richard Dalloway's would almost certainly have been based at the House of Commons. And just how Clarissa and Peter Walsh respectively get home from Bond Street so quickly; and get from Westminster to Regent's Park (pp. 41–7) and from Bloomsbury to Westminster (p. 139) so speedily, must remain either pointless questions, tantalizing conundrums, or evidence of Woolf's occasional loose plotting, depending on the reader's point of view.[2] One obvious rejoinder, of course, is that in a novel which portrays time as an all-pervasive agency of oppressive control, the ability of two of the principal characters to clock off for a while could not be more fitting.

A passing detail which should on no account be passed over, however, is the reference to Septimus's 'crosses' (p. 75). This single word makes it clear that he is not only an extremely fortunate survivor of the War, having enlisted soon after the beginning of the conflict in August 1914 and fought through it until the

---

[2] See e.g. John Sutherland, 'Clarissa's Invisible Taxi', in *Can Jane Eyre be Happy? More Puzzles in Classic Fiction* (Oxford: Oxford World's Classics, 1997), 215–24, and Diderik Roll-Hansen, 'Peter Walsh's Seven-League Boots: A Note on *Mrs Dalloway*', *English Studies*, 50/3 (1969), 301–4.

Armistice of 11 November 1918 (p. 73), but a military hero. We know that Septimus was a 'brave' soldier (p. 20), that he 'won promotion' during the War (pp. 73, 81), and that he 'served with the greatest distinction' (p. 81). But to be decorated with 'crosses' in the context of the 1914–18 War can *only* mean that Septimus's bravery was acknowledged through the conferment on him of *two or more* of the following decorations: the French Croix de Guerre, the Italian Croce di Guerra, the Belgian Military Cross, the Belgian Croix de Guerre, or, if the 'crosses' were British, as they are most likely to have been, the Military Cross and the Victoria Cross, his country's highest award for heroism in battle.[3] In other words, Septimus must have been a remarkably courageous soldier, dedicated to making 'England prosper' (p. 84) with a martial zeal and patriotic fervour to which even Sir William Bradshaw would have to defer. When this is recognized, the treatment he receives at the hands of Bradshaw and Holmes seems all the more callous and unfitting. On discovering that he has leapt from his sitting-room window, Holmes denounces Septimus as a 'coward', but no description of him could be less appropriate. In flinging 'himself vigorously, violently down on to Mrs Filmer's area railings' (p. 127), Septimus ends his life with the same unflinching belligerence with which he must have conducted himself on the battlefield.

Which is not to minimize how sick he is in 1923. Indeed, with his stammer and his loss of memory (p. 83), his delusions and his generally disturbed behaviour, Septimus is a classic case of 'the deferred effects of shell-shock' (p. 155). Lucrezia recognizes that her husband 'had grown stranger and stranger. He said people were talking behind the bedroom walls . . . He saw things too—he had seen an old woman's head in the middle of a fern' (p. 56). He exhibits suicidal tendencies, voices assail him, he jabbers back at them, he sees a Skye terrier turning into a man, and he wants to tell the Cabinet that 'trees are alive . . . there is no crime' (p. 57). Most notably of all, he sees his dead comrade

---

[3] Information from Stanley C. Johnson, *The Medal Collector: A Guide to Naval, Military, Air-Force and Civil Medals and Ribbons* (London: Herbert Jenkins, 1921).

Evans coming towards him from amongst the Regent's Park shrubbery. 'The symptoms [of shell-shock] were wildly diverse,' Wendy Holden has written, 'from total paralysis and blindness to loss of speech, vivid nightmares, hallucinations and memory loss. Some patients declined eventually into schizophrenia, chronic depression and even suicide.'[4] There were some 200,000 cases of this kind of nervous breakdown during and after the War, and at the end of 1922 there were still 16,771 soldiers hospitalized with shattered nerves and around 50,000 neurasthenic and other types of war pensioner at large in Britain.[5] Interestingly, when the Government launched an official Inquiry into shell-shock in 1920 under the chairmanship of Lord Southborough, it gathered evidence from, among others, a Dr Holmes, formerly Consultant Neurologist to the British Expeditionary Force.[6]

Sir William Bradshaw's reputation is based on his 'almost infallible accuracy in diagnosis . . . sympathy; tact; understanding of the human soul' (p. 81), but these last three qualities are not in evidence during his interview with Septimus. For example, Bradshaw interprets his patient's stuttering over the first person pronoun as evidence of his dangerous egotism: '"Try to think as little about yourself as possible," said Sir William kindly. Really, he was not fit to be about' (p. 83). But in a number of ways Septimus shows that he is. Although he is clearly mentally ill, Septimus is far from wholly deranged. He displays a taste for low-level linguistic playfulness when he makes his pun about 'Holmes's homes' (p. 82) and he is sufficiently well attuned to the real world to remark to his wife on leaving Bradshaw's premises that the 'upkeep of that motor car alone must cost him quite a lot' (p. 84). Above all, Septimus's cool analysis of how best to kill himself, as Holmes ascends the stairs to his room, could not be more rational (p. 126). There is, then, evidence to suggest that Septimus is what his appearance

---

[4] Wendy Holden, *Shell Shock* (London and Basingstoke: Channel 4 Books, 1998), 7.

[5] Anthony Babington, *Shell-Shock: A History of the Changing Attitudes to War Neurosis* (London: Leo Cooper, 1997), 121.

[6] Ibid. 124–8.

implies, 'a border case, neither one thing nor the other' (p. 71), who, had he been treated more sympathetically and less harassingly, may have begun to recover his mind. While Septimus is understandably intimidated by Bradshaw during their interview, and his stammer prevents him speaking up for himself, the consultant's opinion that 'attaching meanings to words of a symbolical kind' is a 'serious symptom' of mental unbalance (p. 81) is by some margin the interview's most disturbing revelation.

The 'Bill' which Bradshaw and Richard Dalloway (a Conservative MP) want 'to get through the Commons' (p. 155) is intended to deal with, among other things, 'the deferred effects of shell-shock' (p. 155). From what we know of their politics and their intolerance, it seems likely that Bradshaw is lobbying to have the proposed powers of the legislation extended in order that the State and its doctors would have the authority to deal with the most severely shell-shocked by forcibly immuring them in asylums in Surrey and elsewhere: a 'provision' (p. 155), in short, not only to seclude '[Britain's] lunatics' (p. 85), but her shell-shocked ex-servicemen as well. Though Bradshaw knows exactly what is wrong with Septimus, he shows little compassion for his patient and merely addresses him on the dangers of succumbing to unmanly 'moments of depression' (p. 83). He seems to have no real grasp of the field in which he is supposedly expert, and his desire to segregate Septimus may be viewed as the characteristic response of a man who has dedicated his life to erecting a 'wall of gold' (p. 80) between his wife and himself and the rest of the world.

Holmes, on the other hand, even gets the diagnosis wrong. Although the War, and even more dramatically the influenza pandemic of 1918–19[7] (of which the weak-hearted and ghostly

---

[7] The pandemic killed 228,917 Britons and well over twenty million people worldwide. One commentator has written of 'those 120 days when the fate of civilisation hung in the balance . . . All told, over a billion people—more than half the world's population—are thought to have been attacked' during the pandemic. Richard Collier, *The Plague of the Spanish Lady: The Influenza Pandemic of 1918–1919* (London and Basingstoke: Macmillan, 1974), 305.

Clarissa—she had 'grown very white since her illness' (pp. 3, 31)—is almost certainly a survivor) had shown decisively otherwise, Holmes still insists that 'health is largely a matter in our own control' (p. 78). He is adamant that Septimus is just 'a little out of sorts' (p. 18) and that there is really 'nothing the matter' with him (pp. 20, 57, 77, 78). He prescribes a regimen of cricket (p. 22), golf (p. 77), music hall attendance (pp. 22, 77) and porridge (p. 78), and when those fail he resorts to bromide (pp. 77, 81), a noun, pointedly, which means both a sedative and 'a trite remark' (*OED*). Whether Holmes is antipathetic to the shell-shocked or just cluelessly incompetent is hard to say, but by 1923 the approach of both him and Bradshaw would have been regarded as highly questionable by those who were really in the know about the condition. 'It was perhaps the First World War that most effectively brought home the artificiality of the distinction between the normal mind on the one hand and its abnormal conditions on the other,' the psychologist Cyril Burt remarked in 1935.[8]

London's medical men do brisk business in *Mrs Dalloway*. Before the War, it seems, 'you could buy almost perfect gloves' (p. 9) in Bond Street, but in the London of 1923 nothing quite fits as snugly as it did, either materially or mentally. For the umpteenth time, Hugh Whitbread has come up 'to see doctors' (p. 5). 'Other people came to see pictures; go to the opera; take their daughters out; the Whitbreads came "to see doctors". Times without number Clarissa had visited Evelyn Whitbread in a nursing home . . . Evelyn was a good deal out of sorts' (p. 5), while at other points in the novel, invalids are glimpsed 'huddled up in Bath chairs' in Regent's Park (pp. 20, 23) and 'a maimed file of lunatics' is spotted by Septimus in the Tottenham Court Road (p. 76). Most conspicuous of all, the 'stream of patients' attending Bradshaw's Harley Street consulting room is 'incessant' (p. 81).

Mrs Dalloway was written at a time when Woolf herself was

[8] Quoted in Elaine Showalter, *Hystories: Hysterical Epidemics and Modern Culture* (London: Picador, 1997), 73.

both ill and misdiagnosed. She had suffered breakdowns in the past and had attempted suicide in 1913. During 1921 she was again unstable, suffering hallucinations. 'In the bitterly cold spring of 1922, she had had the 'flu, and [her doctor] had told her that her pulse was "insane" and that "the rhythm of her heart was wrong"' and that she might die imminently, but these proved to be ' "entirely false verdicts" . . . [and *Mrs Dalloway*] was powerfully affected by this brush with mortality. "Suppose the idea of the book is the contrast between life and death", she noted in November [1922]',[9] while an 'idea' which is just as prominent in the finished novel is the folly of seeking to enforce rigid constructions of madness and sanity in a society which had suffered such deep psychological wounds.

Unhinging Things

The reference to taking doors off their hinges in the second and third lines of the novel most evidently relates to the preparations for Clarissa's party, but it may also be a cue to readers to ask themselves which character or characters, if any, *are* 'unhinged' (as a verb meaning 'to unsettle, unbalance, disorder in mind, throw into confusion' (*OED*), unhinge had been in use since the early seventeenth century) in *Mrs Dalloway*. In a diary entry for 14 October 1922, Woolf commented that her work in progress would be 'a study of insanity & suicide: the world seen by the sane & the insane side by side—something like that'.[10] But who is which in the novel?

Is Clarissa, for instance, simply eccentric or precariously unbalanced? Before Septimus is even mentioned, her acute strangeness is carefully established. 'She felt very young; at the same time unspeakably aged. She sliced like a knife through everything; at the same time was outside, looking on. She had a perpetual sense . . . of being out, out, far out to sea and alone; she always had the feeling that it was very, very dangerous to live even

---

[9] Hermione Lee, *Virginia Woolf* (London: Chatto and Windus, 1996), 454–5.
[10] *Diary*, ii. 207.

one day' (p. 7). In that this day in particular is the day of her party, Clarissa is peculiarly uncertain of the time of year: is it 'the middle of June' (p. 4) as she states, or is June 'still untouched . . . almost whole' (p. 31) as she also says? Clarissa feels 'the oddest sense of being herself invisible; unseen; unknown' (p. 9), and when she notices a 'salmon on an iceblock' in a Bond Street fishmonger's window she comments out loud 'That is all . . . That is all' (p. 9). Not knowing 'what the Equator was' (p. 104) might be thought a tad unusual for someone of Clarissa's age and background, but in view of her husband's profession, the prolonged and widespread coverage which the Turkish slaughters of Armenians in 1894–6 and 1915 received in the British press, and the way in which the continuing persecution of Armenians in Turkey was closely monitored in British newspapers between 1915 and the early 1920s, Clarissa's 'muddl[ing] Armenians and Turks' (p. 103) in 1923 is only a little less bizarre than muddling Jews and Nazis would be in the latter half of the following decade.

In Clarissa's eyes, the 'degradingly poor' (p. 104) Doris Kilman is nothing less than a dangerous incubus, 'one of those spectres with which one battles in the night; one of those spectres who stand astride us and suck up half our life-blood, dominators and tyrants' (p. 10). She sees her as 'Elizabeth's seducer; the woman who had crept in to steal and defile' (p. 148). Clarissa is aware that a hatred, a 'brutal monster' (p. 10) lurks inside her with 'icy claws' (p. 31). Unlike the War, the influenza did not leave its survivors mentally impaired, but 'this hatred':

especially since her illness, had power to make her feel scraped, hurt in her spine; gave her physical pain, and made all pleasure in beauty, in friendship, in being well, in being loved and making her home delightful, rock, quiver, and bend as if indeed there were a monster grubbing at the roots, as if the whole panoply of content were nothing but self love! this hatred! (pp. 10–11)

Septimus's affliction is expressed in similar terms and both he and Clarissa are at once homicidal and suicidal, with the perilousness of Clarissa's life underscored by her husband's gift of red and white roses. 'Richard's first duty was to his country' (p. 94), so it is entirely proper that the roses he has chosen are in the same two colours as the cross of St George, the patron saint of England. But red and white flowers together are also 'omens of death'.[11] Dalloway, highly ambiguously, is 'eager, yes, very eager, to travel that spider's thread of attachment between himself and Clarissa' (p. 97), and in doing so he exposes what Woolf saw as the essentially deathly connection between women and patriarchy, the individual and the State. Once home, he has little to say to Clarissa: in a novel of many arresting symmetries, at three o'clock (p. 100) on a hot afternoon in June 1923 Dalloway cannot bring himself to tell his wife, 'in so many words' (pp. 91, 98, 99, 100), that he loves her, just as it was at 'three o'clock in the afternoon of a very hot day' (p. 54) thirty years previously that Clarissa rejected Peter Walsh, unable, in so many words, to say that she loved him.

In her introduction to the Modern Library Edition of *Mrs Dalloway* (1928), Woolf revealed that Septimus 'is intended to be [Clarissa's] double',[12] and as well as being survivors of the two greatest catastrophes to beset mankind in their era, another obvious link between them is that Septimus's mind is locked into what happened during the eighteenth year of the twentieth century no less inextricably than Clarissa's is detained by what happened in the eighteenth year of her life. By acquainting the reader with Clarissa's strangeness in advance of Septimus's, the latter's abnormality is to some extent normalized and the response of the medical establishment made to seem all the more arbitrary and unjust.

Peter Walsh is another 'cranky' (p. 132) character. When Clarissa first sees him she notices that he has 'the same queer look' (p. 34) he has always had, and no sooner has Peter kissed Clarissa's hands than he withdraws 'a large pocket-knife and half opened the blade' (p. 34). 'What an extraordinary habit that was, Clarissa thought; always playing with a knife' (p. 37). Two

---

[11] Iona Opie and Moira Tatem (eds.), *A Dictionary of Superstitions* (London and New York: Oxford University Press, 1989), 164.

[12] Repr. in *The Essays of Virginia Woolf*, ed. Andrew McNeillie (6 vols.; London: Hogarth Press, 1986–), iv. 548–50; quote from p. 549.

pages further on he 'run[s] his finger along the blade of his knife' (p. 39) while talking to Clarissa before, 'to his utter surprise', he bursts into tears. Having rushed from Clarissa's house in a distressed state, he catches sight of a young woman in Trafalgar Square and proceeds to stalk her, 'stealthily fingering his pocket-knife' (p. 45) as he sets off. That evening, on his arrival at Clarissa's party, he opens up 'the big blade of his pocket-knife' (p. 140) before entering her house. One can be certain that if Septimus had a proclivity to caress knives in the presence of women Holmes would have been 'on him' (p. 78) even more rapidly, and Woolf seems at pains to contrast the disturbing behaviour which is tolerated as eccentric within the 'governing-class' (p. 65) with the socially harmless behaviour which is deemed insane and quasi-criminal lower down the social scale.

Peter Walsh likes to see himself as an 'adventurer . . . a romantic buccaneer' (pp. 45–6), and some critics have argued that his penknife equates with his sexual menace. This may be so, but it seems unlikely as he is hardly an accomplished philanderer and he comes across as sexually innocuous. He seems more in awe of the woman he follows than a threat to her, just as he failed to win Clarissa in the 1890s. Moreover, from what the reader learns of Daisy, the young married woman with whom he is infatuated and on whose behalf he has come to London to arrange a divorce, it seems likely that by the time Peter returns to India his flighty lover may well have flown to someone like Major Simmons, the Indian Army officer with whom she is wont to compare Peter to his disadvantage (p. 133), or Major Orde, whom she has 'been meeting' (p. 68) in Peter's absence. Peter is 'attractive to women', but it is because they 'liked the sense that he was not altogether manly' (p. 132). Rather than a symbol of his sexual predatoriness, Peter's penknife more eloquently represents the knife-edge equilibrium of his mind, and, as such, it links him with Clarissa, who slices 'like a knife through everything' (p. 7) and who, according to Lady Bruton, has a habit of 'cutting people up' (p. 88), and Lucrezia, the milliner from Milan who cuts up materials as the fabric of her marriage falls apart.

Like influenza, mental instability is no respecter of rank, and if the imposing car with 'dove-grey upholstery' (p. 12) which pauses in Bond Street on its way to Buckingham Palace is the same 'low, powerful, grey [car] with plain initials interlocked on the panel' (p. 80) which is parked in front of Bradshaw's consulting room, it is possible that even the Royal Family has summoned the assistance of the distinguished nerve specialist. It seems likely that the two cars *are* the same because the 'curious pattern like a tree' (p. 13) on the drawn blinds of the Bond Street vehicle is probably either the staff of Asclepius, the universal emblem of the medical profession, or a caduceus, which is also frequently used as a medical symbol.[13] There is 'a photograph of Lady Bradshaw in Court dress' (p. 82) in Bradshaw's office, and husband and wife may be driving to Buckingham Palace to attend a Court function, but their visit could be of a more professional kind. That 'a face of the very greatest importance' (p. 12) is glimpsed 'only once by three people for a few seconds' (p. 14), and that the pedestrians think the car could be the Queen's or 'The Proime Minister's kyar' (p. 12), is surely Woolf's way of debunking Bradshaw's self-importance and the kudos which neurologists had come to enjoy in post-War society. 'But there could be no doubt', the narrator observes with mock awe and solemnity, 'that greatness was seated within; greatness was passing, hidden, down Bond Street, removed only by a hand's-breadth from ordinary people who might now, for the first time and last, be within speaking distance of the majesty of England . . . ' (p. 14).

If Bradshaw believes that 'health is proportion' (p. 84), and 'not having a sense of proportion' (p. 82) betokens insanity, what light do these guidelines throw on his own mind? For a doctor who likes to see things in black and white, he is surprisingly wedded to grey. If the two cars are the same car, then its 'dove-grey upholstery' (p. 12), 'dove grey' blinds (p. 12), and the 'grey

[13] Asclepius was the Graeco-Roman god of medicine, and his staff is usually portrayed as being branched at the top and entwined by a serpent coiling upwards which is bound more tightly at the base of the staff than at the top. A caduceus, a similar but unrelated symbol, is a winged staff ending in two prongs (or two serpents' heads) twined into a knot. Both symbols could be described as looking roughly 'like a tree' to the casual observer.

furs and silver grey rugs' (p. 80) which are heaped inside it, should not be overlooked by the reader. Bradshaw himself is grey-haired (pp. 81, 155), his wife's apparel is 'grey and silver' (p. 154) and the décor of his consulting room is also grey (p. 86). Inoffensive though it may be, does not Bradshaw's apparently exclusive attraction to grey suggest a monomania akin to Septimus's obsession with Evans?

The girl who serves Miss Kilman in the Army and Navy Stores thinks she is 'mad' (p. 110), such extreme concentration does Miss Kilman devote to the petticoats on display, and it is the habit not only of Doris Kilman, but also Clarissa, Peter Walsh (p. 50), and Septimus 'to talk aloud' (p. 109). In view of the War and the influenza pandemic; in view of the imponderable queerness of the everyday, is it really possible, Woolf seems to be asking the reader, to determine with Bradshavian exactitude where clinical insanity begins and human idiosyncrasy ends?

The Dominions and the Mother Country

If 'Health is proportion' as Bradshaw maintains, where does this leave Millicent, Lady Bruton, *Mrs Dalloway*'s most ardent monomaniac? She has 'lost her sense of proportion' (p. 92) in pursuit of her scheme to export surplus Britons to Canada—so much so, indeed, that 'Emigration had become, in short, largely Lady Bruton' (p. 92). Having nodded off to sleep following the departure of Richard Dalloway and Hugh Whitbread from her lunch-table, Lady Bruton dreams of 'commanding battalions marching to Canada' (p. 95).

Lady Bruton's is an important role in the novel, in that it is through this character that Woolf draws an analogy between the State's treatment of the mentally sick and Britain's treatment of her Empire and dominions. Backed up by the 'police and the good of society' (p. 86), Bradshaw's patriotic toil is unending:

Worshipping proportion, Sir William not only prospered himself but made England prosper, secluded her lunatics, forbade childbirth, penalized despair, made it impossible for the unfit to propagate their views until they, too, shared his sense of proportion . . . But Proportion has a sister, less smiling, more formidable, a Goddess even now engaged—in the heat and sands of India, the mud and swamp of Africa . . . in dashing down shrines, smashing idols, and setting up in their place her own stern countenance. Conversion is her name and she feasts on the wills of the weakly, loving to impress, to impose, adoring her own features stamped on the face of the populace. (pp. 84–5)

It is in this spirit that the 'formidable' Lady Bruton devises her own 'feast' (turbot in a rich sauce, chicken casserole, wine, and coffee) with the sole intention of getting Dalloway and Whitbread to help her 'impress' her patriotic and eugenicist ideology on 'the face of the populace' of Canada. Her pet scheme is a project 'for emigrating young people of both sexes *born of respectable parents* and setting them up with a fair prospect of doing well in Canada' (p. 92; emphasis added). When Hugh Whitbread frames this scheme in slightly different terms in redrafting her letter to the editor of *The Times*, it is important to note that he is representing her nostrum with a specific audience in mind, not altering its substance: even though Lady Bruton hardly recognizes her own thoughts, so brightly has Whitbread polished them, her ideas have been skilfully reformulated, not completely rejigged. Whitbread 'possessed—no one could doubt it—the art of writing letters to *The Times*' (p. 93); his 'name at the end of letters to *The Times*, asking for funds, appealing to the public to protect, to preserve, to clear up litter, to abate smoke, and stamp out immorality in parks, commanded respect' (p. 87). He 'marvellously reduced Lady Bruton's tangles to sense, to grammar such as the editor of *The Times*, Lady Bruton felt, watching the marvellous transformation, must respect' (p. 93).

As Woolf must have been well aware, dispatching a letter to the editor of *The Times* (in the periods 1912–19 and 1922–41 it was Geoffrey Dawson) in June 1923 which advocated the emigration of eugenically sound men and women to Canada would have gone down famously. Canada experienced severe economic, political, and social difficulties in the early 1920s, and Canadian eugenicists were inclined to blame the mental deficiencies of immigrants in general and British immigrants in particular for ' "the unrest which is disturbing Canada at the present moment" '.[14] The British Government, on the other hand, wanted to increase emigration to Canada in order to reduce unemployment and the pressures it was placing on the domestic economy and to repopulate the Empire and Dominions after the depredations of the War. When Charles Clarke, Professor of Psychiatry at the University of Toronto, and the most eminent Canadian eugenicist of his day, gave the fourth Maudsley Lecture to the Medico-Psychological Association of Great Britain in London on 24 May 1923 he did not pull his punches. 'Wasting no time getting to the topic he considered most important, [Clarke] told his audience that immigration had pushed Canada to the brink of crisis. The country was being "bled white" by immigration to the United States and pumped full of defective and "mentally diseased" immigrants, many of whom were British'.[15]

The following day, in its account of his lecture, *The Times* reported that Clarke had 'entered a strong plea for the introduction to Canada of the best Nordic types. He was not at all anxious to see his country flooded by hosts of people of inferior type. "It is all very well," he said, "for Rudyard Kipling and other enthusiasts to say that what Canada must do is to pump in the population. That is true; but at the same time, it is necessary to put the suction-pipe in waters not polluted by defect, physical degeneracy and social failure." '[16] On 26 May 1923, *The Times* roundly endorsed Clarke's position on emigration to Canada in one of its leaders, noting that 'Issues of great importance both to the Dominions and the Mother Country' had been aired in his lecture. The newspaper adopted an uncompromisingly hereditarian line, addressing in particular the problem of 'weak or degenerate, and therefore potentially immoral, types. These types are, without question, the architects of slums and the perpetuators of the

---

[14] Ian Robert Dowbiggin, *Keeping America Sane: Psychiatry and Eugenics in the United States and Canada, 1880–1940* (Ithaca, NY and London: Cornell University Press, 1997), 172–8, quote from p. 173.

[15] Ibid. 176.

[16] 'Canada's Nordic Needs', *The Times* (25 May 1923), 11.

worst side of city life [and whose children] tend to reproduce their evil traits. To exclude them from a population, is, therefore, to secure that population against innumerable dangers and disasters.'[17] The reader of *Mrs Dalloway* is given only three brief excerpts from Whitbread's rewrite of Lady Bruton's letter: 'how, therefore, we are of opinion that the times are ripe ... the superfluous youth of our ever-increasing population ... what we owe to the dead ... ' (p. 93). Filling in the gaps, Whitbread's letter probably argues that 'the times are ripe' for a scheme such as Lady Bruton's for reasons similar to or identical with those which Clarke had outlined in his recent lecture, and that merely 'to pump in' to Canada the 'superfluous youth of our ever-increasing population' would be a betrayal of the great sacrifice which Canada and Britain had made in terms of lives lost in the War—'what we owe to the dead'.

As Woolf got into her stride with *Mrs Dalloway* she wrote in her diary that she wanted to 'criticise the social system', in her fourth novel '& to show it at work, at its most intense',[18] and just as Clarissa's house needs to be partially deconstructed in order to make room for her party—'doors would be taken off their hinges' and 'Rumpelmayer's men' will reconfigure the layout of her furniture (p. 3)—Woolf strives in her novel to expose every aspect of the culture of coercion which she saw as bolstering the 'triumphs of civilization' (p. 128). Personified by Bradshaw and Holmes on the one hand, and Lady Bruton, her acolytes, and *The Times* editorials on the other, Woolf shows how the maintenance of 'the efficiency, the organization, the communal spirit of London' (p. 128), which Peter Walsh so admires on his return to the capital, is predicated on the State's exclusion or marginalization of those who are inefficient, disorganized, communally off-line, or (like Miss Kilman) the wrong gender. Whitbread and Lady Bruton refer quite openly to 'superfluous' people and Whitbread has previously written to *The Times* wanting to 'stamp out' certain kinds of behaviour in public parks. Bradshaw aims to 'seclude' Septimus and *The Times* thought it desirable to

[17] 'Immigration and the Unfit', *The Times* (26 May 1923), 11.
[18] *Diary*, ii. 248.

'exclude' slum children from the population (presumably through such measures as compulsory sterilization). In contrast, the 'battered old woman' (p. 69) who sings in the street embodies the novel's challenge to such hygienic, segregationist, and hereditarian attitudes and gives voice to Woolf's conviction that life cannot be silenced, made tidy, or tucked away. As Clarissa puts it: 'the most dejected of miseries sitting on doorsteps . . . can't be dealt with . . . by Acts of Parliament for that very reason: they love life' (p. 4).

Lady Bruton, who 'never spoke of England, but this isle of men, this dear, dear land' and who has 'the thought of Empire always at hand', is also exercised by 'the state of India' (p. 153). Other countries of the Empire, such as Nigeria (p. 8), South Africa (pp. 88, 92), and Ceylon (p. 153), warrant a mention in *Mrs Dalloway*, but it is Canada and India which stand for the Empire as a whole. Peter Walsh has not returned home from the sub-continent for five years (p. 34): 'All India lay behind him; plains, mountains; epidemics of cholera; a district twice as big as Ireland' (p. 41). He is from 'a respectable Anglo–Indian family which for at least three generations had administered the affairs of a continent', yet he dislikes 'India, and empire, and army' (p. 47). His own and his culture's alien place in India is emphasized when he orders 'wheel-barrows from England, but the coolies wouldn't use them' (pp. 41–2).

Walsh convinces himself that he will go to Clarissa's party only because, like Lady Bruton, 'he wanted to ask Richard what they were doing in India—the conservative duffers . . . What did the Government mean—Richard Dalloway would know—to do about India?' (p. 136). These were urgent questions in 1923. Under the inspired leadership of M. K. Gandhi (1869–1948), the Raj had just about survived a period of intensive opposition, with Gandhi's policy of *satyagraha*, or non-violent non-cooperation (launched on 1 August 1920), and the boycotting of British imports (including, in November 1921, the Prince of Wales) proving very effective. Although this 1919–22 civil disobedience campaign led to Gandhi being jailed for conspiracy in 1922–4 (the first of four spells he was to spend in prison), the independence movement had found a momentum which it would not lose.[19] India's defiance of imperial control corresponds to the various domestic acts of resistance in the novel, most notably Septimus's suicide, and it is striking that a novel which is so carefully mapped on to the streets of London should disclose so colonial a spectacle as 'a retired Judge, presumably, sitting four square at his house door dressed all in white. An Anglo-Indian presumably' (p. 139). Judging by his stance and apparel, this elderly resident of Westminster seems to think that he is still laying down the law in India, and, as such, he could not more neatly personify the timeliness of Indian self-determination, the justice of its being led to eventual independence by Gandhi, a London-educated barrister.

The Empire and patriotism are shown to wield almost as unhealthy a power over the British as the Indians. The shoppers of Bond Street, for example, at one point look 'at each other and [think] of the dead; of the flag; of Empire' (p. 15), in the same way that a breeze in the Mall 'lifted some flag flying in the British breast of Mr Bowley' (p. 17), whereas a 'Colonial''s insulting remark about the Royal Family results in 'words, broken beer glasses, and a general shindy' in a back-street pub (p. 15). Symbolically, when Miss Kilman loses her way in the Army and Navy Stores she becomes 'hemmed in by trunks specially prepared for taking to India' (p. 113). The restriction of her life is shown to be systemically connected with the limitations which Britain has imposed on her Empire.

Swinging Dumb-bells

Physical bulk looms large in *Mrs Dalloway*. Looking more like 'a general of dragoons' (p. 89) or 'a spectral grenadier' (p. 152) than 'an old woman' (p. 153), Lady Bruton is an imposing figure

[19] Anthony Read and David Fisher, *The Proudest Day: India's Long Road to Independence* (London: Pimlico, 1997), 162–210; quote from p. 196. See also Stanley Wolpert, *A New History of India* (4th edn; Oxford and New York: Oxford University Press, 1993), 301–28.

with 'her ramrod bearing, her *robustness* of demeanour' (p. 153; emphasis added). She would not look out of place among the 'Tall men, men of *robust* physique' (p. 15; emphasis added) who peer out of the windows of White's and other gentlemen's clubs, while it is wholly ironic, in view of Septimus's treatment at the hands of Holmes and Bradshaw, that 'the doctors and men of business and capable women all going about their business, punctual, alert, *robust*' (p. 47; emphasis added) seem 'wholly admirable' to Peter Walsh, 'good fellows, to whom one would entrust one's life, companions in the art of living, who would see one through' (p. 47). In contrast to these assorted sturdy types, the young men who parade up Whitehall from the Cenotaph do 'not look robust. They were weedy for the most part' (p. 43). Similarly, the 'perfectly upholstered' (p. 5) Hugh Whitbread is noticeably more corpulent than his wife Evelyn, an 'obscure mouse-like little wom[a]n' (p. 63); Clarissa, who, with her 'narrow pea-stick figure' (p. 9) always feels 'skimpy' (p. 5) beside him; the gaunt Doris Kilman; the wraith-like Ellie Henderson, 'a wisp of a creature, with her thin hair and meagre profile' (p. 143); Septimus, who is 'not one of the large Englishmen [Lucrezia's] sister admired, for he was always thin' (p. 124); and Lucrezia herself, whose wedding ring no longer fits her finger, 'so thin' (pp. 20, 57) has she grown with worry.

Whitbread is said to be cognizant of 'the obligations which size, wealth, health entail' (p. 88), yet the abuse of physical power is a key component of Holmes's and Bradshaw's approach to their work. 'Large, fresh-coloured, handsome' (p. 77), Holmes is a 'powerfully built man' (p. 126) who pushes Lucrezia aside with ease on his visits to Septimus. After Septimus has killed himself, he sedates her and as she passes out of consciousness she sees 'the large outline of his body dark against the window. So that was Dr Holmes' (p. 128). He and Bradshaw 'never weighed less than eleven stone six' (pp. 126, 77), which does not sound heavy by today's standards, but which was far from negligible in 1923 and was distinctly bulky in comparison with Woolf's own frame. Bradshaw's way of restoring a sense of proportion to his patients involves fattening them up, just as Woolf's own doctors had immobilized and '"overfed"' her during her recurrent bouts of mental ill-health.[20] Bradshaw's intention is to transform his patients from 'seven stone six' weaklings to twelve stones of sturdy and submissive normality (p. 84). Likewise, the relentless entertaining which has fuelled Bradshaw's rise up the social and professional ladder has taken a heavy toll on Lady Bradshaw and resulted in her 'conversion' into an exemplary professional wife, remarkable only for her 'stoutness':

Fifteen years ago she had gone under. It was nothing you could put your finger on; there had been no scene, no snap; only the slow sinking, water-logged, of her will into his. Sweet was her smile, swift her submission; dinner in Harley Street, numbering eight or nine courses, feeding ten or fifteen guests of the professional classes, was smooth and urbane. Only as the evening wore on a very slight dullness, or uneasiness perhaps, a nervous twitch, fumble, stumble and confusion indicated, what it was really painful to believe—that the poor lady lied. (p. 85)

Like Lady Bruton, Bradshaw is a hereditarian eugenicist in that he believes that 'unsocial impulses' such as those he discerns in Septimus are 'bred more than anything by the lack of good blood' (p. 86). He has 'a natural respect for breeding' (p. 83) in the same way that Richard Dalloway admires Lady Bruton, a 'well set-up old wom[a]n of pedigree' (p. 89), a 'strong martial woman, well nourished, well descended' (p. 92), and would like to research her family history. Yet is Dalloway's own family as racially and genetically pure as he would wish it to be? Peter Walsh thinks Elizabeth Dalloway is a 'queer-looking girl' (p. 48) and the noteworthiness of her appearance is stressed on more than one occasion:

Was it that some Mongol had been wrecked on the coast of Norfolk (as Mrs Hilbery said), had mixed with the Dalloway ladies, perhaps a hundred years ago? For the Dalloways, in general, were fair-haired;

[20] Typically, after just over a week of drinking 'four or five pints [of milk] daily', Woolf was made to swallow 'progressively, three complete meals with three or four pints of milk a day and with the additions of liquid-malt extract, cod liver oil, and beef tea', Lee, *Virginia Woolf*, 183.

blue-eyed; Elizabeth, on the contrary, was dark; had Chinese eyes in a pale face; an Oriental mystery . . . (p. 104)

Subsequent references to Elizabeth highlight her 'oriental bearing, her inscrutable mystery' (p. 111) and her 'fine, Chinese, oriental' (p. 114) eyes. In a review entitled 'Dostoevsky the Father', Woolf complained in 1922 of Dostoevsky's daughter's obsession with heredity and racial purity, her knack of 'detecting strains of Slav, Norman, Ukrainian, Negro, Mongol, and Swedish blood' in her close relations,[21] but Richard Dalloway seems completely unaware that such 'strains' may feature in his own family history. 'Mongol' and 'oriental' were used interchangeably in the 1920s, but in 1924 the word 'Mongol' was brought into sharper definition when F. G. Crookshank's *The Mongol in Our Midst* linked those whom we would now describe as victims of Down's syndrome with theories of racial atavism and biological recapitulation.[22] While it would be going much too far to suggest that Woolf envisages Elizabeth as a Down's syndrome case, it is possible that she may have had at least something of Crookshank's recessive nuance of 'Mongol' in mind when she conceived the appearance of the Dalloways' offspring, and, if so, Woolf's point is surely that, *pace* Bradshaw and Dalloway, pure breeding is pure tosh.

If Holmes has all the tenacity of Sir Arthur Conan Doyle's world-famous sleuth—'Holmes is on you,' Septimus ruminates at one point, 'Their only chance was to escape, without letting Holmes know; to Italy—anywhere, anywhere, away from Dr Holmes' (p. 78)—but none of his perspicacity, Bradshaw, who allocates a strict 'three-quarters of an hour' to each of his patients (p. 84), takes his name from what was in 1923 a world-famous passenger train timetable, *Bradshaw's Railway Guide* (1839–1961). Like medicine and the law, clock time is associated with the regulation and restraint of the individual in the novel, and it

---

[21] 'Dostoevsky the Father', in *Essays*, iii. 327–31; quote from p. 328.

[22] F. G. Crookshank, *The Mongol in Our Midst: A Study of Man and his Three Faces* (London: Kegan Paul, Trench, Trubner, 1924), 97, *passim*. See also Daniel Jo Kevles, *In the Name of Eugenics: Genetics and the Uses of Human Heredity* (1985; Harmondsworth, Middlesex: Penguin, 1986), 160–2.

is significant that Woolf endows it with the same 'robust' physicality as Holmes, Lady Bruton, and the clubmen of St James's. When the 'sound of Big Ben striking the half-hour' intervenes just as Elizabeth Dalloway steps forward to greet Peter Walsh, for example, it does so 'with extraordinary vigour, as if a young man, strong, indifferent, inconsiderate, were swinging dumb-bells this way and that' (p. 41). This image of time working out shows just how closely Woolf related clocks and physical coercion:

Shredding and slicing, dividing and subdividing, the clocks of Harley Street nibbled at the June day, *counselled submission, upheld authority*, and pointed out in chorus the supreme advantages of a sense of proportion . . . (p. 87; emphasis added)

Tellingly, the Warren Smiths are slightly late for their Harley Street appointment (p. 80), and Clarissa says at one point that she 'feared time itself' (p. 26). The 'great booming voice' (p. 42) of Big Ben is of a piece with 'the voice of authority' (p. 12) which the pedestrians hear as Bradshaw's grey car passes by. Time, like medicine, is an 'exacting science' (p. 84) which cannot waver, and in *Mrs Dalloway* Big Ben is associated with the forceful manipulation of people, and 'laying down the law' (p. 108). Arrestingly, Clarissa reads 'on Lady Bruton's face, as if it had been a dial cut in impassive stone, the dwindling of life' (p. 26).

First heard in 1859, 'Big Ben was first heard over the radio on New Year's Eve, 1923, when its chimes were broadcast at midnight to announce the New Year', and from 17 February 1924, it could be heard every hour on BBC radio, along with 'a regular time signal service from the Greenwich Observatory [which] was broadcast as a series of six electronically produced "pips" ':[23] henceforward, time in Britain was 'ratified by Greenwich' (p. 87) every hour that the BBC was on air. In other words, at the time Woolf was writing *Mrs Dalloway* the growing number of Britons listening in to the increasingly popular wireless were becoming more than ever aware of time's unrelenting march.

[23] Paula Goddard, 'Chimes of Big Ben Broadcast for the First Time: December 31st, 1923', *History Today*, 48/12 (Dec. 1998), 49.

It is worth spending one last moment on time, noting how the 'thin long cloak' of the young woman whom Peter Walsh pursues is stirred by the wind as she walks past 'Dent's shop in Cockspur Street'. The cloak blows out 'with an enveloping kindness, a mournful tenderness, as of arms that would open and take the tired——' (p. 45) and in doing so it not only responds figuratively to Walsh's lukewarm desire for the woman but, more importantly, it foreshadows the blowing-out of Clarissa's curtains during her party, registered on three occasions by the narrator (see below, p. xxxviii), signalling the arrival of Septimus's soul at the gathering. Septimus's twin oppressors are the legislators who have given Bradshaw and his medical colleagues the authority to deprive him of his liberty and the clock time which harries him no less mercilessly. It is significant, therefore, that the founder of Dent's shop, E. J. Dent, was the man who built both Big Ben's clock for the Palace of Westminster and the primary Standard Timekeeper of the United Kingdom at the Royal Observatory, Greenwich.

Living in Each Other

Even by Woolf's extraordinary standards, *Mrs Dalloway* is a deeply organized novel. She expressed her happiness with the novel's 'design' on a number of occasions[24] and one of its most designed aspects is the extent to which connections between Septimus and Clarissa proliferate as the novel unfolds. That their minds are disordered in a similar manner; that he suffered a traumatic experience in the eighteenth year of the century whereas she underwent one in the eighteenth year of her life; and that they are survivors of the two most deathly visitations the twentieth century had then known has been mentioned already. But there are further links and resemblances to be observed. For instance, Clarissa spends her nights in a 'narrow' bed with the sheets 'tight stretched in a broad white band from side to side' where her husband has 'insisted, after her illness, that she must

---

[24] See e.g. *Diary*, ii. 272, 289.

sleep undisturbed' (pp. 26–7), and in a sense she is hospitalized in her own home in precisely the same clinical and isolated fashion as Bradshaw would like to keep Septimus 'in bed in a beautiful house in the country' (p. 82). Clarissa's repetition of the line from *Cymbeline*, 'Fear no more the heat o' the sun' (pp. 8, 25, 34, 158), which Septimus also half-quotes to himself (p. 118), articulates both her probable post-menopausal condition (there would be 'no more having of children now' (p. 9)) and her protective frigidity, her almost relish for the bare room which encapsulates her sense of 'an emptiness about the heart of life' (p. 26). She is as 'cold' (p. 42) with Peter Walsh and her husband as Septimus is with Lucrezia. Septimus's face was once 'a pink innocent oval' (p. 72) and Clarissa still has a 'small pink face' (p. 106), while the 'old man' (p. 127) in the house across the street who sees Septimus about to leap from his window has his counterpart in the 'old lady' who lives opposite Clarissa and whom she sees on two occasions (pp. 107, 157). Alone in his sitting-room, Septimus recalls when he was once bathing hearing 'dogs barking and barking far away' (p. 118), just as, alone in her sitting-room, Clarissa 'listens to . . . the dog barking, far away barking and barking' (p. 34).

For all her sense of isolation, Clarissa is happier reading and sleeping alone than sleeping with her husband, just as Septimus has no interest in sex with his wife, and this correlation in particular brings into focus the question of Clarissa's and Septimus's sexuality. It is intriguingly unclear, for instance, whether Clarissa is most grieved by her failure to marry Peter or the lost opportunity of a life with Sally. Unquestionably, 'the most exquisite moment of her whole life' (p. 30) was when she was kissed by Sally at Bourton. In contrast to her coldness towards Peter Walsh and her husband, Sally's kiss almost makes the earth move for Clarissa—'The whole world might have turned upside down!'—and she has never forgotten that 'infinitely precious' (p. 30) moment. At Bourton, Clarissa 'could not take her eyes off Sally' (p. 28), and was ecstatic that she was sleeping under the same roof as her friend (p. 29). She felt 'in love' (p. 30) with Sally, and in the years which have intervened Clarissa has yielded to the allure of other women. The language of rapturous arousal she uses to describe her feelings on these occasions, when she feels for women 'what men felt' for women, is plainly erotic and practically orgasmic:

It was a sudden revelation, a tinge like a blush which one tried to check and then, as it spread, one yielded to its expansion, and rushed to the farthest verge and there quivered and felt the world come closer, swollen with some astonishing significance, some pressure of rapture, which split its thin skin and gushed and poured with an extraordinary alleviation over the cracks and sores. Then, for that moment, she had seen an illumination; a match burning in a crocus; an inner meaning almost expressed. But the close withdrew; the hard softened. It was over—the moment. (p. 27)

As young women, Clarissa and Sally 'spoke of marriage always as a catastrophe' (p. 29), yet they both end up making prudent ones. However, in the same way that Clarissa is fundamentally a girl of 18, Sally's heart has remained 'like a girl's of twenty' (p. 164), their respective ages at Bourton.

The writing of *Mrs Dalloway* coincided with the erotically charged build-up to Woolf's affair with Vita Sackville-West, and the relationship between Clarissa and Sally reflects the growing excitement Virginia felt in Vita's company. They had first met in 1922, but their affair only began in December 1925. 'They cast each other, and themselves, in dramatic roles,' Hermione Lee has written, 'Virginia set the terms, but Vita played up . . . Virginia was the will o' the wisp, the frail virgin, the "ragamuffin" or "scallywag", the puritan, the sharp-eyed intellectual . . . Vita was the rich, supple, luxurious, high-coloured, glowing, dusky, fruity, fiery, winy, passionate, striding, adventuring traveller . . . Virginia was the one with the head, Vita was the one with the legs.'[25]

Given the novel's insistent parallels between Clarissa and Septimus, the reader should consider whether Clarissa's homoerotic feelings for Sally are mirrored in Septimus's feelings for Evans. It is likely, for instance, that the balance of Septimus's mind has gone, not because of shell-shock per se, but because of the depth

[25] Lee, *Virginia Woolf*, 484–511; quote from p. 485.

of his grief for Evans, the officer who had shown him 'affection' (p. 73) and in whom Septimus 'had seen beauty' (p. 123). 'These are men whose minds the Dead have ravished,' Wilfred Owen wrote in 'Mental Cases', his poem about the shell-shocked, and it is a line which seems perfectly applicable to Septimus. He was unable to feel after Evans's death (p. 73) and it is possible that he then recoiled into heterosexuality (before the War he had idealized Miss Isabel Pole) and marriage with Lucrezia as a reaction to his feelings of grief and guilt about his compatriot. Woolf encourages the reader to see things in this way by stressing the Greek tie between the two men. When Septimus imagines the sparrows singing in Regent's Park, immediately before Evans appears behind the railings, they sing 'freshly and piercingly in Greek words . . . they sang in voices prolonged and piercing in Greek words, from trees in the meadow of life beyond a river where the dead walk, how there is no death' (p. 21). Further on in the novel, just prior to Evans appearing from the bushes, he communicates with Septimus from behind a tree: 'The dead were in Thessaly [a region of ancient Greece], Evans sang, among the orchids' (p. 59; 'orchid' comes from the Greek word for testicle), and when Lucrezia brings home roses, Septimus thinks they have 'been picked by [Evans] in the fields of Greece' (p. 79). We know that Evans was 'undemonstrative in the company of women' (p. 73) and this may have been because they held no attraction for him. As Linda Dowling has written, in the days before the legalization of homosexuality, 'The "love that dare not speak its name" could be spoken of, to those who knew their ancient history, as *paiderastia*, Greek love,' and Chris White adduces sources as diverse as John Addington Symonds, Oscar Wilde, and Aleister Crowley to show how ubiquitous the term 'Greek love' was in the nineteenth century as a code for homosexuality.[26] It is inconceivable that Woolf was unaware of this connotation of the

[26] Linda Dowling, *Hellenism and Homosexuality in Victorian Oxford* (Ithaca, NY and London: Cornell University Press, 1994), 28; see also, pp. 73–5, 78–9, 94–99; Chris White (ed.), *Nineteenth-Century Writings on Homosexuality: A Sourcebook* (London and New York: Routledge, 1999), esp. 161, 214, 315. See also Richard Jenkyns, *The Victorians and Ancient Greece* (Oxford: Basil Blackwell, 1980), 280–93.

word 'Greek' when she chose to use it in the context of Septimus's grief for Evans, and if the reader is inclined to gloss the Hellenic references in this way, then the irony of segregating Septimus to prevent his having children is made all the more tragic.

There are a number of further connections between Septimus and Clarissa which could be discussed, but by far the most important of these is the projection of both characters as birds. Septimus is 'beak-nosed' (p. 12) and reminds Lucrezia of 'a young hawk' (p. 124), while Clarissa's face is 'beaked like a bird's' (p. 9); according to Scrope Purvis she has 'a touch of the bird about her, of the jay' (p. 3). The screen in Septimus's room has 'blue swallows' on it (p. 123) and is matched by Clarissa's drawing-room curtains depicting 'a flight of birds of Paradise' (pp. 144, 143). Septimus is described as 'hopping . . . from foot to foot' (p. 126) before taking flight through his open window, and, following his suicide, in the first reference to Clarissa's curtain, we read that it 'blew out and it seemed as if there were a flight of wings into the room' (p. 143). This symbolic moment of admission occurs prior to Clarissa hearing about Septimus's suicide from the Bradshaws, but it is as if his soul has arrived at the party through the open window (to reinforce this, the curtain blows out twice more: pp. 144, 145). Clarissa's 'birds of Paradise' curtains evoke the abode of the blessed, the Elysian fields from where the sparrows call to Septimus in Regent's Park and sing to him 'in Greek words, from trees in the meadow of life beyond a river where the dead walk, how there is no death ' (p. 21). So strong is the affinity between Clarissa and Septimus that on hearing an account of the circumstances of his death, Clarissa relives his violent end (p. 156), before connecting it with her own experience:

Then (she had felt it only this morning) there was the terror; the overwhelming incapacity, one's parents giving it into one's hands, this life, to be lived to the end . . . there was in the depths of her heart an awful fear. Even now, quite often if Richard had not been there reading *The Times*, so that she could crouch like a bird and gradually revive, send roaring up that immeasurable delight, rubbing stick to stick, one thing with another, she must have perished. (p. 157)

The final image recalls one of Septimus's 'designs, little men and women brandishing sticks for arms, with wings—were they? —on their backs' (p. 125), while Clarissa's 'awful fear' provides further evidence of the Septimus-like vulnerability of her mind.

There are always competing tensions in a Woolf novel. Though *Mrs Dalloway* foregrounds the psychological lesions and social schisms of London, there is an almost equally strong emphasis on the underlying communality of the city, the latent 'universal love' (pp. 57, 125) which Septimus apprehends and in which Woolf passionately believed.[27] This two-way pull is embodied in the contrast between the composed, 'worldly' (p. 65), party-giving, well-connected, and snobbish (pp. 103, 161) Mrs Richard Dalloway, and the frail, retiring, unworldly, more considerate, and fragmentary Clarissa. Significantly, Lady Bruton, the Bradshaws, Hugh Whitbread, and Richard Dalloway are at no point given avian characteristics—other than when Bradshaw is likened, perhaps, to a bird of prey—'He swooped; he devoured' (pp. 86–7)— whereas the bird imagery which links Septimus and Clarissa is shared by many of the other characters in the novel, such as Sally Seton (p. 30), the 'battered old woman' (p. 69), Lucrezia (pp. 76, 124, 126), Peter Walsh (p. 139), Lord Gayton (p. 150) and Helena Parry (p. 138). Appropriately, 'the dead' are also associated with birds. As the pedestrians look up at the sky-writing aeroplane, the clocks strike the hour at which the annual Remembrance service begins at the Cenotaph, and 'the whole world became perfectly silent, and a flight of gulls crossed the sky, first one gull leading, then another, and in this extraordinary silence and peace, in this pallor, in this purity, bells struck eleven times, the sound fading up there among the gulls' (p. 18). Birds fly above London's social and economic divisions and accentuate the oneness of things, and the resonant sound of Big Ben and other bells is portrayed in a similar way. The 'leaden circles' which 'dissolved in the air' (pp. 4, 41, 80, 158) probably have their literal source in the con-

---

[27] See Mark Hussey, *The Singing of the Real World: The Philosophy of Virginia Woolf's Fiction* (Columbus, Ohio: Ohio State University Press, 1986), and Allen McLaurin, 'Consciousness and Group Consciousness in Virginia Woolf', in Eric Warner (ed.), *Virginia Woolf: A Centenary Perspective* (London and Basingstoke: Macmillan, 1984), 28–40.

centric cast iron rings on Big Ben's four 23-ft.-diameter dials,[28] but Woolf's phrase highlights the figurative dissolution of the coercive power which emanates from the Houses of Parliament. It is possible that Woolf wants the reader to think of the sound of Parliament's bell contaminating the sky as lead poisons water, but the image of it 'dissolv[ing]' in the air seems more closely related to the avian, un-policed, and timeless freedoms which lie beyond the control of Britain's Parliamentary lawmakers.

Walking in Regent's Park, Peter Walsh grows ever more conscious of the way in which the old order has altered since he was last in London five years ago. He notices that women of all classes wear make-up, for instance, that sexual mores seem freer, and he is convinced that 'a change of some sort had undoubtedly taken place' (p. 61). 'Those five years—1918 to 1923—had been, he suspected, somehow very important. People looked different. Newspapers seemed different. Now, for instance, there was a man writing quite openly . . . about water-closets' (p. 61). This comparative social openness, inscribed in the uninhibited article on lavatories, represents a 'shift in the whole pyramidal accumulation which in his youth had seemed immovable. On top of them it had pressed; weighed them down, the women especially' (pp. 137–8). This change is also perceived (and in similar terms) by Elizabeth Dalloway, who, when walking along the Strand, notices that although the clouds 'had all the appearance of settled habitations assembled for the conference of gods above the world, there was a perpetual movement among them' and occasionally 'a whole block of *pyramidal* size which had kept its station inalterably' changes its position and transforms the '*accumulated robustness*' of the sky (p. 118; emphases added). As a young woman, Clarissa only received a 'few twigs of knowledge [from] Fräulein Daniels' (p. 7) and Lady Bruton has no idea how to write a letter to *The Times* (p. 153), but at least for Elizabeth, having been 'at a High School' (p. 67) and now under the tutelage of Miss Kilman (who has a 'degree' and whose 'knowledge of modern history was more than respectable' (p. 112)), the outlook is more promising: 'all

---

[28] John Darwin, *The Triumphs of Big Ben* (London: Robert Hale, 1986), 20–1.

professions are open to women of your generation, said Miss Kilman' (p. 111). The opening reference to taking doors off their hinges, therefore, could not be more suitable as a way of beginning this novel not only because it immediately introduces the central theme of mental health, but also because it symbolizes the greater social and intellectual liberties, the comparative unrestrictedness, which the novel both registers and promotes. Even the first line of the book, in which the relationship between mistress and servant, controller and controlled is set aside in an act of sympathetic understanding, signposts the possibility of a less hierarchical and more enlightened future. This is underlined by Clarissa's occupation of 'an attic room' (p. 26), a space intended for servants, in which there is no electricity.

Just as Clarissa and Peter 'lived in each other' and Clarissa feels 'part of people she had never met' (p. 8), so Woolf thought we all could do, regardless of our place in the social hierarchy. So 'the smoke winding off' the trees at Bourton (p. 3) becomes mingled with the smoke of London when the derelict old woman's 'invincible thread of sound wound up into the air like the smoke from a cottage chimney, winding up clean beech trees and issuing in a tuft of blue smoke among the topmost leaves' (p. 70). Clarissa feels 'quite continuously' a sense of the 'existence' of her friends and acquaintances scattered about west London and her parties are 'an offering; to combine, to create' (p. 103). 'Odd affinities she had with people she had never spoken to, some woman in the street, some man behind a counter—even trees, or barns' (p. 129), while Elizabeth Dalloway gets a similar lift from 'the geniality, sisterhood, motherhood, brotherhood' of Fleet Street's 'uproar' (p. 117). The essential unanimity of Londoners is most plainly stressed in their collective response to the car which travels from Bond Street to Buckingham Palace and the aeroplane which swoops and soars above it, while the theme of communality is sustained by the novel's dominant narrative technique. Free indirect discourse, in which an omniscient narrator takes on the idiolect of the character in focus, is employed to great effect in *Mrs Dalloway*. It is a technique which allowed Woolf to fuse a number of discrete narrative perspectives and so draw together an assembly of characters (who are in more obvious ways either unconnected or disconnected) on a single day.

Mining and Meaning

The novel Woolf published in 1925 turned out to be very close to the one she first envisaged in 1922. A character named Clarissa Dalloway appears in Woolf's first novel, *The Voyage Out* (1915), but *Mrs Dalloway* had its most direct origins in a short story called 'Mrs Dalloway in Bond Street', written in 1922 and published in July 1923: its first words are 'Mrs Dalloway said she would buy the gloves herself'.[29] Before the story's publication, on 6 October 1922, Woolf wrote two pages of notes in which she recorded her:

Thoughts upon beginning a book to be called, perhaps, At Home: or The Party.

This is to be a short book consisting of six or seven chapters, each complete separately. In them must be some fusion. And all must converge upon the party at the end. My idea is to have some characters, like Mrs Dalloway, much in relief; then to have some interludes of thought or reflection, or moments of digression (which must be related, logically, to the next) all compact, yet not jerked.

The chapters might be

1. Mrs Dalloway in Bond Street
2. The Prime Minister
3. Ancestors
4. A dialogue
5. The old ladies
6. Country house?
7. Cut flowers
8. The party

One, roughly to be done in a month; but this plan is to consist of some very short intervals, not whole chapters. There should be fun.[30]

[29] *The Complete Shorter Fiction of Virginia Woolf*, ed. Susan Dick (1985; London: The Hogarth Press, rev. edn. 1989), 152–9.

[30] Quoted in Jane Novak, *The Razor Edge of Balance: A Study of Virginia Woolf* (Coral Gables, Fla.: University of Miami Press, 1975), 110–11.

In the event, only three of these 'short intervals' were completed by Woolf—'Mrs Dalloway in Bond Street', 'The Prime Minister' (in effect a discarded draft chapter of the novel),[31] and 'Ancestors'[32]—and by 14 October 1922 Woolf was noting in her diary that 'Mrs Dalloway has branched into a book . . .'.[33]

At some point in the late spring of 1923 Woolf decided to call her novel 'The Hours',[34] and, although its emergence was to be dictated, as usual, by the occasional peak and many chasms of her fragile self-confidence, by 9 February 1924 she was able to write in her diary:

I'm working at The Hours, & think it a very interesting attempt; I may have found my mine this time I think. I may get all my gold out . . . And my vein of gold lies so deep, in such bent channels. To get it I must forge ahead, stoop & grope. But it is gold of a kind I think.[35]

It was only very near the end of this 'mining' process that Woolf decided to call the novel 'Mrs Dalloway'. On 17 October 1924 she noted in her diary that she had written 'the last words of the last page of Mrs Dalloway . . . "For there she was"' eight days earlier on 9 October.[36] Woolf immediately set about revising the novel and she also embarked on eight short stories which centre on the Dalloways' party: 'Ancestors', 'The New Dress', 'The Man Who Loved his Kind', 'Together and Apart', 'The Introduction', 'Happiness', 'A Simple Melody', and 'A Summing Up', only one of which was published in her lifetime.

Mrs Dalloway was first published in London on 14 May 1925. With *To the Lighthouse* it has been the most consistently praised of all Woolf's novels, though in the 1920s its complex subtlety and experimental technique left some commentators stranded.

---

[31] Published for the first time in 1989 as appendix B of the rev. edn. of *Complete Shorter Fiction*, 316–23.

[32] *Complete Shorter Fiction*, 181–3.

[33] *Diary*, ii. 207.

[34] See Helen M. Wussow (ed.), *Virginia Woolf 'The Hours': The British Museum Manuscript of* Mrs Dalloway (New York and London: Pace University Press, 1997).

[35] *Diary*, ii. 292.

[36] Ibid. 316.

The *TLS* had the perception to realize that 'something real has been achieved; for, having the courage of her theme and setting free her vision, Mrs Woolf steeps it in an emotion and irony and delicate imagination which enhance the consciousness and zest of living', while the influential *Calendar of Modern Letters* deemed it 'considerably the best book [Woolf] has written; in it her gifts achieve their full effect, and her capacity to say what she wants to is almost complete'. 'How then', the reviewer went on to ask in a way which shows how far criticism of the novel has developed since 1925, ' . . . can such talent co-exist with a sentimentality that would be remarkable in a stockbroker, and inconceivable among educated people?'.[37]

'It is difficult—perhaps impossible—for a writer to say anything about his own work,' Woolf wrote in her introduction to the Modern Library Edition of the novel. 'All he has to say has been said as fully and as well as he can in the body of the book itself . . . once a book is printed and published it ceases to be the property of its author; he commits it to the care of other people . . . '.[38] But if the author of a text has no control over its interpretation, few contemporary readers of *Mrs Dalloway* would claim to have mined its every meaning and even fewer would discover in it a damaging sentimentality. The challenge of this novel, its reader's exhilarating, discomforting switchback ride, is brought to mind when the crowd of onlookers offer different renditions of the sky-writing aeroplane's words. The crowd outside Buckingham Palace, Septimus, Lucrezia, and Clarissa all recognize, in their different ways, that the aeroplane is conveying a message to them. But what words do the smoky letters form? 'A C was it? an E, then an L? Only for a moment did they lie still; then they moved and melted and were rubbed out up in the sky, and the aeroplane shot further away and again, in a fresh space of sky, began writing a K, and E, a Y perhaps?' (p. 17). It is as if the aeroplane teases the spectators with its message, just as the 'K . . . E . . . Y' to *Mrs*

---

[37] For these two and other reviews, see Robin Majumdar and Allen McLaurin (eds.), *Virginia Woolf: The Critical Heritage* (1975; London: Routledge, 1997), 17–18, 158–92; quotes from pp. 162 and 170 respectively.

[38] *Essays*, iv. 548–9.

Dalloway can seem too complex to grasp at first reading. In a novel like this there will always be new interpretations to ponder, and, like the sky-scanning Londoners, the onus will always lie with the individual reader not only to absorb the signs on the page but to fill in the missing letters that make up the missing words.

NOTE ON THE TEXT

Mrs Dalloway was first published in London on 14 May 1925 by
Leonard and Virginia Woolf at the Hogarth Press. On the same
day, the first American edition of the novel was published in New
York by Harcourt, Brace and Co. This Oxford World's Classics
edition is based on the Second Uniform Edition of the novel,
published in London by the Hogarth Press in 1942.

For a full list of articles concerned with the manuscripts,
textual revisions, and variants of the novel, see B. J. Kirkpatrick and Stuart N. Clarke, *A Bibliography of Virginia Woolf*
(4th edn.; Oxford: Clarendon Press, 1997), 38. No one has
done more work on the text of *Mrs Dalloway* than G. Patton
Wright, and the four appendices to his 'Definitive Collected
Edition' (London: Hogarth Press, 1990) of the novel should be
consulted by any reader wishing to form a comprehensive view
of this subject. Wright's first appendix, 'List of Textual Variants' (pp. 183–99), represents an exhaustive collation of all the
United Kingdom editions of the novel which had appeared at
the time he went to press, the three American editions, and
the two extant sets of page proofs with Woolf's autograph
corrections.

For this edition, a number of emendations have been made.
The most important are these: 'Lords' has been corrected to
'Lord's' on pages 4, 14, and 150, whereas on page 151 'Lord's' has
been changed to 'Lords'; 'Hatchards'' has been corrected to
'Hatchard's' (p. 8), and 'Jorrocks'' has been changed to 'Jorrocks's' (p. 8) and italicized as part of the title. 'Kinloch-Jones's'
has been changed to 'Kinloch-Joneses'' on page 28, and 'Kinlock
Jones's' has been changed to 'Kinloch-Joneses' on page 61 of this
edition; in both instances the change is justified grammatically.

I would like to record my gratitude to Stuart N. Clarke for allowing me to draw on his
expertise as both a textual scholar and keen reader of Woolf. I have also benefited from
his advice in a number of other ways during the preparation of this edition, though any
deficiencies it may have are mine alone.

The same justification has resulted in 'patient's' being changed to 'patients'' on page 86.

This edition also makes minor adjustments to the Second Uniform Edition's hyphenation, italicization (e.g. 'the *Times*' has now been changed to '*The Times*' throughout the text), and word division ('tomorrow', 'tonight', 'someone', etc.). Similarly, '-ize' is preferred to '-ise', full points have been dropped after 'Mr', 'Mrs', and 'Dr', and single rather than double quotation marks have been used in order to be consistent and to follow current standard usage.

SELECT BIBLIOGRAPHY

Bibiliography

Kirkpatrick, B. J., and Clarke, Stuart N., *A Bibliography of Virginia Woolf* (4th edn.; Oxford: Clarendon Press, 1997).

Biography

Bell, Quentin, *Virginia Woolf: A Biography* (1972; London: Pimlico, 1996).

Briggs, Julia, *Virginia Woolf: An Inner Life* (London: Allen Lane, 2005).

Gordon, Lyndall, *Virginia Woolf: A Writer's Life* (Oxford: Oxford University Press, 1984).

Leaska, Mitchell A., *Granite and Rainbow: The Hidden Life of Virginia Woolf* (London: Picador, 1998).

Lee, Hermione, *Virginia Woolf* (London: Chatto and Windus, 1996).

Mepham, John, *Virginia Woolf: A Literary Life* (London and Basingstoke: Macmillan, 1991).

Poole, Roger, *The Unknown Virginia Woolf* (4th edn.; Cambridge: Cambridge University Press, 1995).

Woolf, Leonard, *An Autobiography* (2 vols.; Oxford: Oxford University Press, 1980).

Editions

The Complete Shorter Fiction of Virginia Woolf, ed. Susan Dick (1985; London: Hogarth Press, rev. edn., 1989).

The Diary of Virginia Woolf, ed. Anne Olivier Bell, assisted by Andrew McNeillie (5 vols.; London: Hogarth Press, 1977–84).

The Essays of Virginia Woolf, ed. Andrew McNeillie (6 vols.; London: Hogarth Press, 1986–).

Letters of Leonard Woolf, ed. Frederic Spotts (London: Weidenfeld and Nicolson, 1989).

The Letters of Virginia Woolf, ed. Nigel Nicolson and Joanne Trautmann (6 vols.; London: Hogarth Press, 1975–80).

A Passionate Apprentice: The Early Journals 1897–1909, ed. Mitchell A. Leaska (London: Hogarth Press, 1990).

General Criticism

Abel, Elizabeth, *Virginia Woolf and the Fictions of Psychoanalysis* (Chicago: University of Chicago Press, 1989).

Beer, Gillian, *Virginia Woolf: The Common Ground* (Edinburgh: Edinburgh University Press, 1996).

Bowlby, Rachel (ed.), *Virginia Woolf* (London: Longman, 1992). Longman Critical Readers series.

—— *Virginia Woolf: Feminist Destinations and Further Essays on Virginia Woolf* (Edinburgh: Edinburgh University Press, 1997).

Briggs, Julia (ed.), *Virginia Woolf: Introductions to the Major Works* (London: Virago Press, 1994).

Clements, Patricia, and Grundy, Isobel (eds.), *Virginia Woolf: New Critical Essays* (London: Vision Press, 1983).

Di Battista, Maria, *Virginia Woolf's Major Novels* (New Haven and London: Yale University Press, 1980).

Fleishman, Avrom, *Virginia Woolf: A Critical Reading* (Baltimore: Johns Hopkins University Press, 1975).

Guiguet, Jean, *Virginia Woolf and her Works*, trans. Jean Stewart (London: Hogarth Press, 1965).

Harper, Howard, *Between Language and Silence: The Novels of Virginia Woolf* (Baton Rouge, La.: Louisiana State University Press, 1982).

Hussey, Mark, *The Singing of the Real World: The Philosophy of Virginia Woolf's Fiction* (Columbus, Ohio: Ohio State University Press, 1986).

—— *Virginia Woolf A to Z: A Comprehensive Reference for Students, Teachers and Common Readers to her Life, Work and Critical Reception* (New York: Facts on File Inc., 1995).

—— (ed.), *Virginia Woolf and War: Fiction, Reality, and Myth* (Syracuse, NY: Syracuse University Press, 1991).

Leaska, Mitchell A., *The Novels of Virginia Woolf: From Beginning to End* (London: Weidenfeld and Nicolson, 1977).

Lee, Hermione, *The Novels of Virginia Woolf* (London: Methuen, 1977).

McLaurin, Allen, *Virginia Woolf: The Echoes Enslaved* (Cambridge: Cambridge University Press, 1973).

Majumdar, Robin, and McLaurin, Allen (eds.), *Virginia Woolf: The Critical Heritage* (1975; London: Routledge, 1997).

Marcus, Jane (ed.), *New Feminist Essays on Virginia Woolf* (Lincoln, Nebr.: University of Nebraska Press, 1981).

Marcus, Jane (ed.), *Virginia Woolf: A Feminist Slant* (Lincoln, Nebr.: University of Nebraska Press, 1983).

—— *Virginia Woolf and the Languages of Patriarchy* (Bloomington, Ind.: Indiana University Press, 1987).

Marder, Herbert, *Virginia Woolf: Feminism and Art* (Chicago and London: University of Chicago Press, 1968).

Minow-Pinkney, Makiko, *Virginia Woolf and the Problem of the Subject* (Brighton: Harvester Wheatsheaf, 1987).

Moore, Madeline, *The Short Season between Two Silences: The Mystical and the Political in the Novels of Virginia Woolf* (Boston and London: George Allen and Unwin, 1984).

Naremore, James, *The World Without a Self: Virginia Woolf and the Novel* (New Haven: Yale University Press, 1973).

Phillips, Kathy J., *Virginia Woolf Against Empire* (Knoxville, Tenn.: University of Tennessee Press, 1994).

Richter, Harvena, *Virginia Woolf: The Inward Voyage* (Princeton: Princeton University Press, 1970).

Warner, Eric (ed.), *Virginia Woolf: A Centenary Perspective* (London and Basingstoke: Macmillan, 1984).

Wilson, Jean Moorcroft, *Virginia Woolf: Life and London. A Biography of Place* (London: Cecil Woolf, 1987).

Zwerdling, Alex, *Virginia Woolf and the Real World* (Berkeley, Los Angeles, and London: University of California Press, 1986).

Criticism of Mrs Dalloway

Barrett, Eileen, 'Unmasking Lesbian Passion: The Inverted World of *Mrs Dalloway*', in Eileen Barrett and Patricia Cramer (eds.), *Virginia Woolf: Lesbian Readings* (New York and London: New York University Press, 1997), 146–64.

Beer, Gillian, 'The Island and the Aeroplane: The Case of Virginia Woolf', in Homi K. Bhabha (ed.), *Nation and Narration* (London: Routledge, 1991), 265–90.

Bishop, Edward, 'Writing, Speech, and Silence in *Mrs Dalloway*', *English Studies in Canada*, 12/4 (Dec. 1986), 397–423.

Bloom, Harold (ed.), *Clarissa Dalloway* (New York and Philadelphia: Chelsea House, 1990). Major Literary Characters series.

Edwards, Lee R., 'War and Roses: The Politics of *Mrs Dalloway*', in Arlyn Diamond and Lee R. Edwards (eds.), *The Authority of Experience: Essays in Feminist Criticism* (Amherst, Mass.: University of Massachusetts Press, 1977), 160–77.

Hoffmann, Charles G., 'From Short Story to Novel: The Manuscript Revisions of Virginia Woolf's *Mrs Dalloway*', *Modern Fiction Studies*, 14/2 (Summer 1968), 171–86.

Miller, J. Hillis, *Fiction and Repetition: Seven English Novels* (Cambridge, Mass.: Harvard University Press, 1982).

Novak, Jane, *The Razor Edge of Balance: A Study of Virginia Woolf* (Coral Gables, Fla.: University of Florida Press, 1975).

Richter, Harvena, 'The *Ulysses* Connection: Clarissa Dalloway's Bloomsday', *Studies in the Novel*, 21/3 (Fall 1989), 305–19.

Squier, Susan, *Virginia Woolf and London* (Chapel Hill, NC: University of North Carolina Press, 1985).

Tambling, Jeremy, 'Repression in Mrs. Dalloway's London', *Essays in Criticism*, 39/2 (Apr. 1989), 137–55.

Tate, Trudi, '*Mrs Dalloway* and the Armenian Question', *Textual Practice*, 8/3 (Winter 1994), 467–86.

Thomas, Sue, 'Virginia Woolf's Septimus Smith and Contemporary Perceptions of Shell Shock', *English Language Notes*, 25/2 (Dec. 1987), 49–57.

Wussow, Helen M. (ed.), *Virginia Woolf 'The Hours': The British Museum Manuscript of* Mrs Dalloway (New York and London: Pace University Press, 1997).

Further Reading in Oxford World's Classics

Woolf, Virginia, *Between the Acts*, ed. Frank Kermode.

—— *Flush*, ed. Kate Flint.

—— *Jacob's Room*, ed. Kate Flint.

—— *Night and Day*, ed. Suzanne Raitt.

—— *Orlando: A Biography*, ed. Rachel Bowlby.

—— *A Room of One's Own* and *Three Guineas*, ed. Morag Shiach.

—— *Selected Essays*, ed. David Bradshaw.

—— *To the Lighthouse*, ed. David Bradshaw.

—— *The Voyage Out*, ed. Lorna Sage.

—— *The Waves*, ed. Gillian Beer.

—— *The Years*, ed. Hermione Lee, with notes by Sue Ashbee.

A CHRONOLOGY OF VIRGINIA WOOLF

Life	*Historical and Cultural Background*
1882 (25 Jan.) Adeline Virginia Stephen (VW) born at 22 Hyde Park Gate, London.	Deaths of Darwin, Trollope, D. G. Rossetti; Joyce born; Stravinsky born; Married Women's Property Act; Society for Psychical Research founded.
1895 (5 May) Death of mother, Julia Stephen; VW's first breakdown occurs soon afterwards.	Death of T. H. Huxley; X-rays discovered; invention of the cinematograph; wireless telegraphy invented; arrest, trials, and conviction of Oscar Wilde. Hardy, *Jude the Obscure* Wilde, *The Importance of Being Earnest* and *An Ideal Husband* Wells, *The Time Machine*
1896 (Nov.) Travels in France with sister Vanessa.	Death of William Morris; *Daily Mail* started. Housman, *A Shropshire Lad*
1897 (10 April) Marriage of half-sister Stella; (19 July) death of Stella; (Nov.) VW learning Greek and History at King's College, London.	Queen Victoria's Diamond Jubilee; Tate Gallery opens. Stoker, *Dracula* James, *What Maisie Knew*
1898	Deaths of Gladstone and Lewis Carroll; radium and plutonium discovered. Wells, *The War of the Worlds*
1899 (30 Oct.) VW's brother Thoby goes up to Trinity College, Cambridge, where he forms friendships with Lytton Strachey, Leonard Woolf, Clive Bell, and others of the future Bloomsbury Group (VW's younger brother Adrian follows him to Trinity in 1902).	Boer War begins. Births of Bowen and Coward. Symons, *The Symbolist Movement in Literature* James, *The Awkward Age* Freud, *The Interpretation of Dreams*
1900	Deaths of Nietzsche, Wilde, and Ruskin; *Daily Express* started; Planck announces quantum theory; Boxer Rising. Conrad, *Lord Jim*

1901		Death of Queen Victoria; accession of Edward VII; first wireless communication between Europe and USA; 'World's Classics' series begun. Kipling, *Kim*
1902	VW starts private lessons in Greek with Janet Case.	End of Boer War; British Academy founded; *Encyclopaedia Britannica* (10th edn.); *TLS* started. Bennett, *Anna of the Five Towns* James, *The Wings of the Dove*
1903		Deaths of Gissing and Spencer; *Daily Mirror* started; Wright brothers make their first aeroplane flight; Emmeline Pankhurst founds Women's Social and Political Union. Butler, *The Way of All Flesh* James, *The Ambassadors* Moore, *Principia Ethica*
1904	(22 Feb.) Death of father, Sir Leslie Stephen. In spring, VW travels to Italy with Vanessa and friend Violet Dickinson. (10 May) VW has second nervous breakdown and is ill for three months. Moves to 46, Gordon Square. (14 Dec.) VW's first publication appears.	Deaths of Christina Rossetti and Chekhov; Russo–Japanese War; *Entente Cordiale* between Britain and France. Chesterton, *The Napoleon of Notting Hill* Conrad, *Nostromo* James, *The Golden Bowl*
1905	(March, April) Travels in Portugal and Spain. Writes reviews and teaches once a week at Morley College, London.	Einstein, *Special Theory of Relativity*; Sartre born. Shaw, *Major Barbara* and *Man and Superman* Wells, *Kipps* Forster, *Where Angels Fear to Tread*
1906	(Sept. and Oct.) Travels in Greece. (20 Nov.) death of Thoby Stephen.	Death of Ibsen; Beckett born; Liberal Government elected; Campbell-Bannerman Prime Minister; launch of HMS *Dreadnought*.
1907	(7 Feb.) Marriage of Vanessa to Clive Bell. VW moves with Adrian to 29 Fitzroy Square. At work on her first novel, 'Melymbrosia' (working title for *The Voyage Out*).	Auden born; Anglo-Russian Entente. Synge, *The Playboy of the Western World* Conrad, *The Secret Agent* Forster, *The Longest Journey*

1908 (Sept.) Visits Italy with the Bells.

Asquith Prime Minister; Old Age Pensions Act; Elgar's First Symphony.
Bennett, *The Old Wives' Tale*
Forster, *A Room with a View*
Chesterton, *The Man Who Was Thursday*

1909 (17 Feb.) Lytton Strachey proposes marriage. (30 March) First meets Lady Ottoline Morrell. (April) Visits Florence. (Aug.) Visits Bayreuth and Dresden.

Death of Meredith; 'People's Budget'; English Channel flown by Blériot.
Wells, *Tono-Bungay*
Masterman, *The Condition of England*
Marinetti, *Futurist Manifesto*

1910 (Jan.) Works for women's suffrage. (June–Aug.) Spends time in a nursing home at Twickenham.

Deaths of Edward VII, Tolstoy, and Florence Nightingale; accession of George V; *Encyclopaedia Britannica* (11th edn.); Roger Fry's Post-Impressionist Exhibition.
Bennett, *Clayhanger*
Forster, *Howards End*
Yeats, *The Green Helmet*
Wells, *The History of Mr Polly*

1911 (April) Travels to Turkey, where Vanessa is ill. (Nov.) Moves to 38 Brunswick Square, sharing house with Adrian, John Maynard Keynes, Duncan Grant, and Leonard Woolf.

National Insurance Act; Suffragette riots.
Conrad, *Under Western Eyes*
Wells, *The New Machiavelli*
Lawrence, *The White Peacock*

1912 Rents Asheham House. (Feb.) Spends some days in Twickenham nursing home. (10 Aug.) Marriage of Leonard Woolf. Honeymoon in Provence, Spain, and Italy. (Oct.) Moves to 13 Clifford's Inn, London.

Second Post-Impressionist Exhibition; Suffragettes active; strikes by dockers, coal-miners, and transport workers; Irish Home Rule Bill again rejected by Lords; sinking of SS *Titanic*; death of Scott in the Antarctic; *Daily Herald* started. English translations of Chekhov and Dostoevsky begin to appear.

1913 (March) MS of *The Voyage Out* delivered to publisher. Unwell most of summer. (9 Sept.) Suicide attempt. Remains under care of nurses and husband for rest of year.

New Statesman started; Suffragettes active.
Lawrence, *Sons and Lovers*

1914 (16 Feb.) Last nurse leaves. Moves to Richmond, Surrey.

Irish Home Rule Bill passed by Parliament; First World War begins (4 Aug.); Dylan Thomas born.
Lewis, *Blast*
Joyce, *Dubliners*
Yeats, *Responsibilities*
Hardy, *Satires of Circumstance*
Bell, *Art*

1915 Purchase of Hogarth House, Richmond. (26 March) *The Voyage Out* published. (April, May) Bout of violent madness; under care of nurses until November.

Death of Rupert Brooke; Einstein, *General Theory of Relativity*; Second Battle of Ypres; Dardanelles Campaign; sinking of SS *Lusitania*; air attacks on London.
Ford, *The Good Soldier*
Lawrence, *The Rainbow*
Brooke, *1914 and Other Poems*
Richardson, *Pointed Roofs*

1916 (17 Oct.) Lectures to Richmond branch of the Women's Co-operative Guild. Regular work for *TLS*.

Death of James; Lloyd George Prime Minister; First Battle of the Somme; Battle of Verdun; Gallipoli Campaign; Easter Rising in Dublin.
Joyce, *Portrait of the Artist as a Young Man*

1917 (July) Hogarth Press commences publication with *The Mark on the Wall*. VW begins work on *Night and Day*.

Death of Edward Thomas. Third Battle of Ypres (Passchendaele); T.E. Lawrence's campaigns in Arabia; USA enters the War; Revolution in Russia (Feb., Oct.); Balfour Declaration.
Eliot, *Prufrock and Other Observations*

1918 Writes reviews and *Night and Day;* also sets type for the Hogarth Press. (15 Nov.) First meets T. S. Eliot.

Death of Owen; Second Battle of the Somme; final German offensive collapses; Armistice with Germany (11 Nov.); Franchise Act grants vote to women over 30; influenza pandemic kills millions.
Lewis, *Tarr*
Hopkins, *Poems*
Strachey, *Eminent Victorians*

1919 (1 July) Purchase of Monk's House, Rodmell, Sussex. (20 Oct.) *Night and Day* published.

Treaty of Versailles; Alcock and Brown fly the Atlantic; National Socialists founded in Germany.
Sinclair, *Mary Olivier*
Shaw, *Heartbreak House*

1920 Works on journalism and *Jacob's Room*.

League of Nations established.
Pound, *Hugh Selwyn Mauberley*
Lawrence, *Women in Love*
Eliot, *The Sacred Wood*
Fry, *Vision and Design*

1921	Ill for summer months. (4 Nov.) Finishes *Jacob's Room*.	Irish Free State founded. Huxley, *Crome Yellow*
1922	(Jan. to May) Ill. (14 Dec.) First meets Vita Sackville-West. (24 Oct.) *Jacob's Room* published.	Bonar Law Prime Minister; Mussolini forms Fascist Government in Italy; death of Proust; *Encyclopaedia Britannica* (12th edn.); *Criterion* founded; BBC founded; Irish Free State proclaimed. Eliot, *The Waste Land* Galsworthy, *The Forsyte Saga* Joyce, *Ulysses* Mansfield, *The Garden Party* Wittgenstein, *Tractatus Logico-Philosophicus*
1923	(March, April) Visits Spain. Works on 'The Hours', the first version of *Mrs Dalloway*.	Baldwin Prime Minister; BBC radio begins broadcasting (Nov.); death of K. Mansfield.
1924	Purchase of lease on 52 Tavistock Square, Bloomsbury. Gives lecture that becomes 'Mr Bennett and Mrs Brown'. (8 Oct.) Finishes *Mrs Dalloway*.	First (minority) Labour Government; Ramsay MacDonald Prime Minister; deaths of Lenin, Kafka, and Conrad. Ford, *Some Do Not* Forster, *A Passage to India* O'Casey, *Juno and the Paycock* Coward, *The Vortex*
1925	(23 April) *The Common Reader* published. (14 May) *Mrs Dalloway* published. Ill during summer.	Gerhardie, *The Polyglots* Ford, *No More Parades* Huxley, *Those Barren Leaves* Whitehead, *Science and the Modern World*
1926	(Jan) Unwell with German measles. Writes *To the Lighthouse*.	General Strike (3–12 May); *Encyclopaedia Britannica* (13th edn.); first television demonstration. Ford, *A Man Could Stand Up* Tawney, *Religion and the Rise of Capitalism*
1927	(March, April) Travels in France and Italy. (5 May) *To the Lighthouse* published. (5 Oct.) Begins *Orlando*.	Lindburgh flies solo across the Atlantic; first 'talkie' films.
1928	(11 Oct.) *Orlando* published. Delivers lectures at Cambridge on which she bases *A Room of One's Own*.	Death of Hardy; votes for women over 21. Yeats, *The Tower* Lawrence, *Lady Chatterley's Lover* Waugh, *Decline and Fall* Sherriff, *Journey's End* Ford, *Last Post* Huxley, *Point Counter Point* Bell, *Civilization*

1929 (Jan.) Travels to Berlin. (24 Oct.) *A Room of One's Own* published.

2nd Labour Government, MacDonald Prime Minister; collapse of New York Stock Exchange; start of world economic depression.
Graves, *Goodbye to All That*
Aldington, *Death of a Hero*
Green, *Living*

1930 (20 Feb.) First meets Ethel Smyth; (29 May) Finishes first version of *The Waves*.

Mass unemployment; television starts in USA; deaths of Lawrence and Conan Doyle.
Auden, *Poems*
Eliot, *Ash Wednesday*
Waugh, *Vile Bodies*
Coward, *Private Lives*
Lewis, *Apes of God*

1931 (April) Car tour through France. (8 Oct.) *The Waves* published. Writes *Flush*.

Formation of National Government; abandonment of Gold Standard; death of Bennett; Japan invades China.

1932 (21 Jan.) Death of Lytton Strachey. (13 Oct.) *The Common Reader*, 2nd series, published. Begins *The Years*, at this point called 'The Pargiters'.

Roosevelt becomes President of USA; hunger marches start in Britain; *Scrutiny* starts.
Huxley, *Brave New World*

1933 (May) Car tour of France and Italy. (5 Oct.) *Flush* published.

Deaths of Galsworthy and George Moore; Hitler becomes Chancellor of Germany.
Orwell, *Down and Out in Paris and London*
Wells, *The Shape of Things to Come.*

1934 Works on *The Years*. (9 Sept.) Death of Roger Fry.

Waugh, *A Handful of Dust*
Graves, *I, Claudius*
Beckett, *More Pricks than Kicks*
Toynbee, *A Study of History*

1935 Rewrites *The Years*. (May) Car tour of Holland, Germany, and Italy.

George V's Silver Jubilee; Baldwin Prime Minister of National Government; Germany re-arms; Italian invasion of Abyssinia (Ethiopia).
Isherwood, *Mr Norris Changes Trains*
T. S. Eliot, *Murder in the Cathedral*

1936 (May–Oct.) Ill. Finishes *The Years*. Begins *Three Guineas*.

Death of George V; accession of Edward VIII; abdication crisis; accession of George VI; Civil War breaks out in Spain; first of the Moscow show trials; Germany re-occupies the Rhineland; BBC television begins (2 Nov); deaths of Chesterton, Kipling, and Housman.
Orwell, *Keep the Aspidistra Flying*

1937 (15 March) *The Years* published. Begins *Roger Fry: A Biography*. (18 July) Death in Spanish Civil War of Julian Bell, son of Vanessa.

Chamberlain Prime Minister; destruction of Guernica; death of Barrie.
Orwell, *The Road to Wigan Pier*

1938 (2 June) *Three Guineas* published. Works on *Roger Fry*, and begins to envisage *Between the Acts*.

German *Anschluss* with Austria; Munich agreement; dismemberment of Czechoslovakia; first jet engine.
Beckett, *Murphy*
Bowen, *The Death of the Heart*
Greene, *Brighton Rock*

1939 VW moves to 37 Mecklenburgh Square, but lives mostly at Monk's House. Works on *Between the Acts*. Meets Freud in London.

End of Civil War in Spain; Russo–German pact; Germany invades Poland (Sept.); Britain and France declare war on Germany (3 Sept.); deaths of Freud, Yeats, and Ford.
Joyce, *Finnegans Wake*
Isherwood, *Goodbye to Berlin*

1940 (25 July) *Roger Fry* published. (10 Sept.) Mecklenburgh Square house bombed. (18 Oct.) witnesses the ruins of 52 Tavistock Square, destroyed by bombs. (23 Nov.) Finishes *Between the Acts*.

Germany invades north-west Europe; fall of France; evacuation of British troops from Dunkirk; Battle of Britain; beginning of 'the Blitz'; National Government under Churchill.

1941 (26 Feb.) Revises *Between the Acts*. Becomes ill. (28 March) Drowns herself in River Ouse, near Monk's House. (July) *Between the Acts* published.

Germany invades USSR; Japanese destroy US Fleet at Pearl Harbor; USA enters war; death of Joyce.

A Map of Mrs Dalloway's London

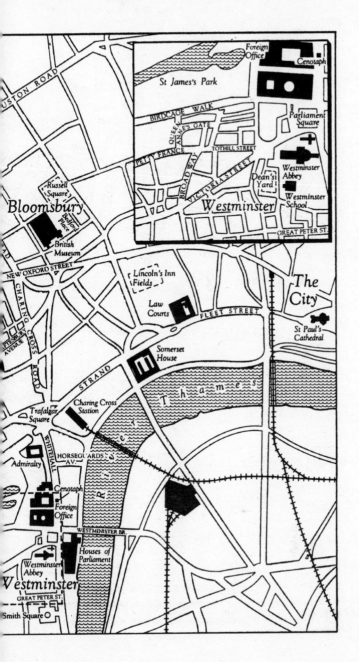

MRS DALLOWAY

MRS DALLOWAY

Mrs Dalloway said she would buy the flowers herself.

For Lucy had her work cut out for her. The doors would be taken off their hinges; Rumpelmayer's* men were coming. And then, thought Clarissa Dalloway, what a morning—fresh as if issued to children on a beach.

What a lark! What a plunge! For so it had always seemed to her when, with a little squeak of the hinges, which she could hear now, she had burst open the French windows and plunged at Bourton* into the open air. How fresh, how calm, stiller than this of course, the air was in the early morning; like the flap of a wave; the kiss of a wave; chill and sharp and yet (for a girl of eighteen as she then was) solemn, feeling as she did, standing there at the open window, that something awful was about to happen; looking at the flowers, at the trees with the smoke winding off them and the rooks rising, falling; standing and looking until Peter Walsh said, 'Musing among the vegetables?'—was that it?—'I prefer men to cauliflowers'—was that it? He must have said it at breakfast one morning when she had gone out on to the terrace—Peter Walsh. He would be back from India one of these days, June or July, she forgot which, for his letters were awfully dull; it was his sayings one remembered; his eyes, his pocket-knife, his smile, his grumpiness and, when millions of things had utterly vanished—how strange it was!—a few sayings like this about cabbages.

She stiffened a little on the kerb, waiting for Durtnall's* van to pass. A charming woman, Scrope Purvis thought her (knowing her as one does know people who live next door to one in Westminster);* a touch of the bird about her, of the jay, blue-green, light, vivacious, though she was over fifty, and grown very white since her illness. There she perched, never seeing him, waiting to cross, very upright.

For having lived in Westminster—how many years now? over twenty,—one feels even in the midst of the traffic, or waking at night, Clarissa was positive, a particular hush, or solemnity; an indescribable pause; a suspense (but that might be her heart, affected, they said, by influenza*) before Big Ben* strikes. There! Out it boomed. First a warning, musical; then the hour, irrevocable. The leaden circles dissolved in the air. Such fools we are, she thought, crossing Victoria Street.* For Heaven only knows why one loves it so, how one sees it so, making it up, building it round one, tumbling it, creating it every moment afresh; but the veriest frumps, the most dejected of miseries sitting on doorsteps (drink their downfall) do the same; can't be dealt with, she felt positive, by Acts of Parliament for that very reason: they love life. In people's eyes, in the swing, tramp, and trudge; in the bellow and the uproar; the carriages, motor cars, omnibuses, vans, sandwich men shuffling and swinging; brass bands; barrel organs; in the triumph and the jingle and the strange high singing of some aeroplane overhead was what she loved; life; London; this moment of June.

For it was the middle of June. The War was over, except for some one like Mrs Foxcroft at the Embassy last night eating her heart out because that nice boy was killed and now the old Manor House must go to a cousin; or Lady Bexborough who opened a bazaar, they said, with the telegram in her hand, John, her favourite, killed; but it was over; thank Heaven—over. It was June. The King and Queen were at the Palace.* And everywhere, though it was still so early, there was a beating, a stirring of galloping ponies, tapping of cricket bats; Lord's, Ascot, Ranelagh* and all the rest of it; wrapped the soft mesh of the grey-blue morning air, which, as the day wore on, would unwind them, and set down on their lawns and pitches the bouncing ponies, whose forefeet just struck the ground and up they sprung, the whirling young men, and laughing girls in their transparent muslins who, even now, after dancing all night, were taking their absurd woolly dogs for a run; and even now, at this hour, discreet old dowagers were shooting out in their motor cars on errands of mystery; and the shop-keepers were fidgeting in their windows with their paste and diamonds, their lovely old sea-green brooches in eighteenth-century settings to tempt Americans (but one must economize, not buy things rashly for Elizabeth), and she, too, loving it as she did with an absurd and faithful passion, being part of it, since her people were courtiers once in the time of the Georges,* she, too, was going that very night to kindle and illuminate; to give her party. But how strange, on entering the Park,* the silence; the mist; the hum; the slow-swimming happy ducks; the pouched birds waddling; and who should be coming along with his back against the Government buildings, most appropriately, carrying a despatch box stamped with the Royal Arms, who but Hugh Whitbread; her old friend Hugh—the admirable Hugh!

'Good-morning to you, Clarissa!' said Hugh, rather extravagantly, for they had known each other as children. 'Where are you off to?'

'I love walking in London,' said Mrs Dalloway. 'Really, it's better than walking in the country.'

They had just come up—unfortunately—to see doctors. Other people came to see pictures; go to the opera; take their daughters out; the Whitbreads came 'to see doctors'. Times without number Clarissa had visited Evelyn Whitbread in a nursing home. Was Evelyn ill again? Evelyn was a good deal out of sorts, said Hugh, intimating by a kind of pout or swell of his very well-covered, manly, extremely handsome, perfectly upholstered body (he was almost too well dressed always, but presumably had to be, with his little job at Court) that his wife had some internal ailment, nothing serious, which, as an old friend, Clarissa Dalloway would quite understand without requiring him to specify. Ah yes, she did of course; what a nuisance; and felt very sisterly and oddly conscious at the same time of her hat. Not the right hat for the early morning, was that it? For Hugh always made her feel, as he bustled on, raising his hat rather extravagantly and assuring her that she might be a girl of eighteen, and of course he was coming to her party tonight, Evelyn absolutely insisted, only a little late he might be after the party at the Palace to which he had to take one of Jim's boys,—she always felt a little skimpy beside Hugh; schoolgirlish; but attached to him, partly from having known him always, but she did think him a good sort in his own way, though Richard was nearly driven mad by him, and as for Peter Walsh, he had never to this day forgiven her for liking him.

She could remember scene after scene at Bourton—Peter furious; Hugh not, of course, his match in any way, but still not a positive imbecile as Peter made out; not a mere barber's block. When his old mother wanted him to give up shooting or to take her to Bath* he did it, without a word; he was really unselfish, and as for saying, as Peter did, that he had no heart, no brain, nothing but the manners and breeding of an English gentleman, that was only her dear Peter at his worst; and he could be intolerable; he could be impossible; but adorable to walk with on a morning like this.

(June had drawn out every leaf on the trees. The mothers of Pimlico* gave suck to their young. Messages were passing from the Fleet to the Admiralty.* Arlington Street and Piccadilly* seemed to chafe the very air in the Park and lift its leaves hotly, brilliantly, on waves of that divine vitality which Clarissa loved. To dance, to ride, she had adored all that.)

For they might be parted for hundreds of years, she and Peter; she never wrote a letter and his were dry sticks; but suddenly it would come over her, if he were with me now what would he say?—some days, some sights bringing him back to her calmly, without the old bitterness; which perhaps was the reward of having cared for people; they came back in the middle of St James's Park on a fine morning—indeed they did. But Peter—however beautiful the day might be, and the trees and the grass, and the little girl in pink—Peter never saw a thing of all that. He would put on his spectacles, if she told him to; he would look. It was the state of the world that interested him; Wagner, Pope's poetry,* people's characters eternally, and the defects of her own soul. How he scolded her! How they argued! She would marry a Prime Minister and stand at the top of a staircase; the perfect hostess he called her (she had cried over it in her bedroom), she had the makings of the perfect hostess, he said.

So she would still find herself arguing in St James's Park, still making out that she had been right—and she had too—not to marry him. For in marriage a little licence, a little independence there must be between people living together day in day out in the same house; which Richard gave her, and she him. (Where was he this morning, for instance? Some committee, she never asked what.) But with Peter everything had to be shared; everything gone into. And it was intolerable, and when it came to that scene in the little garden by the fountain, she had to break with him or they would have been destroyed, both of them ruined, she was convinced; though she had borne about her for years like an arrow sticking in her heart the grief, the anguish: and then the horror of the moment when someone told her at a concert that he had married a woman met on the boat going to India! Never should she forget all that. Cold, heartless, a prude, he called her. Never could she understand how he cared. But those Indian women* did presumably—silly, pretty, flimsy nincompoops. And she wasted her pity. For he was quite happy, he assured her—perfectly happy, though he had never done a thing that they talked of; his whole life had been a failure. It made her angry still.

She had reached the Park gates. She stood for a moment, looking at the omnibuses in Piccadilly.

She would not say of anyone in the world now that they were this or were that. She felt very young; at the same time unspeakably aged. She sliced like a knife through everything; at the same time was outside, looking on. She had a perpetual sense, as she watched the taxicabs, of being out, out, far out to sea and alone; she always had the feeling that it was very, very dangerous to live even one day. Not that she thought herself clever, or much out of the ordinary. How she had got through life on the few twigs of knowledge Fräulein Daniels gave them she could not think. She knew nothing; no language, no history; she scarcely read a book now, except memoirs in bed; and yet to her it was absolutely absorbing; all this; the cabs passing; and she would not say of Peter, she would not say of herself, I am this, I am that.

Her only gift was knowing people almost by instinct, she thought, walking on. If you put her in a room with someone, up went her back like a cat's; or she purred. Devonshire House, Bath House,* the house with the china cockatoo,* she had seen them all lit up once; and remembered Sylvia, Fred, Sally Seton—such hosts of people; and dancing all night; and the waggons plodding past to market; and driving home across the Park. She remembered once throwing a shilling into the Serpentine.* But everyone remembered; what she loved was this, here, now, in front of her; the fat lady in the cab. Did it matter then, she asked herself, walking towards Bond Street,* did it matter that she must inevitably cease completely; all this must go on without her; did she resent it; or did it not become consoling to believe that death ended absolutely? but that somehow in the streets of London, on the ebb and flow of things, here, there, she survived, Peter survived, lived in each other, she being part, she was positive, of the trees at home; of the house there, ugly, rambling all to bits and pieces as it was; part of people she had never met; being laid out like a mist between the people she knew best, who lifted her on their branches as she had seen the trees lift the mist, but it spread ever so far, her life, herself. But what was she dreaming as she looked into Hatchard's* shop window? What was she trying to recover? What image of white dawn in the country, as she read in the book spread open:

> Fear no more the heat o' the sun,
>   Nor the furious winter's rages.*

This late age of world's experience had bred in them all, all men and women, a well of tears. Tears and sorrows; courage and endurance; a perfectly upright and stoical bearing. Think, for example, of the woman she admired most, Lady Bexborough, opening the bazaar.

There were *Jorrocks's Jaunts and Jollities*; there were *Soapy Sponge* and Mrs Asquith's *Memoirs* and *Big Game Shooting in Nigeria*,* all spread open. Ever so many books there were; but none that seemed exactly right to take to Evelyn Whitbread in her nursing home. Nothing that would serve to amuse her and make that indescribably dried-up little woman look, as Clarissa came in, just for a moment cordial; before they settled down for the usual interminable talk of women's ailments. How much she wanted it—that people should look pleased as she came in, Clarissa thought and turned and walked back towards Bond

Street, annoyed, because it was silly to have other reasons for doing things. Much rather would she have been one of those people like Richard who did things for themselves, whereas, she thought, waiting to cross, half the time she did things not simply, not for themselves; but to make people think this or that; perfect idiocy she knew (and now the policeman held up his hand) for no one was ever for a second taken in. Oh if she could have had her life over again! she thought, stepping on to the pavement, could have looked even differently!

She would have been, in the first place, dark like Lady Bexborough, with a skin of crumpled leather and beautiful eyes. She would have been, like Lady Bexborough, slow and stately; rather large; interested in politics like a man; with a country house; very dignified, very sincere. Instead of which she had a narrow pea-stick figure; a ridiculous little face, beaked like a bird's. That she held herself well was true; and had nice hands and feet; and dressed well, considering that she spent little. But often now this body she wore (she stopped to look at a Dutch picture), this body, with all its capacities, seemed nothing—nothing at all. She had the oddest sense of being herself invisible; unseen; unknown; there being no more marrying, no more having of children now, but only this astonishing and rather solemn progress with the rest of them, up Bond Street, this being Mrs Dalloway; not even Clarissa any more; this being Mrs Richard Dalloway.

Bond Street fascinated her; Bond Street early in the morning in the season; its flags flying; its shops; no splash; no glitter; one roll of tweed in the shop where her father had bought his suits for fifty years; a few pearls; salmon on an iceblock.*

'That is all,' she said, looking at the fishmonger's. 'That is all,' she repeated, pausing for a moment at the window of a glove shop* where, before the War, you could buy almost perfect gloves. And her old Uncle William used to say a lady is known by her shoes and her gloves. He had turned on his bed one morning in the middle of the War. He had said, 'I have had enough.' Gloves and shoes; she had a passion for gloves; but her own daughter, her Elizabeth, cared not a straw for either of them.

Not a straw, she thought, going on up Bond Street to a shop where they kept flowers for her when she gave a party. Elizabeth really cared for her dog most of all. The whole house this morning smelt of tar. Still, better poor Grizzle than Miss Kilman; better distemper and tar and all the rest of it than sitting mewed in a stuffy bedroom with a prayer book! Better anything, she was inclined to say. But it might be only a phase, as Richard said, such as all girls go through. It might be falling in love. But why with Miss Kilman? who had been badly treated of course; one must make allowances for that, and Richard said she was very able, had a really historical mind. Anyhow they were inseparable, and Elizabeth, her own daughter, went to Communion; and how she dressed, how she treated people who came to lunch she did not care a bit, it being her experience that the religious ecstasy made people callous (so did causes); dulled their feelings, for Miss Kilman would do anything for the Russians, starve herself for the Austrians,* but in private inflicted positive torture, so insensitive was she, dressed in a green mackintosh coat. Year in year out she wore that coat; she perspired; she was never in the room five minutes without making you feel her superiority, your inferiority; how poor she was; how rich you were; how she lived in a slum without a cushion or a bed or a rug or whatever it might be, all her soul rusted with that grievance sticking in it, her dismissal from school during the War—poor, embittered, unfortunate creature! For it was not her one hated but the idea of her, which undoubtedly had gathered into itself a great deal that was not Miss Kilman; had become one of those spectres with which one battles in the night; one of those spectres who stand astride us and suck up half our life-blood, dominators and tyrants; for no doubt with another throw of the dice, had the black been uppermost and not the white, she would have loved Miss Kilman! But not in this world. No.

It rasped her, though, to have stirring about in her this brutal monster! to hear twigs cracking and feel hooves planted down in the depths of that leaf-encumbered forest, the soul; never to be content quite, or quite secure, for at any moment the brute would be stirring, this hatred, which, especially since her illness, had power to make her feel scraped, hurt in her spine; gave her physical pain, and made all pleasure in beauty, in friendship, in being well, in being loved and making her home delightful, rock, quiver, and bend as if indeed there were a monster grubbing at the roots, as if the whole panoply of content were nothing but self love! this hatred!

Nonsense, nonsense! she cried to herself, pushing through the swing doors of Mulberry's the florists.*

She advanced, light, tall, very upright, to be greeted at once by button-faced Miss Pym, whose hands were always bright red, as if they had been stood in cold water with the flowers.

There were flowers: delphiniums, sweet peas, bunches of lilac; and carnations, masses of carnations. There were roses; there were irises. Ah yes—so she breathed in the earthy-garden sweet smell as she stood talking to Miss Pym who owed her help, and thought her kind, for kind she had been years ago; very kind, but she looked older, this year, turning her head from side to side among the irises and roses and nodding tufts of lilac with her eyes half closed, snuffing in, after the street uproar, the delicious scent, the exquisite coolness. And then, opening her eyes, how fresh, like frilled linen clean from a laundry laid in wicker trays, the roses looked; and dark and prim the red carnations, holding their heads up; and all the sweet peas spreading in their bowls, tinged violet, snow white, pale—as if it were the evening and girls in muslin frocks came out to pick sweet peas and roses after the superb summer's day, with its almost blue-black sky, its delphiniums, its carnations, its arum lilies, was over; and it was the moment between six and seven when every flower—roses, carnations, irises, lilac—glows; white, violet, red, deep orange; every flower seems to burn by itself, softly, purely in the misty beds; and how she loved the grey white moths spinning in and out, over the cherry pie, over the evening primroses!

And as she began to go with Miss Pym from jar to jar, choosing, nonsense, nonsense, she said to herself, more and more gently, as if this beauty, this scent, this colour, and Miss Pym liking her, trusting her, were a wave which she let flow over her and surmount that hatred, that monster, surmount it all; and it lifted her up and up when—oh! a pistol shot in the street outside!

'Dear, those motor cars,' said Miss Pym, going to the window to look, and coming back and smiling apologetically with her hands full of sweet peas, as if those motor cars, those tyres of motor cars, were all *her* fault.

The violent explosion which made Mrs Dalloway jump and Miss Pym go to the window and apologize came from a motor car which had drawn to the side of the pavement precisely opposite Mulberry's shop window. Passers-by, who, of course, stopped and stared, had just time to see a face of the very greatest importance against the dove-grey upholstery, before a male hand drew the blind and there was nothing to be seen except a square of dove grey.

Yet rumours were at once in circulation from the middle of Bond Street to Oxford Street* on one side, to Atkinson's scent shop* on the other, passing invisibly, inaudibly, like a cloud, swift, veil-like upon hills, falling indeed with something of a cloud's sudden sobriety and stillness upon faces which a second before had been utterly disorderly. But now mystery had brushed them with her wing; they had heard the voice of authority; the spirit of religion was abroad with her eyes bandaged tight and her lips gaping wide. But nobody knew whose face had been seen. Was it the Prince of Wales's,* the Queen's, the Prime Minister's?* Whose face was it? Nobody knew.

Edgar J. Watkiss, with his roll of lead piping round his arm, said audibly, humorously of course: 'The Proime Minister's kyar.'

Septimus Warren Smith, who found himself unable to pass, heard him.

Septimus Warren Smith, aged about thirty, pale-faced, beak-nosed, wearing brown shoes and a shabby overcoat, with hazel eyes which had that look of apprehension in them which makes complete strangers apprehensive too. The world has raised its whip; where will it descend?

Everything had come to a standstill. The throb of the motor

engines sounded like a pulse irregularly drumming through an entire body. The sun became extraordinarily hot because the motor car had stopped outside Mulberry's shop window; old ladies on the tops of omnibuses spread their black parasols; here a green, here a red parasol opened with a little pop. Mrs Dalloway, coming to the window with her arms full of sweet peas, looked out with her little pink face pursed in inquiry. Everyone looked at the motor car. Septimus looked. Boys on bicycles sprang off. Traffic accumulated. And there the motor car stood, with drawn blinds, and upon them a curious pattern like a tree, Septimus thought, and this gradual drawing together of everything to one centre before his eyes, as if some horror had come almost to the surface and was about to burst into flames, terrified him. The world wavered and quivered and threatened to burst into flames. It is I who am blocking the way, he thought. Was he not being looked at and pointed at; was he not weighted there, rooted to the pavement, for a purpose? But for what purpose?

'Let us go on, Septimus,' said his wife, a little woman, with large eyes in a sallow pointed face; an Italian girl.

But Lucrezia herself could not help looking at the motor car and the tree pattern on the blinds. Was it the Queen in there—the Queen going shopping?

The chauffeur, who had been opening something, turning something, shutting something, got on to the box.

'Come on,' said Lucrezia.

But her husband, for they had been married four, five years now, jumped, started, and said, 'All right!' angrily, as if she had interrupted him.

People must notice; people must see. People, she thought, look-ing at the crowd staring at the motor car; the English people, with their children and their horses and their clothes, which she admired in a way; but they were 'people' now, because Septimus had said, 'I will kill myself'; an awful thing to say. Suppose they had heard him? She looked at the crowd. Help, help! she wanted to cry out to butchers' boys and women. Help! Only last autumn she and Septimus had stood on the Embankment* wrapped in the same cloak and, Septimus reading a paper instead of talking, she had snatched it from him and laughed in the old man's face who saw them! But failure one conceals. She must take him away into some park.

'Now we will cross,' she said.

She had a right to his arm, though it was without feeling. He would give her, who was so simple, so impulsive, only twenty-four, without friends in England, who had left Italy for his sake, a piece of bone.

The motor car with its blinds drawn and an air of inscrutable reserve proceeded towards Piccadilly, still gazed at, still ruffling the faces on both sides of the street with the same dark breath of veneration whether for Queen, Prince, or Prime Minister nobody knew. The face itself had been seen only once by three people for a few seconds. Even the sex was now in dispute. But there could be no doubt that greatness was seated within; greatness was passing, hidden, down Bond Street, removed only by a hand's-breadth from ordinary people who might now, for the first time and last, be within speaking distance of the majesty of England, of the enduring symbol of the state which will be known to curious antiquaries, sifting the ruins of time, when London is a grass-grown path and all those hurrying along the pavement this Wednesday morning are but bones with a few wedding rings mixed up in their dust and the gold stoppings of innumerable decayed teeth. The face in the motor car will then be known.

It is probably the Queen, thought Mrs Dalloway, coming out of Mulberry's with her flowers: the Queen. And for a second she wore a look of extreme dignity standing by the flower shop in the sunlight while the car passed at a foot's pace, with its blinds drawn. The Queen going to some hospital; the Queen opening some bazaar, thought Clarissa.

The crush was terrific for the time of day. Lord's, Ascot, Hurlingham, what was it? she wondered, for the street was blocked. The British middle classes sitting sideways on the tops of omnibuses with parcels and umbrellas, yes, even furs on a day like this, were, she thought, more ridiculous, more unlike anything there has ever been than one could conceive; and the Queen herself held up; the Queen herself unable to pass. Clarissa was suspended on one side of Brook Street; Sir John Buckhurst, the old Judge, on the other, with the car between them (Sir John had laid down the law for years and liked a well-dressed woman) when the chauffeur, leaning ever so slightly, said or showed something to the policeman, who saluted and raised his arm and jerked his head and moved the omnibus to the side and the car passed through. Slowly and very silently it took its way.

Clarissa guessed; Clarissa knew of course; she had seen something white, magical, circular, in the footman's hand, a disc inscribed with a name,—the Queen's, the Prince of Wales's, the Prime Minister's?—which, by force of its own lustre, burnt its way through (Clarissa saw the car diminishing, disappearing), to blaze among candelabras, glittering stars, breasts stiff with oak leaves,* Hugh Whitbread and all his colleagues, the gentlemen of England, that night in Buckingham Palace. And Clarissa, too, gave a party. She stiffened a little; so she would stand at the top of her stairs.

The car had gone, but it had left a slight ripple which flowed through glove shops and hat shops and tailors' shops on both sides of Bond Street. For thirty seconds all heads were inclined the same way—to the window. Choosing a pair of gloves—should they be to the elbow or above it, lemon or pale grey?—ladies stopped; when the sentence was finished something had happened. Something so trifling in single instances that no mathematical instrument, though capable of transmitting shocks in China, could register the vibration; yet in its fullness rather formidable and in its common appeal emotional; for in all the hat shops and tailors' shops strangers looked at each other and thought of the dead; of the flag; of Empire. In a public-house in a back street a Colonial insulted the House of Windsor,* which led to words, broken beer glasses, and a general shindy, which echoed strangely across the way in the ears of girls buying white underlinen threaded with pure white ribbon for their weddings. For the surface agitation of the passing car as it sunk grazed something very profound.

Gliding across Piccadilly, the car turned down St James's Street.* Tall men, men of robust physique, well-dressed men with their tail-coats and their white slips and their hair raked back, who, for reasons difficult to discriminate, were standing in the bow window of White's* with their hands behind the tails of their coats, looking out, perceived instinctively that greatness was passing, and the pale light of the immortal presence fell upon them as it had fallen upon Clarissa Dalloway. At once they stood even straighter, and removed their hands, and seemed ready to attend their Sovereign, if need be, to the cannon's mouth, as their ancestors had done before them. The white busts and the little tables in the background covered with copies of the *Tatler** and bottles of soda water seemed to approve; seemed to indicate the flowing corn and the manor houses of England; and to return the frail hum of the motor wheels as the walls of a whispering gallery* return a single voice expanded and made sonorous by the might of a whole cathedral. Shawled Moll Pratt with her flowers on the pavement wished the dear boy well (it was the Prince of Wales for certain) and would have tossed the price of a pot of beer—a bunch of roses—into St James's Street out of sheer lightheartedness and contempt of poverty had she not seen the constable's eye upon her, discouraging an old Irishwoman's loyalty. The sentries at St James's saluted; Queen Alexandra's* policeman approved.

A small crowd, meanwhile, had gathered at the gates of Buckingham Palace. Listlessly, yet confidently, poor people all of them, they waited; looked at the Palace itself with the flag flying; at Victoria, billowing on her mound,* admired her shelves of running water, her geraniums; singled out from the motor cars in the Mall first this one, then that; bestowed emotion, vainly, upon commoners out for a drive; recalled their tribute to keep it unspent while this car passed and that; and all the time let rumour accumulate in their veins and thrill the nerves in their thighs at the thought of Royalty looking at them; the Queen bowing; the Prince saluting; at the thought of the heavenly life divinely bestowed upon Kings; of the equerries and deep curtsies; of the Queen's old doll's house;* of Princess Mary married to an Englishman;* and the Prince—ah! the Prince! who took wonderfully, they said, after old King Edward,* but was ever so much slimmer. The Prince lived at St James's; but he might come along in the morning to visit his mother.

So Sarah Bletchley said with her baby in her arms, tipping her foot up and down as though she were by her own fender in Pimlico, but keeping her eyes on the Mall,* while Emily Coates ranged over the Palace windows and thought of the housemaids, the innumerable housemaids, the bedrooms, the innumerable bedrooms. Joined by an elderly gentleman with an Aberdeen terrier, by men without occupation, the crowd increased. Little Mr Bowley, who had rooms in the Albany* and was sealed with wax over the deeper sources of life, but could be unsealed suddenly, inappropriately, sentimentally, by this sort of thing—poor women waiting to see the Queen go past—poor women, nice little children, orphans, widows, the War—tut-tut—actually had tears in his eyes. A breeze flaunting ever so warming down the Mall through the thin trees, past the bronze heroes,* lifted some flag flying in the British breast of Mr Bowley and he raised his hat as the car turned into the Mall and held it high as the car approached and let the poor mothers of Pimlico press close to him, and stood very upright. The car came on.

Suddenly Mrs Coates looked up into the sky. The sound of an aeroplane bored ominously into the ears of the crowd. There it was coming over the trees, letting out white smoke from behind, which curled and twisted, actually writing something! making letters in the sky! Everyone looked up.

Dropping dead down, the aeroplane soared straight up, curved in a loop, raced, sank, rose, and whatever it did, wherever it went, out fluttered behind it a thick ruffled bar of white smoke which curled and wreathed upon the sky in letters. But what letters? A C was it? an E, then an L? Only for a moment did they lie still; then they moved and melted and were rubbed out up in the sky, and the aeroplane shot further away and again, in a fresh space of sky, began writing a K, and E, a Y perhaps?

'Glaxo,'* said Mrs Coates in a strained, awestricken voice, gazing straight up, and her baby, lying stiff and white in her arms, gazed straight up.

'Kreemo,' murmured Mrs Bletchley, like a sleepwalker. With

his hat held out perfectly still in his hand, Mr Bowley gazed straight up. All down the Mall people were standing and looking up into the sky. As they looked the whole world became perfectly silent, and a flight of gulls crossed the sky, first one gull leading, then another, and in this extraordinary silence and peace, in this pallor, in this purity, bells struck eleven times, the sound fading up there among the gulls.

The aeroplane turned and raced and swooped exactly where it liked, swiftly, freely, like a skater—

'That's an E,' said Mrs Bletchley—

or a dancer—

'It's toffee,' murmured Mr Bowley—

(and the car went in at the gates and nobody looked at it), and shutting off the smoke, away and away it rushed, and the smoke faded and assembled itself round the broad white shapes of the clouds.

It had gone; it was behind the clouds. There was no sound. The clouds to which the letters E, G, or L had attached themselves moved freely, as if destined to cross from West to East on a mission of the greatest importance which would never be revealed, and yet certainly so it was—a mission of the greatest importance. Then suddenly, as a train comes out of a tunnel, the aeroplane rushed out of the clouds again, the sound boring into the ears of all people in the Mall, in the Green Park, in Piccadilly, in Regent Street, in Regent's Park, and the bar of smoke curved behind and it dropped down, and it soared up and wrote one letter after another—but what word was it writing?

Lucrezia Warren Smith, sitting by her husband's side on a seat in Regent's Park in the Broad Walk,* looked up.

'Look, look, Septimus!' she cried. For Dr Holmes had told her to make her husband (who had nothing whatever seriously the matter with him but was a little out of sorts) take an interest in things outside himself.

So, thought Septimus, looking up, they are signalling to me. Not indeed in actual words; that is, he could not read the language yet; but it was plain enough, this beauty, this exquisite beauty, and tears filled his eyes as he looked at the smoke words languishing and melting in the sky and bestowing upon him, in their inexhaustible charity and laughing goodness, one shape after another of unimaginable beauty and signalling their intention to provide him, for nothing, for ever, for looking merely, with beauty, more beauty! Tears ran down his cheeks.

It was toffee; they were advertising toffee, a nursemaid told Rezia. Together they began to spell t . . . o . . . f . . .

'K . . . R . . .' said the nursemaid, and Septimus heard her say 'Kay Arr' close to his ear, deeply, softly, like a mellow organ, but with a roughness in her voice like a grasshopper's, which rasped his spine deliciously and sent running up into his brain waves of sound, which, concussing, broke. A marvellous discovery indeed—that the human voice in certain atmospheric conditions (for one must be scientific, above all scientific) can quicken trees into life! Happily Rezia put her hand down with a tremendous weight on his knee so that he was weighted down, transfixed, or the excitement of the elm trees rising and falling, rising and falling with all their leaves alight and the colour thinning and thickening from blue to the green of a hollow wave, like plumes on horses' heads, feathers on ladies', so proudly they rose and fell, so superbly, would have sent him mad. But he would not go mad. He would shut his eyes; he would see no more.

But they beckoned; leaves were alive; trees were alive. And the leaves being connected by millions of fibres with his own body, there on the seat, fanned it up and down; when the branch stretched he, too, made that statement. The sparrows fluttering, rising, and falling in jagged fountains were part of the pattern; the white and blue, barred with black branches. Sounds made harmonies with premeditation; the spaces between them were as significant as the sounds. A child cried. Rightly far away a horn sounded. All taken together meant the birth of a new religion——

'Septimus!' said Rezia. He started violently. People must notice.

'I am going to walk to the fountain and back,' she said.

For she could stand it no longer. Dr Holmes might say there was nothing the matter. Far rather would she that he were dead! She could not sit beside him when he stared so and did not see her and made everything terrible; sky and tree, children playing, dragging carts, blowing whistles, falling down; all were terrible. And he would not kill himself; and she could tell no one. 'Septimus has been working too hard'—that was all she could say to her own mother. To love makes one solitary, she thought. She could tell nobody, not even Septimus now, and looking back, she saw him sitting in his shabby overcoat alone, on the seat, hunched up, staring. And it was cowardly for a man to say he would kill himself, but Septimus had fought; he was brave; he was not Septimus now. She put on her lace collar. She put on her new hat and he never noticed; and he was happy without her. Nothing could make her happy without him! Nothing! He was selfish. So men are. For he was not ill. Dr Holmes said there was nothing the matter with him. She spread her hand before her. Look! Her wedding ring slipped—she had grown so thin. It was she who suffered—but she had nobody to tell.

Far was Italy and the white houses and the room where her sisters sat making hats, and the streets crowded every evening with people walking, laughing out loud, not half alive like people here, huddled up in Bath chairs, looking at a few ugly flowers stuck in pots!

'For you should see the Milan gardens,' she said aloud. But to whom?

There was nobody. Her words faded. So a rocket fades. Its sparks, having grazed their way into the night, surrender to it, dark descends, pours over the outlines of houses and towers; bleak hillsides soften and fall in. But though they are gone, the night is full of them; robbed of colour, blank of windows, they exist more ponderously, give out what the frank daylight fails to transmit—the trouble and suspense of things conglomerated there in the darkness; huddled together in the darkness; reft of the relief which dawn brings when, washing the walls white and grey, spotting each window-pane, lifting the mist from the fields, showing the red-brown cows peacefully grazing, all is once more decked out to the eye; exists again. I am alone; I am alone! she cried, by the fountain in Regent's Park (staring at the Indian and his cross*), as perhaps at midnight, when all boundaries are lost, the country reverts to its ancient shape, as the Romans saw it, lying cloudy, when they landed, and the hills had no names and rivers wound they knew not where—such was her darkness; when suddenly, as if a shelf were shot forth and she stood on it, she said how she was his wife, married years ago in Milan, his wife, and would never, never tell that he was mad! Turning, the shelf fell; down, down she dropped. For he was gone, she thought—gone, as he threatened, to kill himself—to throw himself under a cart! But no; there he was; still sitting alone on the seat, in his shabby overcoat, his legs crossed, staring, talking aloud.

Men must not cut down trees. There is a God. (He noted such revelations on the backs of envelopes.) Change the world. No one kills from hatred. Make it known (he wrote it down). He waited. He listened. A sparrow perched on the railing opposite chirped Septimus, Septimus, four or five times over and went on, drawing its notes out to sing freshly and piercingly in Greek words* how there is no crime and, joined by another sparrow, they sang in voices prolonged and piercing in Greek words, from trees in the meadow of life beyond a river where the dead walk, how there is no death.

There was his hand; there the dead. White things were assembling behind the railings opposite. But he dared not look. Evans was behind the railings!

'What are you saying?' said Rezia suddenly, sitting down by him.

Interrupted again! She was always interrupting.

Away from people—they must get away from people, he said (jumping up), right away over there, where there were chairs beneath a tree and the long slope of the park dipped like a length of green stuff with a ceiling cloth of blue and pink smoke high above, and there was a rampart of far, irregular houses, hazed in smoke, the traffic hummed in a circle, and on the right, dun-coloured animals stretched long necks over the Zoo* palings, barking, howling. There they sat down under a tree.

'Look,' she implored him, pointing at a little troop of boys carrying cricket stumps, and one shuffled, spun round on his heel and shuffled, as if he were acting a clown at the music hall.

'Look,' she implored him, for Dr Holmes had told her to make him notice real things, go to a music hall, play cricket—that was the very game, Dr Holmes said, a nice out-of-door game, the very game for her husband.

'Look,' she repeated.

Look, the unseen bade him, the voice which now communicated with him who was the greatest of mankind, Septimus, lately taken from life to death, the Lord who had come to renew society, who lay like a coverlet, a snow blanket smitten only by the sun, for ever unwasted, suffering for ever, the scapegoat, the eternal sufferer, but he did not want it, he moaned, putting from him with a wave of his hand that eternal suffering, that eternal loneliness.

'Look,' she repeated, for he must not talk aloud to himself out of doors.

'Oh, look,' she implored him. But what was there to look at? A few sheep. That was all.

The way to Regent's Park Tube station—could they tell her the way to Regent's Park Tube station—Maisie Johnson wanted to know. She was only up from Edinburgh two days ago.

'Not this way—over there!' Rezia exclaimed, waving her aside, lest she should see Septimus.

Both seemed queer, Maisie Johnson thought. Everything seemed very queer. In London for the first time, come to take up a post at her uncle's in Leadenhall Street, and now walking through Regent's Park in the morning, this couple on the chairs gave her quite a turn: the young woman seeming foreign, the man looking queer, so that should she be very old she would still remember and make it jangle again among her memories how she had walked through Regent's Park on a fine summer's morning fifty years ago. For she was only nineteen and had got her way at last, to come to London; and now how queer it was, this couple she had asked the way of, and the girl started and jerked her hand, and the man—he seemed awfully odd; quarrelling, perhaps; parting for ever, perhaps; something was up, she knew; and now all these people (for she returned to the Broad Walk), the stone basins, the prim flowers, the old men and women, invalids most of them in Bath chairs—all seemed, after Edinburgh, so queer. And Maisie Johnson, as she joined that gently trudging, vaguely gazing, breeze-kissed company—squirrels perching and preening, sparrow fountains fluttering for crumbs, dogs busy with the railings, busy with each other, while the soft warm air washed over them and lent to the fixed unsurprised gaze with which they received life, something whimsical and mollified—Maisie Johnson positively felt she must cry Oh! (for that young man on the seat had given her quite a turn. Something was up, she knew).

Horror! horror! she wanted to cry. (She had left her people; they had warned her what would happen.)

Why hadn't she stayed at home? she cried, twisting the knob of the iron railing.

That girl, thought Mrs Dempster (who saved crusts for the squirrels and often ate her lunch in Regent's Park), don't know a thing yet; and really it seemed to her better to be a little stout, a little slack, a little moderate in one's expectations. Percy drank. Well, better to have a son, thought Mrs Dempster. She had had a hard time of it, and couldn't help smiling at a girl like that. You'll get married, for you're pretty enough, thought Mrs Dempster. Get married, she thought, and then you'll know. Oh, the cooks, and so on. Every man has his ways. But whether I'd have chosen quite like that if I could have known, thought Mrs Dempster, and could not help wishing to whisper a word to Maisie Johnson; to feel on the creased pouch of her worn old face the kiss of pity. For it's been a hard life, thought Mrs Dempster. What hadn't she given to it? Roses; figure; her feet too. (She drew the knobbed lumps beneath her skirt.)

Roses, she thought sardonically. All trash, m'dear. For really, what with eating, drinking, and mating, the bad days and good, life had been no mere matter of roses, and what was more, let me tell you, Carrie Dempster had no wish to change her lot with any woman's in Kentish Town!* But, she implored, pity. Pity, for the loss of roses. Pity she asked of Maisie Johnson, standing by the hyacinth beds.

Ah, but that aeroplane! Hadn't Mrs Dempster always longed to see foreign parts? She had a nephew, a missionary. It soared and shot. She always went on the sea at Margate,* not out of sight of land, but she had no patience with women who were afraid of water. It swept and fell. Her stomach was in her mouth. Up again. There's a fine young feller aboard of it, Mrs Dempster wagered, and away and away it went, fast and fading, away and away the aeroplane shot: soaring over Greenwich and all the masts;* over the little island of grey churches, St Paul's and the rest,* till, on either side of London, fields spread out and dark brown woods where adventurous thrushes, hopping boldly, glancing quickly, snatched the snail and tapped him on a stone, once, twice, thrice.

Away and away the aeroplane shot, till it was nothing but a bright spark; an aspiration; a concentration; a symbol (so it seemed to Mr Bentley, vigorously rolling his strip of turf at Greenwich) of man's soul; of his determination, thought Mr Bentley, sweeping round the cedar tree, to get outside his body, beyond his house, by means of thought, Einstein, speculation, mathematics, the Mendelian theory*—away the aeroplane shot.

Then, while a seedy-looking nondescript man carrying a lea-ther bag stood on the steps of St Paul's Cathedral, and hesitated, for within was what balm, how great a welcome, how many tombs with banners waving over them, tokens of victories not over armies, but over, he thought, that plaguy spirit of truth seeking which leaves me at present without a situation, and more than that, the cathedral offers company, he thought, invites you to membership of a society; great men belong to it; martyrs have died for it; why not enter in, he thought, put this leather bag stuffed with pamphlets before an altar, a cross, the symbol of something, which has soared beyond seeking and questing and knocking of words together and has become all spirit, dis-embodied, ghostly—why not enter in? he thought, and while he hesitated out flew the aeroplane over Ludgate Circus.*

It was strange; it was still. Not a sound was to be heard above the traffic. Unguided it seemed; sped of its own free will. And now, curving up and up, straight up, like something mounting in ecstasy, in pure delight, out from behind poured white smoke looping, writing a T, and O, an F.

*

'What are they looking at?' said Clarissa Dalloway to the maid who opened her door.

The hall of the house was cool as a vault. Mrs Dalloway raised her hand to her eyes, and, as the maid shut the door to, and she heard the swish of Lucy's skirts, she felt like a nun who has left the world and feels fold round her the familiar veils and the response to old devotions. The cook whistled in the kitchen. She heard the click of the typewriter. It was her life, and, bending her head over the hall table, she bowed beneath the influence, felt blessed and purified, saying to her-self, as she took the pad with the telephone message on it, how moments like this are buds on the tree of life, flowers of dark-ness they are, she thought (as if some lovely rose had blossomed for her eyes only); not for a moment did she believe in God; but all the more, she thought, taking up the pad, must one repay in daily life to servants, yes, to dogs and canaries, above all to Richard her husband, who was the foundation of it—of the gay sounds, of the green lights, of the cook even whistling, for Mrs Walker was Irish and whistled all day long—one must pay back from this secret deposit of exquisite moments, she thought, lifting the pad, while Lucy stood by her, trying to explain how

'Mr Dalloway, ma'am——'

Clarissa read on the telephone pad, 'Lady Bruton wishes to know if Mr Dalloway will lunch with her today.'

'Mr Dalloway, ma'am, told me to tell you he would be lunching out.'

'Dear!' said Clarissa, and Lucy shared as she meant her to her disappointment (but not the pang); felt the concord between them; took the hint; thought how the gentry love; gilded her own future with calm; and taking Mrs Dalloway's parasol, handled it like a sacred weapon which a goddess, having acquitted herself honourably in the field of battle, sheds, and placed it in the umbrella stand.

'Fear no more,' said Clarissa. Fear no more the heat o' the sun; for the shock of Lady Bruton asking Richard to lunch without her made the moment in which she had stood shiver, as a plant on the riverbed feels the shock of a passing oar and shivers: so she rocked: so she shivered.

Millicent Bruton, whose lunch parties were said to be extraordinarily amusing, had not asked her. No vulgar jealousy could separate her from Richard. But she feared time itself, and read on Lady Bruton's face, as if it had been a dial cut in impassive stone, the dwindling of life; how year by year her share was sliced; how little the margin that remained was capable any longer of stretching, of absorbing, as in the youthful years, the colours, salts, tones of existence, so that she filled the room she entered, and felt often, as she stood hesitating one moment on the threshold of her drawing-room, an exquisite suspense, such as might stay a diver before plunging while the sea darkens and brightens beneath him, and the waves which threaten to break, but only gently split their surface, roll and conceal and encrust as they just turn over the weeds with pearl.

She put the pad on the hall table. She began to go slowly upstairs, with her hand on the banisters, as if she had left a party, where now this friend now that had flashed back her face, her voice; had shut the door and gone out and stood alone, a single figure against the appalling night, or rather, to be accurate, against the stare of this matter-of-fact June morning; soft with the glow of rose petals for some, she knew, and felt it, as she paused by the open staircase window which let in blinds flapping, dogs barking, let in, she thought, feeling herself suddenly shrivelled, aged, breastless, the grinding, blowing, flowering of the day, out of doors, out of the window, out of her body and brain which now failed, since Lady Bruton, whose lunch parties were said to be extraordinarily amusing, had not asked her.

Like a nun withdrawing, or a child exploring a tower, she went, upstairs, paused at the window, came to the bathroom. There was the green linoleum and a tap dripping. There was an emptiness about the heart of life; an attic room. Women must put off their rich apparel. At midday they must disrobe. She pierced the pincushion and laid her feathered yellow hat on the bed. The sheets were clean, tight stretched in a broad white band from side to side. Narrower and narrower would her bed be. The candle was half burnt down and she had read deep in Baron Marbot's *Memoirs*.* She had read late at night of the retreat from Moscow. For the House* sat so long that Richard insisted, after her illness, that she must sleep undisturbed. And really she preferred to read of the retreat from Moscow. He knew it. So the room was an attic; the bed narrow; and lying there reading, for she slept badly, she could not dispel a virginity preserved through childbirth which clung to her like a sheet. Lovely in girlhood, suddenly there came a moment—for example on the river beneath the woods at Clieveden*—when, through some contraction of this cold spirit, she had failed him. And then at Constantinople,* and again and again. She could see what she lacked. It was not beauty; it was not mind. It was something central which permeated; something warm which broke up surfaces and rippled the cold contact of man and woman, or of women together. For *that* she could dimly perceive. She resented it, had a scruple picked up Heaven knows where, or, as she felt, sent by Nature (who is invariably wise); yet she could not resist sometimes yielding to the charm of a woman, not a girl, of a woman confessing, as to her they often did, some scrape, some folly. And whether it was pity, or their beauty, or that she was older, or some accident—like a faint scent, or a violin next door (so strange is the power of sounds at certain moments), she did undoubtedly then feel what men felt. Only for a moment; but it was enough. It was a sudden revelation, a tinge like a blush which one tried to check and then, as it spread, one yielded to its expansion, and rushed to the farthest verge and there quivered and felt the world come closer, swollen with some astonishing significance, some pressure of rapture, which split its thin skin and gushed and poured with an extraordinary alleviation over the cracks and sores. Then, for that moment, she had seen an illumination; a match burning in a crocus; an inner meaning almost expressed. But the close withdrew; the hard softened. It was over—the moment. Against such moments (with women too) there contrasted (as she laid her hat down) the bed and Baron Marbot and the candle half-burnt. Lying awake, the floor creaked; the lit house was suddenly darkened, and if she raised her head she could just hear the click of the handle released as gently as possible by Richard, who slipped upstairs in his socks and then, as often as not, dropped his hot-water bottle and swore! How she laughed!

But this question of love (she thought, putting her coat away), this falling in love with women. Take Sally Seton; her relation in the old days with Sally Seton. Had not that, after all, been love?

She sat on the floor—that was her first impression of Sally— she sat on the floor with her arms round her knees, smoking a cigarette. Where could it have been? The Mannings'? The Kinloch-Joneses'? At some party (where she could not be certain), for she had a distinct recollection of saying to the man she was with, 'Who is *that*?' And he had told her, and said that Sally's parents did not get on (how that shocked her—that one's parents should quarrel!). But all that evening she could not take her eyes off Sally. It was an extraordinary beauty of the kind she most admired, dark, large-eyed, with that quality which, since she hadn't got it herself, she always envied—a sort of abandonment, as if she could say anything, do anything; a quality much commoner in foreigners than in Englishwomen. Sally always said she had French blood in her veins, an ancestor had been with Marie Antoinette,* had his head cut off, left a ruby ring. Perhaps that summer she came to stay at Bourton, walking in quite unexpectedly without a penny in her pocket, one night after dinner, and upsetting poor Aunt Helena to such an extent that she never forgave her. There had been some awful quarrel at home. She literally hadn't a penny that night when she came to them—had pawned a brooch to come down. She had rushed off in a passion. They sat up till all hours of the night talking. Sally it was who made her feel, for the first time, how sheltered the life at Bourton was. She knew nothing about sex—nothing about social problems. She had once seen an old man who had dropped dead in a field—she had seen cows just after their calves were born. But Aunt Helena never liked discussion of anything (when Sally gave her William Morris, it had to be wrapped in brown paper).* There they sat, hour after hour, talking in her bedroom at the top of the house, talking about life, how they were to reform the world. They meant to found a society to abolish private property, and actually had a letter written, though not sent out. The ideas were Sally's, of course—but very soon she was just as excited—read Plato* in bed before breakfast; read Morris; read Shelley* by the hour.

Sally's power was amazing, her gift, her personality. There was her way with flowers, for instance. At Bourton they always had stiff little vases all the way down the table. Sally went out, picked hollyhocks, dahlias—all sorts of flowers that had never been seen together—cut their heads off, and made them swim on the top of water in bowls. The effect was extraordinary—coming into dinner in the sunset. (Of course Aunt Helena thought it wicked to treat flowers like that.) Then she forgot her sponge, and ran along the passage naked. That grim old housemaid, Ellen Atkins, went about grumbling—'Suppose any of the gentlemen had seen?' Indeed she did shock people. She was untidy, Papa said.

The strange thing, on looking back, was the purity, the integrity, of her feeling for Sally. It was not like one's feeling for a man. It was completely disinterested, and besides, it had a quality which could only exist between women, between women just grown up. It was protective, on her side; sprang from a sense of being in league together, a presentiment of something that was bound to part them (they spoke of marriage always as a catastrophe), which led to this chivalry, this protective feeling which was much more on her side than Sally's. For in those days she was completely reckless; did the most idiotic things out of bravado; bicycled round the parapet on the terrace: smoked cigars. Absurd, she was—very absurd. But the charm was over-powering, to her at least, so that she could remember standing in her bedroom at the top of the house holding the hot-water can in her hands and saying aloud, 'She is beneath this roof . . . She is beneath this roof!'

No, the words meant absolutely nothing to her now. She could not even get an echo of her old emotion. But she could remember going cold with excitement and doing her hair in a kind of ecstasy (now the old feeling began to come back to her, as she took out her hairpins, laid them on the dressing-table, began to do her hair), with the rooks flaunting up and down in the pink evening light, and dressing, and going downstairs, and feeling as she crossed the hall 'if it were now to die, 'twere now to be most happy'.* That was her feeling—Othello's feeling, and she felt it, she was convinced, as strongly as Shakespeare meant Othello to feel it, all because she was coming down to dinner in a white frock to meet Sally Seton!

She was wearing pink gauze—was that possible? She *seemed*, anyhow, all light, glowing, like some bird or air-ball* that has flown in, attached itself for a moment to a bramble. But nothing is so strange when one is in love (and what was this except being in love?) as the complete indifference of other people. Aunt Helena just wandered off after dinner; Papa read the paper. Peter Walsh might have been there, and old Miss Cummings; Joseph Breitkopf certainly was, for he came every summer, poor old man, for weeks and weeks, and pretended to read German with her, but really played the piano and sang Brahms* without any voice.

All this was only a background for Sally. She stood by the fireplace talking, in that beautiful voice which made everything she said sound like a caress, to Papa, who had begun to be attracted rather against his will (he never got over lending her one of his books and finding it soaked on the terrace), when suddenly she said, 'What a shame to sit indoors!' and they all went out on to the terrace and walked up and down. Peter Walsh and Joseph Breitkopf went on about Wagner. She and Sally fell a little behind. Then came the most exquisite moment of her whole life passing a stone urn with flowers in it. Sally stopped; picked a flower; kissed her on the lips. The whole world might have turned upside down! The others disappeared; there she was alone with Sally. And she felt that she had been given a present, wrapped up, and told just to keep it, not to look at it—a diamond, something infinitely precious, wrapped up, which, as they walked (up and down, up and down), she uncovered, or the radiance burnt through, the revelation, the religious feeling!—when old Joseph and Peter faced them:

'Star-gazing?' said Peter.

It was like running one's face against a granite wall in the darkness! It was shocking; it was horrible!

Not for herself. She felt only how Sally was being mauled already, maltreated; she felt his hostility; his jealousy; his determination to break into their companionship. All this she saw as one sees a landscape in a flash of lightning—and Sally (never had she admired her so much!) gallantly taking her way unvanquished. She laughed. She made old Joseph tell her the names of the stars, which he liked doing very seriously. She stood there: she listened. She heard the names of the stars.

'Oh this horror!' she said to herself, as if she had known all along that something would interrupt, would embitter her moment of happiness.

Yet how much she owed Peter Walsh later. Always when she thought of him she thought of their quarrels for some reason— because she wanted his good opinion so much, perhaps. She owed him words: 'sentimental', 'civilized'; they started up every day of her life as if he guarded her. A book was sentimental; an attitude to life sentimental. 'Sentimental', perhaps she was to be thinking of the past. What would he think, she wondered, when he came back?

That she had grown older? Would he say that, or would she see him thinking when he came back, that she had grown older? It was true. Since her illness she had turned almost white.

Laying her brooch on the table, she had a sudden spasm, as if, while she mused, the icy claws had had the chance to fix in her. She was not old yet. She had just broken into her fifty-second year. Months and months of it were still untouched. June, July, August! Each still remained almost whole, and, as if to catch the falling drop, Clarissa (crossing to the dressing-table) plunged into the very heart of the moment, transfixed it, there—the moment of this June morning on which was the pressure of all the other mornings, seeing the glass, the dressing-table, and all the bottles afresh, collecting the whole of her at one point (as she looked into the glass), seeing the delicate pink face of the woman who was that very night to give a party; of Clarissa Dalloway; of herself.

How many million times she had seen her face, and always with the same imperceptible contraction! She pursed her lips when she looked in the glass. It was to give her face point. That was her self—pointed; dart-like; definite. That was her self when some effort, some call on her to be her self, drew the parts together, she alone knew how different, how incompatible and composed so for the world only into one centre, one diamond, one woman who sat in her drawing-room and made a meeting-point, a radiancy no doubt in some dull lives, a refuge for the lonely to come to, perhaps; she had helped young people, who were grateful to her; had tried to be the same always, never showing a sign of all the other sides of her—faults, jealousies, vanities, suspicions, like this of Lady Bruton not asking her to lunch; which, she thought (combing her hair finally), is utterly base! Now, where was her dress?

Her evening dresses hung in the cupboard. Clarissa, plunging her hand into the softness, gently detached the green dress and carried it to the window. She had torn it. Some one had trod on the skirt. She had felt it give at the Embassy party at the top among the folds. By artificial light the green shone, but lost its colour now in the sun. She would mend it. Her maids had too much to do. She would wear it tonight. She would take her silks, her scissors, her—what was it?—her thimble, of course, down into the drawing-room, for she must also write, and see that things generally were more or less in order.

Strange, she thought, pausing on the landing, and assembling that diamond shape, that single person, strange how a mistress knows the very moment, the very temper of her house! Faint sounds rose in spirals up the well of the stairs; the swish of a mop; tapping; knocking; a loudness when the front door opened; a voice repeating a message in the basement; the chink of silver on a tray; clean silver for the party. All was for the party.

(And Lucy, coming into the drawing-room with her tray held out, put the giant candlesticks on the mantelpiece, the silver casket in the middle, turned the crystal dolphin towards the clock. They would come; they would stand; they would talk in the mincing tones which she could imitate, ladies and gentlemen. Of all, her mistress was loveliest—mistress of silver, of linen, of china, for the sun, the silver, doors off their hinges, Rumpelmayer's men, gave her a sense, as she laid the paper-knife on the inlaid table, of something achieved. Behold! Behold! she said, speaking to her old friends in the baker's shop, where she had first seen service at Caterham,* prying into the glass. She was Lady Angela, attending Princess Mary, when in came Mrs Dalloway.)

'Oh, Lucy,' she said, 'the silver does look nice!'

'And how,' she said, turning the crystal dolphin to stand straight, 'how did you enjoy the play last night?' 'Oh, they had to go before the end!' she said. 'They had to be back at ten!' she said. 'So they don't know what happened,' she said. 'That does seem hard luck,' she said (for her servants stayed later, if they asked her). 'That does seem rather a shame,' she said, taking the old bald-looking cushion in the middle of the sofa and putting it in Lucy's arms, and giving her a little push, and crying:

'Take it away! Give it to Mrs Walker with my compliments! Take it away!' she cried.

And Lucy stopped at the drawing-room door, holding the cushion, and said, very shyly, turning a little pink, couldn't she help to mend that dress?

But, said Mrs Dalloway, she had enough on her hands already, quite enough of her own to do without that.

'But, thank you, Lucy, oh, thank you,' said Mrs Dalloway, and thank you, thank you, she went on saying (sitting down on the sofa with her dress over her knees, her scissors, her silks), thank you, thank you, she went on saying in gratitude to her servants generally for helping her to be like this, to be what she wanted, gentle, generous-hearted. Her servants liked her. And then this dress of hers—where was the tear? and now her needle to be threaded. This was a favourite dress, one of Sally Parker's, the last almost she ever made, alas, for Sally had now retired, lived at Ealing,* and if ever I have a moment, thought Clarissa (but never would she have a moment any more), I shall go and see her at Ealing. For she was a character, thought Clarissa, a real artist. She thought of little out-of-the-way things; yet her dresses were never queer. You could wear them at Hatfield;* at Buckingham Palace. She had worn them at Hatfield; at Buckingham Palace.

Quiet descended on her, calm, content, as her needle, drawing the silk smoothly to its gentle pause, collected the green folds together and attached them, very lightly, to the belt. So on a summer's day waves collect, overbalance, and fall; collect and fall; and the whole world seems to be saying 'that is all' more and more ponderously, until even the heart in the body which lies in the sun on the beach says too, that is all. Fear no more, says the heart. Fear no more, says the heart, committing its burden to some sea, which sighs collectively for all sorrows, and renews, begins, collects, lets fall. And the body alone listens to the passing bee; the wave breaking, the dog barking, far away barking and barking.

'Heavens, the front-door bell!' exclaimed Clarissa, staying her needle. Roused, she listened.

'Mrs Dalloway will see me,' said the elderly man in the hall. 'Oh yes, she will see *me*,' he repeated, putting Lucy aside very benevolently, and running upstairs ever so quickly. 'Yes, yes, yes,' he muttered as he ran upstairs. 'She will see me. After five years in India, Clarissa will see me.'

'Who can—what can—' asked Mrs Dalloway (thinking it was outrageous to be interrupted at eleven o'clock on the morning of the day she was giving a party), hearing a step on the stairs. She heard a hand upon the door. She made to hide her dress, like a virgin protecting chastity, respecting privacy. Now the brass knob slipped. Now the door opened, and in came—for a single second she could not remember what he was called! so surprised she was to see him, so glad, so shy, so utterly taken aback to have Peter Walsh come to her unexpectedly in the morning! (She had not read his letter.)

'And how are you?' said Peter Walsh, positively trembling; taking both her hands; kissing both her hands. She's grown older, he thought, sitting down. I shan't tell her anything about it, he thought, for she's grown older. She's looking at me, he thought, a sudden embarrassment coming over him, though he had kissed her hands. Putting his hand into his pocket, he took out a large pocket-knife and half opened the blade.

Exactly the same, thought Clarissa; the same queer look; the same check suit; a little out of the straight his face is, a little thinner, dryer, perhaps, but he looks awfully well, and just the same.

'How heavenly it is to see you again!' she exclaimed. He had his knife out. That's so like him, she thought.

He had only reached town last night, he said; would have to go down into the country at once; and how was everything, how was everybody—Richard? Elizabeth?

'And what's all this?' he said, tilting his pen-knife towards her green dress.

He's very well dressed, thought Clarissa; yet he always criticizes *me*.

Here she is mending her dress; mending her dress as usual, he thought; here she's been sitting all the time I've been in India; mending her dress; playing about; going to parties; running to the House and back and all that, he thought, growing more and more irritated, more and more agitated, for there's nothing in the world so bad for some women as marriage, he thought; and politics; and having a Conservative husband, like the admirable Richard. So it is, so it is, he thought, shutting his knife with a snap.

'Richard's very well. Richard's at a Committee,' said Clarissa.

And she opened her scissors, and said, did he mind her just finishing what she was doing to her dress, for they had a party that night?

'Which I shan't ask you to,' she said. 'My dear Peter!' she said.

But it was delicious to hear her say that—my dear Peter! Indeed, it was all so delicious—the silver, the chairs; all so delicious!

Why wouldn't she ask him to her party? he asked.

Now of course, thought Clarissa, he's enchanting! perfectly enchanting! Now I remember how impossible it was ever to make up my mind—and why did I make up my mind—not to marry him, she wondered, that awful summer?

'But it's so extraordinary that you should have come this morning!' she cried, putting her hands, one on top of another, down on her dress.

'Do you remember', she said, 'how the blinds used to flap at Bourton?'

'They did,' he said; and he remembered breakfasting alone, very awkwardly, with her father; who had died; and he had not written to Clarissa. But he had never got on well with old Parry, that querulous, weak-kneed old man, Clarissa's father, Justin Parry.

'I often wish I'd got on better with your father,' he said.

'But he never liked anyone who—our friends,' said Clarissa; and could have bitten her tongue for thus reminding Peter that he had wanted to marry her.

Of course I did, thought Peter; it almost broke my heart too, he thought; and was overcome with his own grief, which rose like a moon looked at from a terrace, ghastly beautiful with light from the sunken day. I was more unhappy than I've ever been since, he thought. And as if in truth he were sitting there on the terrace he edged a little towards Clarissa; put his hand out; raised it; let it fall. There above them it hung, that moon. She too seemed to be sitting with him on the terrace, in the moonlight.

'Herbert has it now,' she said. 'I never go there now,' she said.

Then, just as happens on a terrace in the moonlight, when one person begins to feel ashamed that he is already bored, and yet as the other sits silent, very quiet, sadly looking at the moon, does not like to speak, moves his foot, clears his throat, notices some iron scroll on a table leg, stirs a leaf, but says nothing—so Peter Walsh did now. For why go back like this to the past? he thought. Why make him think of it again? Why make him suffer, when she had tortured him so infernally? Why?

'Do you remember the lake?' she said, in an abrupt voice, under the pressure of an emotion which caught her heart, made the muscles of her throat stiff, and contracted her lips in a spasm as she said 'lake'. For she was a child throwing bread to the ducks, between her parents, and at the same time a grown woman coming to her parents who stood by the lake, holding her life in her arms which, as she neared them, grew larger and larger in her arms, until it became a whole life, a complete life, which she put down by them and said, 'This is what I have made of it! This!' And what had she made of it? What, indeed? sitting there sewing this morning with Peter.

She looked at Peter Walsh; her look, passing through all that time and that emotion, reached him doubtfully; settled on him tearfully; and rose and fluttered away, as a bird touches a branch and rises and flutters away. Quite simply she wiped her eyes.

'Yes,' said Peter. 'Yes, yes, yes,' he said, as if she drew up to the surface something which positively hurt him as it rose. Stop! Stop! he wanted to cry. For he was not old; his life was not over; not by any means. He was only just past fifty. Shall I tell her, he thought, or not? He would like to make a clean breast of it all. But she is too cold, he thought; sewing, with her scissors; Daisy would look ordinary beside Clarissa. And she would think me a failure, which I am in their sense, he thought; in the Dalloways' sense. Oh yes, he had no doubt about that; he was a failure, compared with all this—the inlaid table, the mounted paper-knife, the dolphin and the candlesticks, the chair-covers and the old valuable English tinted prints—he was a failure! I detest the smugness of the whole affair, he thought; Richard's doing, not Clarissa's; save that she married him. (Here Lucy came into the room, carrying silver, more silver, but charming, slender, graceful she looked, he thought, as she stooped to put it down.) And this has been going on all the time! he thought; week after week; Clarissa's life; while I—he thought; and at once everything seemed to radiate from him; journeys; rides; quarrels; adventures; bridge parties; love affairs; work; work, work! and he took out his knife quite openly—his old horn-handled knife which Clarissa could swear he had had these thirty years—and clenched his fist upon it.

What an extraordinary habit that was, Clarissa thought; always playing with a knife. Always making one feel, too, frivolous; empty-minded; a mere silly chatterbox, as he used. But I too, she thought, and, taking up her needle, summoned, like a Queen whose guards have fallen asleep and left her unprotected (she had been quite taken aback by this visit—it had upset her) so that anyone can stroll in and have a look at her where she lies with the brambles curving over her, summoned to her help the things she did; the things she liked; her husband; Elizabeth; her self, in short, which Peter hardly knew now, all to come about her and beat off the enemy.

'Well, and what's happened to you?' she said. So before a

battle begins, the horses paw the ground; toss their heads; the light shines on their flanks; their necks curve. So Peter Walsh and Clarissa, sitting side by side on the blue sofa, challenged each other. His powers chafed and tossed in him. He assembled from different quarters all sorts of things; praise; his career at Oxford; his marriage, which she knew nothing whatever about; how he had loved; and altogether done his job.

'Millions of things!' he exclaimed, and, urged by the assembly of powers which were now charging this way and that and giving him the feeling at once frightening and extremely exhilarating of being rushed through the air on the shoulders of people he could no longer see, he raised his hands to his forehead.

Clarissa sat very upright; drew in her breath.

'I am in love,' he said, not to her however, but to someone raised up in the dark so that you could not touch her but must lay your garland down on the grass in the dark.

'In love,' he repeated, now speaking rather dryly to Clarissa Dalloway; 'in love with a girl in India.' He had deposited his garland. Clarissa could make what she would of it.

'In love!' she said. That he at his age should be sucked under in his little bow-tie by that monster! And there's no flesh on his neck; his hands are red; and he's six months older than I am! her eye flashed back to her; but in her heart she felt, all the same; he is in love. He has that, she felt; he is in love.

But the indomitable egotism which for ever rides down the hosts opposed to it, the river which says on, on, on; even though, it admits, there may be no goal for us whatever, still on, on; this indomitable egotism charged her cheeks with colour; made her look very young; very pink; very bright-eyed as she sat with her dress upon her knee, and her needle held to the end of green silk, trembling a little. He was in love! Not with her. With some younger woman, of course.

'And who is she?' she asked.

Now this statue must be brought from its height and set down between them.

'A married woman, unfortunately,' he said; 'the wife of a Major in the Indian Army.'

And with a curious ironical sweetness he smiled as he placed her in this ridiculous way before Clarissa.

(All the same, he is in love, thought Clarissa.)

'She has', he continued, very reasonably, 'two small children; a boy and a girl; and I have come over to see my lawyers about the divorce.'

There they are! he thought. Do what you like with them, Clarissa! There they are! And second by second it seemed to him that the wife of the Major in the Indian Army (his Daisy) and her two small children became more and more lovely as Clarissa looked at them; as if he had set light to a grey pellet on a plate and there had risen up a lovely tree in the brisk sea-salted air of their intimacy (for in some ways no one understood him, felt with him, as Clarissa did)—their exquisite intimacy.

She flattered him; she fooled him, thought Clarissa; shaping the woman, the wife of the Major in the Indian Army, with three strokes of a knife. What a waste! What a folly! All his life long Peter had been fooled like that; first getting sent down from Oxford;* next marrying the girl on the boat going out to India; now the wife of a Major—thank Heaven she had refused to marry him! Still, he was in love; her old friend, her dear Peter, he was in love.

'But what are you going to do?' she asked him. Oh, the lawyers and solicitors, Messrs Hooper and Grateley of Lincoln's Inn,* they were going to do it, he said. And he actually pared his nails with his pocket-knife.

For Heaven's sake, leave your knife alone! she cried to herself in irrepressible irritation; it was his silly unconventionality, his weakness; his lack of the ghost of a notion what anyone else was feeling that annoyed her, had always annoyed her; and now at his age, how silly!

I know all that, Peter thought; I know what I'm up against, he thought, running his finger along the blade of his knife, Clarissa and Dalloway and all the rest of them; but I'll show Clarissa—and then to his utter surprise, suddenly thrown by those uncontrollable forces, thrown through the air, he burst into tears; wept; wept without the least shame, sitting on the sofa, the tears running down his cheeks.

And Clarissa had leant forward, taken his hand, drawn him to her, kissed him,—actually had felt his face on hers before she could down the brandishing of silver-flashing plumes like pampas grass in a tropic gale in her breast, which, subsiding, left her holding his hand, patting his knee, and feeling as she sat back extraordinarily at her ease with him and light-hearted, all in a clap it came over her, If I had married him, this gaiety would have been mine all day!

It was all over for her. The sheet was stretched and the bed narrow. She had gone up into the tower alone and left them blackberrying in the sun. The door had shut, and there among the dust of fallen plaster and the litter of birds' nests how distant the view had looked, and the sounds came thin and chill (once on Leith Hill,* she remembered), and Richard, Richard! she cried, as a sleeper in the night starts and stretches a hand in the dark for help. Lunching with Lady Bruton, it came back to her. He has left me; I am alone for ever, she thought, folding her hands upon her knee.

Peter Walsh had got up and crossed to the window and stood with his back to her, flicking a bandanna handkerchief from side to side. Masterly and dry and desolate he looked, his thin shoulder-blades lifting his coat slightly; blowing his nose violently. Take me with you, Clarissa thought impulsively, as if he were starting directly upon some great voyage; and then, next moment, it was as if the five acts of a play that had been very exciting and moving were now over and she had lived a lifetime in them and had run away, had lived with Peter, and it was now over.

Now it was time to move, and, as a woman gathers her things together, her cloak, her gloves, her opera-glasses, and gets up to go out of the theatre into the street, she rose from the sofa and went to Peter.

And it was awfully strange, he thought, how she still had the power, as she came tinkling, rustling, still had the power, as she came across the room, to make the moon, which he detested, rise at Bourton on the terrace in the summer sky.

'Tell me,' he said, seizing her by the shoulders. 'Are you happy, Clarissa? Does Richard——'

The door opened.

'Here is my Elizabeth,' said Clarissa, emotionally, histrionic-ally, perhaps.

'How d'y do?' said Elizabeth coming forward.

The sound of Big Ben striking the half-hour struck out between them with extraordinary vigour, as if a young man, strong, indifferent, inconsiderate, were swinging dumb-bells this way and that.

'Hullo, Elizabeth!' cried Peter, stuffing his handkerchief into his pocket, going quickly to her, saying 'Good-bye, Clarissa' without looking at her, leaving the room quickly, and running downstairs and opening the hall door.

'Peter! Peter!' cried Clarissa, following him out on to the land-ing. 'My party! Remember my party tonight!' she cried, having to raise her voice against the roar of the open air, and, overwhelmed by the traffic and the sound of all the clocks striking, her voice crying 'Remember my party tonight!' sounded frail and thin and very far away as Peter Walsh shut the door.

Remember my party, remember my party, said Peter Walsh as he stepped down the street, speaking to himself rhythmically, in time with the flow of the sound, the direct downright sound of Big Ben striking the half-hour. (The leaden circles dissolved in the air.) Oh these parties? he thought; Clarissa's parties. Why does she give these parties? he thought. Not that he blamed her or this effigy of a man in a tail-coat with a carnation in his button-hole coming towards him. Only one person in the world could be as he was, in love. And there he was, this fortunate man, himself, reflected in the plate-glass window of a motor-car manufacturer in Victoria Street.* All India lay behind him; plains, mountains; epidemics of cholera; a district twice as big as Ireland; decisions he had come to alone—he, Peter Walsh; who was now really for the first time in his life in love. Clarissa had grown hard, he thought; and a trifle sentimental into the bargain, he suspected, looking at the great motor cars capable of doing—how many miles on how many gallons? For he had a turn for mechanics; had invented a plough in his district, had ordered wheel-barrows from England,

Mrs Dalloway

but the coolies wouldn't use them, all of which Clarissa knew nothing whatever about.

The way she said 'Here is my Elizabeth!'—that annoyed him. Why not 'Here's Elizabeth' simply? It was insincere. And Elizabeth didn't like it either. (Still the last tremors of the great booming voice shook the air round him; the half-hour; still early; only half-past eleven still.) For he understood young people; he liked them. There was always something cold in Clarissa, he thought. She had always, even as a girl, a sort of timidity, which in middle age becomes conventionality, and then it's all up, it's all up, he thought, looking rather drearily into the glassy depths, and wondering whether by calling at that hour he had annoyed her; overcome with shame suddenly at having been a fool; wept; been emotional; told her everything, as usual, as usual.

As a cloud crosses the sun, silence falls on London; and falls on the mind. Effort ceases. Time flaps on the mast. There we stop; there we stand. Rigid, the skeleton of habit alone upholds the human frame. Where there is nothing, Peter Walsh said to himself; feeling hollowed out, utterly empty within. Clarissa refused me, he thought. He stood there thinking, Clarissa refused me.

Ah, said St Margaret's,* like a hostess who comes into her drawing-room on the very stroke of the hour and finds her guests there already. I am not late. No, it is precisely half-past eleven, she says. Yet, though she is perfectly right, her voice, being the voice of the hostess, is reluctant to inflict its individuality. Some grief for the past holds it back; some concern for the present. It is half-past eleven, she says, and the sound of St Margaret's glides into the recesses of the heart and buries itself in ring after ring of sound, like something alive which wants to confide itself, to disperse itself, to be, with a tremor of delight, at rest—like Clarissa herself, thought Peter Walsh, coming downstairs on the stroke of the hour in white. It is Clarissa herself, he thought, with a deep emotion, and an extraordinarily clear, yet puzzling, recollection of her, as if this bell had come into the room years ago, where they sat at some moment of great intimacy, and had gone from one to the other and had left, like a bee with honey, laden with the moment. But what room? What moment?

And why had he been so profoundly happy when the clock was striking? Then, as the sound of St Margaret's languished, he thought, she has been ill, and the sound expressed languor and suffering. It was her heart, he remembered; and the sudden loudness of the final stroke tolled for death that surprised in the midst of life, Clarissa falling where she stood, in her drawing-room. No! No! he cried. She is not dead! I am not old, he cried, and marched up Whitehall,* as if there rolled down to him, vigorous, unending, his future.

He was not old, or set, or dried in the least. As for caring what they said of him—the Dalloways, the Whitbreads, and their set, he cared not a straw—not a straw (though it was true he would have, some time or other, to see whether Richard couldn't help him to some job). Striding, staring, he glared at the statue of the Duke of Cambridge.* He had been sent down from Oxford—true. He had been a Socialist, in some sense a failure—true. Still the future of civilization lies, he thought, in the hands of young men like that; of young men such as he was, thirty years ago; with their love of abstract principles; getting books sent out to them all the way from London to a peak in the Himalayas; reading science; reading philosophy. The future lies in the hands of young men like that, he thought.

A patter like the patter of leaves in a wood came from behind, and with it a rustling, regular thudding sound, which as it over-took him drummed his thoughts, strict in step, up Whitehall, without his doing. Boys in uniform, carrying guns, marched with their eyes ahead of them, marched, their arms stiff, and on their faces an expression like the letters of a legend written round the base of a statue praising duty, gratitude, fidelity, love of England.

It is, thought Peter Walsh, beginning to keep step with them, a very fine training. But they did not look robust. They were weedy for the most part, boys of sixteen, who might, tomorrow, stand behind bowls of rice, cakes of soap on counters. Now they wore on them unmixed with sensual pleasure or daily preoccupations the solemnity of the wreath which they had fetched from Finsbury Pavement to the empty tomb.* They had taken their vow. The traffic respected it; vans were stopped.

I can't keep up with them, Peter Walsh thought, as they marched up Whitehall, and sure enough, on they marched, past him, past everyone, in their steady way, as if one will worked legs and arms uniformly, and life, with its varieties, its irreticences, had been laid under a pavement of monuments and wreaths and drugged into a stiff yet staring corpse by discipline. One had to respect it; one might laugh; but one had to respect it, he thought. There they go, thought Peter Walsh, pausing at the edge of the pavement; and all the exalted statues, Nelson, Gordon, Havelock,* the black, the spectacular images of great soldiers stood looking ahead of them, as if they too had made the same renunciation (Peter Walsh felt he, too, had made it the great renunciation), trampled under the same temptations, and achieved at length a marble stare. But the stare Peter Walsh did not want for himself in the least; though he could respect it in others. He could respect it in boys. They don't know the troubles of the flesh yet, he thought, as the marching boys disappeared in the direction of the Strand*—all that I've been through, he thought, crossing the road, and standing under Gordon's statue, Gordon whom as a boy he had worshipped; Gordon standing lonely with one leg raised and his arms crossed,—poor Gordon, he thought.

And just because nobody yet knew he was in London, except Clarissa, and the earth, after the voyage, still seemed an island to him, the strangeness of standing alone, alive, unknown, at half-past eleven in Trafalgar Square overcame him. What is it? Where am I? And why, after all, does one do it? he thought, the divorce seeming all moonshine. And down his mind went flat as a marsh, and three great emotions bowled over him; understanding; a vast philanthropy; and finally, as if the result of the others, an irrepressible, exquisite delight; as if inside his brain, by another hand, strings were pulled, shutters moved, and he, having noth-ing to do with it, yet stood at the opening of endless avenues down which if he chose he might wander. He had not felt so young for years.

He had escaped! was utterly free—as happens in the downfall of habit when the mind, like an unguarded flame, bows and bends and seems about to blow from its holding. I haven't felt so young for years! thought Peter, escaping (only of course for an hour or so) from being precisely what he was, and feeling like a child who runs out of doors, and sees, as he runs, his old nurse waving at the wrong window. But she's extraordinarily attractive, he thought, as, walking across Trafalgar Square in the direction of the Haymarket, came a young woman who, as she passed Gordon's statue, seemed, Peter Walsh thought (susceptible as he was), to shed veil after veil, until she became the very woman he had always had in mind; young, but stately; merry, but discreet; black, but enchanting.

Straightening himself and stealthily fingering his pocket-knife he started after her to follow this woman, this excitement, which seemed even with its back turned to shed on him a light which connected them, which singled him out, as if the random uproar of the traffic had whispered through hollowed hands his name, not Peter, but his private name which he called himself in his own thoughts. 'You,' she said, only 'you', saying it with her white gloves and her shoulders. Then the thin long cloak which the wind stirred as she walked past Dent's shop in Cockspur Street* blew out with an enveloping kindness, a mournful tenderness, as of arms that would open and take the tired——

But she's not married; she's young; quite young, thought Peter, the red carnation he had seen her wear as she came across Trafalgar Square burning again in his eyes and making her lips red. But she waited at the kerbstone. There was a dignity about her. She was not worldly, like Clarissa; not rich, like Clarissa. Was she, he wondered as she moved, respectable? Witty, with a lizard's flickering tongue, he thought (for one must invent, must allow oneself a little diversion), a cool waiting wit, a darting wit; not noisy.

She moved; she crossed; he followed her. To embarrass her was the last thing he wished. Still if she stopped he would say 'Come and have an ice,' he would say, and she would answer, perfectly simply, 'Oh yes.'

But other people got between them in the street, obstructing him, blotting her out. He pursued; she changed. There was colour in her cheeks; mockery in her eyes; he was an adventurer, reckless, he thought, swift, daring, indeed (landed as he was last night from India) a romantic buccaneer, careless of all these damned proprieties, yellow dressing-gowns, pipes, fishing-rods, in the shop windows; and respectability and evening parties and spruce old men wearing white slips beneath their waistcoats. He was a buccaneer. On and on she went, across Piccadilly, and up Regent Street, ahead of him, her cloak, her gloves, her shoulders combining with the fringes and the laces and the feather boas in the windows to make the spirit of finery and whimsy which dwindled out of the shops on to the pavement, as the light of a lamp goes wavering at night over hedges in the darkness.

Laughing and delightful, she had crossed Oxford Street and Great Portland Street and turned down one of the little streets, and now, and now, the great moment was approaching, for now she slackened, opened her bag, and with one look in his direction, but not at him, one look that bade farewell, summed up the whole situation and dismissed it triumphantly, for ever, had fitted her key, opened the door, and gone! Clarissa's voice saying, Remember my party, Remember my party, sang in his ears. The house was one of those flat red houses with hanging flower-baskets of vague impropriety. It was over.

Well, I've had my fun; I've had it, he thought, looking up at the swinging baskets of pale geraniums. And it was smashed to atoms—his fun, for it was half made up, as he knew very well; invented, this escapade with the girl; made up, as one makes up the better part of life, he thought—making oneself up; making her up; creating an exquisite amusement, and something more. But odd it was, and quite true; all this one could never share—it smashed to atoms.

He turned; went up the street, thinking to find somewhere to sit, till it was time for Lincoln's Inn—for Messrs Hooper and Grateley. Where should he go? No matter. Up the street, then, towards Regent's Park. His boots on the pavement struck out 'no matter'; for it was early, still very early.

It was a splendid morning too. Like the pulse of a perfect heart, life struck straight through the streets. There was no fumbling—no hesitation. Sweeping and swerving, accurately, punctually, noiselessly, there, precisely at the right instant, the motor car stopped at the door. The girl, silk-stockinged, feathered, evanescent, but not to him particularly attractive (for he had had his fling), alighted. Admirable butlers, tawny chow dogs, halls laid in black and white lozenges with white blinds blowing, Peter saw through the opened door and approved of. A splendid achievement in its own way, after all, London; the season; civilization. Coming as he did from a respectable Anglo-Indian family which for at least three generations had administered the affairs of a continent (it's strange, he thought, what a sentiment I have about that, disliking India, and empire, and army as he did), there were moments when civilization, even of this sort, seemed dear to him as a personal possession; moments of pride in England; in butlers; chow dogs; girls in their security. Ridiculous enough, still there it is, he thought. And the doctors and men of business and capable women all going about their business, punctual, alert, robust, seemed to him wholly admirable, good fellows, to whom one would entrust one's life, companions in the art of living, who would see one through. What with one thing and another, the show was really very tolerable; and he would sit down in the shade and smoke.

There was Regent's Park. Yes. As a child he had walked in Regent's Park—odd, he thought, how the thought of childhood keeps coming back to me—the result of seeing Clarissa, perhaps; for women live much more in the past than we do, he thought. They attach themselves to places; and their fathers—a woman's always proud of her father. Bourton was a nice place, a very nice place, but I could never get on with the old man, he thought. There was quite a scene one night—an argument about something or other, what, he could not remember. Politics presumably.

Yes, he remembered Regent's Park; the long straight walk; the little house where one bought air-balls to the left; an absurd statue with an inscription somewhere or other.* He looked for an empty seat. He did not want to be bothered (feeling a little drowsy as he did) by people asking him the time. An elderly grey nurse, with a baby asleep in its perambulator—that was the best he could do for himself; sit down at the far end of the seat by that nurse.

She's a queer-looking girl, he thought, suddenly remembering Elizabeth as she came into the room and stood by her mother. Grown big; quite grown-up, not exactly pretty; handsome rather; and she can't be more than eighteen. Probably she doesn't get on with Clarissa. 'There's my Elizabeth'—that sort of thing—why not 'Here's Elizabeth' simply?—trying to make out, like most mothers, that things are what they're not. She trusts to her charm too much, he thought. She overdoes it.

The rich benignant cigar smoke eddied coolly down his throat; he puffed it out again in rings which breasted the air bravely for a moment; blue, circular—I shall try and get a word alone with Elizabeth tonight, he thought—then began to wobble into hour-glass shapes and taper away; odd shapes they take, he thought. Suddenly he closed his eyes, raised his hand with an effort, and threw away the heavy end of his cigar. A great brush swept smooth across his mind, sweeping across it moving branches, children's voices, the shuffle of feet, and people passing, and humming traffic, rising and falling traffic. Down, down he sank into the plumes and feathers of sleep, sank, and was muffled over.

The grey nurse resumed her knitting as Peter Walsh, on the hot seat beside her, began snoring. In her grey dress, moving her hands indefatigably yet quietly, she seemed like the champion of the rights of sleepers, like one of those spectral presences which rise in twilight in woods made of sky and branches. The solitary traveller, haunter of lanes, disturber of ferns, and devastator of great hemlock plants, looking up suddenly, sees the giant figure at the end of the ride.

By conviction an atheist perhaps, he is taken by surprise with moments of extraordinary exaltation. Nothing exists outside us except a state of mind, he thinks; a desire for solace, for relief, for something outside these miserable pigmies, these feeble, these ugly, these craven men and women. But if he can conceive of her, then in some sort she exists, he thinks, and advancing down the path with his eyes upon sky and branches he rapidly endows them with womanhood; sees with amazement how grave they become; how majestically, as the breeze stirs them, they dispense with a dark flutter of the leaves, charity, comprehension, absolution, and then, flinging themselves suddenly aloft, confound the piety of their aspect with a wild carouse.

Such are the visions which proffer great cornucopias full of fruit to the solitary traveller, or murmur in his ear like sirens lolloping away on the green sea waves, or are dashed in his face like bunches of roses, or rise to the surface like pale faces which fishermen flounder through floods to embrace.

Such are the visions which ceaselessly float up, pace beside, put their faces in front of, the actual thing; often overpowering the solitary traveller and taking away from him the sense of the earth, the wish to return, and giving him for substitute a general peace, as if (so he thinks as he advances down the forest ride) all this fever of living were simplicity itself; and myriads of things merged in one thing; and this figure, made of sky and branches as it is, had risen from the troubled sea (he is elderly, past fifty now) as a shape might be sucked up out of the waves to shower down from her magnificent hands, compassion, comprehension, absolution. So, he thinks, may I never go back to the lamplight; to the sitting-room; never finish my book; never knock out my pipe; never ring for Mrs Turner to clear away; rather let me walk straight on to this great figure, who will, with a toss of her head, mount me on her streamers and let me blow to nothingness with the rest.

Such are the visions. The solitary traveller is soon beyond the wood; and there, coming to the door with shaded eyes, possibly to look for his return, with hands raised, with white apron blowing, is an elderly woman who seems (so powerful is this infirmity) to seek, over the desert, a lost son; to search for a rider destroyed; to be the figure of the mother whose sons have been killed in the battles of the world. So, as the solitary traveller advances down the village street where the women stand knitting and the men dig in the garden, the evening seems ominous; the figures still; as if some august fate, known to them, awaited without fear, were about to sweep them into complete annihilation.

Indoors among ordinary things, the cupboard, the table, the window-sill with its geraniums, suddenly the outline of the land-lady, bending to remove the cloth, becomes soft with light, an adorable emblem which only the recollection of cold human contacts forbids us to embrace. She takes the marmalade; she shuts it in the cupboard.

'There is nothing more tonight, sir?'

But to whom does the solitary traveller make reply?

So the elderly nurse knitted over the sleeping baby in Regent's Park. So Peter Walsh snored. He woke with extreme suddenness, saying to himself, 'The death of the soul.'

'Lord, Lord!' he said to himself out loud, stretching and opening his eyes. 'The death of the soul.' The words attached themselves to some scene, to some room, to some past he had been dreaming of. It became clearer; the scene, the room, the past he had been dreaming of.

It was at Bourton that summer, early in the 'nineties, when he was so passionately in love with Clarissa. There were a great many people there, laughing and talking, sitting round a table after tea, and the room was bathed in yellow light and full of cigarette smoke. They were talking about a man who had married his housemaid, one of the neighbouring squires, he had forgotten his name. He had married his housemaid, and she had been brought to Bourton to call—an awful visit it had been. She was absurdly overdressed, 'like a cockatoo,' Clarissa had said, imitating her, and she never stopped talking. On and on she went, on and on. Clarissa imitated her. Then somebody said—Sally Seton it was—did it make any real difference to one's feelings to know that before they'd married she had had a baby? (In those days, in mixed company, it was a bold thing to say.) He could see Clarissa now, turning bright pink; somehow contracting; and saying, 'Oh, I shall never be able to speak to her again!' Whereupon the whole party sitting round the tea-table seemed to wobble. It was very uncomfortable.

He hadn't blamed her for minding the fact, since in those days a girl brought up as she was knew nothing, but it was her manner that annoyed him; timid; hard; arrogant; prudish. 'The death of the soul.' He had said that instinctively, ticketing the moment as he used to do—the death of her soul.

Everyone wobbled; everyone seemed to bow, as she spoke, and

then to stand up different. He could see Sally Seton, like a child who has been in mischief, leaning forward, rather flushed, wanting to talk, but afraid, and Clarissa did frighten people. (She was Clarissa's greatest friend, always about the place, an attractive creature, handsome, dark, with the reputation in those days of great daring, and he used to give her cigars, which she smoked in her bedroom, and she had either been engaged to somebody or quarrelled with her family, and old Parry disliked them both equally, which was a great bond.) Then Clarissa, still with an air of being offended with them all, got up, made some excuse, and went off, alone. As she opened the door, in came that great shaggy dog which ran after sheep. She flung herself upon him, went into raptures. It was as if she said to Peter—it was all aimed at him, he knew—'I know you thought me absurd about that woman just now; but see how extraordinarily sympathetic I am; see how I love my Rob!'

They had always this queer power of communicating without words. She knew directly he criticized her. Then she would do something quite obvious to defend herself, like this fuss with the dog—but it never took him in, he always saw through Clarissa. Not that he said anything, of course; just sat looking glum. It was the way their quarrels often began.

She shut the door. At once he became extremely depressed. It all seemed useless—going on being in love; going on quarrelling; going on making it up, and he wandered off alone, among out-houses, stables, looking at the horses. (The place was quite a humble one; the Parrys were never very well off; but there were always grooms and stable-boys about—Clarissa loved riding—and an old coachman—what was his name?—an old nurse, old Moody, old Goody, some such name they called her, whom one was taken to visit in a little room with lots of photographs, lots of bird-cages.)

It was an awful evening! He grew more and more gloomy, not about that only; about everything. And he couldn't see her; couldn't explain to her; couldn't have it out. There were always people about—she'd go on as if nothing had happened. That was the devilish part of her—this coldness, this woodenness, something very profound in her, which he had felt again this morning talking to her; an impenetrability. Yet Heaven knows he loved her. She had some queer power of fiddling on one's nerves, turning one's nerves to fiddle-strings, yes.

He had gone into dinner rather late, from some idiotic idea of making himself felt, and had sat down by old Miss Parry—Aunt Helena—Mr Parry's sister, who was supposed to preside. There she sat in her white Cashmere shawl, with her head against the window—a formidable old lady, but kind to him, for he had found her some rare flower, and she was a great botanist, marching off in thick boots with a black tin collecting box slung between her shoulders. He sat down beside her, and couldn't speak. Everything seemed to race past him; he just sat there, eating. And then half-way through dinner he made himself look across at Clarissa for the first time. She was talking to a young man on her right. He had a sudden revelation. 'She will marry that man,' he said to himself. He didn't even know his name.

For of course it was that afternoon, that very afternoon, that Dalloway had come over; and Clarissa called him 'Wickham'; that was the beginning of it all. Somebody had brought him over; and Clarissa got his name wrong. She introduced him to everybody as Wickham. At last he said 'My name is Dalloway!'—that was his first view of Richard—a fair young man, rather awkward, sitting on a deckchair, and blurting out 'My name is Dalloway!' Sally got hold of it; always after that she called him 'My name is Dalloway!'

He was a prey to revelations at that time. This one—that she would marry Dalloway—was blinding—overwhelming at the moment. There was a sort of—how could he put it?—a sort of ease in her manner to him; something maternal; something gentle. They were talking about politics. All through dinner he tried to hear what they were saying.

Afterwards he could remember standing by old Miss Parry's chair in the drawing-room. Clarissa came up, with her perfect manners, like a real hostess, and wanted to introduce him to someone—spoke as if they had never met before, which enraged him. Yet even then he admired her for it. He admired her courage; her social instinct; he admired her power of carrying things through. 'The perfect hostess,' he said to her, whereupon she winced all over. But he meant her to feel it. He would have done anything to hurt her, after seeing her with Dalloway. So she left him. And he had a feeling that they were all gathered together in a conspiracy against him—laughing and talking—behind his back. There he stood by Miss Parry's chair as though he had been cut out of wood, talking about wild flowers. Never, never had he suffered so infernally! He must have forgotten even to pretend to listen; at last he woke up; he saw Miss Parry looking rather disturbed, rather indignant, with her prominent eyes fixed. He almost cried out that he couldn't attend because he was in Hell! People began going out of the room. He heard them talking about fetching cloaks; about its being cold on the water, and so on. They were going boating on the lake by moonlight—one of Sally's mad ideas. He could hear her describing the moon. And they all went out. He was left quite alone.

'Don't you want to go with them?' said Aunt Helena—poor old lady!—she had guessed. And he turned round and there was Clarissa again. She had come back to fetch him. He was overcome by her generosity—her goodness.

'Come along,' she said. 'They're waiting.'

He had never felt so happy in the whole of his life! Without a word they made it up. They walked down to the lake. He had twenty minutes of perfect happiness. Her voice, her laugh, her dress (something floating, white, crimson), her spirit, her adventurousness; she made them all disembark and explore the island; she startled a hen; she laughed; she sang. And all the time, he knew perfectly well, Dalloway was falling in love with her; she was falling in love with Dalloway; but it didn't seem to matter. Nothing mattered. They sat on the ground and talked—he and Clarissa. They went in and out of each other's minds without any effort. And then in a second it was over. He said to himself as they were getting into the boat, 'She will marry that man,' dully, without any resentment; but it was an obvious thing. Dalloway would marry Clarissa.

Dalloway rowed them in. He said nothing But somehow as

they watched him start, jumping on to his bicycle to ride twenty miles through the woods, wobbling off down the drive, waving his hand and disappearing, he obviously did feel, instinctively, tremendously, strongly, all that; the night; the romance; Clarissa. He deserved to have her.

For himself, he was absurd. His demands upon Clarissa (he could see it now) were absurd. He asked impossible things. He made terrible scenes. She would have accepted him still, perhaps, if he had been less absurd. Sally thought so. She wrote him all that summer long letters; how they had talked of him; how she had praised him, how Clarissa burst into tears! It was an extraordinary summer—all letters, scenes, telegrams—arriving at Bourton early in the morning, hanging about till the servants were up; appalling *tête-à-têtes* with old Mr Parry at breakfast; Aunt Helena formidable but kind; Sally sweeping him off for talks in the vegetable garden; Clarissa in bed with headaches.

The final scene, the terrible scene which he believed had mattered more than anything in the whole of his life (it might be an exaggeration—but still, so it did seem now), happened at three o'clock in the afternoon of a very hot day. It was a trifle that led up to it—Sally at lunch saying something about Dalloway, and calling him 'My name is Dalloway'; whereupon Clarissa suddenly stiffened, coloured, in a way she had, and rapped out sharply, 'We've had enough of that feeble joke.' That was all; but for him it was as if she had said, 'I'm only amusing myself with you; I've an understanding with Richard Dalloway.' So he took it. He had not slept for nights. 'It's got to be finished one way or the other,' he said to himself. He sent a note to her by Sally asking her to meet him by the fountain at three. 'Something very important has happened,' he scribbled at the end of it.

The fountain was in the middle of a little shrubbery, far from the house, with shrubs and trees all round it. There she came, even before the time, and they stood with the fountain between them, the spout (it was broken) dribbling water incessantly. How sights fix themselves upon the mind! For example, the vivid green moss.

She did not move. 'Tell me the truth, tell me the truth,' he kept on saying. He felt as if his forehead would burst. She seemed contracted, petrified. She did not move. 'Tell me the truth,' he repeated, when suddenly that old man Breitkopf popped his head in carrying *The Times*; stared at them; gaped; and went away. They neither of them moved. 'Tell me the truth,' he repeated. He felt that he was grinding against something physically hard; she was unyielding. She was like iron, like flint, rigid up the backbone. And when she said, 'It's no use. It's no use. This is the end'—after he had spoken for hours, it seemed, with the tears running down his cheeks—it was as if she had hit him in the face. She turned, she left him, she went away.

'Clarissa!' he cried. 'Clarissa!' But she never came back. It was over. He went away that night. He never saw her again.

It was awful, he cried, awful, awful!

Still, the sun was hot. Still, one got over things. Still, life had a way of adding day to day. Still, he thought, yawning and beginning to take notice—Regent's Park had changed very little since he was a boy, except for the squirrels—still, presumably there were compensations—when little Elise Mitchell, who had been picking up pebbles to add to the pebble collection which she and her brother were making on the nursery mantelpiece, plumped her handful down on the nurse's knee and scudded off again full tilt into a lady's legs. Peter Walsh laughed out.

But Lucrezia Warren Smith was saying to herself, It's wicked; why should I suffer? she was asking, as she walked down the broad path. No; I can't stand it any longer, she was saying, having left Septimus, who wasn't Septimus any longer, to say hard, cruel, wicked things, to talk to himself, to talk to a dead man, on the seat over there; when the child ran full tilt into her, fell flat, and burst out crying.

That was comforting rather. She stood her upright, dusted her frock, kissed her.

But for herself she had done nothing wrong; she had loved Septimus; she had been happy; she had had a beautiful home, and there her sisters lived still, making hats. Why should *she* suffer?

The child ran straight back to its nurse, and Rezia saw her scolded, comforted, taken up by the nurse who put down her

knitting, and the kind-looking man gave her his watch to blow
open to comfort her—but why should *she* be exposed? Why not
left in Milan? Why tortured? Why?

Slightly waved by tears, the broad path, the nurse, the man in
grey, the perambulator, rose and fell before her eyes. To be rocked
by this malignant torturer was her lot. But why? She was like a
bird sheltering under the thin hollow of a leaf, who blinks at the
sun when the leaf moves; starts at the crack of a dry twig. She was
exposed; she was surrounded by the enormous trees, vast clouds
of an indifferent world, exposed; tortured; and why should she
suffer? Why?

She frowned; she stamped her foot. She must go back again to
Septimus since it was almost time for them to be going to Sir
William Bradshaw. She must go back and tell him, go back to him
sitting there on the green chair under the tree, talking to himself,
or to that dead man Evans, whom she had only seen once for a
moment in the shop. He had seemed a nice quiet man; a great
friend of Septimus's, and he had been killed in the War. But such
things happen to everyone. Everyone has friends who were killed
in the War. Everyone gives up something when they marry. She
had given up her home. She had come to live here, in this awful
city. But Septimus let himself think about horrible things, as she
could too, if she tried. He had grown stranger and stranger. He
said people were talking behind the bedroom walls. Mrs Filmer
thought it odd. He saw things too—he had seen an old woman's
head in the middle of a fern. Yet he could be happy when he
chose. They went to Hampton Court* on top of a bus, and they
were perfectly happy. All the little red and yellow flowers were
out on the grass, like floating lamps he said, and talked and chat-
tered and laughed, making up stories. Suddenly he said, 'Now we
will kill ourselves,' when they were standing by the river, and he
looked at it with a look which she had seen in his eyes when a
train went by, or an omnibus—a look as if something fascinated
him; and she felt he was going from her and she caught him by
the arm. But going home he was perfectly quiet—perfectly reasonable. He would argue with her about killing themselves; and
explain how wicked people were; how he could see them making

up lies as they passed in the street. He knew all their thoughts, he said; he knew everything. He knew the meaning of the world, he said.

Then when they got back he could hardly walk. He lay on the sofa and made her hold his hand to prevent him from falling down, down, he cried, into the flames! and saw faces laughing at him, calling him horrible disgusting names, from the walls and hands pointing round the screen. Yet they were quite alone. But he began to talk aloud, answering people, arguing, laughing, crying, getting very excited and making her write things down. Perfect nonsense it was; about death; about Miss Isabel Pole. She could stand it no longer. She would go back.

She was close to him now, could see him staring at the sky, muttering, clasping his hands. Yet Dr Holmes said there was nothing the matter with him. What, then, had happened—why had he gone, then, why, when she sat by him, did he start, frown at her, move away, and point at her hand, take her hand, look at it terrified?

Was it that she had taken off her wedding ring? 'My hand has grown so thin,' she said; 'I have put it in my purse,' she told him.

He dropped her hand. Their marriage was over, he thought, with agony, with relief. The rope was cut; he mounted; he was free, as it was decreed that he, Septimus, the lord of men, should be free; alone (since his wife had thrown away her wedding ring; since she had left him), he, Septimus, was alone, called forth in advance of the mass of men to hear the truth, to learn the meaning, which now at last, after all the toils of civilization—Greeks, Romans, Shakespeare, Darwin, and now himself—was to be given whole to . . . 'To whom?' he asked aloud, 'To the Prime Minister,' the voices which rustled above his head replied. The supreme secret must be told to the Cabinet; first, that trees are alive; next, there is no crime; next, love, universal love, he muttered, gasping, trembling, painfully drawing out these profound truths which needed, so deep were they, so difficult, an immense effort to speak out, but the world was entirely changed by them for ever.

No crime; love; he repeated, fumbling for his card and pencil, when a Skye terrier snuffed his trousers and he started in an agony of fear. It was turning into a man! He could not watch it happen! It was horrible, terrible to see a dog become a man! At once the dog trotted away.

Heaven was divinely merciful, infinitely benignant. It spared him, pardoned his weakness. But what was the scientific explanation (for one must be scientific above all things)? Why could he see through bodies, see into the future, when dogs will become men? It was the heatwave presumably, operating upon a brain made sensitive by eons of evolution. Scientifically speaking, the flesh was melted off the world. His body was macerated until only the nerve fibres were left. It was spread like a veil upon a rock.

He lay back in his chair, exhausted but upheld. He lay resting, waiting, before he again interpreted, with effort, with agony, to mankind. He lay very high, on the back of the world. The earth thrilled beneath him. Red flowers grew through his flesh; their stiff leaves rustled by his head. Music began clanging against the rocks up here. It is a motor horn down in the street, he muttered; but up here it cannoned from rock to rock, divided, met in shocks of sound which rose in smooth columns (that music should be visible was a discovery) and became an anthem, an anthem twined round now by a shepherd boy's piping (That's an old man playing a penny whistle by the public-house, he muttered) which, as the boy stood still, came bubbling from his pipe, and then, as he climbed higher, made its exquisite plaint while the traffic passed beneath. This boy's elegy is played among the traffic, thought Septimus. Now he withdraws up into the snows, and roses hang about him—the thick red roses which grow on my bedroom wall, he reminded himself. The music stopped. He has his penny, he reasoned it out, and has gone on to the next public-house.

But he himself remained high on his rock, like a drowned sailor on a rock. I leant over the edge of the boat and fell down, he thought. I went under the sea. I have been dead, and yet am now alive, but let me rest still, he begged (he was talking to himself again—it was awful, awful!); and as, before waking, the voices of birds and the sound of wheels chime and chatter in a queer harmony, grow louder and louder, and the sleeper feels himself drawing to the shores of life, so he felt himself drawing towards life, the sun growing hotter, cries sounding louder, something tremendous about to happen.

He had only to open his eyes; but a weight was on them; a fear. He strained; he pushed; he looked; he saw Regent's Park before him. Long streamers of sunlight fawned at his feet. The trees waved, brandished. We welcome, the world seemed to say; we accept; we create. Beauty, the world seemed to say. And as if to prove it (scientifically) wherever he looked, at the houses, at the railings, at the antelopes stretching over the palings, beauty sprang instantly. To watch a leaf quivering in the rush of air was an exquisite joy. Up in the sky swallows swooping, swerving, flinging themselves in and out, round and round, yet always with perfect control as if elastics held them; and the flies rising and falling; and the sun spotting now this leaf, now that, in mockery, dazzling it with soft gold in pure good temper; and now and again some chime (it might be a motor horn) tinkling divinely on the grass stalks—all of this, calm and reasonable as it was, made out of ordinary things as it was, was the truth now; beauty, that was the truth now. Beauty was everywhere.

'It is time,' said Rezia.

The word 'time' split its husk; poured its riches over him; and from his lips fell like shells, like shavings from a plane, without his making them, hard, white, imperishable, words, and flew to attach themselves to their places in an ode to Time; an immortal ode to Time. He sang. Evans answered from behind the tree. The dead were in Thessaly,* Evans sang, among the orchids. There they waited till the War was over, and now the dead, now Evans himself—

'For God's sake don't come!' Septimus cried out. For he could not look upon the dead.

But the branches parted. A man in grey was actually walking towards them. It was Evans! But no mud was on him; no wounds; he was not changed. I must tell the whole world, Septimus cried, raising his hand (as the dead man in the grey suit came nearer), raising his hand like some colossal figure who has lamented the fate of man for ages in the desert alone with his hands pressed to his forehead, furrows of despair on his cheeks, and now sees light on the desert's edge which broadens and strikes the iron-black figure (and Septimus half rose from his chair), and with legions of men prostrate behind him he, the giant mourner, receives for one moment on his face the whole—

'But I am so unhappy, Septimus,' said Rezia, trying to make him sit down.

The millions lamented; for ages they had sorrowed. He would turn round, he would tell them in a few moments, only a few moments more, of this relief, of this joy, of this astonishing revelation—

'The time, Septimus,' Rezia repeated. 'What is the time?'

He was talking, he was starting, this man must notice him. He was looking at them.

'I will tell you the time,' said Septimus, very slowly, very drowsily, smiling mysteriously at the dead man in the grey suit. As he sat smiling, the quarter struck—the quarter to twelve.

And that is being young, Peter Walsh thought as he passed them. To be having an awful scene—the poor girl looked absolutely desperate—in the middle of the morning. But what was it about? he wondered; what had the young man in the overcoat been saying to her to make her look like that; what awful fix had they got themselves into, both to look so desperate as that on a fine summer morning? The amusing thing about coming back to England, after five years, was the way it made, anyhow the first days, things stand out as if one had never seen them before; lovers squabbling under a tree; the domestic family life of the parks. Never had he seen London look so enchanting—the softness of the distances; the richness; the greenness; the civilization, after India, he thought, strolling across the grass.

This susceptibility to impressions had been his undoing, no doubt. Still at his age he had, like a boy or a girl even, these alternations of mood; good days, bad days, for no reason whatever, happiness from a pretty face, downright misery at the sight of a frump. After India of course one fell in love with every woman one met. There was a freshness about them; even the poorest dressed better than five years ago surely; and to his eye the fashions had never been so becoming; the long black cloaks; the slimness; the elegance; and then the delicious and apparently universal habit of paint. Every woman, even the most respectable, had roses blooming under glass; lips cut with a knife; curls of Indian ink; there was design, art, everywhere; a change of some sort had undoubtedly taken place. What did the young people think about? Peter Walsh asked himself.

Those five years—1918 to 1923—had been, he suspected, somehow very important. People looked different. Newspapers seemed different. Now, for instance, there was a man writing quite openly in one of the respectable weeklies about water-closets. That you couldn't have done ten years ago—written quite openly about water-closets in a respectable weekly. And then this taking out a stick of rouge, or a powder-puff, and making up in public. On board ship coming home there were lots of young men and girls—Betty and Bertie he remembered in particular—carrying on quite openly; the old mother sitting and watching them with her knitting, cool as a cucumber. The girl would stand still and powder her nose in front of everyone. And they weren't engaged: just having a good time; no feelings hurt on either side. As hard as nails she was—Betty Whatshername—but a thorough good sort. She would make a very good wife at thirty—she would marry when it suited her to marry; marry some rich man and live in a large house near Manchester.

Who was it now who had done that? Peter Walsh asked himself, turning into the Broad Walk—married a rich man and lived in a large house near Manchester? Somebody who had written him a long, gushing letter quite lately about 'blue hydrangeas'. It was seeing blue hydrangeas that made her think of him and the old days—Sally Seton, of course! It was Sally Seton—the last person in the world one would have expected to marry a rich man and live in a large house near Manchester, the wild, the daring, the romantic Sally!

But of all that ancient lot, Clarissa's friends—Whitbreads, Kindersleys, Cunninghams, Kinloch-Joneses—Sally was probably the best. She tried to get hold of things by the right end

anyhow. She saw through Hugh Whitbread anyhow—the
admirable Hugh—when Clarissa and the rest were at his feet.

'The Whitbreads?' he could hear her saying. 'Who are the
Whitbreads? Coal merchants. Respectable trades-people.'

Hugh she detested for some reason. He thought of nothing but
his own appearance, she said. He ought to have been a Duke. He
would be certain to marry one of the Royal Princesses. And of
course Hugh had the most extraordinary, the most natural, the
most sublime respect for the British aristocracy of any human
being he had ever come across. Even Clarissa had to own that. Oh,
but he was such a dear, so unselfish, gave up shooting to please
his old mother—remembered his aunts' birthdays, and so on.

Sally, to do her justice, saw through all that. One of the things
he remembered best was an argument one Sunday morning at
Bourton about women's rights (that antediluvian topic), when
Sally suddenly lost her temper, flared up, and told Hugh that he
represented all that was most detestable in British middle-class
life. She told him that she considered him responsible for the
state of 'those poor girls in Piccadilly'*—Hugh, the perfect
gentleman, poor Hugh!—never did a man look more horrified!
She did it on purpose, she said afterwards (for they used to get
together in the vegetable garden and compare notes). 'He's read
nothing, thought nothing, felt nothing,' he could hear her saying
in that very emphatic voice which carried so much farther than
she knew. The stable boys had more life in them than Hugh, she
said. He was a perfect specimen of the public-school type, she
said. No country but England could have produced him. She was
really spiteful, for some reason; had some grudge against him.
Something had happened—he forgot what—in the smoking-
room. He had insulted her—kissed her? Incredible! Nobody
believed a word against Hugh, of course. Who could? Kissing
Sally in the smoking-room! If it had been some Honourable
Edith or Lady Violet, perhaps; but not that ragamuffin Sally
without a penny to her name, and a father or a mother gambling
at Monte Carlo. For of all the people he had ever met Hugh was
the greatest snob—the most obsequious—no, he didn't cringe
exactly. He was too much of a prig for that. A first-rate valet was

the obvious comparison—somebody who walked behind carrying suitcases; could be trusted to send telegrams—indispensable to hostesses. And he'd found his job—married his Honourable Evelyn; got some little post at Court, looked after the King's cellars, polished the Imperial shoe-buckles, went about in knee-breeches and lace ruffles. How remorseless life is! A little job at Court!

He had married this lady, the Honourable Evelyn, and they lived hereabouts, so he thought (looking at the pompous houses overlooking the Park), for he had lunched there once in a house which had, like all Hugh's possessions, something that no other house could possibly have—linen cupboards it might have been. You had to go and look at them—you had to spend a great deal of time always admiring whatever it was—linen cupboards, pillow-cases, old oak furniture, pictures, which Hugh had picked up for an old song. But Mrs Hugh sometimes gave the show away. She was one of those obscure mouse-like little women who admire big men. She was almost negligible. Then suddenly she would say something quite unexpected—something sharp. She had the relics of the grand manner, perhaps. The steam coal was a little too strong for her—it made the atmosphere thick. And so there they lived, with their linen cupboards and their old masters and their pillow-cases fringed with real lace, at the rate of five or ten thousand a year presumably, while he, who was two years older than Hugh, cadged for a job.

At fifty-three he had to come and ask them to put him into some secretary's office, to find him some usher's job teaching little boys Latin, at the beck and call of some mandarin in an office, something that brought in five hundred a year; for if he married Daisy, even with his pension, they could never do on less. Whitbread could do it presumably; or Dalloway. He didn't mind what he asked Dalloway. He was a thorough good sort; a bit limited; a bit thick in the head; yes; but a thorough good sort. Whatever he took up he did in the same matter-of-fact sensible way; without a touch of imagination, without a spark of brilliancy, but with the inexplicable niceness of his type. He ought to have been a country gentleman—he was wasted on politics. He was at his best out of doors, with horses and dogs—how good he was, for instance, when that great shaggy dog of Clarissa's got caught in a trap and had its paw half torn off, and Clarissa turned faint and Dalloway did the whole thing; bandaged, made splints; told Clarissa not to be a fool. That was what she liked him for, perhaps—that was what she needed. 'Now, my dear, don't be a fool. Hold this—fetch that,' all the time talking to the dog as if it were a human being.

But how could she swallow all that stuff about poetry? How could she let him hold forth about Shakespeare? Seriously and solemnly Richard Dalloway got on his hind legs and said that no decent man ought to read Shakespeare's sonnets because it was like listening at keyholes (besides, the relationship was not one that he approved).* No decent man ought to let his wife visit a deceased wife's sister.* Incredible! The only thing to do was to pelt him with sugared almonds—it was at dinner. But Clarissa sucked it all in; thought it so honest of him; so independent of him; Heaven knows if she didn't think him the most original mind she'd ever met!

That was one of the bonds between Sally and himself. There was a garden where they used to walk, a walled-in place, with rose-bushes and giant cauliflowers—he could remember Sally tearing off a rose, stopping to exclaim at the beauty of the cabbage leaves in the moonlight (it was extraordinary how vividly it all came back to him, things he hadn't thought of for years), while she implored him, half laughing of course, to carry off Clarissa, to save her from the Hughs and the Dalloways and all the other 'perfect gentlemen' who would 'stifle her soul' (she wrote reams of poetry in those days), make a mere hostess of her, encourage her worldliness. But one must do Clarissa justice. She wasn't going to marry Hugh anyhow. She had a perfectly clear notion of what she wanted. Her emotions were all on the surface. Beneath, she was very shrewd—a far better judge of character than Sally, for instance, and with it all, purely feminine; with that extraordinary gift, that woman's gift, of making a world of her own wherever she happened to be. She came into a room; she stood, as he had often seen her, in a doorway with lots of people round her.

But it was Clarissa one remembered. Not that she was striking; not beautiful at all; there was nothing picturesque about her; she never said anything specially clever; there she was, however; there she was.

No, no, no! He was not in love with her any more! He only felt, after seeing her that morning, among her scissors and silks, making ready for the party, unable to get away from the thought of her; she kept coming back and back like a sleeper jolting against him in a railway carriage; which was not being in love, of course; it was thinking of her, criticizing her, starting again, after thirty years, trying to explain her. The obvious thing to say of her was that she was worldly; cared too much for rank and society and getting on in the world—which was true in a sense; she had admitted it to him. (You could always get her to own up if you took the trouble; she was honest.) What she would say was that she hated frumps, fogies, failures, like himself presumably; thought people had no right to slouch about with their hands in their pockets; must do something, be something; and these great swells, these Duchesses, these hoary old Countesses one met in her drawing-room, unspeakably remote as he felt them to be from anything that mattered a straw, stood for something real to her. Lady Bexborough, she said once, held herself upright (so did Clarissa herself; she never lounged in any sense of the word; she was straight as a dart, a little rigid in fact). She said they had a kind of courage which the older she grew the more she respected. In all this there was a great deal of Dalloway, of course; a great deal of the public-spirited, British Empire, tariff-reform, governing-class spirit, which had grown on her, as it tends to do. With twice his wits, she had to see things through his eyes—one of the tragedies of married life. With a mind of her own, she must always be quoting Richard—as if one couldn't know to a tittle what Richard thought by reading the *Morning Post** of a morning! These parties, for example, were all for him, or for her idea of him (to do Richard justice he would have been happier farming in Norfolk). She made her drawing-room a sort of meeting-place; she had a genius for it. Over and over again he had seen her take some raw youth, twist him, turn him, wake him up; set him going. Infinite numbers of dull people conglomerated round her, of course. But odd unexpected people turned up; an artist sometimes; sometimes a writer; queer fish in that atmosphere. And behind it all was that network of visiting, leaving cards, being kind to people; running about with bunches of flowers, little presents; So-and-so was going to France—must have an air-cushion; a real drain on her strength; all that interminable traffic that women of her sort keep up; but she did it genuinely, from a natural instinct.

Oddly enough, she was one of the most thorough-going sceptics he had ever met, and possibly (this was a theory he used to make up to account for her, so transparent in some ways, so inscrutable in others), possibly she said to herself, As we are a doomed race, chained to a sinking ship (her favourite reading as a girl was Huxley and Tyndall,* and they were fond of these nautical metaphors), as the whole thing is a bad joke, let us, at any rate, do our part; mitigate the sufferings of our fellow-prisoners (Huxley again); decorate the dungeon with flowers and air-cushions; be as decent as we possibly can. Those ruffians, the Gods, shan't have it all their own way—her notion being that the Gods, who never lost a chance of hurting, thwarting and spoiling human lives, were seriously put out if, all the same, you behaved like a lady. That phase came directly after Sylvia's death—that horrible affair. To see your own sister killed by a falling tree (all Justin Parry's fault—all his carelessness) before your very eyes, a girl too on the verge of life, the most gifted of them, Clarissa always said, was enough to turn one bitter. Later she wasn't so positive, perhaps; she thought there were no Gods; no one was to blame; and so she evolved this atheist's religion of doing good for the sake of goodness.

And of course she enjoyed life immensely. It was her nature to enjoy (though, goodness only knows, she had her reserves; it was a mere sketch, he often felt, that even he, after all these years, could make of Clarissa). Anyhow there was no bitterness in her; none of that sense of moral virtue which is so repulsive in good women. She enjoyed practically everything. If you walked with her in Hyde Park, now it was a bed of tulips, now a child in a perambulator, now some absurd little drama she made up on the spur of the moment. (Very likely she would have talked to those lovers, if she had thought them unhappy.) She had a sense of comedy that was really exquisite, but she needed people, always people, to bring it out, with the inevitable result that she frittered her time away, lunching, dining, giving these incessant parties of hers, talking nonsense, saying things she didn't mean, blunting the edge of her mind, losing her discrimination. There she would sit at the head of the table taking infinite pains with some old buffer who might be useful to Dalloway—they knew the most appalling bores in Europe—or in came Elizabeth and everything must give way to *her*. She was at a High School, at the inarticulate stage last time he was over, a round-eyed, pale-faced girl, with nothing of her mother in her, a silent, stolid creature, who took it all as a matter of course, let her mother make a fuss of her, and then said 'May I go now?' like a child of four; going off, Clarissa explained, with that mixture of amusement and pride which Dalloway himself seemed to rouse in her, to play hockey. And now Elizabeth was 'out',* presumably; thought him an old fogy, laughed at her mother's friends. Ah well, so be it. The compensation of growing old, Peter Walsh thought, coming out of Regent's Park, and holding his hat in his hand, was simply this; that the passions remain as strong as ever, but one has gained—at last!—the power which adds the supreme flavour to existence—the power of taking hold of experience, of turning it round, slowly, in the light.

A terrible confession it was (he put his hat on again), but now, at the age of fifty-three, one scarcely needed people any more. Life itself, every moment of it, every drop of it, here, this instant, now, in the sun, in Regent's Park, was enough. Too much, indeed. A whole lifetime was too short to bring out, now that one had acquired the power, the full flavour; to extract every ounce of pleasure, every shade of meaning; which both were so much more solid than they used to be, so much less personal. It was impossible that he should ever suffer again as Clarissa had made him suffer. For hours at a time (pray God that one might say these things without being overheard!), for hours and days he never thought of Daisy.

Could it be that he was in love with her, then, remembering the misery, the torture, the extraordinary passion of those days? It was a different thing altogether—a much pleasanter thing— the truth being, of course, that now *she* was in love with *him*. And that perhaps was the reason why, when the ship actually sailed, he felt an extraordinary relief, wanted nothing so much as to be alone; was annoyed to find all her little attentions—cigars, notes, a rug for the voyage—in his cabin. Everyone if they were honest would say the same; one doesn't want people after fifty; one doesn't want to go on telling women they are pretty; that's what most men of fifty would say, Peter Walsh thought, if they were honest.

But then these astonishing accesses of emotion—bursting into tears this morning, what was all that about? What could Clarissa have thought of him? thought him a fool presumably, not for the first time. It was jealousy that was at the bottom of it—jealousy which survives every other passion of mankind, Peter Walsh thought, holding his pocket-knife at arm's length. She had been meeting Major Orde, Daisy said in her last letter; said it on purpose, he knew; said it to make him jealous; he could see her wrinkling her forehead as she wrote, wondering what she could say to hurt him; and yet it made no difference; he was furious! All this pother of coming to England and seeing lawyers wasn't to marry her, but to prevent her from marrying anybody else. That was what tortured him, that was what came over him when he saw Clarissa so calm, so cold, so intent on her dress or whatever it was; realizing what she might have spared him, what she had reduced him to—a whimpering, snivelling old ass. But women, he thought, shutting his pocket-knife, don't know what passion is. They don't know the meaning of it to men. Clarissa was as cold as an icicle. There she would sit on the sofa by his side, let him take her hand, give him one kiss on the cheek——Here he was at the crossing.

A sound interrupted him; a frail quivering sound, a voice bubbling up without direction, vigour, beginning or end, running weakly and shrilly and with an absence of all human meaning into

ee um fah um so
foo swee too eem oo—

the voice of no age or sex, the voice of an ancient spring spouting
from the earth; which issued, just opposite Regent's Park Tube
Station, from a tall quivering shape, like a funnel, like a rusty
pump, like a wind-beaten tree for ever barren of leaves which lets
the wind run up and down its branches singing

ee um fah um so
foo swee too eem oo,

and rocks and creaks and moans in the eternal breeze.

Through all ages—when the pavement was grass, when it was
swamp, through the age of tusk and mammoth, through the age
of silent sunrise—the battered woman*—for she wore a skirt—
with her right hand exposed, her left clutching at her side, stood
singing of love—love which has lasted a million years, she sang,
love which prevails, and millions of years ago her lover, who had
been dead these centuries, had walked, she crooned, with her in
May; but in the course of ages, long as summer days, and flaming,
she remembered, with nothing but red asters, he had gone;
death's enormous sickle had swept those tremendous hills, and
when at last she laid her hoary and immensely aged head on the
earth, now become a mere cinder of ice, she implored the Gods to
lay by her side a bunch of purple heather, there on her high burial
place which the last rays of the last sun caressed; for then the
pageant of the universe would be over.

As the ancient song bubbled up opposite Regent's Park Tube
Station, still the earth seemed green and flowery; still, though it
issued from so rude a mouth, a mere hole in the earth, muddy too,
matted with root fibres and tangled grasses, still the old bubbling
burbling song, soaking through the knotted roots of infinite ages,
and skeletons and treasure, streamed away in rivulets over the
pavement and all along the Marylebone Road, and down towards
Euston, fertilizing, leaving a damp stain.

Still remembering how once in some primeval May she had
walked with her lover, this rusty pump, this battered old woman

with one hand exposed for coppers, the other clutching her side, would still be there in ten million years, remembering how once she had walked in May, where the sea flows now, with whom it did not matter—he was a man, oh yes, a man who had loved her. But the passage of ages had blurred the clarity of that ancient May day; the bright-petalled flowers were hoar and silver frosted; and she no longer saw, when she implored him (as she did now quite clearly) 'look in my eyes with thy sweet eyes intently', she no longer saw brown eyes, black whiskers or sunburnt face, but only a looming shape, a shadow shape, to which, with the bird-like freshness of the very aged, she still twittered 'give me your hand and let me press it gently' (Peter Walsh couldn't help giving the poor creature a coin as he stepped into his taxi), 'and if someone should see, what matter they?'* she demanded; and her fist clutched at her side, and she smiled, pocketing her shilling, and all peering inquisitive eyes seemed blotted out, and the passing generations—the pavement was crowded with bustling middle-class people—vanished, like leaves, to be trodden under, to be soaked and steeped and made mould of by that eternal spring—

ee um fah um so
foo swee too eem oo.

'Poor old woman,' said Rezia Warren Smith.

Oh, poor old wretch! she said, waiting to cross.

Suppose it was a wet night? Suppose one's father, or somebody who had known one in better days had happened to pass, and saw one standing there in the gutter? And where did she sleep at night?

Cheerfully, almost gaily, the invincible thread of sound wound up into the air like the smoke from a cottage chimney, winding up clean beech trees and issuing in a tuft of blue smoke among the topmost leaves. 'And if someone should see, what matter they?'

Since she was so unhappy, for weeks and weeks now, Rezia had given meanings to things that happened, almost felt sometimes that she must stop people in the street, if they looked good, kind people, just to say to them 'I am unhappy'; and this old woman singing in the street 'if someone should see, what matter they?' made her suddenly quite sure that everything was going to be right. They were going to Sir William Bradshaw; she thought his name sounded nice; he would cure Septimus at once. And then there was a brewer's cart; and the grey horses had upright bristles of straw in their tails; there were newspaper placards. It was a silly, silly dream, being unhappy.

So they crossed, Mr and Mrs Septimus Warren Smith, and was there, after all, anything to draw attention to them, anything to make a passer-by suspect here is a young man who carries in him the greatest message in the world, and is, moreover, the happiest man in the world, and the most miserable? Perhaps they walked more slowly than other people, and there was something hesitating, trailing, in the man's walk, but what more natural for a clerk, who has not been in the West End on a weekday at this hour for years, than to keep looking at the sky, looking at this, that and the other, as if Portland Place were a room he had come into when the family are away, the chandeliers being hung in holland bags, and the caretaker, as she lets in long shafts of dusty light upon deserted, queer-looking armchairs, lifting one corner of the long blinds, explains to the visitors what a wonderful place it is; how wonderful, but at the same time, he thinks, how strange.

To look at, he might have been a clerk, but of the better sort; for he wore brown boots; his hands were educated; so, too, his profile—his angular, big-nosed, intelligent, sensitive profile; but not his lips altogether, for they were loose; and his eyes (as eyes tend to be), eyes merely; hazel, large; so that he was, on the whole, a border case, neither one thing nor the other; might end with a house at Purley* and a motor car, or continue renting apartments in back streets all his life; one of those half-educated, self-educated men whose education is all learnt from books borrowed from public libraries, read in the evening after the day's work, on the advice of well-known authors consulted by letter.

As for the other experiences, the solitary ones, which people go through alone, in their bedrooms, in their offices, walking the fields and the streets of London, he had them; had left home, a mere boy, because of his mother; she lied; because he came down to tea for the fiftieth time with his hands unwashed; because he could see no future for a poet in Stroud;* and so, making a confidant of his little sister, had gone to London leaving an absurd note behind him, such as great men have written, and the world has read later when the story of their struggles has become famous.

London has swallowed up many millions of young men called Smith; thought nothing of fantastic Christian names like Septimus with which their parents have thought to distinguish them. Lodging off the Euston Road, there were experiences, again experiences, such as change a face in two years from a pink innocent oval to a face lean, contracted, hostile. But of all this what could the most observant of friends have said except what a gardener says when he opens the conservatory door in the morning and finds a new blossom on his plant: It has flowered; flowered from vanity, ambition, idealism, passion, loneliness, courage, laziness, the usual seeds, which all muddled up (in a room off the Euston Road), made him shy, and stammering, made him anxious to improve himself, made him fall in love with Miss Isabel Pole, lecturing in the Waterloo Road* upon Shakespeare.

Was he not like Keats? she asked; and reflected how she might give him a taste of *Antony and Cleopatra* and the rest; lent him books; wrote him scraps of letters; and lit in him such a fire as burns only once in a lifetime, without heat, flickering a red-gold flame infinitely ethereal and insubstantial over Miss Pole; *Antony and Cleopatra*; and the Waterloo Road. He thought her beautiful, believed her impeccably wise; dreamed of her, wrote poems to her, which, ignoring the subject, she corrected in red ink; he saw her, one summer evening, walking in a green dress in a square; 'It has flowered,' the gardener might have said, had he opened the door; had he come in, that is to say, any night about this time, and found him writing; found him tearing up his writing; found him finishing a masterpiece at three o'clock in the morning and running out to pace the streets, and visiting churches, and fasting one day, drinking another, devouring Shakespeare, Darwin, *The History of Civilisation*,* and Bernard Shaw.

Something was up, Mr Brewer knew; Mr Brewer, managing

clerk at Sibleys and Arrowsmiths,* auctioneers, valuers, land and estate agents; something was up, he thought, and, being paternal with his young men, and thinking very highly of Smith's abilities, and prophesying that he would, in ten or fifteen years, succeed to the leather armchair in the inner room under the skylight with the deed-boxes round him, 'if he keeps his health,' said Mr Brewer, and that was the danger—he looked weakly; advised football, invited him to supper and was seeing his way to consider recommending a rise of salary, when something happened which threw out many of Mr Brewer's calculations, took away his ablest young fellows, and eventually, so prying and insidious were the fingers of the European War, smashed a plaster cast of Ceres,* ploughed a hole in the geranium beds, and utterly ruined the cook's nerves at Mr Brewer's establishment at Muswell Hill.*

Septimus was one of the first to volunteer. He went to France to save an England which consisted almost entirely of Shakespeare's plays and Miss Isabel Pole in a green dress walking in a square. There in the trenches the change which Mr Brewer desired when he advised football was produced instantly; he developed manliness; he was promoted; he drew the attention, indeed the affection of his officer, Evans by name. It was a case of two dogs playing on a hearth-rug; one worrying a paper screw, snarling, snapping, giving a pinch, now and then, at the old dog's ear; the other lying somnolent, blinking at the fire, raising a paw, turning and growling good-temperedly. They had to be together, share with each other, fight with each other, quarrel with each other. But when Evans (Rezia, who had only seen him once, called him 'a quiet man', a sturdy red-haired man, undemonstrative in the company of women), when Evans was killed, just before the Armistice, in Italy, Septimus, far from showing any emotion or recognizing that here was the end of a friendship, congratulated himself upon feeling very little and very reasonably. The War had taught him. It was sublime. He had gone through the whole show, friendship, European War, death, had won promotion, was still under thirty and was bound to survive. He was right there. The last shells missed him. He watched them explode with indifference. When peace came he was in Milan, billeted in the house of an innkeeper with a courtyard, flowers in tubs, little tables in the open, daughters making hats, and to Lucrezia, the younger daughter, he became engaged one evening when the panic was on him—that he could not feel.

For now that it was all over, truce signed, and the dead buried, he had, especially in the evening, these sudden thunder-claps of fear. He could not feel. As he opened the door of the room where the Italian girls sat making hats, he could see them; could hear them; they were rubbing wires among coloured beads in saucers; they were turning buckram shapes this way and that; the table was all strewn with feathers, spangles, silks, ribbons; scissors were rapping on the table; but something failed him; he could not feel. Still, scissors rapping, girls laughing, hats being made protected him; he was assured of safety; he had a refuge. But he could not sit there all night. There were moments of waking in the early morning. The bed was falling; he was falling. Oh for the scissors and the lamplight and the buckram shapes! He asked Lucrezia to marry him, the younger of the two, the gay, the frivolous, with those little artist's fingers that she would hold up and say 'It is all in them.' Silk, feathers, what not, were alive to them.

'It is the hat that matters most,' she would say, when they walked out together. Every hat that passed she would examine; and the cloak and the dress and the way the woman held herself. Ill-dressing, over-dressing she stigmatized, not savagely, rather with impatient movements of the hands, like those of a painter who puts from him some obvious well-meant glaring imposture; and then, generously, but always critically, she would welcome a shop-girl who had turned her little bit of stuff gallantly, or praise, wholly, with enthusiastic and professional understanding, a French lady descending from her carriage, in chinchilla, robes, pearls.

'Beautiful!' she would murmur, nudging Septimus, that he might see. But beauty was behind a pane of glass. Even taste (Rezia liked ices, chocolates, sweet things) had no relish to him. He put down his cup on the little marble table. He looked at people outside; happy they seemed, collecting in the middle of the street, shouting, laughing, squabbling over nothing. But he could not taste, he could not feel. In the teashop among the tables and the chattering waiters the appalling fear came over him—he could not feel. He could reason; he could read, Dante for example, quite easily ('Septimus, do put down your book,' said Rezia, gently shutting the *Inferno**), he could add up his bill; his brain was perfect; it must be the fault of the world then—that he could not feel.

'The English are so silent,' Rezia said. She liked it, she said. She respected these Englishmen, and wanted to see London, and the English horses, and the tailor-made suits, and could remember hearing how wonderful the shops were, from an aunt who had married and lived in Soho.*

It might be possible, Septimus thought, looking at England from the train window, as they left Newhaven;* it might be possible that the world itself is without meaning.

At the office they advanced him to a post of considerable responsibility. They were proud of him; he had won crosses. 'You have done your duty; it is up to us——' began Mr Brewer; and could not finish, so pleasurable was his emotion. They took admirable lodgings off the Tottenham Court Road.*

Here he opened Shakespeare once more. That boy's business of the intoxication of language—*Antony and Cleopatra*—had shrivelled utterly. How Shakespeare loathed humanity—the putting on of clothes, the getting of children, the sordidity of the mouth and the belly! This was now revealed to Septimus; the message hidden in the beauty of words. The secret signal which one generation passes, under disguise, to the next is loathing, hatred, despair. Dante the same. Aeschylus* (translated) the same. There Rezia sat at the table trimming hats. She trimmed hats for Mrs Filmer's friends; she trimmed hats by the hour. She looked pale, mysterious, like a lily, drowned, under water, he thought.

'The English are so serious,' she would say, putting her arms round Septimus, her cheek against his.

Love between man and woman was repulsive to Shakespeare. The business of copulation was filth to him before the end. But, Rezia said, she must have children. They had been married five years.

They went to the Tower* together; to the Victoria and Albert Museum;* stood in the crowd to see the King open Parliament.* And there were the shops—hat shops, dress shops, shops with leather bags in the windows, where she would stand staring. But she must have a boy.

She must have a son like Septimus, she said. But nobody could be like Septimus; so gentle; so serious; so clever. Could she not read Shakespeare too? Was Shakespeare a difficult author? she asked.

One cannot bring children into a world like this. One cannot perpetrate suffering, or increase the breed of these lustful animals, who have no lasting emotions, but only whims and vanities, eddying them now this way, now that.

He watched her snip, shape, as one watches a bird hop, flit in the grass, without daring to move a finger. For the truth is (let her ignore it) that human beings have neither kindness, nor faith, nor charity beyond what serves to increase the pleasure of the moment. They hunt in packs. Their packs scour the desert and vanish screaming into the wilderness. They desert the fallen. They are plastered over with grimaces. There was Brewer at the office, with his waxed moustache, coral tie-pin, white slip, and pleasurable emotions—all coldness and clamminess within,—his geraniums ruined in the War—his cook's nerves destroyed; or Amelia Whatshername, handing round cups of tea punctually at five—a leering, sneering, obscene little harpy; and the Toms and Berties in their starched shirt fronts oozing thick drops of vice. They never saw him drawing pictures of them naked at their antics in his notebook. In the street, vans roared past him; brutality blared out on placards; men were trapped in mines; women burnt alive; and once a maimed file of lunatics being exercised or displayed for the diversion of the populace (who laughed aloud) ambled and nodded and grinned past him, in the Tottenham Court Road, each half apologetically, yet triumphantly, inflicting his hopeless woe. And would *he* go mad?

At tea Rezia told him that Mrs Filmer's daughter was expecting a baby. *She* could not grow old and have no children! She was very lonely, she was very unhappy! She cried for the first time since they were married. Far away he heard her sobbing; he heard it accurately, he noticed it distinctly; he compared it to a piston thumping. But he felt nothing.

His wife was crying, and he felt nothing; only each time she sobbed in this profound, this silent, this hopeless way, he descended another step into the pit.

At last, with a melodramatic gesture which he assumed mechanically and with complete consciousness of its insincerity, he dropped his head on his hands. Now he had surrendered; now other people must help him. People must be sent for. He gave in.

Nothing could rouse him. Rezia put him to bed. She sent for a doctor—Mrs Filmer's Dr Holmes. Dr Holmes examined him. There was nothing whatever the matter, said Dr Holmes. Oh, what a relief! What a kind man, what a good man! thought Rezia. When he felt like that he went to the Music Hall, said Dr Holmes. He took a day off with his wife and played golf. Why not try two tabloids of bromide dissolved in a glass of water at bedtime? These old Bloomsbury houses, said Dr Holmes, tapping the wall, are often full of very fine panelling, which the landlords have the folly to paper over. Only the other day, visiting a patient, Sir Somebody Something, in Bedford Square*—

So there was no excuse; nothing whatever the matter, except the sin for which human nature had condemned him to death; that he did not feel. He had not cared when Evans was killed; that was worst; but all the other crimes raised their heads and shook their fingers and jeered and sneered over the rail of the bed in the early hours of the morning at the prostrate body which lay real-izing its degradation; how he had married his wife without loving her; had lied to her; seduced her; outraged Miss Isabel Pole, and was so pocked and marked with vice that women shuddered when they saw him in the street. The verdict of human nature on such a wretch was death.

Dr Holmes came again. Large, fresh-coloured, handsome, flicking his boots, looking in the glass, he brushed it all aside—headaches, sleeplessness, fears, dreams—nerve symptoms and nothing more, he said. If Dr Holmes found himself even half a pound below eleven stone six, he asked his wife for another plate of porridge at breakfast. (Rezia would learn to cook porridge.) But, he continued, health is largely a matter in our own control. Throw yourself into outside interests; take up some hobby. He opened Shakespeare—*Antony and Cleopatra*; pushed Shakespeare aside. Some hobby, said Dr Holmes, for did he not owe his own excellent health (and he worked as hard as any man in London) to the fact that he could always switch off from his patients on to old furniture? And what a very pretty comb, if he might say so, Mrs Warren Smith was wearing!

When the damned fool came again, Septimus refused to see him. Did he indeed? said Dr Holmes, smiling agreeably. Really he had to give that charming little lady, Mrs Smith, a friendly push before he could get past her into her husband's bedrooms.

'So you're in a funk,' he said agreeably, sitting down by his patient's side. He had actually talked of killing himself to his wife, quite a girl, a foreigner, wasn't she? Didn't that give her a very odd idea of English husbands? Didn't one owe perhaps a duty to one's wife? Wouldn't it be better to do something instead of lying in bed? For he had had forty years' experience behind him; and Septimus could take Dr Holmes's word for it—there was nothing whatever the matter with him. And next time Dr Holmes came he hoped to find Smith out of bed and not making that charming little lady his wife anxious about him.

Human nature, in short, was on him—the repulsive brute, with the blood-red nostrils. Holmes was on him. Dr Holmes came quite regularly every day. Once you stumble, Septimus wrote on the back of a postcard, human nature is on you. Holmes is on you. Their only chance was to escape, without letting Holmes know; to Italy—anywhere, anywhere, away from Dr Holmes.

But Rezia could not understand him. Dr Holmes was such a kind man. He was so interested in Septimus. He only wanted to help them, he said. He had four little children and he had asked her to tea, she told Septimus.

So he was deserted. The whole world was clamouring: Kill yourself, kill yourself, for our sakes. But why should he kill himself for their sakes? Food was pleasant; the sun hot; and this killing oneself, how does one set about it, with a table knife, uglily, with floods of blood,—by sucking a gas-pipe? He was too weak; he could scarcely raise his hand. Besides, now that he was quite alone, condemned, deserted, as those who are about to die are alone, there was a luxury in it, an isolation full of sublimity; a freedom which the attached can never know. Holmes had won of course; the brute with the red nostrils had won. But even Holmes himself could not touch this last relic straying on the edge of the world, this outcast, who gazed back at the inhabited regions, who lay, like a drowned sailor, on the shore of the world.

It was at that moment (Rezia had gone shopping) that the great revelation took place. A voice spoke from behind the screen. Evans was speaking. The dead were with him.

'Evans, Evans!' he cried.

Mr Smith was talking aloud to himself, Agnes the servant girl cried to Mrs Filmer in the kitchen. 'Evans, Evans!' he had said as she brought in the tray. She jumped, she did. She scuttled downstairs.

And Rezia came in, with her flowers, and walked across the room, and put the roses in a vase, upon which the sun struck directly, and went laughing, leaping round the room.

She had had to buy the roses, Rezia said, from a poor man in the street. But they were almost dead already, she said, arranging the roses.

So there was a man outside; Evans presumably; and the roses, which Rezia said were half dead, had been picked by him in the fields of Greece. Communication is health; communication is happiness. Communication, he muttered.

'What are you saying, Septimus?' Rezia asked, wild with terror, for he was talking to himself.

She sent Agnes running for Dr Holmes. Her husband, she said, was mad. He scarcely knew her.

'You brute! You brute!' cried Septimus, seeing human nature, that is Dr Holmes, enter the room.

'Now what's all this about,' said Dr Holmes in the most amiable way in the world. 'Talking nonsense to frighten your wife?' But he would give him something to make him sleep. And if they were rich people, said Dr Holmes, looking ironically round the room, by all means let them go to Harley Street;* if they had no confidence in him, said Dr Holmes, looking not quite so kind.

It was precisely twelve o'clock; twelve by Big Ben; whose stroke was wafted over the northern part of London; blent with that of other clocks, mixed in a thin ethereal way with the clouds and wisps of smoke and died up there among the seagulls—twelve o'clock struck as Clarissa Dalloway laid her green dress on her bed, and the Warren Smiths walked down Harley Street. Twelve was the hour of their appointment. Probably, Rezia thought, that was Sir William Bradshaw's house with the grey motor car in front of it. (The leaden circles dissolved in the air.)

Indeed it was—Sir William Bradshaw's motor car; low, powerful, grey with plain initials interlocked on the panel, as if the pomps of heraldry were incongruous, this man being the ghostly helper, the priest of science; and, as the motor car was grey, so, to match its sober suavity, grey furs, silver grey rugs were heaped in it, to keep her ladyship warm while she waited. For often Sir William would travel sixty miles or more down into the country to visit the rich, the afflicted, who could afford the very large fee which Sir William very properly charged for his advice. Her ladyship waited with the rugs about her knees an hour or more, leaning back, thinking sometimes of the patient, sometimes, excusably, of the wall of gold, mounting minute by minute while she waited; the wall of gold that was mounting between them and all shifts and anxieties (she had borne them bravely; they had had their struggles), until she felt wedged on a calm ocean, where only spice winds blow; respected, admired, envied, with scarcely anything left to wish for, though she regretted her stoutness; large dinner-parties every Thursday night to the profession; an occasional bazaar to be opened; Royalty greeted; too little time, alas, with her husband, whose work grew and grew; a boy doing well at Eton;* she would have liked a daughter too; interests she had, however, in plenty; child welfare; the after-care of the epileptic, and photography, so that if there was a church building, or a church decaying, she bribed the sexton, got the key and took photographs, which were scarcely to be distinguished from the work of professionals, while she waited.

Sir William himself was no longer young. He had worked very hard; he had won his position by sheer ability (being the son of a shop-keeper); loved his profession; made a fine figurehead at ceremonies and spoke well—all of which had by the time he was knighted given him a heavy look, a weary look (the stream of patients being so incessant, the responsibilities and privileges of his profession so onerous), which weariness, together with his grey hairs, increased the extraordinary distinction of his presence and gave him the reputation (of the utmost importance in dealing with nerve cases) not merely of lightning skill and almost infallible accuracy in diagnosis, but of sympathy; tact; understanding of the human soul. He could see the first moment they came into the room (the Warren Smiths they were called); he was certain directly he saw the man; it was a case of extreme gravity. It was a case of complete breakdown—complete physical and nervous breakdown, with every symptom in an advanced stage, he ascertained in two or three minutes (writing answers to questions, murmured discreetly, on a pink card).

How long had Dr Holmes been attending him?

Six weeks.

Prescribed a little bromide? Said there was nothing the matter? Ah yes (those general practitioners! thought Sir William. It took half his time to undo their blunders. Some were irreparable).

'You served with great distinction in the War?'

The patient repeated the word 'war' interrogatively.

He was attaching meanings to words of a symbolical kind. A serious symptom to be noted on the card.

'The War?' the patient asked. The European War— that little shindy of schoolboys with gunpowder? Had he served with distinction? He really forgot. In the War itself he had failed.

'Yes, he served with the greatest distinction,' Rezia assured the doctor; 'he was promoted.'

'And they have the very highest opinion of you at your office?' Sir William murmured, glancing at Mr Brewer's very generously worded letter. 'So that you have nothing to worry you, no financial anxiety, nothing?'

He had committed an appalling crime and been condemned to death by human nature.

'I have—I have', he began, 'committed a crime——'

'He has done nothing wrong whatever,' Rezia assured the doctor. If Mr Smith would wait, said Sir William, he would speak to Mrs Smith in the next room. Her husband was very seriously ill, Sir William said. Did he threaten to kill himself?

Oh, he did, she cried. But he did not mean it, she said. Of course not. It was merely a question of rest, said Sir William; of rest, rest, rest; a long rest in bed. There was a delightful home down in the country where her husband would be perfectly looked after. Away from her? she asked. Unfortunately, yes; the people we care for most are not good for us when we are ill. But he was not mad, was he? Sir William said he never spoke of 'madness'; he called it not having a sense of proportion.* But her husband did not like doctors. He would refuse to go there. Shortly and kindly Sir William explained to her the state of the case. He had threatened to kill himself. There was no alternative. It was a question of law. He would lie in bed in a beautiful house in the country. The nurses were admirable. Sir William would visit him once a week. If Mrs Warren Smith was quite sure she had no more questions to ask—he never hurried his patients— they would return to her husband. She had nothing more to ask—not of Sir William.

So they returned to the most exalted of mankind; the criminal who faced his judges; the victim exposed on the heights; the fugitive; the drowned sailor; the poet of the immortal ode; the Lord who had gone from life to death; to Septimus Warren Smith, who sat in the armchair under the skylight staring at a photograph of Lady Bradshaw in Court dress, muttering messages about beauty.

'We have had our little talk,' said Sir William.

'He says that you are very, very ill,' Rezia cried.

'We have been arranging that you should go into a home,' said Sir William.

'One of Holmes's homes?' sneered Septimus.

The fellow made a distasteful impression. For there was in Sir William, whose father had been a tradesman, a natural respect for breeding and clothing, which shabbiness nettled; again, more profoundly, there was in Sir William, who had never had time for reading, a grudge, deeply buried, against cultivated people who came into his room and intimated that doctors, whose profession is a constant strain upon all the highest faculties, are not educated men.

'One of *my* homes, Mr Warren Smith,' he said, 'where we will teach you to rest.'

And there was just one thing more.

He was quite certain that when Mr Warren Smith was well he was the last man in the world to frighten his wife. But he had talked of killing himself.

'We all have our moments of depression,' said Sir William.

Once you fall, Septimus repeated to himself, human nature is on you. Holmes and Bradshaw are on you. They scour the desert. They fly screaming into the wilderness. The rack and the thumbscrew are applied. Human nature is remorseless.

'Impulses came upon him sometimes?' Sir William asked, with his pencil on a pink card.

That was his own affair, said Septimus.

'Nobody lives for himself alone,' said Sir William, glancing at the photograph of his wife in Court dress.

'And you have a brilliant career before you,' said Sir William. There was Mr Brewer's letter on the table. 'An exceptionally brilliant career.'

But if he confessed? If he communicated? Would they let him off then, Holmes, Bradshaw?

'I—I——' he stammered.

But what was his crime? He could not remember it.

'Yes?' Sir William encouraged him. (But it was growing late.)

Love, trees, there is no crime—what was his message?

He could not remember it.

'I—I——' Septimus stammered.

'Try to think as little about yourself as possible,' said Sir William kindly. Really, he was not fit to be about.

Was there anything else they wished to ask him? Sir William would make all arrangements (he murmured to Rezia) and he would let her know between five and six that evening.

'Trust everything to me,' he said, and dismissed them.

Never, never had Rezia felt such agony in her life! She had asked for help and been deserted! He had failed them! Sir William Bradshaw was not a nice man.

The upkeep of that motor car alone must cost him quite a lot, said Septimus, when they got out into the street.

She clung to his arm. They had been deserted.

But what more did she want?

To his patients he gave three-quarters of an hour; and if in this exacting science which has to do with what, after all, we know nothing about—the nervous system, the human brain—a doctor loses his sense of proportion, as a doctor he fails. Health we must have; and health is proportion; so that when a man comes into your room and says he is Christ (a common delusion), and has a message, as they mostly have, and threatens, as they often do, to kill himself, you invoke proportion; order rest in bed; rest in solitude; silence and rest; rest without friends, without books, without messages; six months' rest; until a man who went in weighing seven stone six comes out weighing twelve.

Proportion, divine proportion, Sir William's goddess, was acquired by Sir William walking hospitals, catching salmon, begetting one son in Harley Street by Lady Bradshaw, who caught salmon herself and took photographs scarcely to be distinguished from the work of professionals. Worshipping proportion, Sir William not only prospered himself but made England prosper, secluded her lunatics, forbade childbirth, penalized despair, made it impossible for the unfit to propagate their views until they, too, shared his sense of proportion—his, if they were men, Lady Bradshaw's if they were women (she embroidered, knitted, spent four nights out of seven at home with her son), so that not only did his colleagues respect him, his subordinates fear him, but the friends and relations of his patients felt for him the keenest gratitude for insisting that these prophetic Christs and Christesses, who prophesied the end of the world, or the advent of God, should drink milk in bed, as Sir William ordered; Sir William with his thirty years' experience of these kinds of cases, and his infallible instinct, this is madness, this sense; his sense of proportion.

But Proportion has a sister, less smiling, more formidable, a Goddess even now engaged—in the heat and sands of India, the mud and swamp of Africa, the purlieus of London, wherever, in short, the climate or the devil tempts men to fall from the true belief which is her own—is even now engaged in dashing down shrines, smashing idols, and setting up in their place her own stern countenance. Conversion is her name and she feasts on the wills of the weakly, loving to impress, to impose, adoring her own features stamped on the face of the populace. At Hyde Park Corner* on a tub she stands preaching; shrouds herself in white and walks penitentially disguised as brotherly love through factories and parliaments; offers help, but desires power; smites out of her way roughly the dissentient, or dissatisfied; bestows her blessing on those who, looking upward, catch submissively from her eyes the light of their own. This lady too (Rezia Warren Smith divined it) had her dwelling in Sir William's heart, though concealed, as she mostly is, under some plausible disguise; some venerable name; love, duty, self-sacrifice. How he would work—how toil to raise funds, propagate reforms, initiate institutions! But Conversion, fastidious Goddess, loves blood better than brick, and feasts most subtly on the human will. For example, Lady Bradshaw. Fifteen years ago she had gone under. It was nothing you could put your finger on; there had been no scene, no snap; only the slow sinking, water-logged, of her will into his. Sweet was her smile, swift her submission; dinner in Harley Street, numbering eight or nine courses, feeding ten or fifteen guests of the professional classes, was smooth and urbane. Only as the evening wore on a very slight dullness, or uneasiness perhaps, a nervous twitch, fumble, stumble and confusion indicated, what it was really painful to believe—that the poor lady lied. Once, long ago, she had caught salmon freely: now, quick to minister to the craving which lit her husband's eye so oilily for dominion, for power, she cramped, squeezed, pared, pruned, drew back, peeped through: so that without knowing precisely what made the evening disagreeable, and caused this pressure on the top of the head (which might well be imputed to the professional conversation, or the fatigue of a great doctor whose life, Lady Bradshaw said, 'is not his own but his patients''), disagreeable it was: so that guests, when the clock struck ten, breathed in the air of Harley Street even with rapture; which relief, however, was denied to his patients.

There in the grey room, with the pictures on the wall, and the valuable furniture, under the ground-glass skylight, they learnt the extent of their transgressions: huddled up in armchairs, they watched him go through, for their benefit, a curious exercise with the arms, which he shot out, brought sharply back to his hip, to prove (if the patient was obstinate) that Sir William was master of his own actions, which the patient was not. There some weakly broke down; sobbed, submitted; others, inspired by Heaven knows what intemperate madness, called Sir William to his face a damnable humbug; questioned, even more impiously, life itself. Why live? they demanded. Sir William replied that life was good. Certainly Lady Bradshaw in ostrich feathers hung over the mantelpiece, and as for his income it was quite twelve thousand a year. But to us, they protested, life has given no such bounty. He acquiesced. They lacked a sense of proportion. And perhaps, after all, there is no God? He shrugged his shoulders. In short, this living or not living is an affair of our own? But there they were mistaken. Sir William had a friend in Surrey where they taught, what Sir William frankly admitted was a difficult art—a sense of proportion. There were, moreover, family affection; honour; courage; and a brilliant career. All of these had in Sir William a resolute champion. If they failed, he had to support him police and the good of society, which, he remarked very quietly, would take care, down in Surrey, that these unsocial impulses, bred more than anything by the lack of good blood, were held in control. And then stole out from her hiding-place and mounted her throne that Goddess whose lust is to override opposition, to stamp indelibly in the sanctuaries of others the image of herself. Naked, defenceless, the exhausted, the friend-less received the impress of Sir William's will. He swooped; he devoured. He shut people up. It was this combination of decision and humanity that endeared Sir William so greatly to the relations of his victims.

But Rezia Warren Smith cried, walking down Harley Street, that she did not like that man.

Shredding and slicing, dividing and subdividing, the clocks of Harley Street nibbled at the June day, counselled submission, upheld authority, and pointed out in chorus the supreme advantages of a sense of proportion, until the mound of time was so far diminished that a commercial clock, suspended above a shop in Oxford Street, announced, genially and fraternally, as if it were a pleasure to Messrs Rigby and Lowndes* to give the information gratis, that it was half-past one.

Looking up, it appeared that each letter of their names stood for one of the hours; subconsciously one was grateful to Rigby and Lowndes for giving one time ratified by Greenwich; and this gratitude (so Hugh Whitbread ruminated, dallying there in front of the shop window) naturally took the form later of buying off Rigby and Lowndes socks or shoes. So he ruminated. It was his habit. He did not go deeply. He brushed surfaces; the dead languages, the living, life in Constantinople, Paris, Rome; riding, shooting, tennis, it had been once. The malicious asserted that he now kept guard at Buckingham Palace, dressed in silk stockings and knee-breeches, over what nobody knew. But he did it extremely efficiently. He had been afloat on the cream of English society for fifty-five years. He had known Prime Ministers. His affections were understood to be deep. And if it were true that he had not taken part in any of the great movements of the time or held important office, one or two humble reforms stood to his credit; an improvement in public shelters was one; the protection of owls in Norfolk another; servant girls had reason to be grateful to him; and his name at the end of letters to *The Times*, asking for funds, appealing to the public to protect, to preserve, to clear up litter, to abate smoke, and stamp out immorality in parks, commanded respect.

A magnificent figure he cut too, pausing for a moment (as the sound of the half-hour died away) to look critically, magisterially, at socks and shoes; impeccable, substantial, as if he beheld the world from a certain eminence, and dressed to match; but realized the obligations which size, wealth, health entail, and observed punctiliously, even when not absolutely necessary, little courtesies, old-fashioned ceremonies, which gave a quality to his manner, something to imitate, something to remember him by, for he would never lunch, for example, with Lady Bruton, whom he had known these twenty years, without bringing her in his outstretched hand a bunch of carnations, and asking Miss Brush, Lady Bruton's secretary, after her brother in South Africa, which, for some reason, Miss Brush, deficient though she was in every attribute of female charm, so much resented that she said 'Thank you, he's doing very well in South Africa,' when, for half-a-dozen years, he had been doing badly in Portsmouth.*

Lady Bruton herself preferred Richard Dalloway, who arrived at the same moment. Indeed they met on the doorstep.

Lady Bruton preferred Richard Dalloway of course. He was made of much finer material. But she wouldn't let them run down her poor dear Hugh. She could never forget his kindness—he had been really remarkably kind—she forgot precisely upon what occasion. But he had been—remarkably kind. Anyhow, the difference between one man and another does not amount to much. She had never seen the sense of cutting people up, as Clarissa Dalloway did—cutting them up and sticking them together again; not at any rate when one was sixty-two. She took Hugh's carnations with her angular grim smile. There was nobody else coming, she said. She had got them there on false pretences, to help her out of a difficulty—

'But let us eat first,' she said.

And so there began a soundless and exquisite passing to and fro through swing doors of aproned, white-capped maids, handmaidens not of necessity, but adepts in a mystery or grand deception practised by hostesses in Mayfair from one-thirty to two, when, with a wave of the hand, the traffic ceases, and there rises instead this profound illusion in the first place about the food—how it is not paid for; and then that the table spreads itself voluntarily with glass and silver, little mats, saucers of red fruit; films of brown cream mask turbot; in casseroles severed chickens swim; coloured, undomestic, the fire burns; and with the wine and the coffee (not paid for) rise jocund visions before musing eyes; gently speculative eyes; eyes to whom life appears musical, mysterious; eyes now kindled to observe genially the beauty of the red carnations which Lady Bruton (whose movements were always angular) had laid beside her plate, so that Hugh Whitbread, feeling at peace with the entire universe and at the same time completely sure of his standing, said, resting his fork:

'Wouldn't they look charming against your lace?'

Miss Brush resented this familiarity intensely. She thought him an underbred fellow. She made Lady Bruton laugh.

Lady Bruton raised the carnations, holding them rather stiffly with much the same attitude with which the General held the scroll in the picture behind her; she remained fixed, tranced. Which was she now, the General's great-grand-daughter? great-great-grand-daughter? Richard Dalloway asked himself. Sir Roderick, Sir Miles, Sir Talbot—that was it. It was remarkable how in that family the likeness persisted in the women. She should have been a general of dragoons herself. And Richard would have served under her, cheerfully; he had the greatest respect for her; he cherished these romantic views about well-set-up old women of pedigree, and would have liked, in his good-humoured way, to bring some young hot-heads of his acquaintance to lunch with her; as if a type like hers could be bred of amiable tea-drinking enthusiasts! He knew her country. He knew her people. There was a vine, still bearing, which either Lovelace or Herrick*—she never read a word of poetry herself, but so the story ran—had sat under. Better wait to put before them the question that bothered her (about making an appeal to the public; if so, in what terms and so on), better wait until they have had their coffee, Lady Bruton thought; and so laid the carnations down beside her plate.

'How's Clarissa?' she asked abruptly.

Clarissa always said that Lady Bruton did not like her. Indeed, Lady Bruton had the reputation of being more interested in politics than people; of talking like a man; of having had a finger in some notorious intrigue of the eighties, which was now beginning to be mentioned in memoirs. Certainly there was an alcove in her drawing-room, and a table in that alcove, and a photograph upon that table of General Sir Talbot Moore, now deceased, who had written there (one evening in the eighties) in Lady Bruton's presence, with her cognisance, perhaps advice, a telegram ordering the British troops to advance upon an historical occasion. (She kept the pen and told the story.) Thus, when she said in her offhand way 'How's Clarissa?' husbands had difficulty in persuading their wives, and indeed, however devoted, were secretly doubtful themselves, of her interest in women who often got in their husbands' way, prevented them from accepting posts abroad, and had to be taken to the seaside in the middle of the session to recover from influenza. Nevertheless her inquiry, 'How's Clarissa?' was known by women infallibly to be a signal from a well-wisher, from an almost silent companion, whose utterances (half a dozen perhaps in the course of a lifetime) signified recognition of some feminine comradeship which went beneath masculine lunch parties and united Lady Bruton and Mrs Dalloway, who seldom met, and appeared when they did meet indifferent and even hostile, in a singular bond.

'I met Clarissa in the Park this morning,' said Hugh Whitbread, diving into the casserole, anxious to pay himself this little tribute, for he had only to come to London and he met everybody at once; but greedy, one of the greediest men she had ever known, Milly Brush thought, who observed men with unflinching rectitude, and was capable of everlasting devotion, to her own sex in particular, being knobbed, scraped, angular, and entirely without feminine charm.

'D'you know who's in town?' said Lady Bruton, suddenly bethinking her. 'Our old friend, Peter Walsh.'

They all smiled. Peter Walsh! And Mr Dalloway was genuinely glad, Milly Brush thought; and Mr Whitbread thought only of his chicken.

Peter Walsh! All three, Lady Bruton, Hugh Whitbread, and Richard Dalloway, remembered the same thing—how passionately Peter had been in love; been rejected; gone to India; come a cropper; made a mess of things; and Richard Dalloway had a very great liking for the dear old fellow too. Milly Brush saw that; saw a depth in the brown of his eyes; saw him hesitate; consider; which interested her, as Mr Dalloway always interested her, for what was he thinking, she wondered, about Peter Walsh?

That Peter Walsh had been in love with Clarissa; that he would go back directly after lunch and find Clarissa; that he would tell her, in so many words, that he loved her. Yes, he would say that.

Milly Brush once might almost have fallen in love with these silences; and Mr Dalloway was always so dependable; such a gentleman too. Now, being forty, Lady Bruton had only to nod, or turn her head a little abruptly, and Milly Brush took the signal, however deeply she might be sunk in these reflections of a detached spirit, of an uncorrupted soul whom life could not bamboozle, because life had not offered her a trinket of the slightest value; not a curl, smile, lip, cheek, nose; nothing whatever; Lady Bruton had only to nod, and Perkins was instructed to quicken the coffee.

'Yes; Peter Walsh has come back,' said Lady Bruton. It was vaguely flattering to them all. He had come back, battered, unsuccessful, to their secure shores. But to help him, they reflected, was impossible; there was some flaw in his character. Hugh Whitbread said one might of course mention his name to So-and-so. He wrinkled lugubriously, consequentially, at the thought of the letters he would write to the heads of Government offices about 'my old friend, Peter Walsh', and so on. But it wouldn't lead to anything—not to anything permanent, because of his character.

'In trouble with some woman,' said Lady Bruton. They had all guessed that *that* was at the bottom of it.

'However,' said Lady Bruton, anxious to leave the subject, 'we shall hear the whole story from Peter himself.'

(The coffee was very slow in coming.)

'The address?' murmured Hugh Whitbread, and there was at once a ripple in the grey tide of service which washed round Lady Bruton day in, day out, collecting, intercepting, enveloping her in a fine tissue which broke concussions, mitigated interruptions, and spread round the house in Brook Street* a fine net where things lodged and were picked out accurately, instantly by grey-haired Perkins, who had been with Lady Bruton these thirty years and now wrote down the address; handed it to Mr Whitbread, who took out his pocket-book, raised his eyebrows, and, slipping it in among documents of the highest importance, said that he would get Evelyn to ask him to lunch.

(They were waiting to bring the coffee until Mr Whitbread had finished.)

Hugh was very slow, Lady Bruton thought. He was getting fat, she noticed. Richard always kept himself in the pink of condition. She was getting impatient; the whole of her being was setting positively, undeniably, domineeringly brushing aside all this unnecessary trifling (Peter Walsh and his affairs) upon that subject which engaged her attention, and not merely her attention, but that fibre which was the ramrod of her soul, that essential part of her without which Millicent Bruton would not have been Millicent Bruton; that project for emigrating young people of both sexes born of respectable parents and setting them up with a fair prospect of doing well in Canada.* She exaggerated. She had perhaps lost her sense of proportion. Emigration was not to others the obvious remedy, the sublime conception. It was not to them (not to Hugh, or Richard, or even to devoted Miss Brush) the liberator of the pent egotism, which a strong martial woman, well nourished, well descended, of direct impulses, downright feelings, and little introspective power (broad and simple—why could not everyone be broad and simple? she asked), feels rise within her, once youth is past, and must eject upon some object— it may be Emigration, it may be Emancipation; but whatever it be, this object round which the essence of her soul is daily secreted becomes inevitably prismatic, lustrous, half looking-glass, half precious stone; now carefully hidden in case people should sneer at it; now proudly displayed. Emigration had become, in short, largely Lady Bruton.

But she had to write. And one letter to *The Times*, she used to say to Miss Brush, cost her more than to organize an expedition to South Africa (which she had done in the war). After a morning's battle, beginning, tearing up, beginning again, she used to feel the futility of her own womanhood as she felt it on no other occasion, and would turn gratefully to the thought of Hugh Whitbread who possessed—no one could doubt it—the art of writing letters to *The Times*.

A being so differently constituted from herself, with such a command of language; able to put things as editors liked them put; had passions which one could not call simply greed. Lady Bruton often suspended judgement upon men in deference to the mysterious accord in which they, but no woman, stood to the laws of the universe; knew how to put things; knew what was said; so that if Richard advised her, and Hugh wrote for her, she was sure of being somehow right. So she let Hugh eat his soufflé; asked after poor Evelyn; waited until they were smoking, and then said,

'Milly, would you fetch the papers?'

And Miss Brush went out, came back; laid papers on the table; and Hugh produced his fountain pen; his silver fountain pen, which had done twenty years' service, he said, unscrewing the cap. It was still in perfect order; he had shown it to the makers; there was no reason, they said, why it should ever wear out; which was somehow to Hugh's credit, and to the credit of the sentiments which his pen expressed (so Richard Dalloway felt) as Hugh began carefully writing capital letters with rings round them in the margin, and thus marvellously reduced Lady Bruton's tangles to sense, to grammar such as the editor of *The Times*, Lady Bruton felt, watching the marvellous transformation, must respect. Hugh was slow. Hugh was pertinacious. Richard said one must take risks. Hugh proposed modifications in deference to people's feelings, which, he said rather tartly when Richard laughed, 'had to be considered', and read out 'how, therefore, we are of opinion that the times are ripe ... the superfluous youth of our ever-increasing population ... what we owe to the dead ...' which Richard thought all stuffing and bunkum, but no harm in it, of course, and Hugh went on drafting sentiments in alphabetical order of the highest nobility, brushing the cigar ash from his waistcoat, and summing up now and then the progress they had made until, finally, he read out the draft of a letter which Lady Bruton felt certain was a masterpiece. Could her own meaning sound like that?

Hugh could not guarantee that the editor would put it in; but he would be meeting somebody at luncheon.

Whereupon Lady Bruton, who seldom did a graceful thing, stuffed all Hugh's carnations into the front of her dress, and flinging her hands out called him 'My Prime Minister!' What she would have done without them both she did not know. They rose. And Richard Dalloway strolled off as usual to have a look at the General's portrait, because he meant, whenever he had a moment of leisure, to write a history of Lady Bruton's family.

And Millicent Bruton was very proud of her family. But they could wait, they could wait, she said, looking at the picture; meaning that her family, of military men, administrators, admirals, had been men of action, who had done their duty; and Richard's first duty was to his country, but it was a fine face, she said; and all the papers were ready for Richard down at Aldmixton whenever the time came; the Labour Government,* she meant. 'Ah, the news from India!'* she cried.

And then, as they stood in the hall taking yellow gloves from the bowl on the malachite table and Hugh was offering Miss Brush with quite unnecessary courtesy some discarded ticket or other compliment, which she loathed from the depths of her heart and blushed brick red, Richard turned to Lady Bruton, with his hat in his hand, and said,

'We shall see you at our party tonight?' whereupon Lady Bruton resumed the magnificence which letter-writing had shattered. She might come; or she might not come. Clarissa had wonderful energy. Parties terrified Lady Bruton. But then, she was getting old. So she intimated, standing at her doorway; handsome; very erect; while her chow stretched behind her, and Miss Brush disappeared into the background with her hands full of papers.

And Lady Bruton went ponderously, majestically, up to her room, lay, one arm extended, on the sofa. She sighed, she snored, not that she was asleep, only drowsy and heavy, drowsy and heavy, like a field of clover in the sunshine this hot June day, with the bees going round and about and the yellow butterflies. Always she went back to those fields down in Devonshire, where she had jumped the brooks on Patty, her pony, with Mortimer and Tom, her brothers. And there were the dogs; there were the rats; there were her father and mother on the lawn under the trees, with the tea-things out, and the beds of dahlias, the hollyhocks, the pampas grass; and they, little wretches, always up to some mischief! stealing back through the shrubbery, so as not to be seen, all bedraggled from some roguery. What old nurse used to say about her frocks!

Ah, dear, she remembered—it was Wednesday in Brook Street. Those kind good fellows, Richard Dalloway, Hugh Whitbread, had gone this hot day through the streets whose growl came up to her lying on the sofa. Power was hers, position, income. She had lived in the forefront of her time. She had had good friends; known the ablest men of her day. Murmuring London flowed up to her, and her hand, lying on the sofa back, curled upon some imaginary baton such as her grandfathers might have held, holding which she seemed, drowsy and heavy, to be commanding battalions marching to Canada, and those good fellows walking across London, that territory of theirs, that little bit of carpet, Mayfair.*

And they went further and further from her, being attached to her by a thin thread (since they had lunched with her) which would stretch and stretch, get thinner and thinner as they walked across London; as if one's friends were attached to one's body, after lunching with them, by a thin thread, which (as she dozed there) became hazy with the sound of bells, striking the hour or ringing to service, as a single spider's thread is blotted with raindrops, and, burdened, sags down. So she slept.

And Richard Dalloway and Hugh Whitbread hesitated at the corner of Conduit Street at the very moment that Millicent Bruton, lying on the sofa, let the thread snap; snored. Contrary winds buffeted at the street corner. They looked in at a shop window; they did not wish to buy or to talk but to part, only with contrary winds buffeting the street corner, with some sort of lapse in the tides of the body, two forces meeting in a swirl, morning and afternoon, they paused. Some newspaper placard went up in the air, gallantly, like a kite at first, then paused, swooped, fluttered; and a lady's veil hung. Yellow awnings trembled. The speed of the morning traffic slackened, and single carts rattled carelessly down half-empty streets. In Norfolk, of which Richard Dalloway was half thinking, a soft warm wind blew back the petals; confused the waters; ruffled the flowering grasses. Haymakers, who had pitched beneath hedges to sleep away the morning toil, parted curtains of green blades; moved trembling globes of cow parsley to see the sky; the blue, the steadfast, the blazing summer sky.

Aware that he was looking at a silver two-handled Jacobean mug, and that Hugh Whitbread admired condescendingly, with airs of connoisseurship, a Spanish necklace which he thought of asking the price of in case Evelyn might like it—still Richard was torpid; could not think or move. Life had thrown up this wreck-age; shop windows full of coloured paste, and one stood stark with the lethargy of the old, stiff with the rigidity of the old, looking in. Evelyn Whitbread might like to buy this Spanish necklace—so she might. Yawn he must. Hugh was going into the shop.

'Right you are!' said Richard, following.

Goodness knows he didn't want to go buying necklaces with Hugh. But there are tides in the body. Morning meets afternoon. Borne like a frail shallop on deep, deep floods, Lady Bruton's great-grandfather and his memoir and his campaigns in North America were whelmed and sunk. And Millicent Bruton too. She went under. Richard didn't care a straw what became of Emigra-tion; about that letter, whether the editor put it in or not. The necklace hung stretched between Hugh's admirable fingers. Let him give it to a girl, if he must buy jewels—any girl, any girl in the street. For the worthlessness of this life did strike Richard pretty forcibly—buying necklaces for Evelyn. If he'd had a boy he'd have said, Work, work. But he had his Elizabeth; he adored his Elizabeth.

'I should like to see Mr Dubonnet,' said Hugh in his curt worldly way. It appeared that this Dubonnet had the measure-ments of Mrs Whitbread's neck, or, more strangely still, knew her views upon Spanish jewellery and the extent of her possessions in that line (which Hugh could not remember). All of which seemed to Richard Dalloway awfully odd. For he never gave Clarissa presents, except a bracelet two or three years ago, which had not been a success. She never wore it. It pained him to remember that she never wore it. And as a single spider's thread after wavering here and there attaches itself to the point of a leaf, so Richard's mind, recovering from its lethargy, set now on his wife, Clarissa, whom Peter Walsh had loved so passionately; and Richard had had a sudden vision of her there at luncheon; of himself and Clarissa; of their life together; and he drew the tray of old jewels towards him, and taking up first this brooch, then that ring, 'How much is that?' he asked, but doubted his own taste. He wanted to open the drawing-room door and come in holding out something; a present for Clarissa. Only what? But Hugh was on his legs again. He was unspeakably pompous. Really, after dealing here for thirty-five years he was not going to be put off by a mere boy who did not know his business. For Dubonnet, it seemed, was out, and Hugh would not buy anything until Mr Dubonnet chose to be in; at which the youth flushed and bowed his correct little bow. It was all perfectly correct. And yet Richard couldn't have said that to save his life! Why these people stood that damned insolence he could not conceive. Hugh was becoming an intolerable ass. Richard Dalloway could not stand more than an hour of his society. And, flicking his bowler hat by way of farewell, Richard turned at the corner of Conduit Street eager, yes, very eager, to travel that spider's thread of attachment between himself and Clarissa; he would go straight to her, in Westminster.

But he wanted to come in holding something. Flowers? Yes, flowers, since he did not trust his taste in gold; any number of flowers, roses, orchids, to celebrate what was, reckoning things as you will, an event; this feeling about her when they spoke of Peter Walsh at luncheon; and they never spoke of it; not for years had they spoken of it; which, he thought, grasping his red and white roses together (a vast bunch in tissue paper), is the greatest mistake in the world. The time comes when it can't be said; one's too shy to say it, he thought, pocketing his sixpence or two of change, setting off with his great bunch held against his body to West-minster, to say straight out in so many words (whatever she might think of him), holding out his flowers, 'I love you.' Why not? Really it was a miracle thinking of the war, and thousands of poor chaps, with all their lives before them, shovelled together, already half forgotten; it was a miracle. Here he was walking across Lon-don to say to Clarissa in so many words that he loved her. Which one never does say, he thought. Partly one's lazy; partly one's shy. And Clarissa—it was difficult to think of her; except in starts, as at luncheon, when he saw her quite distinctly; their whole life. He stopped at the crossing; and repeated—being simple by nature, and undebauched, because he had tramped, and shot; being per-tinacious and dogged, having championed the down-trodden and followed his instincts in the House of Commons; being preserved in his simplicity yet at the same time grown rather speechless, rather stiff—he repeated that it was a miracle that he should have married Clarissa; a miracle—his life had been a miracle, he thought; hesitating to cross. But it did make his blood boil to see little creatures of five or six crossing Piccadilly alone. The police ought to have stopped the traffic at once. He had no illusions about the London police. Indeed, he was collecting evidence of their malpractices; and those costermongers, not allowed to stand their barrows in the streets; and prostitutes, good Lord, the fault wasn't in them, nor in young men either, but in our detestable social system and so forth; all of which he considered, could be seen considering, grey, dogged, dapper, clean, as he walked across the Park to tell his wife that he loved her.

For he would say it in so many words, when he came into the room. Because it is a thousand pities never to say what one feels, he thought, crossing the Green Park* and observing with pleasure how in the shade of the trees whole families, poor families, were sprawling; children kicking up their legs; sucking milk; paper bags thrown about, which could easily be picked up (if people objected) by one of those fat gentlemen in livery; for he was of opinion that every park, and every square, during the summer months should be open to children (the grass of the park flushed and faded, lighting up the poor mothers of Westminster and their crawling babies, as if a yellow lamp were moved beneath). But what could be done for female vagrants like that poor creature, stretched on her elbow (as if she had flung herself on the earth, rid of all ties, to observe curiously, to speculate boldly, to consider the whys and the wherefores, impudent, loose-lipped, humorous), he did not know. Bearing his flowers like a weapon, Richard Dalloway approached her; intent he passed her; still there was time for a spark between them—she laughed at the sight of him, he smiled good humouredly, considering the problem of the female vagrant; not that they would ever speak. But he would tell Clarissa that he loved her, in so many words. He had, once upon a time, been jealous of Peter Walsh; jealous of him and Clarissa. But she had often said to him that she had been right not to marry Peter Walsh; which, knowing Clarissa, was obviously true; she wanted support. Not that she was weak; but she wanted support.

As for Buckingham Palace (like an old prima donna facing the audience all in white) you can't deny it a certain dignity, he considered, nor despise what does, after all, stand to millions of people (a little crowd was waiting at the gate to see the King drive out) for a symbol, absurd though it is; a child with a box of bricks could have done better, he thought; looking at the memorial to Queen Victoria (whom he could remember in her horn spectacles driving through Kensington), its white mound, its billowing motherliness; but he liked being ruled by the descendant of Horsa;* he liked continuity; and the sense of handing on the traditions of the past. It was a great age in which to have lived. Indeed, his own life was a miracle; let him make no mistake about it; here he was, in the prime of life, walking to his house in Westminster to tell Clarissa that he loved her. Happiness is this, he thought.

It is this, he said, as he entered Dean's Yard.* Big Ben was beginning to strike, first the warning, musical; then the hour, irrevocable. Lunch parties waste the entire afternoon, he thought, approaching his door.

The sound of Big Ben flooded Clarissa's drawing-room, where she sat, ever so annoyed, at her writing-table; worried; annoyed. It was perfectly true that she had not asked Ellie Henderson to her party; but she had done it on purpose. Now Mrs Marsham wrote: 'She had told Ellie Henderson she would ask Clarissa— Ellie so much wanted to come.'

But why should she invite all the dull women in London to her parties? Why should Mrs Marsham interfere? And there was Elizabeth closeted all this time with Doris Kilman. Anything more nauseating she could not conceive. Prayer at this hour with that woman. And the sound of the bell flooded the room with its melancholy wave; which receded, and gathered itself together to fall once more, when she heard, distractingly, something fumbling, something scratching at the door. Who at this hour? Three, good Heavens! Three already! For with overpowering directness and dignity the clock struck three; and she heard nothing else; but the door handle slipped round and in came Richard! What a surprise! In came Richard, holding out flowers. She had failed him, once at Constantinople; and Lady Bruton, whose lunch parties were said to be extraordinarily amusing, had not asked her. He was holding out flowers—roses, red and white roses. (But he could not bring himself to say he loved her; not in so many words.)

But how lovely, she said, taking his flowers. She understood; she understood without his speaking; his Clarissa. She put them in vases on the mantelpiece. How lovely they looked, she said. And was it amusing, she asked? Had Lady Bruton asked after her? Peter Walsh was back. Mrs Marsham had written. Must she ask Ellie Henderson? That woman Kilman was upstairs.

'But let us sit down for five minutes,' said Richard.

It all looked so empty. All the chairs were against the wall. What had they been doing? Oh, it was for the party; no, he had not forgotten the party. Peter Walsh was back. Oh yes, she had had him. And he was going to get a divorce; and he was in love with some woman out there. And he hadn't changed in the slightest. There she was, mending her dress . . .

'Thinking of Bourton,' she said.

'Hugh was at lunch,' said Richard. She had met him too! Well, he was getting absolutely intolerable. Buying Evelyn necklaces; fatter than ever; an intolerable ass.

'And it came over me "I might have married you",' she said, thinking of Peter sitting there in his little bow-tie; with that knife, opening it, shutting it. 'Just as he always was, you know.'

They were talking about him at lunch, said Richard. (But he could not tell her he loved her. He held her hand. Happiness is this, he thought.) They had been writing a letter to *The Times* for Millicent Bruton. That was about all Hugh was fit for.

'And our dear Miss Kilman?' he asked. Clarissa thought the roses absolutely lovely; first bunched together; now of their own accord starting apart.

'Kilman arrives just as we've done lunch,' she said. 'Elizabeth turns pink. They shut themselves up. I suppose they're praying.'

Lord! He didn't like it; but these things pass over if you let them.

'In a mackintosh with an umbrella,' said Clarissa.

He had not said 'I love you'; but he held her hand. Happiness is this, is this, he thought.

'But why should I ask all the dull women in London to my parties?' said Clarissa. And if Mrs Marsham gave a party, did *she* invite her guests?

'Poor Ellie Henderson,' said Richard—it was a very odd thing how much Clarissa minded about her parties, he thought.

But Richard had no notion of the look of a room. However—what was he going to say?

If she worried about these parties he would not let her give them. Did she wish she had married Peter? But he must go.

He must be off, he said, getting up. But he stood for a moment as if he were about to say something; and she wondered what? Why? There were the roses.

'Some Committee?' she asked, as he opened the door.

'Armenians,' he said; or perhaps it was 'Albanians'.*

And there is a dignity in people; a solitude; even between husband and wife a gulf; and that one must respect, thought Clarissa, watching him open the door; for one would not part with it oneself, or take it, against his will, from one's husband, without losing one's independence, one's self-respect—something, after all, priceless.

He returned with a pillow and a quilt.

'An hour's complete rest after luncheon,' he said. And he went.

How like him! He would go on saying 'An hour's complete rest after luncheon' to the end of time, because a doctor had ordered it once. It was like him to take what doctors said literally; part of his adorable divine simplicity, which no one had to the same extent; which made him go and do the thing while she and Peter frittered their time away bickering. He was already half-way to the House of Commons, to his Armenians, his Albanians, having settled her on the sofa, looking at his roses. And people would say, 'Clarissa Dalloway is spoilt.' She cared much more for her roses than for the Armenians. Hunted out of existence, maimed, frozen, the victims of cruelty and injustice (she had heard Richard say so over and over again)—no, she could feel nothing for the Albanians, or was it the Armenians? but she loved her roses (didn't that help the Armenians?)—the only flowers she could bear to see cut. But Richard was already at the House of Commons; at his Committee, having settled all her difficulties. But no; alas, that was not true. He did not see the reasons against asking Ellie Henderson. She would do it, of course, as he wished it. Since he had brought the pillow, she would lie down . . . But—but—why did she suddenly feel, for no reason that she could discover, desperately unhappy? As a person who has dropped some grain of pearl or diamond into the grass and parts the tall blades very carefully, this way and that, and searches here and there vainly, and at last spies it there at the roots, so she went through one thing and another; no, it was not Sally Seton saying that Richard would never be in the Cabinet because he had a second-class brain (it came back to her); no, she did not mind that; nor was it to do with Elizabeth either and Doris Kilman; those were facts. It was a feeling, some unpleasant feeling, earlier in the day perhaps; something that Peter had said, combined with some depression of her own, in her bedroom, taking off her hat; and what Richard had said had added to it, but what had he said? There were his roses. Her parties! That was it! Her parties! Both of them criticized her very unfairly, laughed at her very unjustly, for her parties. That was it! That was it!

Well, how was she going to defend herself? Now that she knew what it was, she felt perfectly happy. They thought, or Peter at any rate thought, that she enjoyed imposing herself; liked to have famous people about her; great names; was simply a snob, in short. Well, Peter might think so. Richard merely thought it foolish of her to like excitement when she knew it was bad for her heart. It was childish, he thought. And both were quite wrong. What she liked was simply life.

'That's what I do it for,' she said, speaking aloud, to life.

Since she was lying on the sofa, cloistered, exempt, the presence of this thing which she felt to be so obvious became physically existent; with robes of sound from the street, sunny, with hot breath, whispering, blowing out the blinds. But suppose Peter said to her, 'Yes, yes, but your parties—what's the sense of your parties?' all she could say was (and nobody could be expected to understand): They're an offering; which sounded horribly vague. But who was Peter to make out that life was all plain sailing?— Peter always in love, always in love with the wrong woman? What's your love? she might say to him. And she knew his answer; how it is the most important thing in the world and no woman possibly understood it. Very well. But could any man understand what she meant either? about life? She could not imagine Peter or Richard taking the trouble to give a party for no reason whatever.

But to go deeper, beneath what people said (and these judgements, how superficial, how fragmentary they are!) in her own mind now, what did it mean to her, this thing called life? Oh, it was very queer. Here was So-and-so in South Kensington; someone up in Bayswater; and somebody else, say, in Mayfair. And she felt quite continuously a sense of their existence; and she felt what a waste; and she felt what a pity; and she felt if only they could be brought together; so she did it. And it was an offering; to combine, to create; but to whom?

An offering for the sake of offering, perhaps. Anyhow, it was her gift. Nothing else had she of the slightest importance; could not think, write, even play the piano. She muddled Armenians and Turks; loved success; hated discomfort; must be liked; talked oceans of nonsense; and to this day, ask her what the Equator was, and she did not know.

All the same, that one day should follow another; Wednesday, Thursday, Friday, Saturday; that one should wake up in the morning; see the sky; walk in the park; meet Hugh Whitbread; then suddenly in came Peter; then these roses; it was enough. After that, how unbelievable death was!—that it must end; and no one in the whole world would know how she had loved it all; how, every instant . . .

The door opened. Elizabeth knew that her mother was resting. She came in very quietly. She stood perfectly still. Was it that some Mongol had been wrecked on the coast of Norfolk (as Mrs Hilbery* said), had mixed with the Dalloway ladies, perhaps a hundred years ago? For the Dalloways, in general, were fair-haired; blue-eyed; Elizabeth, on the contrary, was dark; had Chinese eyes in a pale face; an Oriental mystery; was gentle, considerate, still. As a child, she had had a perfect sense of humour; but now at seventeen, why, Clarissa could not in the least understand, she had become very serious; like a hyacinth sheathed in glossy green, with buds just tinted, a hyacinth which has had no sun.

She stood quite still and looked at her mother; but the door was ajar, and outside the door was Miss Kilman, as Clarissa knew; Miss Kilman in her mackintosh listening to whatever they said.

Yes, Miss Kilman stood on the landing, and wore a mackintosh; but had her reasons. First, it was cheap; second, she was over forty; and did not, after all, dress to please. She was poor, moreover; degradingly poor. Otherwise she would not be taking jobs from people like the Dalloways; from rich people, who liked to be kind. Mr Dalloway, to do him justice, had been kind. But Mrs Dalloway had not. She had been merely condescending. She came from the most worthless of all classes—the rich, with a smattering of culture. They had expensive things everywhere; pictures, carpets, lots of servants. She considered that she had a perfect right to anything that the Dalloways did for her.

She had been cheated. Yes, the word was no exaggeration, for surely a girl has a right to some kind of happiness? And she had never been happy, what with being so clumsy and so poor. And then, just as she might have had a chance at Miss Dolby's school, the war came; and she had never been able to tell lies. Miss Dolby thought she would be happier with people who shared her views about the Germans. She had had to go. It was true that the family was of German origin; spelt the name Kiehlman in the eighteenth century; but her brother had been killed. They turned her out because she would not pretend that the Germans were all villains—when she had German friends, when the only happy days of her life had been spent in Germany! And after all, she could read history. She had had to take whatever she could get. Mr Dalloway had come across her working for the Friends.* He had allowed her (and that was really generous of him) to teach his daughter history. Also she did a little Extension lecturing* and so on. Then Our Lord had come to her (and here she always bowed her head). She had seen the light two years and three months ago. Now she did not envy women like Clarissa Dalloway; she pitied them.

She pitied and despised them from the bottom of her heart, as she stood on the soft carpet, looking at the old engraving of a little girl with a muff. With all this luxury going on, what hope was there for a better state of things? Instead of lying on a sofa— 'My mother is resting,' Elizabeth had said—she should have been in a factory; behind a counter; Mrs Dalloway and all the other fine ladies!

Bitter and burning, Miss Kilman had turned into a church two years three months ago. She had heard the Rev. Edward Whittaker preach; the boys sing; had seen the solemn lights descend, and whether it was the music, or the voices (she herself when alone in the evening found comfort in a violin; but the sound was excruciating; she had no ear), the hot and turbulent feelings which boiled and surged in her had been assuaged as she sat there, and she had wept copiously, and gone to call on Mr Whittaker at his private house in Kensington. It was the hand of God, he said. The Lord had shown her the way. So now, when-ever the hot and painful feelings boiled within her, this hatred of Mrs Dalloway, this grudge against the world, she thought of

God. She thought of Mr Whittaker. Rage was succeeded by calm. A sweet savour filled her veins, her lips parted, and, standing formidable upon the landing in her mackintosh, she looked with steady and sinister serenity at Mrs Dalloway, who came out with her daughter.

Elizabeth said she had forgotten her gloves. That was because Miss Kilman and her mother hated each other. She could not bear to see them together. She ran upstairs to find her gloves.

But Miss Kilman did not hate Mrs Dalloway. Turning her large gooseberry-coloured eyes upon Clarissa, observing her small pink face, her delicate body, her air of freshness and fashion, Miss Kilman felt, Fool! Simpleton! You who have known neither sorrow nor pleasure; who have trifled your life away! And there rose in her an overmastering desire to overcome her; to unmask her. If she could have felled her it would have eased her. But it was not the body; it was the soul and its mockery that she wished to subdue; make feel her mastery. If only she could make her weep; could ruin her; humiliate her; bring her to her knees crying, You are right! But this was God's will, not Miss Kilman's. It was to be a religious victory. So she glared; so she glowered.

Clarissa was really shocked. This a Christian—this woman! This woman had taken her daughter from her! She in touch with invisible presences! Heavy, ugly, commonplace, without kindness or grace, she know the meaning of life!

'You are taking Elizabeth to the Stores?'* Mrs Dalloway said.

Miss Kilman said she was. They stood there. Miss Kilman was not going to make herself agreeable. She had always earned her living. Her knowledge of modern history was thorough in the extreme. She did, out of her meagre income, set aside so much for causes she believed in; whereas this woman did nothing, believed nothing; brought up her daughter—but here was Elizabeth, rather out of breath, the beautiful girl.

So they were going to the Stores. Odd it was, as Miss Kilman stood there (and stand she did, with the power and taciturnity of some prehistoric monster armoured for primeval warfare), how, second by second, the idea of her diminished, how hatred (which was for ideas, not people) crumbled, how she lost her malignity, her size, became second by second merely Miss Kilman, in a mackintosh, whom Heaven knows Clarissa would have liked to help.

At this dwindling of the monster, Clarissa laughed. Saying good-bye, she laughed.

Off they went together, Miss Kilman and Elizabeth, downstairs.

With a sudden impulse, with a violent anguish, for this woman was taking her daughter from her, Clarissa leant over the banisters and cried out, 'Remember the party! Remember our party tonight!'

But Elizabeth had already opened the front door; there was a van passing; she did not answer.

Love and religion! thought Clarissa, going back into the drawing-room, tingling all over. How detestable, how detestable they are! For now that the body of Miss Kilman was not before her, it overwhelmed her—the idea. The cruellest things in the world, she thought, seeing them clumsy, hot, domineering, hypocritical, eavesdropping, jealous, infinitely cruel and unscrupulous, dressed in a mackintosh coat, on the landing; love and religion. Had she ever tried to convert anyone herself? Did she not wish everybody merely to be themselves? And she watched out of the window the old lady opposite climbing upstairs. Let her climb upstairs if she wanted to; let her stop; then let her, as Clarissa had often seen her, gain her bedroom, part her curtains, and disappear again into the background. Somehow one respected that—that old woman looking out of the window, quite unconscious that she was being watched. There was something solemn in it—but love and religion would destroy that, whatever it was, the privacy of the soul. The odious Kilman would destroy it. Yet it was a sight that made her want to cry.

Love destroyed too. Everything that was fine, everything that was true went. Take Peter Walsh now. There was a man, charming, clever, with ideas about everything. If you wanted to know about Pope, say, or Addison,* or just to talk nonsense, what people were like, what things meant, Peter knew better than anyone. It was Peter who had helped her; Peter who had lent her books. But look at the women he loved—vulgar, trivial, commonplace. Think of Peter in love—he came to see her after all these years, and what did he talk about? Himself. Horrible passion! she thought. Degrading passion! she thought, thinking of Kilman and her Elizabeth walking to the Army and Navy Stores.

Big Ben struck the half-hour.

How extraordinary it was, strange, yes, touching to see the old lady (they had been neighbours ever so many years) move away from the window, as if she were attached to that sound, that string. Gigantic as it was, it had something to do with her. Down, down, into the midst of ordinary things the finger fell, making the moment solemn. She was forced, so Clarissa imagined, by that sound, to move, to go—but where? Clarissa tried to follow her as she turned and disappeared, and could still just see her white cap moving at the back of the bedroom. She was still there, moving about at the other end of the room. Why creeds and prayers and mackintoshes? when, thought Clarissa, that's the miracle, that's the mystery; that old lady, she meant, whom she could see going from chest of drawers to dressing-table. She could still see her. And the supreme mystery which Kilman might say she had solved, or Peter might say he had solved, but Clarissa didn't believe either of them had the ghost of an idea of solving, was simply this: here was one room; there another. Did religion solve that, or love?

Love—but here the other clock, the clock which always struck two minutes after Big Ben, came shuffling in with its lap full of odds and ends, which it dumped down as if Big Ben were all very well with his majesty laying down the law, so solemn, so just, but she must remember all sorts of little things besides—Mrs Marsham, Ellie Henderson, glasses for ices—all sorts of little things came flooding and lapping and dancing in on the wake of that solemn stroke which lay flat like a bar of gold on the sea. Mrs Marsham, Ellie Henderson, glasses for ices. She must telephone now at once.

Volubly, troublously, the late clock sounded, coming in on the wake of Big Ben, with its lap full of trifles, Beaten up, broken up by the assault of carriages, the brutality of vans, the eager advance of myriads of angular men, of flaunting women, the domes and spires of offices and hospitals, the last relics of this lap full of odds and ends seemed to break, like the spray of an exhausted wave, upon the body of Miss Kilman standing still in the street for a moment to mutter 'It is the flesh.'

It was the flesh that she must control. Clarissa Dalloway had insulted her. That she expected. But she had not triumphed; she had not mastered the flesh. Ugly, clumsy, Clarissa Dalloway had laughed at her for being that; and had revived the fleshly desires, for she minded looking as she did beside Clarissa. Nor could she talk as she did. But why wish to resemble her? Why? She despised Mrs Dalloway from the bottom of her heart. She was not serious. She was not good. Her life was a tissue of vanity and deceit. Yet Doris Kilman had been overcome. She had, as a matter of fact, very nearly burst into tears when Clarissa Dalloway laughed at her. 'It is the flesh, it is the flesh,' she muttered (it being her habit to talk aloud), trying to subdue this turbulent and painful feeling as she walked down Victoria Street. She prayed to God. She could not help being ugly; she could not afford to buy pretty clothes. Clarissa Dalloway had laughed—but she would concentrate her mind upon something else until she had reached the pillar-box. At any rate she had got Elizabeth. But she would think of something else; she would think of Russia; until she reached the pillar-box.

How nice it must be, she said, in the country, struggling, as Mr Whittaker had told her, with that violent grudge against the world which had scorned her, sneered at her, cast her off, beginning with this indignity—the infliction of her unlovable body which people could not bear to see. Do her hair as she might, her forehead remained like an egg, bald, white. No clothes suited her. She might buy anything. And for a woman, of course, that meant never meeting the opposite sex. Never would she come first with anyone. Sometimes lately it had seemed to her that, except for Elizabeth, her food was all that she lived for; her comforts; her dinner, her tea; her hot-water bottle at night. But one must fight; vanquish; have faith in God. Mr Whittaker had said she was there for a purpose. But no one knew the agony! He said, pointing to the crucifix, that God knew. But why should she have to suffer when other women, like Clarissa Dalloway, escaped? Knowledge comes through suffering, said Mr Whittaker.

She had passed the pillar-box, and Elizabeth had turned into the cool brown tobacco department of the Army and Navy Stores while she was still muttering to herself what Mr Whittaker had said about knowledge coming through suffering and the flesh. 'The flesh,' she muttered.

What department did she want? Elizabeth interrupted her.

'Petticoats,' she said abruptly, and stalked straight on to the lift.

Up they went. Elizabeth guided her this way and that; guided her in her abstraction as if she had been a great child, an unwieldy battleship. There were the petticoats, brown, decorous, striped, frivolous, solid, flimsy; and she chose, in her abstraction, portentously, and the girl serving thought her mad.

Elizabeth rather wondered, as they did up the parcel, what Miss Kilman was thinking. They must have their tea, said Miss Kilman, rousing, collecting herself. They had their tea.

Elizabeth rather wondered whether Miss Kilman could be hungry. It was her way of eating, eating with intensity, then look- ing, again and again, at a plate of sugared cakes on the table next them; then, when a lady and a child sat down and the child took the cake, could Miss Kilman really mind it? Yes, Miss Kilman did mind it. She had wanted that cake—the pink one. The pleasure of eating was almost the only pure pleasure left her, and then to be baffled even in that!

When people are happy they have a reserve, she had told Elizabeth, upon which to draw, whereas she was like a wheel without a tyre (she was fond of such metaphors), jolted by every pebble—so she would say, staying on after the lesson, standing by the fireplace with her bag of books, her 'satchel', she called it, on a Tuesday morning, after the lesson was over. And she talked too about the war. After all, there were people who did not think the English invariably right. There were books. There were meetings. There were other points of view. Would Elizabeth like to come with her to listen to So-and-so? (a most extraordinary-looking old man). Then Miss Kilman took her to some church in Kensington and they had tea with a clergyman. She had lent her books. Law, medicine, politics, all professions are open to women of your generation, said Miss Kilman. But for herself, her career was absolutely ruined, and was it her fault? Good gracious, said Elizabeth, no.

And her mother would come calling to say that a hamper had come from Bourton and would Miss Kilman like some flowers? To Miss Kilman she was always very, very nice, but Miss Kilman squashed the flowers all in a bunch, and hadn't any small talk, and what interested Miss Kilman bored her mother, and Miss Kilman and she were terrible together; and Miss Kilman swelled and looked very plain, but Miss Kilman was frightfully clever. Elizabeth had never thought about the poor. They lived with everything they wanted,—her mother had breakfast in bed every day; Lucy carried it up; and she liked old women because they were Duchesses, and being descended from some Lord. But Miss Kilman said (one of those Tuesday mornings when the lesson was over), 'My grandfather kept an oil and colour shop in Kensington.' Miss Kilman was quite different from anyone she knew; she made one feel so small.

Miss Kilman took another cup of tea. Elizabeth, with her oriental bearing, her inscrutable mystery, sat perfectly upright; no, she did not want anything more. She looked for her gloves— her white gloves. They were under the table. Ah, but she must not go! Miss Kilman could not let her go! this youth, that was so beautiful! this girl, whom she genuinely loved! Her large hand opened and shut on the table.

But perhaps it was a little flat somehow, Elizabeth felt. And really she would like to go.

But said Miss Kilman, 'I've not quite finished yet.'

Of course, then, Elizabeth would wait. But it was rather stuffy in here.

'Are you going to the party tonight?' Miss Kilman said. Elizabeth supposed she was going; her mother wanted her to go. She must not let parties absorb her, Miss Kilman said, fingering the last two inches of a chocolate éclair.

She did not much like parties, Elizabeth said. Miss Kilman opened her mouth, slightly projected her chin, and swallowed down the last inches of the chocolate éclair, then wiped her fingers, and washed the tea round in her cup.

She was about to split asunder, she felt. The agony was so terrific. If she could grasp her, if she could clasp her, if she could make her hers absolutely and for ever and then die; that was all she wanted. But to sit here, unable to think of anything to say; to see Elizabeth turning against her; to be felt repulsive even by her—it was too much; she could not stand it. The thick fingers curled inwards.

'I never go to parties,' said Miss Kilman, just to keep Elizabeth from going. 'People don't ask me to parties'—and she knew as she said it that it was this egotism that was her undoing; Mr Whittaker had warned her; but she could not help it. She had suffered so horribly. 'Why should they ask me?' she said. 'I'm plain, I'm unhappy.' She knew it was idiotic. But it was all those people passing—people with parcels who despised her—who made her say it. However, she was Doris Kilman. She had her degree. She was a woman who had made her way in the world. Her knowledge of modern history was more than respectable.

'I don't pity myself,' she said. 'I pity'—she meant to say 'your mother', but no, she could not, not to Elizabeth. 'I pity other people much more.'

Like some dumb creature who has been brought up to a gate for an unknown purpose, and stands there longing to gallop away, Elizabeth Dalloway sat silent. Was Miss Kilman going to say anything more?

'Don't quite forget me,' said Doris Kilman; her voice quivered. Right away to the end of the field the dumb creature galloped in terror.

The great hand opened and shut.

Elizabeth turned her head. The waitress came. One had to pay at the desk, Elizabeth said, and went off, drawing out, so Miss Kilman felt, the very entrails in her body, stretching them as she crossed the room, and then, with a final twist, bowing her head very politely, she went.

She had gone. Miss Kilman sat at the marble table among the éclairs, stricken once, twice, thrice by shocks of suffering. She had gone. Mrs Dalloway had triumphed. Elizabeth had gone. Beauty had gone; youth had gone.

So she sat. She got up, blundered off among the little tables, rocking slightly from side to side, and somebody came after her with her petticoat, and she lost her way, and was hemmed in by trunks specially prepared for taking to India; next got among the accouchement sets and baby linen; through all the commodities of the world, perishable and permanent, hams, drugs, flowers, stationery, variously smelling, now sweet, now sour, she lurched; saw herself thus lurching with her hat askew, very red in the face, full length in a looking-glass; and at last came out into the street.

The tower of Westminster Cathedral rose in front of her, the habitation of God. In the midst of the traffic, there was the habitation of God. Doggedly she set off with her parcel to that other sanctuary, the Abbey,* where, raising her hands in a tent before her face, she sat beside those driven into shelter too; the variously assorted worshippers, now divested of social rank, almost of sex, as they raised their hands before their faces; but once they removed them, instantly reverent, middle-class, English men and women, some of them desirous of seeing the waxworks.*

But Miss Kilman held her tent before her face. Now she was deserted; now rejoined. New worshippers came in from the street to replace the strollers, and still, as people gazed round and shuffled past the tomb of the Unknown Warrior,* still she barred her eyes with her fingers and tried in this double darkness, for the light in the Abbey was bodiless, to aspire above the vanities, the desires, the commodities, to rid herself both of hatred and of love. Her hands twitched. She seemed to struggle. Yet to others God was accessible and the path to Him smooth. Mr Fletcher, retired, of the Treasury, Mrs Gorham, widow of the famous KC, approached Him simply, and having done their praying, leant back, enjoyed the music (the organ pealed sweetly), and saw Miss Kilman at the end of the row, praying, praying, and, being still on the threshold of their underworld, thought of her sympathetically as a soul haunting the same territory; a soul cut out of immaterial substance; not a woman, a soul.

But Mr Fletcher had to go. He had to pass her, and being himself neat as a new pin, could not help being a little distressed by the poor lady's disorder; her hair down; her parcel on the floor. She did not at once let him pass. But, as he stood gazing about him, at the white marbles, grey window panes, and accumulated treasures (for he was extremely proud of the Abbey), her large-ness, robustness, and power as she sat there shifting her knees from time to time (it was so rough the approach to her God— so tough her desires) impressed him, as they had impressed Mrs Dalloway (she could not get the thought of her out of her mind that afternoon), the Rev. Edward Whittaker, and Elizabeth too.

And Elizabeth waited in Victoria Street for an omnibus. It was so nice to be out of doors. She thought perhaps she need not go home just yet. It was so nice to be out in the air. So she would get on to an omnibus. And already, even as she stood there, in her very well-cut clothes, it was beginning . . . People were beginning to compare her to poplar trees, early dawn, hyacinths, fawns, running water, and garden lilies; and it made her life a burden to her, for she so much preferred being left alone to do what she liked in the country, but they would compare her to lilies, and she had to go to parties, and London was so dreary compared with being alone in the country with her father and the dogs.

Buses swooped, settled, were off—garish caravans, glistening with red and yellow varnish. But which should she get on to? She had no preferences. Of course, she would not push her way. She inclined to be passive. It was expression she needed, but her eyes were fine, Chinese, oriental, and, as her mother said, with such nice shoulders and holding herself so straight, she was always charming to look at; and lately, in the evening especially, when she was interested, for she never seemed excited, she looked almost beautiful, very stately, very serene. What could she be thinking? Every man fell in love with her, and she was really awfully bored. For it was beginning. Her mother could see that— the compliments were beginning. That she did not care more about it—for instance for her clothes—sometimes worried Clarissa, but perhaps it was as well with all those puppies and guinea pigs about having distemper, and it gave her a charm. And now there was this odd friendship with Miss Kilman. Well, thought Clarissa about three o'clock in the morning, reading Baron Marbot for she could not sleep, it proves she has a heart.

Suddenly Elizabeth stepped forward and most competently boarded the omnibus, in front of everybody. She took a seat on top. The impetuous creature—a pirate—started forward, sprang away; she had to hold the rail to steady herself, for a pirate it was, reckless, unscrupulous, bearing down ruthlessly, circumventing dangerously, boldly snatching a passenger, or ignoring a passenger, squeezing eel-like and arrogant in between, and then rushing insolently all sails spread up Whitehall. And did Elizabeth give one thought to poor Miss Kilman who loved her without jealousy, to whom she had been a fawn in the open, a moon in a glade? She was delighted to be free. The fresh air was so delicious. It had been so stuffy in the Army and Navy Stores. And now it was like riding, to be rushing up Whitehall; and to each movement of the omnibus the beautiful body in the fawn-coloured coat responded freely like a rider, like the figure-head of a ship, for the breeze slightly disarrayed her; the heat gave her cheeks the pallor of white painted wood; and her fine eyes, having no eyes to meet, gazed ahead, blank, bright, with the staring, incredible innocence of sculpture.

It was always talking about her own sufferings that made Miss Kilman so difficult. And was she right? If it was being on committees and giving up hours and hours every day (she hardly ever saw him in London) that helped the poor, her father did that, goodness knows—if that was what Miss Kilman meant about being a Christian; but it was so difficult to say. Oh, she would like to go a little farther. Another penny, was it, to the Strand? Here was another penny, then. She would go up the Strand.

She liked people who were ill. And every profession is open to the women of your generation, said Miss Kilman. So she might be a doctor. She might be a farmer. Animals are often ill. She might own a thousand acres and have people under her. She would go and see them in their cottages. This was Somerset House.* One might be a very good farmer—and that, strangely enough, though Miss Kilman had her share in it, was almost entirely due to Somerset House. It looked so splendid, so serious, that great grey building. And she liked the feeling of people working. She liked those churches, like shapes of grey paper, breasting the stream of the Strand. It was quite different here from Westminster, she thought, getting off at Chancery Lane. It was so serious; it was so busy. In short, she would like to have a profession. She would become a doctor, a farmer, possibly go into Parliament if she found it necessary, all because of the Strand.

The feet of those people busy about their activities, hands putting stone to stone, minds eternally occupied not with trivial chatterings (comparing women to poplars—which was rather exciting, of course, but very silly), but with thoughts of ships, of business, of law, of administration and with it all so stately (she was in the Temple*), gay (there was the river), pious (there was the Church),* made her quite determined, whatever her mother might say, to become either a farmer or a doctor. But she was, of course, rather lazy.

And it was much better to say nothing about it. It seemed so silly. It was the sort of thing that did sometimes happen, when one was alone—buildings without architects' names, crowds of people coming back from the city having more power than single clergymen in Kensington, than any of the books Miss Kilman had lent her, to stimulate what lay slumbrous, clumsy, and shy on the mind's sandy floor, to break surface, as a child suddenly stretches its arms; it was just that, perhaps, a sigh, a stretch of the arms; an impulse, a revelation, which has its effects for ever, and then down again it went to the sandy floor. She must go home. She must dress for dinner. But what was the time?—where was a clock?

She looked up Fleet Street. She walked just a little way towards St Paul's, shyly, like someone penetrating on tiptoe, exploring a strange house by night with a candle, on edge lest the owner should suddenly fling wide his bedroom door and ask her business, nor did she dare wander off into queer alleys, tempting by-streets, any more than in a strange house open doors which might be bedroom doors, or sitting-room doors, or lead straight to the larder. For no Dalloways came down the Strand daily; she was a pioneer, a stray, venturing, trusting.

In many ways, her mother felt, she was extremely immature, like a child still, attached to dolls, to old slippers; a perfect baby; and that was charming. But then, of course, there was in the Dalloway family the tradition of public service. Abbesses, principals, head mistresses, dignitaries, in the republic of women—without being brilliant, any of them, they were that. She penetrated a little farther in the direction of St Paul's. She liked the geniality, sisterhood, motherhood, brotherhood of this uproar. It seemed to her good. The noise was tremendous; and suddenly there were trumpets (the unemployed) blaring, rattling about in the uproar; military music; as if people were marching; yet had they been dying—had some woman breathed her last, and whoever was watching, opening the window of the room where she had just brought off that act of supreme dignity, looked down on Fleet Street, that uproar, that military music would have come triumphing up to him, consolatory, indifferent.

It was not conscious. There was no recognition in it of one's fortune, or fate, and for that very reason even to those dazed with watching for the last shivers of consciousness on the faces of the dying, consoling.

Forgetfulness in people might wound, their ingratitude corrode, but this voice, pouring endlessly, year in, year out, would take whatever it might be; this vow; this van; this life; this procession; would wrap them all about and carry them on, as in the rough stream of a glacier the ice holds a splinter of bone, a blue petal, some oak trees, and rolls them on.

But it was later than she thought. Her mother would not like her to be wandering off alone like this. She turned back down the Strand.

A puff of wind (in spite of the heat, there was quite a wind) blew a thin black veil over the sun and over the Strand. The faces faded; the omnibuses suddenly lost their glow. For although the clouds were of mountainous white so that one could fancy hacking hard chips off with a hatchet, with broad golden slopes, lawns of celestial pleasure gardens, on their flanks, and had all the appearance of settled habitations assembled for the conference of gods above the world, there was a perpetual movement among them. Signs were interchanged, when, as if to fulfil some scheme arranged already, now a summit dwindled, now a whole block of pyramidal size which had kept its station inalterably advanced into the midst or gravely led the procession to fresh anchorage. Fixed though they seemed at their posts, at rest in perfect unanimity, nothing could be fresher, freer, more sensitive superficially than the snow-white or gold-kindled surface; to change, to go, to dismantle the solemn assemblage was immediately possible; and in spite of the grave fixity, the accumulated robustness and solidity, now they struck light to the earth, now darkness.

Calmly and competently, Elizabeth Dalloway mounted the Westminster omnibus.

Going and coming, beckoning, signalling, so the light and shadow, which now made the wall grey, now the bananas bright yellow, now made the Strand grey, now made the omnibuses bright yellow, seemed to Septimus Warren Smith lying on the sofa in the sitting-room; watching the watery gold glow and fade with the astonishing sensibility of some live creature on the roses, on the wallpaper. Outside the trees dragged their leaves like nets through the depths of the air; the sound of water was in the room, and through the waves came the voices of birds singing. Every power poured its treasures on his head, and his hand lay there on the back of the sofa, as he had seen his hand lie when he was bathing, floating, on the top of the waves, while far away on shore he heard dogs barking and barking far away. Fear no more, says the heart in the body; fear no more.

He was not afraid. At every moment Nature signified by some laughing hint like that gold spot which went round the wall—there, there, there—her determination to show, by brandishing her plumes, shaking her tresses, flinging her mantle this way and that, beautifully, always beautifully, and standing close up to breathe through her hollowed hands Shakespeare's words, her meaning.

Rezia, sitting at the table twisting a hat in her hands, watched him; saw him smiling. He was happy, then. But she could not bear to see him smiling. It was not marriage; it was not being one's husband to look strange like that, always to be starting, laughing, sitting hour after hour silent, or clutching her and telling her to write. The table drawer was full of those writings; about war; about Shakespeare; about great discoveries; how there is no death. Lately he had become excited suddenly for no reason (and both Dr Holmes and Sir William Bradshaw said excitement was the worst thing for him), and waved his hands and cried out that he knew the truth! He knew everything! That man, his friend who was killed, Evans, had come, he said. He was singing behind the screen. She wrote it down just as he spoke it. Some things were very beautiful; others sheer nonsense. And he was always stopping in the middle, changing his mind; wanting to add something; hearing something new; listening with his hand up. But she heard nothing.

And once they found the girl who did the room reading one of these papers in fits of laughter. It was a dreadful pity. For that made Septimus cry out about human cruelty—how they tear each other to pieces. The fallen, he said, they tear to pieces. 'Holmes is on us,' he would say, and he would invent stories about Holmes; Holmes eating porridge; Holmes reading Shakespeare—making himself roar with laughter or rage, for Dr Holmes seemed to stand for something horrible to him. 'Human nature', he called him. Then there were the visions. He was drowned, he used to say, and lying on a cliff with the gulls screaming over him. He would look over the edge of the sofa down into the sea. Or he was hearing music. Really it was only a barrel organ or some man crying in the street. But 'Lovely!' he used to cry, and the tears would run down his cheeks, which was to her the most dreadful thing of all, to see a man like Septimus, who had fought, who was brave, crying. And he would lie listening until suddenly he would cry that he was falling down, down into the flames! Actually she would look for flames, it was so vivid. But there was nothing.

They were alone in the room. It was a dream, she would tell him, and so quiet him at last, but sometimes she was frightened too. She sighed as she sat sewing.

Her sigh was tender and enchanting, like the wind outside a wood in the evening. Now she put down her scissors; now she turned to take something from the table. A little stir, a little crinkling, a little tapping built up something on the table there, where she sat sewing. Through his eyelashes he could see her blurred outline; her little black body; her face and hands; her turning movements at the table, as she took up a reel, or looked (she was apt to lose things) for her silk. She was making a hat for Mrs Filmer's married daughter, whose name was—he had forgotten her name.

'What is the name of Mrs Filmer's married daughter?' he asked.

'Mrs Peters,' said Rezia. She was afraid it was too small, she said, holding it before her. Mrs Peters was a big woman; but she did not like her. It was only because Mrs Filmer had been so good to them—'She gave me grapes this morning,' she said—that Rezia wanted to do something to show that they were grateful. She had come into the room the other evening and found Mrs Peters, who thought they were out, playing the gramophone.

'Was it true?' he asked. She was playing the gramophone? Yes; she had told him about it at the time; she had found Mrs Peters playing the gramophone.

He began, very cautiously, to open his eyes, to see whether a gramophone was really there. But real things—real things were too exciting. He must be cautious. He would not go mad. First he looked at the fashion papers on the lower shelf, then gradually at the gramophone with the green trumpet. Nothing could be more exact. And so, gathering courage, he looked at the sideboard; the plate of bananas; the engraving of Queen Victoria and the Prince Consort;* at the mantelpiece, with the jar of roses. None of these things moved. All were still; all were real.

'She is a woman with a spiteful tongue,' said Rezia.

'What does Mr Peters do?' Septimus asked.

'Ah,' said Rezia, trying to remember. She thought Mrs Filmer had said that he travelled for some company. 'Just now he is in Hull,'* she said.

'Just now!' She said that with her Italian accent. She said that herself. He shaded his eyes so that he might see only a little of her face at a time, first the chin, then the nose, then the forehead, in case it were deformed, or had some terrible mark on it. But no, there she was, perfectly natural, sewing, with the pursed lips that women have, the set, the melancholy expression, when sewing. But there was nothing terrible about it, he assured himself, looking a second time, a third time at her face, her hands, for what was frightening or disgusting in her as she sat there in broad daylight, sewing? Mrs Peters had a spiteful tongue. Mr Peters was in Hull. Why, then, rage and prophesy? Why fly scourged and outcast? Why be made to tremble and sob by the clouds? Why seek truths and deliver messages when Rezia sat sticking pins into the front of her dress, and Mr Peters was in Hull? Miracles, revelations, agonies, loneliness, falling through the sea, down, down into the flames, all were burnt out, for he had a sense, as he watched Rezia trimming the straw hat for Mrs Peters, of a coverlet of flowers.

'It's too small for Mrs Peters,' said Septimus.

For the first time for days he was speaking as he used to do! Of course it was—absurdly small, she said. But Mrs Peters had chosen it.

He took it out of her hands. He said it was an organ grinder's monkey's hat.

How it rejoiced her, that! Not for weeks had they laughed like this together, poking fun privately like married people. What she meant was that if Mrs Filmer had come in, or Mrs Peters or anybody, they would not have understood what she and Septimus were laughing at.

'There,' she said, pinning a rose to one side of the hat. Never had she felt so happy! Never in her life!

But that was still more ridiculous, Septimus said. Now the poor woman looked like a pig at a fair. (Nobody ever made her laugh as Septimus did.)

What had she got in her work box? She had ribbons and beads, tassels, artificial flowers. She tumbled them out on the table. He began putting odd colours together—for though he had no fingers, could not even do up a parcel, he had a wonderful eye, and often he was right, sometimes absurd, of course, but sometimes wonderfully right.

'She shall have a beautiful hat!' he murmured, taking up this and that, Rezia kneeling by his side, looking over his shoulder. Now it was finished—that is to say the design; she must stitch it together. But she must be very, very careful, he said, to keep it just as he had made it.

So she sewed. When she sewed, he thought, she made a sound like a kettle on the hob; bubbling, murmuring, always busy, her strong little pointed fingers pinching and poking; her needle flashing straight. The sun might go in and out, on the tassels, on the wallpaper, but he would wait, he thought, stretching out his feet, looking at his ringed sock at the end of the sofa; he would wait in this warm place, this pocket of still air, which one comes on at the edge of a wood sometimes in the evening, when, because of a fall in the ground, or some arrangement of the trees (one must be scientific above all, scientific), warmth lingers, and the air buffets the cheek like the wing of a bird.

'There it is,' said Rezia, twirling Mrs Peters' hat on the tips of her fingers. 'That'll do for the moment. Later . . .' her sentence bubbled away drip, drip, drip, like a contented tap left running.

It was wonderful. Never had he done anything which made him feel so proud. It was so real, it was so substantial, Mrs Peters' hat.

'Just look at it,' he said.

Yes it would always make her happy to see that hat. He had become himself then, he had laughed then. They had been alone together. Always she would like that hat.

He told her to try it on.

'But I must look so queer!' she cried, running over to the glass and looking first this side, then that. Then she snatched it off again, for there was a tap at the door. Could it be Sir William Bradshaw? Had he sent already?

No! it was only the small girl with the evening paper.

What always happened, then happened—what happened every

night of their lives. The small girl sucked her thumb at the door; Rezia went down on her knees; Rezia cooed and kissed; Rezia got a bag of sweets out of the table drawer. For so it always happened. First one thing, then another. So she built it up, first one thing and then another. Dancing, skipping, round and round the room they went. He took the paper. Surrey was all out,* he read. There was a heat wave. Rezia repeated: Surrey was all out. There was a heat wave, making it part of the game she was playing with Mrs Filmer's grandchild, both of them laughing, chattering at the same time, at their game. He was very tired. He was very happy. He would sleep. He shut his eyes. But directly he saw nothing the sounds of the game became fainter and stranger and sounded like the cries of people seeking and not finding, and passing farther and farther away. They had lost him!

He started up in terror. What did he see? The plate of bananas on the sideboard. Nobody was there (Rezia had taken the child to its mother; it was bedtime). That was it: to be alone for ever. That was the doom pronounced in Milan when he came into the room and saw them cutting out buckram shapes with their scissors; to be alone for ever.

He was alone with the sideboard and the bananas. He was alone, exposed on this bleak eminence, stretched out—but not on a hill-top; not on a crag; on Mrs Filmer's sitting-room sofa. As for the visions, the faces, the voices of the dead, where were they? There was a screen in front of him, with black bulrushes and blue swallows. Where he had once seen mountains, where he had seen faces, where he had seen beauty, there was a screen.

'Evans!' he cried. There was no answer. A mouse had squeaked, or a curtain rustled. Those were the voices of the dead. The screen, the coal-scuttle, the sideboard remained to him. Let him, then, face the screen, the coal-scuttle and the sideboard . . . but Rezia burst into the room chattering.

Some letter had come. Everybody's plans were changed. Mrs Filmer would not be able to go to Brighton* after all. There was no time to let Mrs Williams know, and really Rezia thought it very, very annoying, when she caught sight of the hat and thought . . .

perhaps . . . she—might just make a little . . . Her voice died out in contented melody.

'Ah, damn!' she cried (it was a joke of theirs, her swearing); the needle had broken. Hat, child, Brighton, needle. She built it up; first one thing, then another, she built it up, sewing.

She wanted him to say whether by moving the rose she had improved the hat. She sat on the end of the sofa.

They were perfectly happy now, she said suddenly, putting the hat down. For she could say anything to him now. She could say whatever came into her head. That was almost the first thing she had felt about him, that night in the café when he had come in with his English friends. He had come in, rather shyly, looking round him, and his hat had fallen when he hung it up. That she could remember. She knew he was English, though not one of the large Englishmen her sister admired, for he was always thin; but he had a beautiful fresh colour; and with his big nose, his bright eyes, his way of sitting a little hunched, made her think, she had often told him, of a young hawk, that first evening she saw him, when they were playing dominoes, and he had come in—of a young hawk; but with her he was always very gentle. She had never seen him wild or drunk, only suffering sometimes through this terrible war, but even so, when she came in, he would put it all away. Anything, anything in the whole world, any little bother with her work, anything that struck her to say she would tell him, and he understood at once. Her own family even were not the same. Being older than she was and being so clever—how serious he was, wanting her to read Shakespeare before she could even read a child's story in English!—being so much more experienced, he could help her. And she, too, could help him.

But this hat now. And then (it was getting late) Sir William Bradshaw.

She held her hands to her head, waiting for him to say did he like the hat or not, and as she sat there, waiting, looking down, he could feel her mind, like a bird, falling from branch to branch, and always alighting, quite rightly; he could follow her mind, as she sat there in one of those loose lax poses that came to her naturally, and, if he should say anything, at once she smiled, like a bird alighting with all its claws firm upon the bough.

But he remembered. Bradshaw said, 'The people we are most fond of are not good for us when we are ill.' Bradshaw said he must be taught to rest. Bradshaw said they must be separated.

'Must', 'must', why 'must'? What power had Bradshaw over him? 'What right has Bradshaw to say "must" to me?' he demanded.

'It is because you talked of killing yourself,' said Rezia. (Mercifully, she could now say anything to Septimus.)

So he was in their power! Holmes and Bradshaw were on him! The brute with the red nostrils was snuffling into every secret place! 'Must' it could say! Where were his papers? the things he had written?

She brought him his papers, the things he had written, things she had written for him. She tumbled them out on to the sofa. They looked at them together. Diagrams, designs, little men and women brandishing sticks for arms, with wings—were they?—on their backs; circles traced round shillings and sixpences—the suns and stars; zigzagging precipices with mountaineers ascending roped together, exactly like knives and forks; sea pieces with little faces laughing out of what might perhaps be waves: the map of the world. Burn them! he cried. Now for his writings; how the dead sing behind rhododendron bushes; odes to Time; conversations with Shakespeare; Evans, Evans, Evans—his messages from the dead; do not cut down trees; tell the Prime Minister. Universal love: the meaning of the world. Burn them! he cried.

But Rezia laid her hands on them. Some were very beautiful, she thought. She would tie them up (for she had no envelope) with a piece of silk.

Even if they took him, she said, she would go with him. They could not separate them against their wills, she said.

Shuffling the edges straight, she did up the papers, and tied the parcel almost without looking, sitting close, sitting beside him, he thought, as if all her petals were about her. She was a flowering tree; and through her branches looked out the face of a lawgiver, who had reached a sanctuary where she feared no one; not Holmes; not Bradshaw; a miracle, a triumph, the last and greatest. Staggering he saw her mount the appalling staircase, laden with Holmes and Bradshaw, men who never weighed less than eleven stone six, who sent their wives to court, men who made ten thousand a year and talked of proportion; who differed in their verdicts (for Holmes said one thing, Bradshaw another), yet judges they were; who mixed the vision and the sideboard; saw nothing clear, yet ruled, yet inflicted. Over them she triumphed.

'There!' she said. The papers were tied up. No one should get at them. She would put them away.

And, she said, nothing should separate them. She sat down beside him and called him by the name of that hawk or crow which, being malicious and a great destroyer of crops, was precisely like him. No one could separate them, she said.

Then she got up to go into the bedroom to pack their things, but hearing voices downstairs and thinking that Dr Holmes had perhaps called, ran down to prevent him coming up.

Septimus could hear her talking to Holmes on the staircase.

'My dear lady, I have come as a friend,' Holmes was saying.

'No. I will not allow you to see my husband,' she said.

He could see her, like a little hen, with her wings spread barring his passage. But Holmes persevered.

'My dear lady, allow me . . .' Holmes said, putting her aside (Holmes was a powerfully built man).

Holmes was coming upstairs. Holmes would burst open the door. Holmes would say, 'In a funk, eh?' Holmes would get him. But no; not Holmes; not Bradshaw. Getting up rather unsteadily, hopping indeed from foot to foot, he considered Mrs Filmer's nice clean bread-knife with 'Bread' carved on the handle. Ah, but one mustn't spoil that. The gas fire? But it was too late now. Holmes was coming. Razors he might have got, but Rezia, who always did that sort of thing, had packed them. There remained only the window, the large Bloomsbury lodging-house window; the tiresome, the troublesome, and rather melodramatic business of opening the window and throwing himself out. It was their idea of tragedy, not his or Rezia's (for she was with him). Holmes and Bradshaw liked that sort of thing. (He sat on the sill.) But he would wait till the very last moment. He did not want to die. Life was good. The sun hot. Only human beings? Coming down the staircase opposite an old man stopped and stared at him. Holmes was at the door. 'I'll give it you!' he cried, and flung himself vigorously, violently down on to Mrs Filmer's area railings.

'The coward!' cried Dr Holmes, bursting the door open. Rezia ran to the window, she saw; she understood. Dr Holmes and Mrs Filmer collided with each other. Mrs Filmer flapped her apron and made her hide her eyes in the bedroom. There was a great deal of running up and down stairs. Dr Holmes came in—white as a sheet, shaking all over, with a glass in his hand. She must be brave and drink something, he said (What was it? Something sweet), for her husband was horribly mangled, would not recover consciousness, she must not see him, must be spared as much as possible, would have the inquest to go through, poor young woman. Who could have foretold it? A sudden impulse, no one was in the least to blame (he told Mrs Filmer). And why the devil he did it, Dr Holmes could not conceive.

It seemed to her as she drank the sweet stuff that she was opening long windows, stepping out into some garden. But where? The clock was striking—one, two, three: how sensible the sound was; compared with all this thumping and whispering; like Septimus himself. She was falling asleep. But the clock went on striking, four, five, six, and Mrs Filmer waving her apron (they wouldn't bring the body in here, would they?) seemed part of that garden; or a flag. She had once seen a flag slowly rippling out from a mast when she stayed with her aunt at Venice. Men killed in battle were thus saluted, and Septimus had been through the War. Of her memories, most were happy.

She put on her hat, and ran through cornfields—where could it have been?—on to some hill, somewhere near the sea, for there were ships, gulls, butterflies; they sat on a cliff. In London, too, there they sat, and, half dreaming, came to her through the bedroom door, rain falling, whisperings, stirrings among dry corn, the caress of the sea, as it seemed to her, hollowing them in its arched shell and murmuring to her laid on shore, strewn she felt, like flying flowers over some tomb.

'He is dead,' she said, smiling at the poor old woman who guarded her with her honest light-blue eyes fixed on the door. (They wouldn't bring him in here, would they?) But Mrs Filmer pooh-poohed. Oh no, oh no! They were carrying him away now. Ought she not to be told? Married people ought to be together, Mrs Filmer thought. But they must do as the doctor said.

'Let her sleep,' said Dr Holmes, feeling her pulse. She saw the large outline of his body dark against the window. So that was Dr Holmes.

One of the triumphs of civilization, Peter Walsh thought. It is one of the triumphs of civilization, as the light high bell of the ambulance sounded. Swiftly, cleanly, the ambulance sped to the hospital, having picked up instantly, humanely, some poor devil; some one hit on the head, struck down by disease, knocked over perhaps a minute or so ago at one of these crossings, as might happen to oneself. That was civilization. It struck him coming back from the East—the efficiency, the organization, the communal spirit of London. Every cart or carriage of its own accord drew aside to let the ambulance pass. Perhaps it was morbid; or was it not touching rather, the respect which they showed this ambulance with its victim inside—busy men hurrying home, yet instantly bethinking them as it passed of some wife; or presumably how easily it might have been them there, stretched on a shelf with a doctor and a nurse ... Ah, but thinking became morbid, sentimental, directly one began conjuring up doctors, dead bodies; a little glow of pleasure, a sort of lust, too, over the visual impression warned one not to go on with that sort of thing any more—fatal to art, fatal to friendship. True. And yet, thought Peter Walsh, as the ambulance turned the corner, though the light high bell could be heard down the next street and still farther as it crossed the Tottenham Court Road, chiming constantly, it is the privilege of loneliness; in privacy one may do as one chooses. One might weep if no one saw. It had been his undoing—this susceptibility—in Anglo-Indian society; not weeping at the right time, or laughing either. I have that in me, he thought, standing by the pillar-box, which could now dissolve in tears. Why, heaven knows. Beauty of some sort probably, and the weight of the day, which, beginning with that visit to Clarissa, had exhausted him with its heat, its intensity, and the drip, drip of one impression after another down into that cellar where they stood, deep, dark, and no one would ever know. Partly for that reason, its secrecy, complete and inviolable, he had found life like an unknown garden, full of turns and corners, surprising, yes; really it took one's breath away, these moments; there coming to him by the pillar-box opposite the British Museum* one of them, a moment, in which things came together; this ambulance; and life and death. It was as if he were sucked up to some very high roof by that rush of emotion, and the rest of him, like a white shell-sprinkled beach, left bare. It had been his undoing in Anglo-Indian society—this susceptibility.

Clarissa once, going on top of an omnibus with him some-where, Clarissa superficially at least, so easily moved, now in des-pair, now in the best of spirits, all aquiver in those days and such good company, spotting queer little scenes, names, people from the top of a bus, for they used to explore London and bring back bags full of treasures from the Caledonian Market*—Clarissa had a theory in those days—they had heaps of theories, always theories, as young people have. It was to explain the feeling they had of dissatisfaction; not knowing people; not being known. For how could they know each other? You met every day; then not for six months, or years. It was unsatisfactory, they agreed, how little one knew people. But she said, sitting on the bus going up Shaftesbury Avenue,* she felt herself everywhere; not 'here, here, here'; and she tapped the back of the seat; but everywhere. She waved her hand, going up Shaftesbury Avenue. She was all that. So that to know her, or any one, one must seek out the people who completed them; even the places. Odd affinities she had with people she had never spoken to, some woman in the street, some man behind a counter—even trees, or barns. It ended in a transcendental theory which, with her horror of death, allowed her to believe, or say that she believed (for all her scepticism), that since our apparitions, the part of us which appears, are so momentary compared with the other, the unseen part of us, which spreads wide, the unseen might survive, be recovered somehow attached to this person or that, or even haunting certain places, after death. Perhaps—perhaps.

Looking back over that long friendship of almost thirty years her theory worked to this extent. Brief, broken, often painful as their actual meetings had been, what with his absences and inter-ruptions (this morning, for instance, in came Elizabeth, like a long-legged colt, handsome, dumb, just as he was beginning to talk to Clarissa), the effect of them on his life was immeasurable. There was a mystery about it. You were given a sharp, acute, uncomfortable grain—the actual meeting; horribly painful as often as not; yet in absence, in the most unlikely places, it would flower out, open, shed its scent, let you touch, taste, look about you, get the whole feel of it and understanding, after years of lying lost. Thus she had come to him; on board ship; in the Himalayas; suggested by the oddest things (so Sally Seton, generous, enthusiastic goose! thought of *him* when she saw blue hydrangeas). She had influenced him more than any person he had ever known. And always in this way coming before him without his wishing it, cool, ladylike, critical; or ravishing, romantic, recalling some field or English harvest. He saw her most often in the country, not in London. One scene after another at Bourton . . .

He had reached his hotel. He crossed the hall, with its mounds of reddish chairs and sofas, its spike-leaved, withered-looking plants. He got his key off the hook. The young lady handed him some letters. He went upstairs—he saw her most often at Bourton, in the late summer, when he stayed there for a week, or fortnight even, as people did in those days. First on top of some hill there she would stand, hands clapped to her hair, her cloak blowing out, pointing, crying to them—She saw the Severn* beneath. Or in a wood, making the kettle boil—very ineffective with her fingers; the smoke curtseying, blowing in their faces; her little pink face showing through; begging water from an old woman in a cottage, who came to the door to watch them go. They walked always; the others drove. She was bored driving, disliked all animals, except that dog. They tramped miles along roads. She would break off to get her bearings, pilot him back across country; and all the time they argued, discussed poetry, discussed people, discussed politics (she was a Radical then); never noticing a thing except when she stopped, cried out at a view or a tree, and made him look with her; and so on again, through stubble fields, she walking ahead, with a flower for her aunt, never tired of walking for all her delicacy; to drop down on Bourton in the dusk. Then, after dinner, old Breitkopf would open the piano and sing without any voice, and they would lie sunk in armchairs, trying not to laugh, but always breaking down and laughing, laughing—laughing at nothing. Breitkopf was supposed not to see. And then in the morning, flirting up and down like a wagtail in front of the house . . .

Oh it was a letter from her! This blue envelope; that was her hand. And he would have to read it. Here was another of those meetings, bound to be painful! To read her letter needed the devil of an effort. 'How heavenly it was to see him. She must tell him that.' That was all.

But it upset him. It annoyed him. He wished she hadn't written it. Coming on top of his thoughts, it was like a nudge in the ribs. Why couldn't she let him be? After all, she had married Dalloway, and lived with him in perfect happiness all these years.

These hotels are not consoling places. Far from it. Any number of people had hung up their hats on those pegs. Even the flies, if you thought of it, had settled on other people's noses. As for the cleanliness which hit him in the face, it wasn't cleanliness, so much as bareness, frigidity; a thing that had to be. Some arid matron made her rounds at dawn sniffing, peering, causing blue-nosed maids to scour, for all the world as if the next visitor were a joint of meat to be served on a perfectly clean platter. For sleep, one bed; for sitting in, one armchair; for cleansing one's teeth and shaving one's chin, one tumbler, one looking-glass. Books, letters, dressing-gown, slipped about on the impersonality of the horse-hair like incongruous impertinences. And it was Clarissa's letter that made him see all this. 'Heavenly to see you. She must say so!'

He folded the paper; pushed it away; nothing would induce him to read it again!

To get that letter to him by six o'clock she must have sat down and written it directly he left her; stamped it; sent somebody to the post. It was, as people say, very like her. She was upset by his visit. She had felt a great deal; had for a moment, when she kissed his hand, regretted, envied him even, remembered possibly (for he saw her look it) something he had said—how they would change the world if she married him perhaps; whereas, it was this; it was middle age; it was mediocrity; then forced herself with her indomitable vitality to put all that aside, there being in her a thread of life which for toughness, endurance, power to overcome obstacles and carry her triumphantly through he had never known the like of. Yes; but there would come a reaction directly he left the room. She would be frightfully sorry for him; she would think what in the world she could do to give him pleasure (short always of the one thing), and he could see her with the tears running down her cheeks going to her writing-table and dashing off that one line which he was to find greeting him . . . 'Heavenly to see you!' And she meant it.

Peter Walsh had now unlaced his boots.

But it would not have been a success, their marriage. The other thing, after all, came so much more naturally.

It was odd; it was true; lots of people felt it. Peter Walsh, who had done just respectably, filled the usual posts adequately, was liked, but thought a little cranky, gave himself airs—it was odd that *he* should have had, especially now that his hair was grey, a contented look; a look of having reserves. It was this that made him attractive to women, who liked the sense that he was not altogether manly. There was something unusual about him, or something behind him. It might be that he was bookish—never came to see you without taking up the book on the table (he was now reading, with his bootlaces trailing on the floor); or that he was a gentleman, which showed itself in the way he knocked the ashes out of his pipe, and in his manners of course to women. For it was very charming and quite ridiculous how easily some girl without a grain of sense could twist him round her finger. But at her own risk. That is to say, though he might be ever so easy, and indeed with his gaiety and good-breeding fascinating to be with, it was only up to a point. She said something—no, no; he saw through that. He wouldn't stand that—no, no. Then he could shout and rock and hold his sides together over some joke with men. He was the best judge of cooking in India. He was a man. But not the sort of man one had to respect—which was a mercy; not like Major Simmons, for instance; not in the least, Daisy thought, when, in spite of her two small children, she used to compare them.

He pulled off his boots. He emptied his pockets. Out came with his pocket-knife a snapshot of Daisy on the verandah; Daisy all in white, with a fox-terrier on her knee; very charming, very dark; the best he had ever seen of her. It did come, after all, so naturally; so much more naturally than Clarissa. No fuss. No bother. No finicking and fidgeting. All plain sailing. And the dark, adorably pretty girl on the verandah exclaimed (he could hear her). Of course, of course she would give him everything! she cried (she had no sense of discretion); everything he wanted! she cried, running to meet him, whoever might be looking. And she was only twenty-four. And she had two children. Well, well!

Well indeed he had got himself into a mess at his age. And it came over him when he woke in the night pretty forcibly. Suppose they did marry? For him it would be all very well, but what about her? Mrs Burgess, a good sort and no chatterbox, in whom he had confided, thought this absence of his in England, ostensibly to see lawyers, might serve to make Daisy reconsider, think what it meant. It was a question of her position, Mrs Burgess said; the social barrier; giving up her children. She'd be a widow with a past one of these days, draggling about in the suburbs, or more likely, indiscriminate (you know, she said, what such women get like, with too much paint). But Peter Walsh pooh-poohed all that. He didn't mean to die yet. Anyhow, she must settle for herself; judge for herself, he thought, padding about the room in his socks, smoothing out his dress-shirt for he might go to Clarissa's party, or he might go to one of the Halls, or he might settle in and read an absorbing book written by a man he used to know at Oxford. And if he did retire, that's what he'd do—write books. He would go to Oxford and poke about in the Bodleian.* Vainly the dark, adorably pretty girl ran to the end of the terrace; vainly waved her hand; vainly cried she didn't care a straw what people said. There he was, the man she thought the world of, the perfect gentleman, the fascinating, the distinguished (and his age made not the least difference to her), padding about a room in an hotel in Bloomsbury, shaving, washing, continuing, as he took up cans, put down razors, to poke about in the Bodleian, and get at the truth about one or two little matters that interested him. And he would have a chat with whoever it might be, and so come to disregard more and more precise hours for lunch, and miss engagements; and when Daisy asked him, as she would, for a kiss, a scene, fail to come up to the scratch (though he was genuinely devoted to her)—in short, it might be happier, as Mrs Burgess said, that she should forget him, or merely remember him as he was in August 1922, like a figure standing at the crossroads at dusk, which grows more and more remote as the dog-cart spins away, carrying her securely fastened to the back seat, though her arms are outstretched; and, as she sees the figure dwindle and disappear, still she cries out how she would do anything in the world, anything, anything, anything . . .

He never knew what people thought. It became more and more difficult for him to concentrate. He became absorbed; he became busied with his own concerns; now surly, now gay; dependent on women, absent-minded, moody, less and less able (so he thought as he shaved) to understand why Clarissa couldn't simply find them a lodging and be nice to Daisy; introduce her. And then he could just—just do what? just haunt and hover (he was at the moment actually engaged in sorting out various keys, papers), swoop and taste, be alone, in short, sufficient to himself; and yet nobody of course was more dependent upon others (he buttoned his waistcoat); it had been his undoing. He could not keep out of smoking-rooms, liked colonels, liked golf, liked bridge, and above all women's society, and the fineness of their companionship, and their faithfulness and audacity and greatness in loving which, though it had its drawbacks, seemed to him (and the dark, adorably pretty face was on top of the envelopes) so wholly admirable, so splendid a flower to grow on the crest of human life, and yet he could not come up to the scratch, being always apt to see round things (Clarissa had sapped something in him permanently), and to tire very easily of mute devotion and to want variety in love, though it would make him furious if Daisy loved anybody else, furious! for he was jealous, uncontrollably jealous by temperament. He suffered tortures! But where was his knife; his watch; his seals, his note-case, and Clarissa's letter which he would not read again but liked to think of, and Daisy's photograph? And now for dinner.

They were eating.

Sitting at little tables round vases, dressed or not dressed, with their shawls and bags laid beside them, with their air of false composure, for they were not used to so many courses at dinner; and confidence, for they were able to pay for it; and strain, for they had been running about London all day shopping, sightseeing; and their natural curiosity, for they looked round and up as the nice-looking gentleman in horn-rimmed spectacles came in; and their good nature, for they would have been glad to do any little service, such as lend a time-table or impart useful information; and their desire, pulsing in them, tugging at them subterraneously, somehow to establish connections if it were only a birthplace (Liverpool, for example), in common or friends of the same name; with their furtive glances, odd silences, and sudden withdrawals into family jocularity and isolation; there they sat eating dinner when Mr Walsh came in and took his seat at a little table by the curtain.

It was not that he said anything, for being solitary he could only address himself to the waiter; it was his way of looking at the menu, of pointing his forefinger to a particular wine, of hitching himself up to the table, of addressing himself seriously, not gluttonously, to dinner, that won him their respect; which, having to remain unexpressed for the greater part of the meal, flared up at the table where the Morrises sat when Mr Walsh was heard to say at the end of the meal, 'Bartlett pears'.* Why he should have spoken so moderately yet firmly, with the air of a disciplinarian well within his rights which are founded upon justice, neither young Charles Morris, nor old Charles, neither Miss Elaine nor Mrs Morris knew. But when he said, 'Bartlett pears', sitting alone at his table, they felt that he counted on their support in some lawful demand; was champion of a cause which immediately became their own, so that their eyes met his eyes sympathetically, and when they all reached the smoking-room simultaneously, a little talk between them became inevitable.

It was not very profound—only to the effect that London was crowded; had changed in thirty years; that Mr Morris preferred Liverpool; that Mrs Morris had been to the Westminster flower-show, and that they had all seen the Prince of Wales. Yet, thought Peter Walsh, no family in the world can compare with the Morrises; none whatever; and their relations to each other are perfect, and they don't care a hang for the upper classes, and they like what they like, and Elaine is training for the family business, and the boy has won a scholarship at Leeds, and the old lady (who is about his own age) has three more children at home; and they have two motor cars, but Mr Morris still mends the boots on Sunday: it is superb, it is absolutely superb, thought Peter Walsh, swaying a little backwards and forwards with his liqueur glass in his hand among the hairy red chairs and ash-trays, feeling very well pleased with himself, for the Morrises liked him. Yes; they liked a man who said 'Bartlett pears'. They liked him, he felt.

He would go to Clarissa's party. (The Morrises moved off; but they would meet again.) He would go to Clarissa's party, because he wanted to ask Richard what they were doing in India—the conservative duffers. And what's being acted? And music . . . Oh yes, and mere gossip.

For this is the truth about our soul, he thought, our self, who fish-like inhabits deep seas and plies among obscurities threading her way between the boles of giant weeds, over sun-flickered spaces and on and on into gloom, cold, deep, inscrutable; sud-denly she shoots to the surface and sports on the wind-wrinkled waves; that is, has a positive need to brush, scrape, kindle herself, gossiping. What did the Government mean—Richard Dalloway would know—to do about India?

Since it was a very hot night and the paper boys went by with placards proclaiming in huge red letters that there was a heat wave, wicker chairs were placed on the hotel steps and there, sipping, smoking, detached gentlemen sat. Peter Walsh sat there. One might fancy that day, the London day, was just beginning. Like a woman who had slipped off her print dress and white apron to array herself in blue and pearls, the day changed, put off stuff, took gauze, changed to evening, and with the same sigh of exhilaration that a woman breathes, tumbling petticoats on the floor, it too shed dust, heat, colour; the traffic thinned; motor cars, tinkling, darting, succeeded the lumber of vans; and here and there among the thick foliage of the squares an intense light hung. I resign, the evening seemed to say, as it paled and faded above the battlements and prominences, moulded, pointed, of hotel, flat, and block of shops, I fade, she was beginning, I disappear, but London would have none of it, and rushed her bayonets into the sky, pinioned her, constrained her to partnership in her revelry.

For the great revolution of Mr Willett's summer time* had taken place since Peter Walsh's last visit to England. The prolonged evening was new to him. It was inspiriting, rather. For as the young people went by with their despatch-boxes, awfully glad to be free, proud too, dumbly, of stepping this famous pavement, joy of a kind, cheap, tinselly, if you like, but all the same rapture, flushed their faces. They dressed well too; pink stockings; pretty shoes. They would now have two hours at the pictures. It sharpened, it refined them, the yellow-blue evening light; and on the leaves in the square shone lurid, livid—they looked as if dipped in sea water—the foliage of a submerged city. He was astonished by the beauty; it was encouraging too, for where the returned Anglo-Indian sat by rights (he knew crowds of them) in the Oriental Club* biliously summing up the ruin of the world, here was he, as young as ever; envying young people their summer time and the rest of it, and more than suspecting from the words of a girl, from a housemaid's laughter—intangible things you couldn't lay your hands on—that shift in the whole pyramidal accumulation which in his youth had seemed immovable. On top

of them it had pressed; weighed them down, the women especially, like those flowers Clarissa's Aunt Helena used to press
between sheets of grey blotting-paper with Littré's dictionary* on
top, sitting under the lamp after dinner. She was dead now. He
had heard of her, from Clarissa, losing the sight of one eye. It
seemed so fitting—one of nature's masterpieces—that old Miss
Parry should turn to glass. She would die like some bird in a frost
gripping her perch. She belonged to a different age, but being so
entire, so complete, would always stand up on the horizon, stone-
white, eminent, like a lighthouse marking some past stage on this
adventurous, long, long voyage, this interminable—(he felt for a
copper to buy a paper and read about Surrey and Yorkshire; he
had held out that copper millions of times—Surrey was all out
once more)—this interminable life. But cricket was no mere
game. Cricket was important. He could never help reading about
cricket. He read the scores in the stop press first, then how it was
a hot day; then about a murder case. Having done things millions
of times enriched them, though it might be said to take the surface off. The past enriched, and experience, and having cared for
one or two people, and so having acquired the power which the
young lack, of cutting short, doing what one likes, not caring a
rap what people say and coming and going without any very great
expectations (he left his paper on the table and moved off), which
however (and he looked for his hat and coat) was not altogether
true of him, not tonight, for here he was starting to go to a party,
at his age, with the belief upon him that he was about to have an
experience. But what?

Beauty anyhow. Not the crude beauty of the eye. It was not
beauty pure and simple—Bedford Place leading into Russell
Square. It was straightness and emptiness of course; the sym-
metry of a corridor; but it was also windows lit up, a piano, a
gramophone sounding; a sense of pleasure-making hidden, but
now and again emerging when, through the uncurtained window,
the window left open, one saw parties sitting over tables, young
people slowly circling, conversations between men and women,
maids idly looking out (a strange comment theirs, when work was
done), stockings drying on top ledges, a parrot, a few plants.

Absorbing, mysterious, of infinite richness, this life. And in the large square where the cabs shot and swerved so quick, there were loitering couples, dallying, embracing, shrunk up under the shower of a tree; that was moving; so silent, so absorbed, that one passed, discreetly, timidly, as if in the presence of some sacred ceremony to interrupt which would have been impious. That was interesting. And so on into the flare and glare.

His light overcoat blew open, he stepped with indescribable idiosyncrasy, leant a little forward, tripped, with his hands behind his back and his eyes still a little hawk-like; he tripped through London, towards Westminster, observing.

Was everybody dining out, then? Doors were being opened here by a footman to let issue a high-stepping old dame, in buckled shoes, with three purple ostrich feathers in her hair. Doors were being opened for ladies wrapped like mummies in shawls with bright flowers on them, ladies with bare heads. And in respectable quarters with stucco pillars through small front gardens, lightly swathed, with combs in their hair (having run up to see the children), women came; men waited for them, with their coats blowing open, and the motor started. Everybody was going out. What with these doors being opened, and the descent and the start, it seemed as if the whole of London were embarking in little boats moored to the bank, tossing on the waters, as if the whole place were floating off in carnival. And Whitehall was skated over, silver beaten as it was, skated over by spiders, and there was a sense of midges round the arc lamps; it was so hot that people stood about talking. And here in Westminster was a retired Judge, presumably, sitting four square at his house door dressed all in white. An Anglo-Indian presumably.

And here a shindy of brawling women, drunken women; here only a policeman and looming houses, high houses, domed houses, churches, parliaments, and the hoot of a steamer on the river, a hollow misty cry. But it was her street, this, Clarissa's; cabs were rushing round the corner, like water round the piers of a bridge, drawn together, it seemed to him, because they bore people going to her party, Clarissa's party.

The cold stream of visual impressions failed him now as if the eye were a cup that overflowed and let the rest run down its china walls unrecorded. The brain must wake now. The body must contract now, entering the house, the lighted house, where the door stood open, where the motor cars were standing, and bright women descending: the soul must brave itself to endure. He opened the big blade of his pocket-knife.

Lucy came running full tilt downstairs, having just nipped into the drawing-room to smooth a cover, to straighten a chair, to pause a moment and feel whoever came in must think how clean, how bright, how beautifully cared for, when they saw the beautiful silver, the brass fire-irons, the new chair-covers, and the curtains of yellow chintz: she appraised each; heard a roar of voices; people already coming up from dinner; she must fly!

The Prime Minister was coming, Agnes said: so she had heard them say in the dining-room, she said, coming in with a tray of glasses. Did it matter, did it matter in the least, one Prime Minister more or less? It made no difference at this hour of the night to Mrs Walker among the plates, saucepans, cullenders, frying-pans, chicken in aspic, ice-cream freezers, pared crusts of bread, lemons, soup tureens, and pudding basins which, however hard they washed up in the scullery, seemed to be all on top of her, on the kitchen table, on chairs, while the fire blared and roared, the electric lights glared, and still supper had to be laid. All she felt was, one Prime Minister more or less made not a scrap of difference to Mrs Walker.

The ladies were going upstairs already, said Lucy; the ladies were going up, one by one, Mrs Dalloway walking last and almost always sending back some message to the kitchen, 'My love to Mrs Walker,' that was it one night. Next morning they would go over the dishes—the soup, the salmon; the salmon, Mrs Walker knew, as usual underdone, for she always got nervous about the pudding and left it to Jenny; so it happened, the salmon was always underdone. But some lady with fair hair and silver ornaments had said, Lucy said, about the entrée, was it really made at home? But it was the salmon that bothered Mrs Walker, as she spun the plates round and round, and pushed in dampers and pulled out dampers; and there came a burst of laughter from the dining-room; a voice speaking; then another burst of laughter— the gentlemen enjoying themselves when the ladies had gone. The tokay, said Lucy, running in. Mr Dalloway had sent for the tokay, from the Emperor's cellars, the Imperial Tokay.*

It was borne through the kitchen. Over her shoulder Lucy reported how Miss Elizabeth looked quite lovely; she couldn't take her eyes off her; in her pink dress, wearing the necklace Mr Dalloway had given her. Jenny must remember the dog, Miss Elizabeth's fox-terrier, which, since it bit, had to be shut up and might, Elizabeth thought, want something. Jenny must remember the dog. But Jenny was not going upstairs with all those people about. There was a motor at the door already! There was a ring at the bell—and the gentlemen still in the dining-room, drinking tokay!

There, they were going upstairs; that was the first to come, and now they would come faster and faster, so that Mrs Parkinson (hired for parties) would leave the hall door ajar, and the hall would be full of gentlemen waiting (they stood waiting, sleeking down their hair) while the ladies took their cloaks off in the room along the passage; where Mrs Barnet helped them, old Ellen Barnet, who had been with the family for forty years, and came every summer to help the ladies, and remembered mothers when they were girls, and though very unassuming did shake hands; said 'milady' very respectfully, yet had a humorous way with her, looking at the young ladies, and ever so tactfully helping Lady Lovejoy, who had some trouble with her underbodice. And they could not help feeling, Lady Lovejoy and Miss Alice, that some little privilege in the matter of brush and comb was awarded them having known Mrs Barnet—'thirty years, milady,' Mrs Barnet supplied her. Young ladies did not use to rouge, said Lady Lovejoy, when they stayed at Bourton in the old days. And Miss Alice didn't need rouge, said Mrs Barnet, looking at her fondly. There Mrs Barnet would sit, in the cloakroom, patting down the furs, smoothing out the Spanish shawls, tidying the dressing-table, and knowing perfectly well, in spite of the furs and the embroideries, which were nice ladies, which were not. The dear old body, said Lady Lovejoy, mounting the stairs, Clarissa's old nurse.

And then Lady Lovejoy stiffened. 'Lady and Miss Lovejoy,' she said to Mr Wilkins (hired for parties). He had an admirable manner, as he bent and straightened himself, bent and straightened himself and announced with perfect impartiality 'Lady and Miss Lovejoy . . . Sir John and Lady Needham . . . Miss Weld . . . Mr Walsh'. His manner was admirable; his family life must be irreproachable, except that it seemed impossible that a being with greenish lips and shaven cheeks could ever have blundered into the nuisance of children.

'How delightful to see you!' said Clarissa. She said it to everyone. How delightful to see you! She was at her worst—effusive, insincere. It was a great mistake to have come. He should have stayed at home and read his book, thought Peter Walsh; should have gone to a music hall; he should have stayed at home, for he knew no one.

Oh dear, it was going to be a failure; a complete failure, Clarissa felt it in her bones as dear old Lord Lexham stood there apologizing for his wife who had caught cold at the Buckingham Palace garden party. She could see Peter out of the tail of her eye, criticizing her, there, in that corner. Why, after all, did she do these things? Why seek pinnacles and stand drenched in fire? Might it consume her anyhow! Burn her to cinders! Better anything, better brandish one's torch and hurl it to earth than taper and dwindle away like some Ellie Henderson! It was extraordinary how Peter put her into these states just by coming and standing in a corner. He made her see herself; exaggerate. It was idiotic. But why did he come, then, merely to criticize? Why always take, never give? Why not risk one's one little point of view? There he was wandering off, and she must speak to him. But she would not get the chance. Life was that—humiliation, renunciation. What Lord Lexham was saying was that his wife would not wear her furs at the garden party because 'my dear, you ladies are all alike'—Lady Lexham being seventy-five at least! It was delicious, how they petted each other, that old couple. She did like old Lord Lexham. She did think it mattered, her party, and it made her feel quite sick to know that it was all going wrong, all falling flat. Anything, any explosion, any horror was better than people wandering aimlessly, standing in a bunch at a corner like Ellie Henderson, not even caring to hold themselves upright.

Gently the yellow curtain with all the birds of Paradise blew out and it seemed as if there were a flight of wings into the room, right out, then sucked back. (For the windows were open.) Was it draughty, Ellie Henderson wondered? She was subject to chills. But it did not matter that she should come down sneezing tomorrow; it was the girls with their naked shoulders she thought of, being trained to think of others by an old father, an invalid, late vicar of Bourton, but he was dead now; and her chills never went to her chest, never. It was the girls she thought of, the young girls with their bare shoulders, she herself having always been a wisp of a creature, with her thin hair and meagre profile; though now, past fifty, there was beginning to shine through some mild beam, something purified into distinction by years of self-abnegation but obscured again, perpetually, by her distressing gentility, her panic fear, which arose from three hundred pounds income, and her weaponless state (she could not earn a penny) and it made her timid, and more and more disqualified year by year to meet well-dressed people who did this sort of thing every night of the season, merely telling their maids 'I'll wear so and so,' whereas Ellie Henderson ran out nervously and bought cheap pink flowers, half-a-dozen, and then threw a shawl over her old black dress. For her invitation to Clarissa's party had come at the last moment. She was not quite happy about it. She had a sort of feeling that Clarissa had not meant to ask her this year.

Why should she? There was no reason really, except that they had always known each other. Indeed, they were cousins. But naturally they had rather drifted apart, Clarissa being so sought after. It was an event to her, going to a party. It was quite a treat just to see the lovely clothes. Wasn't that Elizabeth, grown up, with her hair done in the fashionable way, in the pink dress? Yet she could not be more than seventeen. She was very, very handsome. But girls when they first came out didn't seem to wear white as they used. (She must remember everything to tell Edith.) Girls wore straight frocks, perfectly tight, with skirts well above the ankles. It was not becoming, she thought.

So, with her weak eyesight, Ellie Henderson craned rather forward, and it wasn't so much she who minded not having any-one to talk to (she hardly knew anybody there), for she felt that they were all such interesting people to watch; politicians pre-sumably; Richard Dalloway's friends; but it was Richard himself who felt that he could not let the poor creature go on standing there all the evening by herself.

'Well, Ellie, and how's the world treating *you*?' he said in his genial way, and Ellie Henderson, getting nervous and flushing and feeling that it was extraordinarily nice of him to come and talk to her, said that many people really felt the heat more than the cold.

'Yes, they do,' said Richard Dalloway. 'Yes.'

But what more did one say?

'Hullo, Richard,' said somebody, taking him by the elbow, and, good Lord, there was old Peter, old Peter Walsh. He was delighted to see him—ever so pleased to see him! He hadn't changed a bit. And off they went together walking right across the room, giving each other little pats, as if they hadn't met for a long time, Ellie Henderson thought, watching them go, certain she knew that man's face. A tall man, middle aged, rather fine eyes, dark, wearing spectacles, with a look of John Burrows. Edith would be sure to know.

The curtain with its flight of birds of Paradise blew out again. And Clarissa saw—she saw Ralph Lyon beat it back, and go on talking. So it wasn't a failure after all! it was going to be all right now—her party. It had begun. It had started. But it was still touch and go. She must stand there for the present. People seemed to come in a rush.

Colonel and Mrs Garrod ... Mr Hugh Whitbread ... Mr Bowley ... Mrs Hilbery ... Lady Mary Maddox ... Mr Quin ... intoned Wilkins. She had six or seven words with each, and they went on, they went into the rooms; into something now, not nothing, since Ralph Lyon had beat back the curtain.

And yet for her own part, it was too much of an effort. She was not enjoying it. It was too much like being—just anybody, stand-ing there; anybody could do it; yet this anybody she did a little admire, couldn't help feeling that she had, anyhow, made this happen, that it marked a stage, this post that she felt herself to have become, for oddly enough she had quite forgotten what she looked like, but felt herself a stake driven in at the top of her stairs. Every time she gave a party she had this feeling of being something not herself, and that everyone was unreal in one way; much more real in another. It was, she thought, partly their clothes, partly being taken out of their ordinary ways, partly the background; it was possible to say things you couldn't say anyhow else, things that needed an effort; possible to go much deeper. But not for her; not yet anyhow.

'How delightful to see you!' she said. Dear old Sir Harry! He would know everyone.

And what was so odd about it was the sense one had as they came up the stairs one after another, Mrs Mount and Celia, Herbert Ainsty, Mrs Dakers—oh, and Lady Bruton!

'How awfully good of you to come!' she said, and she meant it—it was odd how standing there one felt them going on, going on, some quite old, some . . .

What name? Lady Rosseter? But who on earth was Lady Rosseter?

'Clarissa!' That voice! It was Sally Seton! Sally Seton! after all these years! She loomed through a mist. For she hadn't looked like *that*, Sally Seton, when Clarissa grasped the hot-water can. To think of her under this roof, under this roof! Not like that!

All on top of each other, embarrassed, laughing, words tumbled out—passing through London; heard from Clara Haydon; what a chance of seeing you! So I thrust myself in—without an invitation . . .

One might put down the hot-water can quite composedly. The lustre had left her. Yet it was extraordinary to see her again, older, happier, less lovely. They kissed each other, first this cheek, then that, by the drawing-room door, and Clarissa turned, with Sally's hand in hers, and saw her rooms full, heard the roar of voices, saw the candlesticks, the blowing curtains, and the roses which Richard had given her.

'I have five enormous boys,' said Sally.

She had the simplest egotism, the most open desire to be thought first always, and Clarissa loved her for being still like that. 'I can't believe it!' she cried, kindling all over with pleasure at the thought of the past.

But alas, Wilkins; Wilkins wanted her; Wilkins was emitting in a voice of commanding authority, as if the whole company must be admonished and the hostess reclaimed from frivolity, one name:

'The Prime Minister,' said Peter Walsh.

The Prime Minister? Was it really? Ellie Henderson marvelled. What a thing to tell Edith!

One couldn't laugh at him. He looked so ordinary. You might have stood him behind a counter and bought biscuits—poor chap, all rigged up in gold lace. And to be fair, as he went his rounds, first with Clarissa, then with Richard escorting him, he did it very well. He tried to look somebody. It was amusing to watch. Nobody looked at him. They just went on talking, yet it was perfectly plain that they all knew, felt to the marrow of their bones, this majesty passing; this symbol of what they all stood for, English society. Old Lady Bruton, and she looked very fine too, very stalwart in her lace, swam up, and they withdrew into a little room which at once became spied upon, guarded, and a sort of stir and rustle rippled through everyone openly: the Prime Minister!

Lord, lord, the snobbery of the English! thought Peter Walsh, standing in the corner. How they loved dressing up in gold lace and doing homage! There! That must be—by Jove it was—Hugh Whitbread, snuffling around the precincts of the great, grown rather fatter, rather whiter, the admirable Hugh!

He looked always as if he were on duty, thought Peter, a privileged but secretive being, hoarding secrets which he would die to defend, though it was only some little piece of tittle-tattle dropped by a court footman which would be in all the papers tomorrow. Such were his rattles, his baubles, in playing with which he had grown white, come to the verge of old age, enjoying the respect and affection of all who had the privilege of knowing this type of the English public-school man. Inevitably one made up things like that about Hugh; that was his style; the style of those admirable letters which Peter had read thousands of miles across the sea in *The Times*, and had thanked God he was out of that pernicious hubble-bubble if it were only to hear baboons chatter and coolies beat their wives. An olive-skinned youth from one of the Universities stood obsequiously by. Him he would patronize, initiate, teach how to get on. For he liked nothing better than doing kindnesses, making the hearts of old ladies palpitate with the joy of being thought of in their age, their affliction, thinking themselves quite forgotten, yet here was dear Hugh driving up and spending an hour talking of the past, remembering trifles, praising the home-made cake, though Hugh might eat cake with a Duchess any day of his life, and, to look at him, probably did spend a good deal of time in that agreeable occupation. The All-judging, the All-merciful, might excuse. Peter Walsh had no mercy. Villains there must be, and, God knows, the rascals who get hanged for battering the brains of a girl out in a train do less harm on the whole than Hugh Whitbread and his kindness! Look at him now, on tip-toe, dancing forward, bowing and scraping, as the Prime Minister and Lady Bruton emerged, intimating for all the world to see that he was privileged to say something, something private, to Lady Bruton as she passed. She stopped. She wagged her fine old head. She was thanking him presumably for some piece of servility. She had her toadies, minor officials in Government offices who ran about putting through little jobs on her behalf, in return for which she gave them luncheon. But she derived from the eighteenth century. She was all right.

And now Clarissa escorted her Prime Minister down the room, prancing, sparkling, with the stateliness of her grey hair. She wore ear-rings, and a silver-green mermaid's dress. Lolloping on the waves and braiding her tresses she seemed, having that gift still; to be; to exist; to sum it all up in the moment as she passed; turned, caught her scarf in some other woman's dress, unhitched it, laughed, all with the most perfect ease and air of a creature floating in its element. But age had brushed her; even as a mermaid might behold in her glass the setting sun on some very clear evening over the waves. There was a breath of tenderness; her severity, her prudery, her woodenness were all warmed through now, and she had about her as she said good-bye to the thick gold-laced man who was doing his best, and good luck to him, to look important, an inexpressible dignity; an exquisite cordiality; as if she wished the whole world well, and must now, being on the very verge and rim of things, take her leave. So she made him think. (But he was not in love.)

Indeed, Clarissa felt, the Prime Minister had been good to come. And, walking down the room with him, with Sally there and Peter there and Richard very pleased, with all those people rather inclined, perhaps, to envy, she had felt that intoxication of the moment, that dilatation of the nerves of the heart itself till it seemed to quiver, steeped, upright;—yes, but after all it was what other people felt, that; for, though she loved it and felt it tingle and sting, still these semblances, these triumphs (dear old Peter, for example, thinking her so brilliant), had a hollowness; at arm's length they were, not in the heart; and it might be that she was growing old, but they satisfied her no longer as they used; and suddenly, as she saw the Prime Minister go down the stairs, the gilt rim of the Sir Joshua picture* of the little girl with a muff brought back Kilman with a rush; Kilman her enemy. That was satisfying; that was real. Ah, how she hated her—hot, hypo-critical, corrupt; with all that power; Elizabeth's seducer; the woman who had crept in to steal and defile (Richard would say, What nonsense!). She hated her: she loved her. It was enemies one wanted, not friends—not Mrs Durrant and Clara,* Sir William and Lady Bradshaw, Miss Truelock and Eleanor Gibson (whom she saw coming upstairs). They must find her if they wanted her. She was for the party!

There was her old friend Sir Harry.

'Dear Sir Harry!' she said, going up to the fine old fellow who had produced more bad pictures than any other two Academi-cians in the whole of St John's Wood (they were always of cattle, standing in sunset pools absorbing moisture, or signifying, for he had a certain range of gesture, by the raising of one foreleg and the toss of the antlers, 'the Approach of the Stranger'—all his activities, dining out, racing, were founded on cattle standing absorbing moisture in sunset pools).*

'What are you laughing at?' she asked him. For Willie Titcomb and Sir Harry and Herbert Ainsty were all laughing. But no. Sir Harry could not tell Clarissa Dalloway (much though he liked her; of her type he thought her perfect, and threatened to paint her) his stories of the music-hall stage. He chaffed her about her party. He missed his brandy. These circles, he said, were above him. But he liked her; respected her, in spite of her damnable, difficult, upper-class refinement, which made it impossible to ask Clarissa Dalloway to sit on his knee. And up came that wandering will-o'-the-wisp, that vagous* phosphorescence, old Mrs Hilbery, stretching her hands to the blazes of his laughter (about the Duke and the Lady), which, as she heard it across the room, seemed to reassure her on a point which sometimes bothered her if she woke early in the morning and did not like to call her maid for a cup of tea; how it is certain we must die.

'They won't tell us their stories,' said Clarissa.

'Dear Clarissa!' exclaimed Mrs Hilbery. She looked tonight, she said, so like her mother as she first saw her walking in a garden in a grey hat.

And really Clarissa's eyes filled with tears. Her mother, walking in a garden! But alas, she must go.

For there was Professor Brierly, who lectured on Milton, talking to little Jim Hutton (who was unable even for a party like this to compass both tie and waistcoat or make his hair lie flat), and even at this distance they were quarrelling, she could see. For Professor Brierly was a very queer fish. With all those degrees, honours, lectureships between him and the scribblers, he suspected instantly an atmosphere not favourable to his queer compound; his prodigious learning and timidity; his wintry charm without cordiality; his innocence blent with snobbery; he quivered if made conscious, by a lady's unkempt hair, a youth's boots, of an underworld, very creditable doubtless, of rebels, of ardent young people; of would-be geniuses, and intimated with a little toss of the head, with a sniff—Humph!—the value of moderation; of some slight training in the classics in order to appreciate Milton. Professor Brierly (Clarissa could see) wasn't hitting it off with little Jim Hutton (who wore red socks, his black being at the laundry) about Milton. She interrupted.

She said she loved Bach. So did Hutton. That was the bond between them, and Hutton (a very bad poet) always felt that Mrs Dalloway was far the best of the great ladies who took an interest in art. It was odd how strict she was. About music she was purely impersonal. She was rather a prig. But how charming to look at! She made her house so nice, if it weren't for her Professors. Clarissa had half a mind to snatch him off and set him down at the piano in the back room. For he played divinely.

'But the noise!' she said. 'The noise!'

'The sign of a successful party.' Nodding urbanely, the Professor stepped delicately off.

'He knows everything in the whole world about Milton,' said Clarissa.

'Does he indeed?' said Hutton, who would imitate the Professor throughout Hampstead:* the Professor on Milton; the Professor on moderation; the Professor stepping delicately off.

But she must speak to that couple, said Clarissa, Lord Gayton and Nancy Blow.

Not that *they* added perceptibly to the noise of the party. They were not talking (perceptibly) as they stood side by side by the yellow curtains. They would soon be off elsewhere, together; and never had very much to say in any circumstances. They looked; that was all. That was enough. They looked so clean, so sound, she with an apricot bloom of powder and paint, but he scrubbed, rinsed, with the eyes of a bird, so that no ball could pass him or stroke surprise him. He struck, he leapt, accurately, on the spot. Ponies' mouths quivered at the end of his reins. He had his honours, ancestral monuments, banners hanging in the church at home. He had his duties; his tenants; a mother and sisters; had been all day at Lord's, and that was what they were talking about—cricket, cousins, the movies—when Mrs Dalloway came up. Lord Gayton liked her most awfully. So did Miss Blow. She had such charming manners.

'It is angelic—it is delicious of you to have come!' she said. She loved Lords; she loved youth, and Nancy, dressed at enormous expense by the greatest artists in Paris, stood there looking as if her body had merely put forth, of its own accord, a green frill.

'I had meant to have dancing,' said Clarissa.

For the young people could not talk. And why should they? Shout, embrace, swing, be up at dawn; carry sugar to ponies; kiss and caress the snouts of adorable chows; and then, all tingling and streaming, plunge and swim. But the enormous resources of the English language, the power it bestows, after all, of communicating feelings (at their age, she and Peter would have been arguing all the evening), was not for them. They would solidify young. They would be good beyond measure to the people on the estate, but alone, perhaps, rather dull.

'What a pity!' she said. 'I had hoped to have dancing.'

It was so extraordinarily nice of them to have come! But talk of dancing! The rooms were packed.

There was old Aunt Helena in her shawl. Alas, she must leave them—Lord Gayton and Nancy Blow. There was old Miss Parry, her aunt.

For Miss Helena Parry was not dead: Miss Parry was alive. She was past eighty. She ascended staircases slowly with a stick. She was placed in a chair (Richard had seen to it). People who had known Burma in the 'seventies were always led up to her. Where had Peter got to? They used to be such friends. For at the mention of India, or even Ceylon, her eyes (only one was glass) slowly deepened, became blue, beheld, not human beings—she had no tender memories, no proud illusions about Viceroys, Generals, Mutinies—it was orchids she saw, and mountain passes, and herself carried on the backs of coolies in the 'sixties over solitary peaks; or descending to uproot orchids (startling blossoms, never beheld before) which she painted in water-colour; an indomitable Englishwoman, fretful if disturbed by the war, say, which dropped a bomb at her very door, from her deep meditation over orchids and her own figure journeying in the 'sixties in India— but here was Peter.

'Come and talk to Aunt Helena about Burma,' said Clarissa.

And yet he had not had a word with her all the evening!

'We will talk later,' said Clarissa, leading him up to Aunt Helena, in her white shawl, with her stick.

'Peter Walsh,' said Clarissa.

That meant nothing.

Clarissa had asked her. It was tiring; it was noisy; but Clarissa had asked her. So she had come. It was a pity that they lived in London—Richard and Clarissa. If only for Clarissa's health it would have been better to live in the country. But Clarissa had always been fond of society.

'He has been in Burma,' said Clarissa.

Ah! She could not resist recalling what Charles Darwin had said about her little book on the orchids of Burma.

(Clarissa must speak to Lady Bruton.)

No doubt it was forgotten now, her book on the orchids of Burma, but it went into three editions before 1870, she told Peter. She remembered him now. He had been at Bourton (and he had left her, Peter Walsh remembered, without a word in the drawing-room that night when Clarissa had asked him to come boating).

'Richard so much enjoyed his lunch party,' said Clarissa to Lady Bruton.

'Richard was the greatest possible help,' Lady Bruton replied. 'He helped me to write a letter. And how are you?'

'Oh, perfectly well!' said Clarissa. (Lady Bruton detested illness in the wives of politicians.)

'And there's Peter Walsh!' said Lady Bruton (for she could never think of anything to say to Clarissa; though she liked her. She had lots of fine qualities; but they had nothing in common— she and Clarissa. It might have been better if Richard had married a woman with less charm, who would have helped him more in his work. He had lost his chance of the Cabinet). 'There's Peter Walsh!' she said, shaking hands with that agreeable sinner, that very able fellow who should have made a name for himself but hadn't (always in difficulties with women), and, of course, old Miss Parry. Wonderful old lady!

Lady Bruton stood by Miss Parry's chair, a spectral grenadier, draped in black, inviting Peter Walsh to lunch; cordial; but without small talk, remembering nothing whatever about the flora or fauna of India. She had been there, of course; had stayed with three Viceroys; thought some of the Indian civilians uncommonly fine fellows; but what a tragedy it was—the state of India! The Prime Minister had just been telling her (old Miss Parry, huddled up in her shawl, did not care what the Prime Minister had just been telling her), and Lady Bruton would like to have Peter Walsh's opinion, he being fresh from the centre, and she would get Sir Sampson to meet him, for really it prevented her from sleeping at night, the folly of it, the wickedness she might say, being a soldier's daughter. She was an old woman now, not good for much. But her house, her servants, her good friend Milly Brush—did he remember her?—were all there only asking to be used if—if they could be of help, in short. For she never spoke of England, but this isle of men, this dear, dear land,* was in her blood (without reading Shakespeare), and if ever a woman could have worn the helmet and shot the arrow, could have led troops to attack, ruled with indomitable justice barbarian hordes and lain under a shield noseless in a church, or made a green grass mound on some primeval hillside, that woman was Millicent Bruton. Debarred by her sex, and some truancy, too, of the logical faculty (she found it impossible to write a letter to *The Times*), she had the thought of Empire always at hand, and had acquired from her association with that armoured goddess her ramrod bearing, her robustness of demeanour, so that one could not figure her even in death parted from the earth or roaming territories over which, in some spiritual shape, the Union Jack had ceased to fly. To be not English even among the dead—no, no! Impossible!

But was it Lady Bruton? (whom she used to know). Was it Peter Walsh grown grey? Lady Rosseter asked herself (who had been Sally Seton). It was old Miss Parry certainly—the old aunt who used to be so cross when she stayed at Bourton. Never should she forget running along the passage naked, and being sent for by Miss Parry! And Clarissa! oh Clarissa! Sally caught her by the arm.

Clarissa stopped beside them.

'But I can't stay,' she said. 'I shall come later. Wait,' she said, looking at Peter and Sally. They must wait, she meant, until all these people had gone.

'I shall come back,' she said, looking at her old friends, Sally and Peter, who were shaking hands, and Sally, remembering the past no doubt, was laughing.

But her voice was wrung of its old ravishing richness; her eyes not aglow as they used to be, when she smoked cigars, when she ran down the passage to fetch her sponge bag without a stitch of clothing on her, and Ellen Atkins asked, What if the gentlemen had met her? But everybody forgave her. She stole a chicken from the larder because she was hungry in the night; she smoked cigars in her bedroom; she left a priceless book in the punt. But everybody adored her (except perhaps Papa). It was her warmth; her vitality—she would paint, she would write. Old women in the village never to this day forgot to ask after 'your friend in the red cloak who seemed so bright'. She accused Hugh Whitbread, of all people (and there he was, her old friend Hugh, talking to the Portuguese Ambassador), of kissing her in the smoking-room to punish her for saying that women should have votes. Vulgar men did, she said. And Clarissa remembered having to persuade her not to denounce him at family prayers—which she was capable of doing with her daring, her recklessness, her melodramatic love of being the centre of everything and creating scenes, and it was bound, Clarissa used to think, to end in some awful tragedy; her death; her martyrdom; instead of which she had married, quite unexpectedly, a bald man with a large buttonhole who owned, it was said, cotton mills at Manchester. And she had five boys!

She and Peter had settled down together. They were talking; it seemed so familiar—that they should be talking. They would discuss the past. With the two of them (more even than with Richard) she shared her past; the garden; the trees; old Joseph Breitkopf singing Brahms without any voice; the drawing-room wallpaper; the smell of the mats. A part of this Sally must always be; Peter must always be. But she must leave them. There were the Bradshaws, whom she disliked.

She must go up to Lady Bradshaw (in grey and silver, balancing like a sea-lion at the edge of its tank, barking for invitations, Duchesses, the typical successful man's wife), she must go up to Lady Bradshaw and say . . .

But Lady Bradshaw anticipated her.

'We are shockingly late, dear Mrs Dalloway; we hardly dared to come in,' she said.

And Sir William, who looked very distinguished, with his grey hair and blue eyes, said yes: they had not been able to resist the temptation. He was talking to Richard about that Bill probably, which they wanted to get through the Commons. Why did the sight of him, talking to Richard, curl her up? He looked what he was, a great doctor. A man absolutely at the head of his profession, very powerful, rather worn. For think what cases came before him—people in the uttermost depths of misery; people on the verge of insanity; husbands and wives. He had to decide questions of appalling difficulty. Yet—what she felt was, one wouldn't like Sir William to see one unhappy. No; not that man.

'How is your son at Eton?' she asked Lady Bradshaw.

He had just missed his eleven,* said Lady Bradshaw, because of the mumps. His father minded even more than he did, she thought, 'being', she said, 'nothing but a great boy himself.'

Clarissa looked at Sir William, talking to Richard. He did not look like a boy—not in the least like a boy.

She had once gone with someone to ask his advice. He had been perfectly right; extremely sensible. But Heavens—what a relief to get out to the street again! There was some poor wretch sobbing, she remembered, in the waiting-room. But she did not know what it was about Sir William; what exactly she disliked. Only Richard agreed with her, 'didn't like his taste, didn't like his smell'. But he was extraordinarily able. They were talking about this Bill. Some case Sir William was mentioning, lowering his voice. It had its bearing upon what he was saying about the deferred effects of shell-shock. There must be some provision in the Bill.

Sinking her voice, drawing Mrs Dalloway into the shelter of a common femininity, a common pride in the illustrious qualities of husbands and their sad tendency to overwork, Lady Bradshaw (poor goose—one didn't dislike her) murmured how, 'just as we were starting, my husband was called up on the telephone, a very sad case. A young man (that is what Sir William is telling Mr Dalloway) had killed himself. He had been in the army.' Oh! thought Clarissa, in the middle of my party, here's death, she thought.

She went on, into the little room where the Prime Minister had gone with Lady Bruton. Perhaps there was somebody there. But there was nobody. The chairs still kept the impress of the Prime Minister and Lady Bruton, she turned deferentially, he sitting four-square, authoritatively. They had been talking about India. There was nobody. The party's splendour fell to the floor, so strange it was to come in alone in her finery.

What business had the Bradshaws to talk of death at her party? A young man had killed himself. And they talked of it at her party—the Bradshaws talked of death. He had killed himself— but how? Always her body went through it, when she was told, first, suddenly, of an accident; her dress flamed, her body burnt. He had thrown himself from a window. Up had flashed the ground; through him, blundering, bruising, went the rusty spikes. There he lay with a thud, thud, thud in his brain, and then a suffocation of blackness. So she saw it. But why had he done it? And the Bradshaws talked of it at her party!

She had once thrown a shilling into the Serpentine, never any-thing more. But he had flung it away. They went on living (she would have to go back; the rooms were still crowded; people kept on coming). They (all day she had been thinking of Bourton, of Peter, of Sally), they would grow old. A thing there was that mattered; a thing, wreathed about with chatter, defaced, obscured in her own life, let drop every day in corruption, lies, chatter. This he had preserved. Death was defiance. Death was an attempt to communicate, people feeling the impossibility of reaching the centre which, mystically, evaded them; closeness drew apart; rapture faded; one was alone. There was an embrace in death.

But this young man who had killed himself—had he plunged holding his treasure? 'If it were now to die, 'twere now to be most happy,'* she had said to herself once, coming down, in white.

Or there were the poets and thinkers. Suppose he had had that passion, and had gone to Sir William Bradshaw, a great doctor, yet to her obscurely evil, without sex or lust, extremely polite to women, but capable of some indescribable outrage—forcing your soul, that was it—if this young man had gone to him, and Sir William had impressed him, like that, with his power, might he not then have said (indeed she felt it now), Life is made intolerable; they make life intolerable, men like that?

Then (she had felt it only this morning) there was the terror; the overwhelming incapacity, one's parents giving it into one's hands, this life, to be lived to the end, to be walked with serenely; there was in the depths of her heart an awful fear. Even now, quite often if Richard had not been there reading *The Times*, so that she could crouch like a bird and gradually revive, send roaring up that immeasurable delight, rubbing stick to stick, one thing with another, she must have perished. She had escaped. But that young man had killed himself.

Somehow it was her disaster—her disgrace. It was her punishment to see sink and disappear here a man, there a woman, in this profound darkness, and she forced to stand here in her evening dress. She had schemed; she had pilfered. She was never wholly admirable. She had wanted success, Lady Bexborough and the rest of it. And once she had walked on the terrace at Bourton.

Odd, incredible; she had never been so happy. Nothing could be slow enough; nothing last too long. No pleasure could equal, she thought, straightening the chairs, pushing in one book on the shelf, this having done with the triumphs of youth, lost herself in the process of living, to find it, with a shock of delight, as the sun rose, as the day sank. Many a time had she gone, at Bourton when they were all talking, to look at the sky; or seen it between people's shoulders at dinner; seen it in London when she could not sleep. She walked to the window.

It held, foolish as the idea was, something of her own in it, this country sky, this sky above Westminster. She parted the curtains; she looked. Oh, but how surprising!—in the room opposite the old lady stared straight at her! She was going to bed. And the sky.

It will be a solemn sky, she had thought, it will be a dusky sky, turning away its cheek in beauty. But there it was—ashen pale, raced over quickly by tapering vast clouds. It was new to her. The wind must have risen. She was going to bed, in the room oppo- site. It was fascinating to watch her, moving about, that old lady, crossing the room, coming to the window. Could she see her? It was fascinating, with people still laughing and shouting in the drawing-room, to watch that old woman, quite quietly, going to bed alone. She pulled the blind now. The clock began striking. The young man had killed himself; but she did not pity him; with the clock striking the hour, one, two, three, she did not pity him, with all this going on. There! the old lady had put out her light! the whole house was dark now with this going on, she repeated, and the words came to her, Fear no more the heat of the sun. She must go back to them. But what an extraordinary night! She felt somehow very like him—the young man who had killed himself. She felt glad that he had done it; thrown it away while they went on living. The clock was striking. The leaden circles dissolved in the air. But she must go back. She must assemble. She must find Sally and Peter. And she came in from the little room.

'But where is Clarissa?' said Peter. He was sitting on the sofa with Sally. (After all these years he really could not call her 'Lady Rosseter'.) 'Where's the woman gone to?' he asked. 'Where's Clarissa?'

Sally supposed, and so did Peter for the matter of that, that there were people of importance, politicians, whom neither of them knew unless by sight in the picture papers, whom Clarissa had to be nice to, had to talk to. She was with them. Yet there was Richard Dalloway not in the Cabinet. He hadn't been a success, Sally supposed? For herself, she scarcely ever read the papers. She sometimes saw his name mentioned. But then—well, she lived a very solitary life, in the wilds, Clarissa would say, among great merchants, great manufacturers, men, after all, who did things. She had done things too!

'I have five sons!' she told him.

Lord, lord, what a change had come over her! the softness

of motherhood; its egotism too. Last time they met, Peter remembered, had been among the cauliflowers in the moonlight, the leaves 'like rough bronze' she had said, with her literary turn; and she had picked a rose. She had marched him up and down that awful night, after the scene by the fountain; he was to catch the midnight train. Heavens, he had wept!

That was his old trick, opening a pocket-knife, thought Sally, always opening and shutting a knife when he got excited. They had been very, very intimate, she and Peter Walsh, when he was in love with Clarissa, and there was that dreadful, ridiculous scene over Richard Dalloway at lunch. She had called Richard 'Wickham'. Why not call Richard 'Wickham'? Clarissa had flared up! and indeed they had never seen each other since, she and Clarissa, not more than half-a-dozen times perhaps in the last ten years. And Peter Walsh had gone off to India, and she had heard vaguely that he had made an unhappy marriage, and she didn't know whether he had any children, and she couldn't ask him, for he had changed. He was rather shrivelled-looking, but kinder, she felt, and she had a real affection for him, for he was connected with her youth, and she still had a little Emily Brontë* he had given her, and he was to write, surely? In those days he was to write.

'Have you written?' she asked him, spreading her hand, her firm and shapely hand, on her knee in a way he recalled.

'Not a word!' said Peter Walsh, and she laughed.

She was still attractive, still a personage, Sally Seton. But who was this Rosseter? He wore two camellias on his wedding day—that was all Peter knew of him. 'They have myriads of servants, miles of conservatories,' Clarissa wrote; something like that. Sally owned it with a shout of laughter.

'Yes, I have ten thousand a year'—whether before the tax was paid or after, she couldn't remember, for her husband, 'whom you must meet,' she said, 'whom you would like,' she said, did all that for her.

And Sally used to be in rags and tatters. She had pawned her great-grandfather's ring which Marie Antoinette had given him—had he got it right?—to come to Bourton.

Oh yes. Sally remembered; she had it still, a ruby ring which

Marie Antoinette had given her great-grandfather. She never had a penny to her name in those days, and going to Bourton always meant some frightful pinch. But going to Bourton had meant so much to her—had kept her sane, she believed, so unhappy had she been at home. But that was all a thing of the past—all over now, she said. And Mr Parry was dead; and Miss Parry was still alive. Never had he had such a shock in his life! said Peter. He had been quite certain she was dead. And the marriage had been, Sally supposed, a success? And that very handsome, very self-possessed young woman was Elizabeth, over there, by the curtains, in pink.

(She was like a poplar, she was like a river, she was like a hyacinth, Willie Titcomb was thinking. Oh how much nicer to be in the country and do what she liked! She could hear the poor dog howling, Elizabeth was certain.) She was not a bit like Clarissa, Peter Walsh said.

'Oh, Clarissa!' said Sally.

What Sally felt was simply this. She had owed Clarissa an enormous amount. They had been friends, not acquaintances, friends, and she still saw Clarissa all in white going about the house with her hands full of flowers—to this day tobacco plants made her think of Bourton. But—did Peter understand?—she lacked something. Lacked what was it? She had charm; she had extraordinary charm. But to be frank (and she felt that Peter was an old friend, a real friend—did absence matter? did distance matter? She had often wanted to write to him, but torn it up, yet felt he understood, for people understand without things being said, as one realizes growing old, and old she was, had been that afternoon to see her sons at Eton, where they had the mumps), to be quite frank, then, how could Clarissa have done it?—married Richard Dalloway? a sportsman, a man who cared only for dogs. Literally, when he came into the room he smelt of the stables. And then all this? She waved her hand.

Hugh Whitbread it was, strolling past in his white waistcoat, dim, fat, blind, past everything he looked, except self-esteem and comfort.

'He's not going to recognize *us*,' said Sally, and really she hadn't the courage—so that was Hugh! the admirable Hugh!

'And what does he do?' she asked Peter.

He blacked the King's boots or counted bottles at Windsor, Peter told her. Peter kept his sharp tongue still! But Sally must be frank, Peter said. That kiss now, Hugh's.

On the lips, she assured him, in the smoking-room one evening. She went straight to Clarissa in a rage. Hugh didn't do such things! Clarissa said, the admirable Hugh! Hugh's socks were without exception the most beautiful she had ever seen—and now his evening dress. Perfect! And had he children?

'Everybody in the room has six sons at Eton,' Peter told her, except himself. He thank God, had none. No sons, no daughters, no wife. Well, he didn't seem to mind, said Sally. He looked younger, she thought, than any of them.

But it had been a silly thing to do, in many ways, Peter said, to marry like that; 'a perfect goose she was,' he said, but, he said, 'we had a splendid time of it,' but how could that be? Sally wondered; what did he mean? and how odd it was to know him and yet not know a single thing that had happened to him. And did he say it out of pride? Very likely, for after all it must be galling for him (though he was an oddity, a sort of sprite, not at all an ordinary man), it must be lonely at his age to have no home, nowhere to go to. But he must stay with them for weeks and weeks. Of course he would; he would love to stay with them, and that was how it came out. All these years the Dalloways had never been once. Time after time they had asked them. Clarissa (for it was Clarissa of course) would not come. For, said Sally, Clarissa was at heart a snob—one had to admit it, a snob. And it was that that was between them, she was convinced. Clarissa thought she had married beneath her, her husband being—she was proud of it—a miner's son. Every penny they had he had earned. As a little boy (her voice trembled) he had carried great sacks.

(And so she would go on, Peter felt, hour after hour; the miner's son; people thought she had married beneath her; her five sons; and what was the other thing—plants, hydrangeas, syringas, very very rare hibiscus lilies that never grow north of the Suez Canal,* but she, with one gardener in a suburb near Manchester, had beds of them, positively beds! Now all that Clarissa had escaped, unmaternal as she was.)

A snob was she? Yes, in many ways. Where was she, all this time? It was getting late.

'Yes,' said Sally, 'when I heard Clarissa was giving a party, I felt I couldn't *not* come—must see her again (and I'm staying in Victoria Street, practically next door). So I just came without an invitation. But,' she whispered, 'tell me, do. Who is this?'

It was Mrs Hilbery, looking for the door. For how late it was getting! And, she murmured, as the night grew later, as people went, one found old friends; quiet nooks and corners; and the loveliest views. Did they know, she asked, that they were surrounded by an enchanted garden? Lights and trees and wonderful gleaming lakes and the sky. Just a few fairy lamps, Clarissa Dalloway had said, in the back garden! But she was a magician! It was a park . . . And she didn't know their names, but friends she knew they were, friends without names, songs without words, always the best. But there were so many doors, such unexpected places, she could not find her way.

'Old Mrs Hilbery,' said Peter; but who was that? that lady standing by the curtain all the evening, without speaking? He knew her face; connected her with Bourton. Surely she used to cut up underclothes at the large table in the window? Davidson, was that her name?

'Oh, that is Ellie Henderson,' said Sally. Clarissa was really very hard on her. She was a cousin, very poor. Clarissa *was* hard on people.

She was rather, said Peter. Yet, said Sally, in her emotional way, with a rush of that enthusiasm which Peter used to love her for, yet dreaded a little now, so effusive she might become—how generous to her friends Clarissa was! and what a rare quality one found it, and how sometimes at night or on Christmas Day, when she counted up her blessings, she put that friendship first. They were young; that was it. Clarissa was pure-hearted; that was it. Peter would think her sentimental. So she was. For she had come to feel that it was the only thing worth saying—what one felt. Cleverness was silly. One must say simply what one felt.

'But I do not know', said Peter Walsh, 'what I feel.'

Poor Peter, thought Sally. Why did not Clarissa come and talk to them? That was what he was longing for. She knew it. All the time he was thinking only of Clarissa, and was fidgeting with his knife.

He had not found life simple, Peter said. His relations with Clarissa had not been simple. It had spoilt his life, he said. (They had been so intimate—he and Sally Seton, it was absurd not to say it.) One could not be in love twice, he said. And what could she say? Still, it is better to have loved (but he would think her sentimental—he used to be so sharp). He must come and stay with them in Manchester. That is all very true, he said. All very true. He would love to come and stay with them, directly he had done what he had to do in London.

And Clarissa had cared for him more than she had ever cared for Richard, Sally was positive of that.

'No, no, no!' said Peter (Sally should not have said that—she went too far). That good fellow—there he was at the end of the room, holding forth, the same as ever, dear old Richard. Who was he talking to? Sally asked, that very distinguished-looking man? Living in the wilds as she did, she had an insatiable curiosity to know who people were. But Peter did not know. He did not like his looks, he said, probably a Cabinet Minister. Of them all, Richard seemed to him the best, he said—the most disinterested.

'But what has he done?' Sally asked. Public work, she supposed. And were they happy together? Sally asked (she herself was extremely happy); for, she admitted, she knew nothing about them, only jumped to conclusions, as one does, for what can one know even of the people one lives with every day? she asked. Are we not all prisoners? She had read a wonderful play about a man who scratched on the wall of his cell, and she had felt that was true of life—one scratched on the wall. Despairing of human relationships (people were so difficult), she often went into her garden and got from her flowers a peace which men and women never gave her. But no; he did not like cabbages; he preferred human beings, Peter said. Indeed, the young are beautiful, Sally said, watching Elizabeth cross the room. How unlike Clarissa at her age! Could he make anything of her? She would not open her lips. Not much, not yet, Peter admitted. She was like a lily, Sally said, a lily by the side of a pool. But Peter did not agree that we know nothing. We know everything, he said; at least he did.

But these two, Sally whispered, these two coming now (and really she must go, if Clarissa did not come soon), this distinguished-looking man and his rather common-looking wife who had been talking to Richard—what could one know about people like that?

'That they're damnable humbugs,' said Peter, looking at them casually. He made Sally laugh.

But Sir William Bradshaw stopped at the door to look at a picture. He looked in the corner for the engraver's name. His wife looked too. Sir William Bradshaw was so interested in art.

When one was young, said Peter, one was too much excited to know people. Now that one was old, fifty-two to be precise* (Sally was fifty-five, in body, she said, but her heart was like a girl's of twenty); now that one was mature then, said Peter, one could watch, one could understand, and one did not lose the power of feeling, he said. No, that is true, said Sally. She felt more deeply, more passionately, every year. It increased, he said, alas, perhaps, but one should be glad of it—it went on increasing in his experience. There was someone in India. He would like to tell Sally about her. He would like Sally to know her. She was married, he said. She had two small children. They must all come to Manchester, said Sally—he must promise before they left.

'There's Elizabeth,' he said, 'she feels not half what we feel, not yet.' 'But,' said Sally, watching Elizabeth go to her father, 'one can see they are devoted to each other.' She could feel it by the way Elizabeth went to her father.

For her father had been looking at her, as he stood talking to the Bradshaws, and he had thought to himself who is that lovely girl? And suddenly he realized that it was his Elizabeth, and he had not recognized her, she looked so lovely in her pink frock! Elizabeth had felt him looking at her as she talked to Willie Titcomb. So she went to him and they stood together, now that the party was almost over, looking at the people going, and the rooms getting emptier and emptier, with things scattered on the floor. Even Ellie Henderson was going, nearly last of all, though no one had spoken to her, but she had wanted to see everything, to tell Edith. And Richard and Elizabeth were rather glad it was over, but Richard was proud of his daughter. And he had not meant to tell her, but he could not help telling her. He had looked at her, he said, and he had wondered, who is that lovely girl? and it was his daughter! That did make her happy. But her poor dog was howling.

'Richard has improved. You are right,' said Sally. 'I shall go and talk to him. I shall say good-night. What does the brain matter,' said Lady Rosseter, getting up, 'compared with the heart?'

'I will come,' said Peter, but he sat on for a moment. What is this terror? what is this ecstasy? he thought to himself. What is it that fills me with extraordinary excitement?

It is Clarissa, he said.

For there she was.

EXPLANATORY NOTES

In the notes that follow, all quotations followed by *LE* and a page reference are from Ben Weinreb and Christopher Hibbert, (eds.), *The London Encyclopaedia* (London and Basingstoke: Macmillan, 1993), an indispensable and absorbing companion for anyone tasked with elucidating allusions and references to the city's boroughs, buildings, customs, memorials, statues and thoroughfares. Information or quotations followed by the abbreviation *PO* and a page reference are taken from an equally invaluable work, *The Post Office London Directory with County Suburbs for 1923* (London: Kelly's Directories Ltd, 1923).

Mrs Dalloway contains many references to the topography of London and not all of them require expansion. In this edition, such references have only been glossed where it is thought that the location or character of a district or street, etc., has some kind of thematic or symbolic significance, no matter how slight. Reference should also be made to the map on pp. lx–lxi of this edition.

3 *Rumpelmayer's*: a firm of 'refreshment contractors' (*PO*, p. 1928), Rumpelmayer and Co. were based at 72–3 St James's Street (see notes to p. 15), Westminster (see notes below).

    Bourton: an imaginary country house, the family home of Clarissa Dalloway, née Parry, enjoying an elevated view of the River Severn (see note to p. 130). It is likely, therefore, that Woolf envisages Bourton as lying somewhere among the Cotswold Hills in Gloucestershire, not far from Gloucester itself and not too distant from Stroud, the home town of Septimus (see notes to p. 72).

    Durtnall's: a firm of 'removal and road transport contractors and furniture warehousemen, railway carriers and general cartage agents' (*PO*, p. 1558), Durtnall and Co. were based at 4 Bartholomew Close in the City of London.

    Westminster: the principal borough of London, the City of Westminster on the north bank of the Thames contains within it all the main Government offices, the two Houses of Parliament (collectively known as the Palace of Westminster), Westminster Abbey (see notes to p. 113), and both of the London Royal palaces (Buckingham (see notes to p. 4) and St James's (see notes to p. 16)), etc.

4 *influenza*: see Introduction, p. xvii, n. 7.

    Big Ben: cast in 1858, weighing just over thirteen and a half tons and operational since 1859, officially 'Big Ben' applies only to the bell in the clock tower of the Palace of Westminster. But over the years Big Ben has 'been extended to include the bell, clock and St Stephen's Tower of the Houses of Parliament' (*LE*, p. 65).

Victoria Street: largely built between the 1850s and the 1880s, it 'is now remarkable mainly for its modern blocks' (*LE* p. 942).

the King and Queen were at the Palace: in 1923, George V (1865–1936) was on the throne, having ascended it in 1910. In 1893 he had married Princess Mary of Teck (1867–1953). Buckingham Palace has been the London residence of the sovereign since Victoria became Queen in 1837.

Lord's, Ascot, Ranelagh: in 1787 a Yorkshireman called Thomas Lord formed the Marylebone Cricket Club. It has been based at its present location in the St John's Wood area of north London since 1816. The Middlesex County Cricket Club made Lord's its home ground in 1877 and it is now the national headquarters of the game. The first ever Test (international) Match was played on the Lord's ground in 1884, when England beat Australia. Clarissa, however, is almost certainly thinking not of an international cricket match but of the annual Eton *v.* Harrow match, then more a fixture of the London social 'season' than it is today, played at Lord's each summer since 1805 between two of England's most prestigious public schools, and played in 1923 on Friday and Saturday, 13–14 July. Previous editions have followed Woolf's 'Lords', which was clearly an error on her part. 'Lords' has also been changed to 'Lord's' on pp. 14 and 150. A more important event in the social calendar is Royal Ascot. A racecourse constructed on the orders of Queen Anne in 1711, near the village of Ascot in the county of Berkshire, by tradition Royal Ascot is opened each June when the sovereign drives in an open carriage round the course from nearby Windsor Castle. By 'Ranelagh', Clarissa has in mind either the Ranelagh Club at Barn Elms Park in south-west London, which from 1884 to 1939 provided facilities for polo, tennis, golf, and other sports, or the Hurlingham Club, situated in Ranelagh Gardens in the south-west London district of Fulham: compare 'Lord's, Ascot, Hurlingham' on p. 14 of the novel. Polo was played at Hurlingham from 1874 to 1946, and it still flourishes as a sports and social club today. Woolf enjoyed watching a polo match at the Hurlingham Club on 24 May 1920; see *The Diary of Virginia Woolf*, ed. Anne Olivier Bell and Andrew McNeillie, ii. *1920–1924* (London: Hogarth Press, 1978), 41–2.

5 *the time of the Georges*: that is, any time from the accession of George I in 1714 to the death of George IV in 1830. Throughout this period a Hanoverian king was on the throne of Great Britain and Ireland: George I (1714–27); George II (1727–60); George III (1760–1820); George IV (1820–1830). In this context, however, the phrase most likely connotes 'at some point in the eighteenth century'.

the Park: the oldest of London's Royal Parks, St James's Park covers about 90 acres in central London near Buckingham Palace and the Palace of Westminster.

6 *Bath*: a spa town of architectural distinction on the River Avon in the county of Somerset, south-west England. It became fashionable in

the eighteenth century when many of its finest buildings were erected, including the Royal Crescent and the Assembly Rooms.

6 *Pimlico*: is the area which lies adjacent to Westminster between the Chelsea Bridge Road, Ebury Street, and Vauxhall Bridge Road. In 1923 it was more socially mixed than it is today.

Fleet to the Admiralty: built in 1722–6 by Thomas Ripley, the Admiralty building is in Whitehall (see notes to p. 43). In 1909 it had a 200-ft.-high mast placed on its roof as part of a wireless telegraphy station installed by the Marconi Company. By means of this, the Fleet communicated with the Admiralty and vice versa, enabling centralized Fleet control. See W. J. Baker, *A History of the Marconi Company* (London: Methuen, 1970), p. 128.

Piccadilly: 'Extending from Piccadilly Circus to Hyde Park Corner, this is one of the two ancient highways leading westward out of London, the other being Oxford Street' (*LE*, p. 613).

Wagner, Pope's poetry: the masterwork of the great German Romantic composer Richard Wilhelm Wagner (1813–83), *The Ring of the Nibelung*, was given its first performance in 1876. Alexander Pope, author of *The Rape of the Lock* (1712) and many other neoclassical poems, lived from 1688 to 1744.

7 *those Indian women*: that is, British women in India.

Devonshire House, Bath House: built in 1734–7 for William Cavendish, 3rd Duke of Devonshire, Devonshire House, Piccadilly, was sold by the 9th Duke in 1918, and demolished in 1924. It had been the scene of many lavish parties. Before it was demolished in 1960, Bath House stood at 82 Piccadilly, at the west corner of Bolton Street. Originally built by the Earl of Bath in the eighteenth century, it was rebuilt in 1821 by Alexander Baring, later Lord Ashburton. In 1923 it was occupied by Lord and Lady Ludlow (*PO*, p. 580).

the house with the china cockatoo: now demolished, this was No. 1 Stratton Street, Mayfair (see note to p. 95), home of Angela Georgina Burdett-Coutts, Baroness Burdett-Coutts (1814–1906), an indefatigable philanthropist, friend of Charles Dickens, the Duke of Wellington, and a host of other Victorian notables, the richest woman in England during the nineteenth century, including Queen Victoria, and second only to her in terms of fame. Raised to the peerage in 1871, the Baroness had annexed 80 Piccadilly (bought by her grandfather in 1802, and the house in which she was born) in 1849, thus creating a large mansion on the corner of Stratton Street and Piccadilly. It was here that a white china cockatoo 'hung "on a level with the top of a passing omnibus" on a circular perch in the big bay window looking on to Piccadilly. Like the Royal Standard at Buckingham Palace, the bird's purpose was to indicate that its owner was in residence'. Diana Orton, *Made of Gold: A Biography of Angela Burdett-Coutts* (London: Hamish Hamilton, 1980), 2.

8 *throwing a shilling into the Serpentine*: the lake in Hyde Park, formed in 1730 by the damming of the River Westbourne. Clarissa also recalls doing this on p. 156.

Bond Street: a premier shopping street extending from Oxford Street to Piccadilly through London's exclusive Mayfair district.

Hatchard's: a well-known bookshop at 187 Piccadilly, opened by John Hatchard in 1801, having moved from 173 Piccadilly, where Hatchard opened his first shop in 1797. Previous editions have followed Woolf's 'Hatchards'', but the plural possessive has no authority and was plainly an error on her part.

Fear no more the heat o' the sun . . . rages: the first two lines of the 'Song' sung by Arviragus and Guiderius in Shakespeare's *Cymbeline*, IV. ii. 258–9. See also pp. 25, 34 and 158, where Clarissa repeats these words, and p. 118 where they come into the mind of Septimus. Printed *litteratim* from the First Folio of 1623, the limited edition Players' Shakespeare text of *Cymbeline*, edited and introduced by Harley Granville Barker, illustrated by Albert Rutherston and published in August 1923, was noticed in the *Times Literary Supplement* on 13 September 1923, p. 607 and is just the kind of thing which Hatchard's would have put on display in its front window.

Jorrocks's Jaunts and Jollities . . . Nigeria: Mr Jorrocks, a sporting Cockney grocer, was one of the humorous creations of Robert Smith Surtees (1805–64). Comic sketches involving Mr Jorrocks had first appeared in the *New Sporting Magazine* in 1831 and were subsequently collected as *Jorrocks's Jaunts and Jollities* (1838). Previous editions of *Mrs Dalloway* have followed the first edition's 'Jorrocks' *Jaunts and Jollities*', but this is clearly an error. Surtees's other great comic character was Mr Soapy Sponge, who appears in *Mr Sponge's Sporting Tour* (1853). The two volumes of *The Autobiography of Margot Asquith* were published in 1920 and 1922, but *Big Game Shooting in Nigeria* is an invented example of a popular genre.

9 *salmon on an iceblock*: seen, almost certainly, in the window of Gilsons Ltd., a renowned fishmonger situated at 121 New Bond Street (*PO*, p. 1617).

a glove shop: possibly A. Bide Ltd., Glovers, of 158A New Bond Street (*PO*, p. 1423)

10 *Russians . . . the Austrians*: in the early 1920s there was much hardship and suffering in the Soviet Union (formed in 1920) following the Bolshevik Revolution of October 1917 and the Russian Civil War which ensued (1918–22). After the collapse of Austria-Hungary at the end of the First World War, those German-speaking lands of the old Habsburg Empire not annexed by other successor states constituted themselves on 12 November 1918 as 'German Austria', renamed Austria

on the insistence of the victor powers. In the 1920s Austria endured the same social and economic dislocations which afflicted Germany.

11 *Mulberry's the florists*: an imaginary shop, most likely based on G. Adam and Co., florists and fruiterers to HM the King and HRH the Prince of Wales, situated at 42 New Bond Street (*PO*, p. 1368).

12 *Oxford Street*: runs east–west from St Giles Circus to Marble Arch in London's West End. It is now a busy street of shops and department stores, and Bond Street runs off it to the south.

Atkinson's scent shop: that is J. and E. Atkinson Ltd., purveyors of perfumery and toilet soap, whose retail business was situated at 24 Old Bond Street (*PO*, p. 1390)

Prince of Wales's: in 1923, the Prince of Wales was Prince Edward (1894–1972), who came to throne in 1936 as Edward VIII on the death of his father and abdicated on 11 December of that year because of constitutional objections to his intention to marry the twice-divorced American Mrs Wallis Simpson (1896–1986). They were married in 1937, and for the remainder of their lives were known as the Duke and Duchess of Windsor.

the Prime Minister's?: in June 1923, the Prime Minister was Stanley Baldwin (1867–1947).

13 *the Embankment*: built in 1864–70 by Sir Joseph Bazalgette, the Victoria Embankment runs between Westminster Bridge and Blackfriar's Bridge over 37 acres of reclaimed land on the north bank of the Thames. At night, it was, and still is, a place where London's dispossessed congregate.

15 *breasts stiff with oak leaves*: commemorating Charles II's concealment in 'The Royal Oak' at Boscobel in Shropshire after his defeat at the Battle of Worcester (1651), the birthday of Charles II (29 May), and the day he entered London at the Restoration (1660), was in 1664 commanded by Act of Parliament 'to be observed as a day of thanksgiving. A special service (expunged in 1859) was inserted in the Book of Common Prayer and people wore sprigs of oak with gilded apple-leaves on that day' (*Brewer's Dictionary of Phrase and Fable*).

House of Windsor: Windsor has been the unequivocally English-sounding name of Britain's Royal Family since 1917, when it was changed from the inappropriately German-sounding Saxe-Coburg-Gotha as an act of identification with his British subjects by George V.

St James's Street: celebrated for its gentlemen's clubs and fine shops since the early eighteenth century, it runs from Piccadilly down to St James's Palace (see notes to p. 16).

16 *White's*: the oldest and grandest of London's gentlemen's clubs, White's is situated at 37–8 St James's Street. It was rebuilt in its present form in 1787–8 and its celebrated bow window was created in the middle of its façade in 1811.

the Tatler: subtitled *An Illustrated Journal of Society and the Stage*, the *Tatler* was first published on 3 July 1901 and still exists today. The original *Tatler* was a periodical founded by Richard Steele (1672–1729) in 1709. Part of its purpose was to provide an entertaining account of the gaming, gallantry, and general well-bred brouhaha which took place nightly at White's Chocolate House (as the club was then called: see preceding note), though gradually it adopted a more sober position.

the walls of a whispering gallery: 'Immediately below the 24 windows of the dome [of St Paul's: see notes to p. 24 on St Paul's Cathedral] is the Whispering Gallery . . . It is 100 ft above the floor and is famous for its acoustics. If you whisper against the wall you can be heard clearly on the opposite side the Gallery 107 ft away' (*LE*, p. 780).

St James's . . . Queen Alexandra's: situated at the southern end of St James's Street, St James's Palace was built by Henry VIII (1491–1547; reigned 1509–47) and for over 300 years it was one of the principal residences of the Kings and Queens of England. Queen Alexandra (1844–1925) was the widow of King Edward VII (who died in 1910).

Victoria, billowing on her mound: unveiled by George V in 1911, the Queen Victoria Memorial is 82 ft. high and stands at the end of the Mall (see notes to p. 17) opposite the main entrance to Buckingham Palace. It was created by Sir Thomas Brock and is capped by a 13-ft.-high seated figure of Queen Victoria (who reigned from 1837 to 1901) surrounded by what the writer Osbert Sitwell called '"tons of allegorical females in white wedding cake marble, with whole litters of their cretinous children"' (*LE*, p. 649). See also p. 99, where Richard Dalloway looks at 'the memorial to Queen Victoria . . . its white mound, its billowing motherliness'.

the Queen's old doll's house: 'In 1920, the suggestion was made that it would be very interesting to present to Her Majesty [Queen Mary] as complete and exquisite a model twentieth-century residence as art and craft and devotion could contrive,' E.V. Lucas wrote in his preface to E. V. Lucas, *The Book of the Queen's Dolls' House*, ii (London: Methuen, 1924), p. v. It was designed on a scale of one inch to one foot by the distinguished architect Sir Edwin Lutyens (1869–1944) and presented to Queen Mary in 1923. It included everything, from a scale fountain pen to 'two hundred books written in their author's own hands, and a collection of over seven hundred water-colours by living artists'. See the companion volume to Lucas's, edited by A. C. Benson and Sir Lawrence Weaver, in which every conceivable detail about the dolls' house is documented. Given that Lutyens's dolls' house did not replace a previous one and the Queen possessed more than one doll, 'old' and 'doll's' actually make little sense.

Princess Mary married to an Englishman: another topical allusion. The only daughter of George V and Queen Mary, Princess Mary (1897–1965) married Viscount Lascelles (6th Earl of Harewood, 1929) in 1922.

16 *old King Edward*: that is, Edward VII, who reigned 1901–10.

17 *the Mall*: created around 1660 as part of the post-Restoration improvements to St James's Park, it was transformed in 1903–4 into a processional route, 115 ft. wide, as part of the national memorial to Queen Victoria. It links the Queen Victoria Memorial to Admiralty Arch (which leads on to Trafalgar Square).

Mr Bowley . . . the Albany: it seems that this character, who has previously appeared in *Jacob's Room*, is also a guest at Clarissa's party (p. 144). Built in 1770–4, the Albany is a mansion on the north side of Piccadilly which was converted into chambers for bachelors in 1802. A desirable address, residents (though by no means all bachelors) have included the Prime Ministers Lord Palmerston (1784–1865), William Ewart Gladstone (1809–98), and Edward Heath (b. 1916), and the writers Lord Byron (1788–1824), Aldous Huxley (1894–1963), and Graham Greene (1904–91).

past the bronze heroes: the breeze progresses from the Queen Victoria Memorial (see notes to p. 16) end of the Mall down towards the Admiralty Arch at the other end, past 'Bronze figures by Adrian Jones of two marines, one wounded, in fighting attitudes. A memorial to those who fell in South Africa and China in 1899–1902. Bronze reliefs by Sir Thomas Graham Jackson depict battles in the two campaigns' (*LE*, p. 525).

Glaxo: best known in the 1920s as the proprietary name of a formula milk product, now part of the vast Glaxo–Wellcome pharmaceuticals conglomerate.

18 *the Broad Walk*: the main pedestrian avenue, running north–south, through Regent's Park.

20 *the Indian and his cross*: as Michael Whitworth has remarked, 'Woolf is almost certainly referring to the Readymoney fountain, a drinking fountain at the north end of the Broad Walk in Regent's Park. When the fountain was opened in 1869, a brass tablet explained that it was

> the gift of the Cowasjee Jehangheer Ready-Money, Companion of the Star of India, a wealthy Parsee gentleman of Bombay, for the protection enjoyed by him and his Parsee fellow-countrymen under British rule in India.'

Whitworth goes on to note that the original tablet was replaced in 1931 and he suggests that Woolf's 'reference to a cross must be to the whole structure, which resembles a market-square cross' ('"The Indian and his Cross" in *Mrs Dalloway*', *Virginia Woolf Miscellany*, 49 (Spring 1997), pp. 4–5.

21 *in Greek words*: in 1904, when Woolf suffered a breakdown, she thought 'that the birds were singing Greek choruses' to her as she lay in bed. For an interesting discussion of Woolf's 'Greek-talking birds', see

Hermione Lee, *Virginia Woolf* (London: Chatto and Windus, 1996), 195–7. This passage in the novel also brings to mind the penultimate line of W. J. Cory's celebrated and much anthologized translation of an epigram by the Greek poet Callimachus (*c*.310–240 BC):

> They told me, Heraclitus, they told me you were dead,
> They brought me bitter news to hear and bitter tears to shed.
> I wept as I remembered how often you and I
> Had tired the sun with talking and sent him down the sky
> And now that thou are lying, my dear old Carian guest,
> A handful of grey ashes, long, long ago at rest,
> Still are thy pleasant voices, thy nightingales, awake;
> For death, he hath taken all away, but these he cannot take.

the Zoo: that is, the Zoological Gardens in Regent's Park. The Zoological Society of London was founded in 1826 and the Society's collection of animals in Regent's Park was opened to the public in 1828 'with, amongst other animals, monkeys, bears, emus, kangaroos, llamas, zebras and turtles' (*LE*, p. 1006). Many other species followed, and by the late nineteenth century visiting the Society's gardens—or 'zoo' as they were now universally known—had become immensely popular.

23 *Kentish Town*: a district of north London. 'After the 1860s the middle-class atmosphere vanished as the Midland Railway developed. Huge tracts of land were acquired for railway undertakings, and soon Kentish Town was transformed into a grimy working class district . . . with many houses in multiple occupation . . . ' (*LE*, p. 440).

24 *Margate*: a seaside resort on the north Kent coast then particularly popular with Londoners, its development had begun in the late eighteenth century when Benjamin Beale, a local man, invented the bathing machine.

Greenwich and all the masts: a borough of south-east London on the south bank of the Thames where the Royal Naval College and the Royal Observatory are both located, Greenwich would have had its fair share of masts. But the aeroplane would also pass over the docks of London: West India (1802), London (1805), East India (1805), Surrey (1807), St Katharine's (1828), etc., and the ships moored within them.

St Paul's and the rest: designed by Sir Christopher Wren (1632–1723), begun in 1675 and completed in 1710, the present St Paul's Cathedral is the fourth to occupy its site at the top of Ludgate Hill. The aeroplane is flying over the City of London's many ancient stone churches ('the little island of grey churches') as well as St Paul's.

Mendelian theory: the Moravian monk and botanist Gregor Johann Mendel (1822–84) discovered the fundamental principles governing the inheritance of characters in living things after experimenting with generations of peas. He published his findings in the 1860s, but his work remained unrecognized until 1900.

24 *Ludgate Circus*: constructed in 1864–75, it forms the junction of Ludgate Hill and Fleet Street.

27 *Baron Marbot's Memoirs*: translated into English in 1892 by A. J. Butler, with an abridged version appearing in 1893 and a new edition in 1897, the three volumes of the *Mémoires de général Baron de Marbot* by Jean Baptiste Antoine Marcellin de Marbot, Baron de Marbot, were first published in Paris in 1891. In 1812, Marbot (1782–1854) had been involved in Napoleon's disastrous retreat from Moscow.

the House: that is, the House of Commons. Richard Dalloway is a Conservative Member of Parliament.

Clieveden: an imaginary country house. It is possible that Woolf has in mind Clivedon House on the Thames near Maidenhead in Buckinghamshire, owned for many years by the Astor family and the scene of house parties to which politicians were invariably invited.

Constantinople: the ancient city of Byzantium was renamed Constantinople in 330, when the Emperor Constantine I declared it the capital of the Eastern Roman Empire. It was renamed Istanbul by the Ottoman Turks in 1457, but the city only took this name officially in 1926.

28 *Marie Antoinette*: born in 1755, the daughter of the Emperor Francis II of Austria and Maria Theresa, Marie Antoinette married in 1770 the Dauphin (the eldest son of the King of France) who became king four years later as Louis XVI. An extravagant, frivolous, capricious, and scheming queen consort, she was guillotined in 1793.

William Morris . . . brown paper: educated at Marlborough public school and Oxford University, William Morris (1834–96) was a prolific poet, essayist, and designer. From the late 1870s he turned increasingly towards political activity and in 1883 he joined the Social Democratic Federation. From 1884 onwards he was the leader of the Socialist League and wrote two socialist fantasies, *A Dream of John Ball* (1888) and *News from Nowhere* (1891). In the 1890s, when Sally Seton gives Clarissa a book by Morris, he was at the height of his fame and influence as a socialist and of sufficient notoriety with the older generation to warrant being 'wrapped in brown paper'.

29 *Plato*: the Athenian philosopher Plato (429–347 BC) saw no hope for humanity unless philosophers became rulers or rulers philosophers. His greatest political works are the *Republic* and the *Laws*, both descriptions of ideal states.

Shelley: the work of the Romantic poet Percy Bysshe Shelley (1792–1822), especially *Queen Mab* (1813), *Prometheus Unbound* (1820), and the political essays and pamphlets, was a formative influence on the development of socialism in Great Britain.

30 *'if it were now to die, 'twere now to be most happy'*: from *Othello*, II. i.

187–8. These words are spoken by Othello as he lands at Cyprus and is reunited with Desdemona. See also p. 156, where the quotation is reiterated.

air-ball: a toy balloon.

Brahms: the German composer Johannes Brahms was born in Hamburg in 1833. He died in 1897.

33 *Caterham*: small town in the county of Surrey, south of London.

Ealing: a district of west London.

Hatfield: not the town in Hertfordshire, but the seventeenth-century Hatfield House within it. Built in 1608 for Sir Robert Cecil (1563–1612), 1st Earl of Salisbury. His descendants still live there.

39 *sent down from Oxford*: to be expelled from an Oxford college, either temporarily or permanently, and especially permanently.

Lincoln's Inn: situated off Holborn and founded in the middle of the fourteenth century, it is one of London's four Inns of Court.

40 *Leith Hill*: a beauty spot in Surrey, four miles south-west of Dorking.

41 *a motor-car manufacturer in Victoria Street*: the only Victoria Street entries under 'Motor Car Makers' in the *Post Office London Directory* . . . *for 1923* are Stevens Petrol Electric Vehicles Ltd. at 68 Victoria Street (described in the *Directory* as a firm of 'motor car manufacturers', *PO*, p. 1989) and the Worthmore Motor Co. at 34 Victoria Street (*PO*, p. 2570 for both entries).

42 *St Margaret's*: that is, the bells of St Margaret's, Parliament Square, Westminster. Founded in the twelfth century, 'In 1614 the [House of] Commons made it their parish church . . . Members remain *ex officio* parishioners of St Margaret's' (*LE*, p. 753).

43 *Whitehall*: the London street running from Trafalgar Square to the Houses of Parliament, which is dominated by Government offices (such as the Ministry of Defence and the Treasury) and synonymous with officialdom.

the Duke of Cambridge: sculpted by Adrian Jones and erected in 1907, the equestrian bronze statue of Field-Marshal HRH George, 2nd Duke of Cambridge (1819–1904), Queen Victoria's cousin and the British Army's commander-in-chief from 1856 to 1895, is in Whitehall (see preceding note).

Finsbury Pavement to the empty tomb: Finsbury Pavement now refers to the area which once boasted a fashionable promenade across the marshy district of Moorfields, just outside the City of London, to which the boys are now returning. The 'empty tomb' is the Portland stone Cenotaph (from two Greek words meaning 'empty tomb') in Whitehall, designed by Sir Edwin Lutyens (1869–1944) and erected in 1919–20 as the national memorial to the 'Glorious Dead' of the First World War (and subsequently extended to include all the British and Commonwealth servicemen to have died in the later conflicts of the twentieth century).

An annual service, attended by the monarch and leading politicians, is held at the Cenotaph at 11.00 a.m. on Remembrance Sunday, the Sunday nearest 11 November.

44 *Nelson, Gordon, Havelock*: the 145-ft.-high Nelson Column, erected in 1839–42, stands at the centre of the south side of Trafalgar Square at the top of Whitehall. It commemorates the last great victory of Horatio, Lord Nelson (1758–1805) at the Battle of Trafalgar (1805), during which he was mortally wounded. The 17-ft.-high stone statue of Nelson was raised in 1843 and is by E. H. Baily. On the east side of the Nelson Column there is a bronze statue by William Behnes (1861) of Sir Henry Havelock (1795–1857), a British general who served with distinction in the first Burmese War (1824–6), the first Afghan War (1838–42), and the first Sikh War (1845–6), but who failed to hold Cawnpore or lift the siege of Lucknow during the Indian Mutiny of 1857. He died of dysentery at Lucknow in November 1857. A bronze statue of General Charles George Gordon (1833–85) by Sir Hamo Thorneycroft was erected in Trafalgar Square in 1887, two years after his death during the siege of Khartoum, but it was removed to the Victoria Embankment Gardens in 1953. 'The General is standing holding a Bible and with the cane he habitually carried under one arm' (*LE*, p. 841), not as the statue is described on p. 44 of the novel. The statues of the three military men are 'black' in that from Peter's perspective they are silhouettes and two are made of bronze; ie, 'black' is not a noun.

the Strand: the street which, running east from Trafalgar Square, links the City of Westminster to the City of London. In the early twentieth century 'the Strand was renowned for its restaurants, jolly public-houses, music-halls, and smoking-rooms. Harry Castling's song "Let's all go down the Strand", gave rise to a familiar proposition' (*LE*, p. 853).

45 *Dent's shop in Cockspur Street*: that is, E. Dent and Co. Ltd. the watch- and clockmakers to the Royal Family at No. 28. And not just the Royals: Dent were also the 'makers of the Great Clock of the Houses of Parliament [i.e., Big Ben] & of the primary Standard Timekeeper of the United Kingdom at the Royal Observatory, Greenwich' (*PO*, p. 1542).

47 *an absurd statue with an inscription somewhere or other*: this is almost certainly 'the *Matilda* fountain by Gloucester Gate of [Regent's Park] with the bronze figure of a girl shading her eyes with her hand and standing on a pile of Cornish rocks . . . by Joseph Durham (1878)' (*LE*, p. 664).

56 *Hampton Court*: 'On the banks of the Thames some 15 miles south-west of London, [Hampton Court Palace] contains some of the finest Tudor architecture in Britain, as well as buildings of great splendour by Sir Christopher Wren' (*LE*, p. 370). It was begun by Cardinal Wolsey in 1514 and confiscated by Henry VIII in 1529. Queen Victoria opened it to the

public on certain days of the week, and in 1851 its upkeep was transferred from the Crown to the Government.

59 *Thessaly*: in antiquity, an area of northern Greece noted for its cavalry, its chief cities being Larissa and Pherae.

62 *'those poor girls in Piccadilly'*: Woolf refers to the prostitutes of Piccadilly Circus on a number of occasions in both *The Voyage Out* (1915) and *Jacob's Room* (1922).

64 *Shakespeare's sonnets . . . not one that he approved*: at the sensational first trial of Oscar Wilde (1854–1900) in 1895, Wilde's essay entitled 'The Portrait of Mr W. H.' (first published in 1889, it is an extensive account of Wilde's deep interest in the homoerotic 'Willie Hughes theory of Shakespeare's sonnets') was raised and the nature of the relationship outlined in Shakespeare's sonnets. Wilde was asked by the prosecuting counsel: 'Have you ever adored a young man madly?' and upon being pressed on the matter Wilde answered, 'No. The whole idea was borrowed from Shakespeare, I regret to say—yes, from Shakespeare's sonnets.' Quoted in Richard Ellmann, *Oscar Wilde* (London: Hamish Hamilton, 1987), 422. This is almost certainly why, in the 1890s, Richard Dalloway does not approve of them.

No decent man . . . deceased wife's sister: as Edward Bishop has noted, the background to this is the 1921 Amendment Bill to the Deceased Wife's Sister's Marriage Act of 1907. 'The object of the bill was to remove the anomaly in the existing law which prohibited marriage with a deceased brother's widow while allowing marriage with a deceased wife's sister. A clause was introduced . . . that would have deprived anyone taking advantage of the act from having the marriage solemnized in a church or receiving communion . . . The clause was rejected and the bill passed, 10 June 1921.' 'Writing, Speech, and Silence in *Mrs Dalloway*', *English Studies in Canada*, 12/4 (Dec. 1986), 397–423; quote from p. 420.

65 *Morning Post*: a resolutely Conservative newspaper, first published 1 January 1801 and incorporated with the *Daily Telegraph* 30 September 1937.

66 *Huxley and Tyndall*: the British scientist, humanist, and agnostic Thomas Henry Huxley (1825–95) was popularly known as 'Darwin's Bulldog' due to his being for many years the most prominent and ardent champion of the theory of Evolution. He wrote *Man's Place in Nature* (1863) and many other papers and books. In 1869, he coined the word 'agnostic' to describe his own religious position. The physicist and controversialist John Tyndall (1820–93) was Professor of Natural History at the Royal Institution; later its Superintendent. Like Huxley, he was a great popularizer of science.

67 *Elizabeth was 'out'*: that is, formally launched into upper-class society having been presented at Court.

69 *battered woman*: of a blind 'old beggar woman', whom she saw singing

aloud in a London street, Woolf wrote in her diary on 8 June 1920: 'There was a recklessness about her; much in the spirit of London. Defiant—almost gay, clasping her dog as if for warmth. How many Junes has she sat there, in the heart of London?' *Diary*, ii. 47.

70 *give me your hand . . . what matter they?*: these words were first identified by J. Hillis Miller in 1982 as part of an English version of 'Allerseelen', a song by Richard Strauss (1864–1949) with words by Hermann von Gilm. See '*Mrs Dalloway*: Repetition as the Raising of the Dead', repr. in Morris Beja (ed.), *Critical Essays on Virginia Woolf* (Boston, Mass.: G. K. Hall, 1985), 53–72, esp. 63–4.

71 *Purley*: a town in Surrey, south of Croydon.

72 *Stroud*: a town in Gloucestershire.

Waterloo Road: leading south from the Thames, it was on this road, at Morley College, that Woolf gave voluntary evening classes on various subjects between 1905 and 1907. The College was founded in the 1880s in an effort 'to raise the moral as well as the material standards of the Waterloo Road district. A lease was taken of the Old Vic [theatre] . . . [and] Regular evening classes were started in the theatre dressing rooms in 1885; and in 1889 this educational side of the Old Vic was formally organised as Morley College' (*LE*, p. 543). See also Hermione Lee, *Virginia Woolf*, 222–4. In 1924 Morley College moved to a house on the Westminster Bridge Road where it still exists today.

The History of Civilisation: Septimus has probably been reading Henry Thomas Buckle's two-volume *History of Civilisation in England* (1857–61). There were two copies of this work in Leonard and Virginia Woolf's library. Buckle's *History*, like *Mrs Dalloway*, challenges accepted notions of civilization and social purpose. Furthermore, Buckle, like Septimus, suffered from 'shattered nerves' (to borrow the phrase Woolf's father, Leslie Stephen, used in his *Dictionary of National Biography* entry on Buckle) while preparing his second volume for the press, and he died before his project was completed.

73 *Sibleys and Arrowsmiths*: an imaginary firm.

Ceres: the ancient Roman corn-goddess.

Muswell Hill: a hilly suburb of north London largely created in the period 1897–1914. 'It has a unique Edwardian homogeneity of architectural style—substantial, stone-dressed, brick-built terraces with ornamental plasterwork, served by fine shopping parades' (*LE*, p. 547).

75 *Inferno*: written by the Italian poet Dante Alighieri (1265–1321) as part of his greatest work (and the greatest poem of the medieval world), the *Divine Comedy* (*c*.1307–21) recounts a journey through Hell ('Inferno'), Purgatory, and Paradise.

Soho: a cosmopolitan and bohemian district of central London, nowadays revelling in a tawdry disrepute. From the late seventeenth century until quite recently, it was densely populated with foreign immigrants, many of them French, German, Swiss, or Italian in origin.

Newhaven: a port on the English Channel in East Sussex at the mouth of the River Ouse (a short distance downstream from where Woolf drowned herself in 1941). Septimus and Lucrezia would almost certainly have arrived at Newhaven from the French port of Dieppe.

off the Tottenham Court Road: their lodgings are in Bloomsbury (pp. 77, 126), to the east of the road, traditionally noted for its furniture stores, such as Heal's and Maples, which leads northwards (generally in the direction of Tottenham, a district in north-east London) from the east end of Oxford Street in central London.

Aeschylus: Athenian dramatist (*c.*525–456 BC) who wrote around ninety plays including *Seven Against Thebes* (467 BC) and the *Oresteia* trilogy.

76 *the Tower*: begun in the eleventh century, the Tower of London is a fortress on the north bank of the Thames to the east of the City. For centuries it was a Royal residence and the principal state prison.

the Victoria and Albert Museum: designed by Aston Webb and officially opened by Edward VII in 1909, it occupies a prominent location on the Cromwell Road in the west London district of South Kensington, and is a museum of fine and applied art of all countries, styles, and periods.

the King open Parliament: the State Opening of Parliament, which marks the beginning of the new Parliamentary session each October, is a ceremonial which has changed little since the sixteenth century though reform is in the offing. The public are not admitted to the ceremony in the Palace of Westminster, but Septimus and Lucrezia would have been able to see the King ride by in the Irish State Coach along the Mall or in Whitehall. 'At Westminster the monarch and accompanying members of the Royal Family are greeted by a salute of guns fired by the King's Troop of the Royal Horse Artillery' (*LE*, p. 835) before entering Parliament by the Victoria Tower.

77 *Bedford Square*: a well-known Georgian square in the Bloomsbury district of central north London.

80 *Harley Street*: world famous for its distinguished and expensive practitioners of medicine, it is a short distance south-west of Regent's Park.

Eton: one of the largest and the most famous of the English public schools, Eton College lies just below Windsor Castle in the small town of Eton in Berkshire on the north bank of Thames. The school was founded in 1440 by Henry VI.

82 *not having a sense of proportion*: Woolf herself suffered mental collapses in 1895 (when, like Septimus, she jumped out of a window), 1904, and in 1913–15; and she again attempted to take her own life in 1913. In 1922 she thought she was in for another bout of physical and mental illness and she went to see Harley Street specialists. As one of them bid her

farewell at the end of her consultation he counselled 'Equanimity—equanimity—practise equanimity, Mrs Woolf', a clear model for Bradshaw's 'Proportion' mantra. See *Diary*, ii. 189.

85 *Hyde Park Corner*: the south-east corner of the Park. It is likely that Woolf had in mind Speakers' Corner, the north-east corner of the Park, where, since 1872, 'anyone with a mind so to do may . . . declaim on any subject he chooses, provided he is not obscene or blasphemous, or does not constitute an incitement to a breach of the peace' (*LE*, p. 414).

87 *Messrs Rigby and Lowndes*: an imaginary shop.

88 *Portsmouth*: city and important naval port on the Hampshire coast of southern England, 74 miles south-west of London.

89 *Lovelace or Herrick*: two of the so-called 'Cavalier' poets of the mid-seventeenth century, Richard Lovelace (1618–58) and Robert Herrick (1591–1674) supported Charles I in the civil wars (1642–6; 1648) and wrote poems which are courtly, polished, and lyrical.

91 *Brook Street*: a street in Mayfair extending from Hanover Square to Grosvenor Square. It is apt that such a well-bred and quintessentially eighteenth-century figure as Lady Bruton should live in a street 'described in 1736 as "For the most part nobly built and inhabited by People of Quality"' (*LE*, p. 101).

92 *Canada*: see Introduction, pp. xxiv–xxvii

94 *the Labour Government*: Britain's first Labour Government took office on 22 January 1924, with (James) Ramsay MacDonald (1866–1937) as Prime Minister. His Government was replaced by the Conservative administration of Stanley Baldwin on 4 November 1924.

the news from India!: see Introduction, pp. xxviii–xxix

95 *Mayfair*: 'Now denotes the large area bounded on the north by Oxford Street, on the east by Regent Street, on the south by Piccadilly and on the west by Park Lane . . . Mayfair has always retained its social *cachet*, and even today a good address there is as much sought after as ever' (*LE*, p. 518).

98 *the Green Park*: 'So called because of its verdure of grass and trees, it comprises about 53 acres between Piccadilly and Constitution Hill . . . It was enclosed by Henry VIII and made into a Royal Park by Charles II' (*LE*, pp. 342–3).

99 *Horsa*: Hengist and Horsa are semi-legendary brothers who are said to have led the first Saxons to settle in England. Horsa is reputed to have been slain at the Battle of Aylesford (*c*.AD 455) and he is connected with the English word 'horse', while Hengist is connected to the German word *hengst*, a stallion, so Woolf is probably having some fun at Queen Victoria's and Richard Dalloway's expense as well as indicating the depth of his interest in lineage.

Dean's Yard: a residential area in Westminster, next to Westminster Abbey and Westminster School.

101 *Armenians . . . Albanians*: it was most definitely the (Christian) Armenians, many of whom, in what some historians have identified as the twentieth century's first act of genocide, were massacred by the (Muslim) Turks in 1915. This followed earlier slaughters of Armenians by the Turks in 1894–6. From 1915, the Turks drove out two-thirds of the Armenian population, forcing them to flee to Soviet Armenia, Syria, and Palestine. During this exodus (1915–20), one million Armenians were either killed or died of starvation, prompting a great deal of debate in the British press about how best to protect the Armenians and other ethnic minorities (see p. 103 of the novel). For an interesting discussion of Clarissa's confusion, see Trudi Tate, '*Mrs Dalloway* and the Armenian Question', *Textual Practice*, 8/3 (Winter 1994), 467–86. See also, Akaby Nassibian, *Britain and the Armenian Question, 1915–1923* (London: Croom Helm, 1984). Significantly, the offices of both the British Armenia Committee and the Armenian Refugees (Lord Mayor's) Fund were located round the corner from Clarissa's house at 96 Victoria Street (*PO*, p. 708).

104 *Mrs Hilbery*: a major character in Woolf's second novel, *Night and Day* (1919).

105 *the Friends*: more properly, the Religious Society of Friends, otherwise known as the Quakers. They originated in the 1650s and their headquarters is still located at Friends' House on the Euston Road, London. Quakers refuse military service but are often prominent in the ambulance and medical corps and in charitable work.

Extension lecturing: more properly, university extension lecturing, was in 1923 another name for extramural teaching at the Universities of London and Oxford.

106 *the Stores*: in 1918, the Army and Navy Stores Ltd., which had begun business in 1871 as a co-operative run by a group of army and navy officers to sell provisions at discount to service families, opened its premises in Victoria Street, Westminster, to the general public.

107 *Addison*: a contributor to Steele's *Tatler* between 1709 and 1711 (see notes to p. 16), co-producer with Steele of the *Spectator* (1711–12), and editor of the *Spectator* in 1714, Joseph Addison (1672–1719) was also a neoclassical poet, a dramatist, and a politician.

113 *Westminster Cathedral . . . the Abbey*: a striking, early Christian Byzantine-style brick edifice, Westminster Cathedral was completed in 1903, but its interior is still evolving. It is the centre of the Roman Catholic Church in England and its campanile or bell-tower stands 273 ft. high and is topped by an 11-ft.-high cross. In contrast, Westminster Abbey, begun by Henry III in 1245 in the French style, is one of the great centres of the Anglican Church in England, and is the usual setting for the coronation and burial of British monarchs.

the waxworks: in other words, the wax effigies in Westminster Abbey that were used in the funerals of some of those buried there. See Woolf's 'Waxworks at the Abbey', *Essays* iv. 540–2.

113 *the tomb of the Unknown Warrior*: 'One of the most famous and visited of all tombs [in Westminster Abbey], is that in the nave, of the Unknown Warrior whose body was brought back from France after the 1st World War and buried on 11 November 1920 as a representative of the thousands of dead. The soil for his grave was brought from the battlefields and the marble slab from Belgium' (*LE*, p. 974).

116 *Somerset House*: originally the site of a palace built in 1547–50 for Edward Seymour, Lord Protector Somerset (*c*.1500–52), it was demolished in the late eighteenth century and replaced by the present Somerset House. 'In 1836–1973 the offices of the General Register of Births, Deaths and Marriages were there and the Inland Revenue occupied most of the building' (*LE*, p. 819).

the Temple: there are four Inns of Court, and the Middle Temple and the Inner Temple are two of them (Lincoln's Inn and Gray's Inn are the others). The Temple is the general name for the Inner and Middle Temples. Ownership of the Temple site, which lies north of the Victoria Embankment on the boundary between Westminster and the City of London, was granted to these two Inns in 1609 by James I.

the Church: 'Although the ground plan of the Temple Church is unchanged since its foundation, it is difficult to capture the ancient romance of the building, since the restorers, particularly those of the 19th century, have seen to it that . . . "every ancient surface was repaired away or renewed" . . . In 1608 James I presented the freehold of the church to the lawyers, presenting the southern half to the Inner Temple and the northern half to the Middle Temple on condition that they maintained the church and its service for ever' (*LE*, pp. 881–2).

120 *Prince Consort*: Queen Victoria's husband, Prince Albert (1819–61).

121 *Hull*: more properly Kingston-upon-Hull, is a city and port on the north bank of the Humber estuary in the county of Yorkshire in the north of England, 22 miles from the North Sea. It was once Europe's biggest fishing port.

123 *Surrey was all out*: in what must be the first edition of 'the evening paper' (p. 122), Septimus glances at a headline which indicates that ten of the eleven Surrey county cricket team batsmen have lost their wickets, thus ending their first innings in their match against Yorkshire. In 1923, Yorkshire's game against Surrey took place at Sheffield on Saturday 16, Monday 18, and Tuesday 19 June. Yorkshire won by 25 runs, but Surrey was not 'all out' twice in one day (further on in the novel, after Septimus's death, Peter Walsh reads in what must be the second or final edition of the evening paper that 'Surrey was all out once more', p. 138). The return match, Surrey versus Yorkshire, took place at the Oval cricket ground in south London between 22 and 24 August 1923; the

match was drawn and Surrey only batted once. These facts, gleaned from Sydney H. Pardon (ed.), *John Wisden's Cricketers' Almanack for 1924: Full Scores and Bowling Analyses of all Important Matches Played in 1923* (London: John Wisden and Co, 1924), 43, 104–5, confirm that Woolf sets the novel on an *imaginary* Wednesday in June 1923, not on Wednesday 20 June, as Morris Beja has claimed (*Mrs Dalloway*, ed. Morris Beja (Oxford: The Shakespeare Head Press, 1996), pp. xiv, 147, 157), and not on Wednesday 13 June, as Harvena Richter and, following her lead, Elaine Showalter have argued (Harvena Richter, 'The *Ulysses* Connection: Clarissa Dalloway's Bloomsday', *Studies in the Novel*, 21/3 (Fall 1989), 305–19; Elaine Showalter, 'Introduction' to *Mrs Dalloway*, ed. Stella McNichol (Harmondsworth, Middlesex: Penguin Books, 1992), pp. xi–xlviii; see p. xiii.

Brighton: a holiday centre on the East Sussex coast of England, 51 miles south of London. A fashionable resort from the Regency (1811–20) period onwards.

129 *the British Museum*: begun in 1823 to the classical design of Robert Smirke, the British Museum is on Great Russell Street, Bloomsbury.

Caledonian Market: took place on Fridays among the empty pens of the Metropolitan Cattle Market in the north London borough of Islington. It was synonymous with bargains and in 1924 was extended to Tuesdays. It closed for good during the Second World War.

Shaftesbury Avenue: known as the 'heart of theatreland', it is a major thoroughfare of London's West End.

130 *the Severn*: the Severn is the longest river in the United Kingdom. It rises in central Wales and flows into the Bristol Channel after passing through such towns and cities as Shrewsbury in Shropshire, Worcester, and Gloucester.

134 *the Bodleian*: a copyright library since 1610, entitled to receive a free copy of every book published in the United Kingdom, it is the principal library of Oxford University. It was founded by Humphrey, 1st Duke of Gloucester (1390–1447) in 1409 and restored and enlarged by Sir Thomas Bodley (1545–1613), an English diplomat and scholar, between 1598 and 1602.

135 *'Bartlett pears'*: named after the American merchant Enoch Bartlett (1779–1860), who first distributed this variety in the United States.

137 *Mr Willett's summer time*: first proposed as Daylight Saving Time by William Willett (1856–1915) in 1907, it was adopted in 1916 to save power during the First World War and was still in force in 1923. Now known as British Summer Time (BST), it simply involves putting the clocks forward one hour for the spring and summer months, that is, an hour in advance of Greenwich Mean Time (GMT).

the Oriental Club: in 1923 this was located in Hanover Square (it is now housed in Stratford House, Stratford Place). It was founded in 1824 by officers in the service of the East India Company who were not eligible for the military clubs of Pall Mall.

138 *Littré's dictionary*: a famous dictionary of the French language compiled by Émile Littré (1801–81) and first published in four volumes in 1863–73 with a supplementary volume in 1877.

141 *the Imperial Tokay*: Tokay or Tokaj is a small town in north-east Hungary forty miles from the Ukrainian border. It has given its name to a famous dessert wine which is produced in the area using the Furmint grape. The wine is 'Imperial', most likely, because it has come from the cellars of either Charles I (1887–1922; ruled 1916–18), the last Habsburg Emperor of Austria-Hungary, or the last German Emperor, Wilhelm II (1859–1941; ruled 1888–1918), or the Tsar of Russia, Nicholas II (1868–1918; ruled 1894–1917).

148 *Sir Joshua picture*: a picture by Sir Joshua Reynolds (1723–92), one of the most important English portrait painters of the eighteenth century. Almost every person of note in the second half of the century had their portrait painted by him. Also an influential theoretician, he held the post of first President of the Royal Academy from 1768.

Mrs Durrant and Clara: like Mr Bowley, these two characters first appear in *Jacob's Room*.

149 *Academicians . . . sunset pools*: a Royal Academician, Sir Harry appears to specialize in the kind of sentimental, anthropomorphic, and extremely popular animal subjects with which the painter, sculptor, and Royal Academician Sir Edwin Landseer (1802–73) had made his name and fortune. He died insane.

vagous: like the Latin adjective *vagus* from which it derives, this rare English word means vague, unsettled, wandering, straying, or inconstant.

150 *Hampstead*: a district of north London traditionally associated with the freethinking, mould-breaking, bickering, and posturing of artists, writers, and other intellectuals.

153 *this isle of men, this dear, dear land*: even 'without reading Shakespeare', Lady Bruton manages to evoke John of Gaunt's impassioned words on the state of England in Shakespeare's *Richard II*, II. i. 40–68, and in particular ll. 57–8:

> This land of such dear souls, this dear dear land,
> Dear for her reputation through the world.

155 *his eleven*: that is, the cricket team of his school boarding house.

156 *'If it were now to die . . . most happy,'*: see note to p. 30.

159 *Emily Brontë*: one of the three novel-writing Brontë sisters, Emily (1818–48) was the author of *Wuthering Heights* (1847) and also a poet. Her sisters were Charlotte Brontë (1816–55), author of *Jane Eyre* (1847), *Shirley* (1849), and *Villette* (1853), and Anne Brontë (1820–49), author of *Agnes Grey* (1847) and *The Tenant of Wildfell Hall* (1848).

161 *Suez Canal*: designed by the French engineer Ferdinand de Lesseps and opened in 1869, the Suez Canal is a vitally important Egyptian waterway linking the Mediterranean Sea and the Red Sea. It is 103 miles long.

164 *fifty-two to be precise*: earlier in the novel, Peter Walsh has both ruminated that he is 'only just past fifty' (p. 37) and that he is 53 (p. 63). Clarissa, aged 51 (p. 31), recalls at one point that Peter is 'six months older than I am' (p. 38).

American Literature

British and Irish Literature

Children's Literature

Classics and Ancient Literature

Colonial Literature

Eastern Literature

European Literature

Gothic Literature

History

Medieval Literature

Oxford English Drama

Poetry

Philosophy

Politics

Religion

The Oxford Shakespeare

A complete list of Oxford World's Classics, including Authors in Context, Oxford English Drama, and the Oxford Shakespeare, is available in the UK from the Marketing Services Department, Oxford University Press, Great Clarendon Street, Oxford OX2 6DP, or visit the website at www.oup.com/uk/worldsclassics.

In the USA, visit www.oup.com/us/owc for a complete title list.

Oxford World's Classics are available from all good bookshops. In case of difficulty, customers in the UK should contact Oxford University Press Bookshop, 116 High Street, Oxford OX1 4BR.

	Late Victorian Gothic Tales
JANE AUSTEN	Emma
	Mansfield Park
	Persuasion
	Pride and Prejudice
	Selected Letters
	Sense and Sensibility
MRS BEETON	Book of Household Management
MARY ELIZABETH BRADDON	Lady Audley's Secret
ANNE BRONTË	The Tenant of Wildfell Hall
CHARLOTTE BRONTË	Jane Eyre
	Shirley
	Villette
EMILY BRONTË	Wuthering Heights
ROBERT BROWNING	The Major Works
JOHN CLARE	The Major Works
SAMUEL TAYLOR COLERIDGE	The Major Works
WILKIE COLLINS	The Moonstone
	No Name
	The Woman in White
CHARLES DARWIN	The Origin of Species
THOMAS DE QUINCEY	The Confessions of an English Opium-Eater
	On Murder
CHARLES DICKENS	The Adventures of Oliver Twist
	Barnaby Rudge
	Bleak House
	David Copperfield
	Great Expectations
	Nicholas Nickleby
	The Old Curiosity Shop
	Our Mutual Friend
	The Pickwick Papers

ANTON CHEKHOV   **About Love and Other Stories**
                   Early Stories
                   Five Plays
                   The Princess and Other Stories
                   The Russian Master and Other Stories
                   The Steppe and Other Stories
                   Twelve Plays
                   Ward Number Six and Other Stories

FYODOR DOSTOEVSKY **Crime and Punishment**
                   Devils
                   A Gentle Creature and Other Stories
                   The Idiot
                   The Karamazov Brothers
                   Memoirs from the House of the Dead
                   Notes from the Underground and
                        The Gambler

NIKOLAI GOGOL   **Dead Souls**
                   Plays and Petersburg Tales

ALEXANDER PUSHKIN **Eugene Onegin**
                   The Queen of Spades and Other Stories

LEO TOLSTOY   **Anna Karenina**
                   The Kreutzer Sonata and Other Stories
                   The Raid and Other Stories
                   Resurrection
                   War and Peace

IVAN TURGENEV   **Fathers and Sons**
                   First Love and Other Stories
                   A Month in the Country